NO SON OF MINE

BOOKS BY G. B. STERN

Al mio caro amico—
H. Walter Barnett, questo ricordo
di Samoa Girolamo Pieri Nerli offre—

DRAWING OF STEVENSON BY COUNT NERLI, SENT WITH AN
INSCRIPTION TO H. WALTER BARNETT, IN 1892 OR 1894.

NO SON
OF
MINE

By

G. B. STERN

*"It is very pleasant to dig
into the past of a close friend and find him
at every spadeful shine brighter."*

ROBERT LOUIS STEVENSON

NEW YORK

THE MACMILLAN COMPANY

1948

For

Lloyd Osbourne

in gratitude for the Prefaces

to the

Tusitala Edition

PREFACE

Robert himself would have said "it doesn't make sense" of any foreword to a chronicle of how he came into being. Yet in spite of such a characteristic verdict, a little of his pre-natal career does require urgently to be set down beforehand; even to why in these first few lines I have to introduce him simply as "Robert" without a surname.

For the story of Robert is fiction, although *No Son of Mine* cannot be unequivocally listed under the same heading, for it contains firm biography as well as fiction. And I must vehemently repudiate all idea of running the two into one, and describing the cunning entanglement as "fictional biography", that picturesque form of presentation which, as a matter of individual preference, has always left me oddly uncomfortable. Probably this is my chief reason for a preface: to sever the story of Robert from the biographical matter of quite another man; a man who really did exist; a writer who is rather widely known as Robert Louis Stevenson. Where this book touches on R.L.S. it is as factual, as accurate and conscientious as hard study and perpetual verification can make it. As indeed it should be, for one cannot be too severe over biography, whether or not the subject be still alive to protect himself, or his friends and relatives and the law stand by to protect his memory. Courtesy and duty demand this attitude from the boldest biographer.

On a subsequent page I give my acknowledgments with sincere gratitude. Helped by these, I have not knowingly violated the truth as far as we can ever know the truth; nor in the regions beyond exact knowledge have I invented dialogue, imagined fresh incidents, twisted minor evidence, or, whistling to show how little it really matters, carried a date or a place several months forward in time, a few hundred miles across country in geography, in order to make the quality of the hero more striking and romantic. Not that much need be added to the Life of Robert Louis Stevenson to give it more abundant life. Certainly I may learn that I have tripped up, and I express my sincere contrition; but mistakes are perhaps not so unforgivable when one has faithfully tried to avoid them, as a wanton heightening of colour is unforgivable, or any rapid sleight of hand to alter the shape and contents of a life already steel-engraved by death.

Deliberately, I have only twice tampered with dates, though not with events. The frontispiece could not be other, for my purpose, than a reproduction of a drawing of Stevenson's head made by Count Girolamo Nerli at Samoa in 1894 (or possibly on his first visit in 1892) in preparation for a portrait now to be seen at Edinburgh's National Gallery. The drawing was superbly right; the finished portrait would not do at all. But *No Son of Mine* had to happen in 1911; "had to" by one of those mysterious fierce compulsions which govern the conception of any book (the sentence ends: "or it wouldn't be any good"). Robert could not possibly have seen that drawing in 1911; it had not yet been reproduced anywhere; I believe it did not appear until 1913, in an extra number of *The Bookman* dedicated to Robert Louis Stevenson. On the other hand, he could have chanced upon the portrait, for it stood as a frontispiece to H. Baildon's *Robert Louis Stevenson, A Life Study in Criticism*, published in 1901.

So I confess to a lie: after a brief conflict in which fact went down defeated, I substituted the essential drawing for the painting, in the copy of Baildon which Robert pulled out from a shelf of Miss Gibson's bookshop. I can only repeat that I am sorry, not repentant—but chiefly sorry that Mr. Baildon himself had not elected to choose the drawing.

Also, I quoted from four letters which were not included in the collection until 1926, though three were written in 1874 and one in 1875.

[6]

Otherwise there has been no violation of honesty; for Robert, as I said before, is wholly imagined except in his origin, which by conjecture could be strangely linked with biography; as if green water-meadows on one side of a stream, and a classical garden, formal and restrained, on the other, were linked by one of those little humped bridges that one sees frequently in soft old landscape prints, running up steeply from each side to a high centre, to divide as well as to join.

It occurs to me just not too late, that my conscience is not yet altogether clear; one other piece of despotism has to be recorded:

In Chapter 10, Robert calls on a Scots author living in London in a high terrace of houses overlooking the river. Their dialogue is, of course, invented; therefore I give the author an imaginary name. Yet since I use biographical matter, an authentic letter quoted, and identifiable strips of native bark, sent from Samoa, hanging on the wall, the author can be easily recognized as J. M. Barrie. Where a real character meets and talks with a character of fiction, (a precarious encounter upon the little humped bridge) one can do no less than abjure the impudence of calling the former by his real name, before one begins to take liberties with his conversation. So I did not call him Mr. Barrie (as he was at that date); though taking for granted that had Robert been actual flesh and blood, he would in pursuit of his quest undoubtedly have called on such a worshipper as the man from Kirriemuir who had referred to R.L.S. as "the most beloved initials in recent literature".

The verdict against my work has so often been "flippant" (which few could mind) or "trivial" (which we all do), that you will understand if I repeat that this special book was meant to be neither, and that I was deeply serious at least in respect for my subject, though I appear to have an unfortunate tendency to lapse into a mood seeming to make ducks and drakes of any subject under the visiting moon. It happens that I would care so terribly if in this instance it were again to be the verdict, that I must plead beforehand that my failure would be and easily may be in achievement, for which I can bear to be blamed, but not in any fault of intention.

Here is how I came to write this book which is neither fiction nor biography:

I was crossing the courtyard of the Savoy Hotel one murky evening, when I was hailed by a well-known journalist whom I had not seen for a long time. We halted perilously among the cars and taxis streaming in and dodging out, reversing and advancing at the commissionaire's command, while we talked of this-and-that in the past. Presently he asked me what work I was doing? I replied that I had persuaded a film company to let me make a script on the life of Robert Louis Stevenson; an idea which I had treasured for many years before. The journalist was interested; he plunged into a spate of anecdote and hearsay concerning Stevenson. Later, I discovered that a broken segment of one incident, crumbled off from the rest, had somehow lodged in my mind and I could not evict it. I still cannot tell why I was so haunted, for I did not hear how he began the story . . . of a tramp who arrived at the house among the dripping trees at night. . . . Fir-trees, and the rain pouring down, and the house was a manse— Or had the details filled themselves in later, to heighten the queer excitement which shook me over the few words which passed between the tramp as he left the house and—was it the minister? "Ye'll be Stevenson's son, are ye not?" The tramp said yes, and disappeared into the dark.

Research is a twopence-coloured business; I know few occupations more absorbing. Really, it amounts to detective work: our own personal home-made thrillers in which one thing can never fail to lead to another. It is as deep as it is wide. It is a banquet from which we rise still hungry and avid for further feasting. Therefore when my film-script was finished and delivered, I went on with research; or rather, it went on of its own momentum.

I presently grew to love the work of R.L.S., but at first I explored it less for its own sake than because it could not fail to illumine a thousand odd corners and

[8]

by-ways and passages, and moments heroic or humorous—
often both—of a life that had captured my imagination to
a rare degree.

Even apart from the letters, the existing Stevenson bibliography could be compared with the multitudinous seas; I
felt I need never come to land again. For it so happened
that besides his own revelations, conscious and unconscious,
he was also endowed with a sort of enchanting potentiality
which excited other writers, and tempted those who knew
him to pass on the tidings first-hand to yet more writers
who by time and fortune had not had the same luck. And
not only professionals and scholars, but his family, his
friends, his servants, men of business, men of no temperament, men of different race and creed and colour, all were
moved by the same extraordinary impulse: somehow they
had to get it down about Stevenson before they could be
satisfied.

With all that accumulated material, that storehouse in
which we can rummage to our heart's content, we remain
only partially satisfied ourselves . . . until we too have got
something down.

So there was I, ransacking heaven and earth for the right
literary vehicle to put an end to my restless desire to share
and be rid of all I had found and had not used; or at least
to share, if I could not be rid of it. A straightforward
biography would have been plainly superfluous; among so
many, how could mine be better or even equal? And to
supply a worse biography is foolish labour.

And now I met the journalist in the Savoy courtyard, and
began to be haunted by the tramp who vanished among
the dark trees. . . . Till it flashed across me that through
this vagrant I could convey all that I longed to tell: He
should be a vehicle, no more and no less, for a faithful
biography; nobody's son, anybody's son, struck by the idea
that he was on to a useful racket if he read up his data
and learnt it by heart. For a start, he need know as
little of Stevenson as (by test) ninety-nine people out of
a hundred: "Oh yes, he wrote *Treasure Island*. An
invalid, wasn't he? Went to the South Seas and died

out there, didn't he?'' Occasionally *Jekyll and Hyde* is added to *Treasure Island*, or *A Child's Garden of Verses*; the latter less frequently, perhaps, than had he kept to his better title of "Penny Whistles". So from the lowest motives, my tramp should begin to read up his subject; and through him, with him, at the same gradual pace and growing interest, readers of *No Son of Mine* could progress towards enlightenment.

When already half-way through my first rough draft, a friend picked up George Hellman's *The True Stevenson* second-hand, and brought it to me in the indulgent way that people pander to one's King Charles's Head.

. . . I pass by without offering any opinion on that other question which is concerned with the man who calls himself Robert W. Stevenson and who claims to be Louis' son.

It should not have been such a shock to me to discover in cold print this casual corroboration of the legend which, blurred by dusk and muffled by the throb of car-engines, I had heard in the courtyard of the Savoy. Yet I stared incredulous at such sudden evidence that there had indeed been a man making such a claim, and that his name was indeed Robert. "But *I* called him Robert," was my childish protest . . . before the American idiom dormant in most of us, told me to be my age.

Once more the tramp was to be conjured from the shadows, this third time in a clearer shape, and again when I was off my guard. By then, I was within three chapters of finishing *No Son of Mine*. In a volume of essays just published, I came across a minor but startling theory that slid a shaft of new light on to some of Stevenson's early letters. This had to be pursued, therefore, with all the frenzy of a jig-saw addict after a missing piece, though it had nothing to do with my book. So I wrote to the author and asked him to lunch.

A pleasant meeting duly took place. Just before he left, he added a quite irrelevant "by the way". It concerned . . . a tramp who at one time was reported to have gone about Edinburgh, pretending, on a strong resemblance to Stevenson, that he was actually his son— "And he cashed in on it," said my guileless informant (guileless, of course, only because he could not possibly be aware of that bulk of manuscript in my drawer upstairs). "He used to go along theatre queues telling people to look at his face, and then collect money."

Life versus fiction! Theatre queues had never occurred to me.

Stevenson has written of his Brownies who played odd tricks on him, such as tipping him a glimpse of Jekyll and Hyde in a bogy dream, when he was most in need of an idea for a shilling shocker.

Who are the Little People ? They are near connections of the dreamer's, beyond doubt . . . they can tell him a story piece by piece, like a serial, and keep him all the while in ignorance of where they aim . . . they are somewhat fantastic, like their stories hot and hot, full of passion and the picturesque, alive with incident ; and they have no prejudice against the supernatural . . . my Brownies have not a rudiment of what we call conscience. . . .

Thus the Brownies were to him, as to many of us, not funny little whimsical fellows with peaked caps who squat on mushrooms, but the queer need of mankind to externalize a long procession of freakish mishaps, uncanny coincidences and teasing games; they are related to the goblins and the Puck and the Poltergeist, and latterly to the Gremlins of our own time. The three unrelated incarnations of this nameless tramp who had moved into my life, must surely have been arranged by Stevenson's Brownies when I was questing for an out-of-the-ordinary vehicle for Stevenson's biography. Yet by the time I heard of the fellow jingling coins in his battered old hat along the length of a theatre queue in a cold grey street of Edinburgh, I had already crossed the little humped bridge that linked biography with fiction. These appearances affirmed a real man, a living man ; but many weeks before, in vigorous if ironic protest at being engaged to act as a mere formula, an angle, a vehicle, Robert had already taken possession and made a living man out of himself; a living man who engendered a soul and story of his own, independent of his vicarious uses to the author.

So many readers have a conscience over skipping, that having none myself, I yet hardly dare actually recommend them to skip Chapter 6, if they happen to be already well enough acquainted with the facts of Stevenson's life; or if they can enjoy Robert's story without a guide for reference slanted, according to my first plan, through Robert's need, not theirs, of such a guide. Shortly afterwards, the book was wrested out of its biographical intentions; and though no author has a right to usurp the critic's function, I cannot help knowing that onwards from here, it mysteriously surrenders to what should have been its design from the start.

I have rashly dismissed, in the past, the affectation of writers who declare they do their whole job whilst only semi-conscious. But it is never wise to scoff at a thing which might happen to oneself at any moment. Naturally I am referring only to the first very rough draft of the tale. By the time I wrote it "properly", I was perfectly well aware of all that was happening and likely to happen to Robert. Though even then, my bones were still miraculously informed of what Robert would do and feel and say in any situation, (which in all humility may still mean that I have failed to put it across), in the same way as he himself gradually acquired authority to do more than just guess what R.L.S. might have felt and done and said.

Robert is only just beginning to quicken and grow up when we leave him, in the spring of 1913. I had hoped to let it be understood that in the war of 1914 he would be able to force a way into it, if not as an active combatant, then as a stretcher-bearer. But I fear that a soldier's end on the battlefield was not meant for him . . . either. Not only would it have been too rewarding, too improbably near his own wish, but I know from that deep spring of anonymous information which will not let writers do as they like, that Robert could not live long enough for the trumpets literally to sound at his death, nor for the solace of a warrior's burial.

I am aware, finally, that I should elucidate my own attitude towards the son myth. Do I believe it to be true?

[12]

Strictly within the defined bounds of fiction, yes, I do. Beyond and outside these water-meadows and across the humped bridge into the keener airs of exact biography, I simply do not know. It has been repeated over and over again, with certainly no loss of reverence or devotion, by Stevenson's friends and biographers, as well as in frank confession by R.L.S. himself, that he was a man essentially human. Lloyd Osbourne says, in one of the prefaces of the Tusitala Edition :

> Of course, he was no saint. One would do his memory a poor service by endowing him with all the perfections. His early life had been tempestuously intermixed with those of many women, and I have never heard him express a wish that it might have been otherwise ; on occasions he could swear vociferously, and when roused he had a most violent temper : he loved good wine and the good things of life ; he often championed people who were not worth championing, impulsively believing in them, and getting himself, in consequence, in a false position. He was unduly quick to accept responsibilities or tasks that soon grew extremely irksome, and which, with a moment's reflection, might easily have been avoided. He gave away money with a royal hand and often to arrant impostors.
>
> But when this is said I seem to come to the end. No human being was ever freer from pettiness, meanness, or self-seeking ; none ever more high-minded or sincere ; and none surely was ever possessed of a great indulgence towards the erring and fallen. In this, indeed, one does see a saintly quality. There were no irreparable sins to Stevenson ; nothing that might man or woman do that was not redeemable ; he had an immeasurable tolerance, an immeasurable tenderness for those who had been cast by the world outside the pale.

"Of course, he was no saint." . . . So it is possible that the unverified rumours may be true, that he had a natural son. Possible, not probable. If asked why not, I can only surmise on instinct, and on the knowledge I have acquired during years of research and reading, that he was no hole-and-corner man, and would not be likely to leave a son unacknowledged. According to the dates and place advanced by the theatre-queue claimant (not the same as those I had already invented for Robert) he had been conceived in San Francisco during those utterly derelict and lonely months early in 1880, and would have been fifteen

[13]

years old when Stevenson died in Samoa. As he made his name and parentage known later in Edinburgh (to raise the wind in more senses than one), why not have done so, if they were true, while the father he claimed was still alive and fairly accessible? Stevenson's frequent bitter or sorrowful references to his childless state eliminate any idea that he might have known about this boy and never spoken; a man of high code and courage, he never paid lip tribute to respectability, nor left dark deeds in the dark. Besides, would it not have made him too happy for silence on the subject?

Yet all this is conjecture. I can only repeat that though within the bounds of Robert's story I have rights and responsibilities, and can say "he is authentic" or "he is a fraud", beyond them Robert is a creature of my imagination. I can never hope to analyse why I was compelled to set down this record of how a man suddenly fastened a meaning to what R.L.S. had flung out haphazard on a Penny Whistle.

Finally, my publishers and I would express our indebtedness to the late Lloyd Osbourne and to his sister, Mrs. Salisbury Field, for permission to include so much material from the Letters and other copyright sources, as well as for the photograph of R.L.S. facing page 228. We have sought in vain for the owner of the sketch by Nerli reproduced as a frontispiece. Messrs. Macmillan & Co. Ltd. and W. E. Henley's executors have kindly given permission to quote from his *Poems*. I should also like to acknowledge short quotations made here and there from writings, poems, etc. by Will Low, Richard Le Gallienne, and H. J. Moors; from speeches and writings of J. M. Barrie; from George Hellman's *The True Stevenson* (Little, Brown & Co., Boston); from Graham Balfour's *Life of R. L. Stevenson* (Methuen); and from the poem by W. Robertson Nicoll in the special number of *The Bookman*, 1913.

[14]

1

"Ye'll be Stevenson's son, are ye not?"

"Yes." The man wrenched himself from the Minister's clasp which had so eagerly tightened on his arm, and plunged into the slicing rain.

It was already dark. The sombre wood of fir-trees that dripped close up to the back-door of the Manse, made it darker. In a moment he had gone.

He wanted to be alone and think it out. This thing had happened before, not once alone, but twice since he had landed from California; and that was leaving out an earlier incident at Pop Ernest's Café on Monterey beach, when sick and sunken, skin stretched tight to show the skeleton bones, he had gone on munching his abalone steak, not caring how some old fool of a sailor opposite had babbled like a girl, about eyes that reminded him of someone . . . who was it?

So now: "This fellow Stevenson again, I reckon." The tramp grinned in saturnine amusement.

But what recent change in his looks had sharpened the excitement for those who were seeing a more precise likeness than to a vague someone, out on the Pacific shore? On the voyage home—no, he had no home—on his last voyage, he had let his beard grow; saved trouble for a lazy devil languid after rheumatic fever. Then that skirt on board had coaxed him into borrowing an old razor to shave himself velvet clean, as he told her he used to be. The beard therefore came off, but by the time they docked at Clydeside, he had had enough of her, and for all her taunts and pleadings, had left untouched the long flamboyant moustache that without melancholy shaded his mouth.

"Are you Stevenson's son?" . . . He could hardly help noticing that it meant he fared richer and better by food, money and comfort, bestowed with readiness and even a kind of awe; though he had hesitated in his assent, hardly knowing what was expected of him, nor where advantage lay; he who was usually so ready to take his cue. For always, gipsying up and down England, South Africa, the western states of America, his ingratiating though never humble statement of what he wanted, automatically produced a maddening counter-statement of what his patrons wanted *done*. A job of work? Hell, no! Warmth and whisky and bed and a shelter that at least didn't let the sleet through, that was all. Not enough sun in this blamed land. Fat lot they knew about lying supine and contented in the sun, or they'd drop their everlasting silly cant about work.

"*Ye'll be Stevenson's son?*" And tonight for the first time he answered the wistful question blindly, with a bold "Yes." And after all, had not lingered for the usual proceeds, the chink of coins—silver, not copper—the invitation to sit down and eat, and warm his frozen flesh.

For this was building up to proportions beyond a joke, and he was puzzled by that queer tone in all their voices, never accosting him as in mere casual enquiry—("Any relation to old So-and-so? man I used to know with a boss-eye and ginger hair? Went to New Zealand years ago. Lost sight of him. No? Oh well, just wondered—").

He ran over in his mind the people who had questioned him: that surly ruffian in the shop where he bought a packet of smokes; the lawyerish, professorish old boy whom he had nearly knocked down on an abrupt turn of the path down to the river. And tonight the Minister, keen-eyed, grizzled, a giant in stature, stooping and peering from beneath his lintel at the gaunt, threadbare, mud-splashed mendicant for bread and cheese. All old men, you see, but otherwise nothing to link them together; each pulled from a different pack of cards; except for that incredulous scrutiny and then—was it a cry of welcome suddenly?

He neither knew nor cared. But when scrutiny and question were repeated— Look here, a man had to live by his wits; suppose he were to cash in on it? Suppose in **this**

[16]

bitter weather, bitter or sodden, day after miserable day—
God! suppose his big chance were being offered him at
last? Luck in a whole stunning lump? Smashing, staggering onslaught of luck, and chuck away rags for ever; he
was not too proud to do himself proud on a lie.

He had to sit down for a bit. The bones of his legs were
gnawed with pain, legacy from his fever; fine and useful
for a vagrant, or call it wayfarer, prettier word. To lift his
thoughts away from the gloomy damp wood and the gloomy
damp pain, he put himself to steady examination of the
whole curious business:

For a start, who was this fellow Stevenson? Might be
the writer. Yes, now he came to think of it, the old lawyer,
staring through his goggles, had varied the formula by
stammering a fuller name: "Are you— Can you be a son
of Robert Louis Stevenson?" That was the cove who wrote
Treasure Island. Good yarn; he had read it as a lad; but
the writing part of all this did not matter; find out and
learn by heart the man's life, his wife, his family, his sons,
dates and principal events . . . and for goodness' sake, whether
one son had somehow cut loose from the rest? got himself
lost so that a stranger might profit, had indeed already
profited by—what? What mystery of accidental resemblance
in line or shape or voice had so instantly tricked attention?

A raging curiosity to see a portrait jerked him to his feet
again. Beyond tree-darkness, he must surely strike a road
to the nearest town and a Public Library?

For there was more in this than a lodging for the night,
one hearty meal, a few shillings; far more, if you set about
it in the right way, organized your bluff, thought up beforehand how you would act and what it might be expedient
to pretend to remember. Jove, what a game! Simply
rolling off the cushion into his pocket as easy and inevitable
as a billiard-ball in Perry's Saloon when that damned old
double-crosser Rogers with a twist of the cue sent it up the
smooth green cloth: "Say, how's that?"

Risky, true; but a hundred times nearer his freakish
taste than the usual semi-reproachful offer to swap his
freedom for boring toil. Under his breath he mimicked

[17]

those good respectable people: "Come alang wi' me, my
puir man, to the shed and I'll show ye the wood and the
chopper. Ye'll no' be sorry, I'm thinking, to airn your
meat honestly."

And that's where they were wrong.

So if "Stevenson's son" fetched them off their fixed idea
of supplying him with a chopper in a woodshed, then he
was amiably prepared to be Stevenson's son till all was
blue. "Prepared?" The word muttered a warning. Impostors slipped up sometimes. The Tichborne Case. And
that kid, scullion in a king's kitchen—they called them
Pretenders in history. Anyway, neither of these had pulled
it off as he now swore to pull it off. He was too elated to
make heavy weather of the dangers ahead. A foundling
with no notion of his own parentage and little interest in
the matter, he would be mad casually to throw away this
miracle of reputed birth, for want of an hour's mugging-up
on the subject. He limped along, squelching every now
and then with one foot into a rut between the drier ridges,
till on the road again, faintly a-glitter with rain, he was able
to concentrate on assembling the few bare facts already in
his possession about the writer of *Treasure Island*.

A Scot; an invalid; lungs, wasn't it? Went off to live
on some South Sea island. They'd put up a monument to
him in 'Frisco (he had seen it), a fountain in the open space
of the Old Plaza near Chinatown, topped by a bronze galleon
in full sail; lettering too, but Robert had never bothered
to read that. The monument probably meant the man was
dead.

What else? Nothing else. Squeezing his brains, he
could extract no further juice of biography. To have remembered even as much was gratifying, but he felt that a trifle
more data might be needed to inspire confidence in his
jaying, and for that touch of swagger which was part of his
customary stock-in-trade. For even when he begged, he did
it with zest, never whined, scorning to trade on his usual
damnable health, bankrupt here as well as in pocket; if
they refused, he cursed, and then as often as not, laughed
good-naturedly at his victims for their timid panic. Took

him for a professional tramp with a bludgeon up his sleeve, did they? Well, and so he was, in the lordly sense of being handicapped by no delicate aversion from asking and taking, and when that lot was finished, asking and taking again. Badly brought up? I believe you, my dear Sir; I was brought up first in the workhouse and then transferred to a charity home down in the south of England; and my charity name is Robert Black, which for all I know, for all anyone knows about my origin, might as truthfully have been Julius Caesar. My parents? Whoever you like to bestow on me; I'm of an obliging nature and only too willing, as you can see, to acknowledge any father, alive or dead, who can do me handsome. In fact, as it happens, a writer suits my fancy; they have this elegant knack of earning a living without work. I'd have been disappointed if you'd looked into my face and declared me a son of Big Business.

He whistled as he limped along, well entertained by the mocking dialogue with his future dupes; he was accustomed to provide his own good company, for he preferred it on the whole to any haphazard pal of the road: grumblers and grudgers whose talk was all in envy of comfortable men. If wishes were horses, beggars would ride. . . . And when he was goaded by hunger and black weather into indolent wishing, it was always towards a more fantastic horseback ride, beyond the prosaic immediate need of dry boots and a full stomach.

For luck, not wealth was his desire; wealth had to be achieved after the fashion of an American Success Story, bit by bit, step by step, no occasion missed, no industry too burdensome; but luck travelled swiftly and carelessly in any direction, and you might miss it or hit it full and square. So when slanged, he shrugged his shoulders; but flared up if commiseration took the unbearable form of: "Bad luck, my boy!" *No* luck, my boy, if you like, so far; but that was only a blank space waiting to be filled one day.

His teachers and guardians at the Institution where he grew up, handed in adverse reports of a restless, idle, impudent disposition; painfully irreligious too, and never in the least

[19]

"responsive to good influence". Nor, however, to evil influence; they granted that he did not tremble and weakly succumb when any vicious gang of youngsters at the Home tried to rope him in. A graceless young scamp, they remarked, and drew up a list of his qualities to counter the sterner catalogue: generous, though he had little enough to give; easy-tempered; a good loser. All very fine, but sooner or later during the fourteen years he spent at the Home being trained and educated, they came up against the same disappointment of so many who were to encounter it later on: he was. . . . inaccessible; they thought him "attached" to them, and were grieved and hurt at how easily he could slip cable; it was unfair that in spite of it they continued to remember him; angrily, of course, but still remembered him long after his thankless disappearance. It may have been that this very nonchalance, when obviously he had no justification for it, provoked an over-possessive nerve in those with whom he came in contact; nevertheless, their cross claims to affection failed to interest him; it is doubtful, indeed, whether he noticed them. At all events, they did not tally with his own secret conception of wishes and horses.

Without ambition, creator of nothing and caring for no one, often marvelling why he bothered to keep alive and moving on this abominable earth, he dispensed as far as possible with the dubitable charm of earning his living by fair and strenuous means, and was therefore enchanted at this foul and happy opportunity of perhaps ceasing to earn it at all or ever again. It tickled his mood to exaggerate the fatefulness of his present errand: tell himself that at last, in the Public Library of a small Scottish town, Destiny awaited him; the turn of the tide; the cross-roads; the double six; every other grandiloquence that occurred to him to heighten his solitary drama.

And that brought him to Dumburnock. After closing time.

The next day was Sunday.

On Monday morning, he stood expectant before the Library doors, more impatient for admittance than ever

[20]

while waiting outside a saloon bar. A few minutes later, he was to learn how it felt to jar curiosity against a blank wall, for he was informed that all books on Stevenson's life were out; there had been a run on them, the librarian said, owing to the fresh interest which had sprung up since a second reprinting two months ago of the new edition of the Letters containing one-hundred-and-fifty which had never been published. "This is Stevenson's ain country ye're in," she informed him, thawing slightly at the pleading gaze of the man's brilliant wide-apart dark eyes, "and a' the folk, since his death out there, look on him as belonging to them in a varra special way; I prefair the tales of Crockett, mysel'. In any case, wi'out a form filled up and witnessed by two pairsons of reputable poseetion—"

At that moment, several subscribers claimed her attention; returning books and asking for others. Robert lingered; he could not bear to go away thwarted. Presently, from several piles in front of her, the girl selected a couple of volumes of unequal size and binding, and turned to him with quite a friendly air: "Here are some of the Letters, just come in." Then, going into pedantic detail: "It's the fairst volume of the old 1899 edition, and only Volume Four of the new one. But was it no' the Life that you asked for so specially?"

"The Life doesn't matter." He was surprised how his heart thudded and bruised against his thin ribs. For surely, surely the letters were bound to contain at least one photograph?

"You can sit yersel' doun and look at them, but mind, wi'out a form filled up, they'll no' leave the building."

So these were his primers.

A laconic dandy in rags strolled with them across to a distant table; set them down carelessly. Affected to be in no hurry to open them. Took impudent stock of his neighbours. Yawned. Ran a hand through his unruly hair, colour of a conker but already rusting in streaks. Finally decided that since he had mistakenly committed himself to a passing acquaintance with literature, he might as well take a look. . . .

Seizing the more massive book, he opened it at the page of contents which ended: *Frontispiece—Portrait of R. L. Stevenson, aet. 35. From a photograph by Mr. Lloyd Osbourne.*

The Portrait had been torn out.

His sense of irony temporarily mislaid, Robert swore under his breath against these unscrupulous swine who damaged and stole from public property, without consideration for such respectable citizens (himself) who might also need to avail themselves of the Free Library. Disappointment made him quite an eloquent champion of the cause of these trustful citizens. Half his eager hopes gone, he turned to the frontispiece in the smaller scarlet volume.

"*R. L. Stevenson on his Horse Jack.*"

"And that's about all it is!" muttered Robert, savagely disappointed for the second time. For it might have been any man; thin, with a dark moustache. It looked like a snapshot reproduced very small and without individuality. Robert vainly scrutinized it for a likeness to himself. "Oh well, it doesn't matter"— Better see what useful facts he could pick up out of the book itself.

Pages and pages of print; mainly the light-hearted kind of print, not in solid unreadable blocks. And three other volumes, the woman at the desk had said, equally stuffed full of scribble. Had his pseudo-daddy never anything to do but scrawl hundreds of letters?

Where to begin? At random he lit on a paragraph from the last letter of all:

Come to think of it, Gosse, I believe the main distinction is that you have a family growing up around you, and I am a childless, rather bitter, very clear-eyed, blighted youth—

"*Childless*"—Robert burst into a shout of derisive laughter, forgetting where he was; other readers, mainly of the local paper, stared at him, mute and frowning: *not* the type who should have been allowed in at all.

"Childless be damned! Then look here, who the devil do you suppose *I'm* supposed to be?"

2

So he would have to fake a romantic story from the very start, himself in the centre as the little love-child. But what innocence, Robert mocked at a too sanguine Robert, to contemplate a claim to be the son of a man who officially had no children. The news was a shock, not to his morals certainly, but to his foregone conclusions. He had been so sure of finding in these two books photographs of his apocryphal existence at all ages; had visualized family groups in self-conscious attitudes in their South Sea island setting: Mother and invalid Father complacently seated on a verandah; three or four tall sons erect and stiff behind them; two or three little daughters on the floor at their feet (people in the tropics nearly always had out-size litters). Then he would gather from a few of the letters—(and hoped to be spared from reading them all)—how one of the tall sons, the one who looked most like his Dad, had run away to sea perhaps, or gone off to fight in some minor war, or been sent on a sheep-farm in New Zealand. This particular son had always been the favourite—Robert made a wry grimace at his pretty fancies gone flop—yes, undoubtedly the favourite; he had such engaging ways, but no stability; they trusted it would do him good to leave home at an early age; his mother was inclined to spoil him; he was not strong in the chest, you see ("that's where my cough comes in handy"). They received a couple of letters and then heard no more, till rumours of his death came vaguely drifting in, like sea-weed thrown up in streaks and ringlets on the shore: killed in a brawl—drowned—hanged—anything you like. . . .

And now, in 1911, the glorious resurrection of a prodigal son.

Add a few flourishes and authentic anecdotes to this conventional tale, learn his proper cues about names and ages, and Robert had little doubt but that increment and benefits would rapidly accrue. The life of leisure spread before him in shining panorama.

But now—"childless". Confound it! He really would have to go sleuthing for his data; hardly likely to find in the man's published letters, a compendium set forth legibly about an escapade which had brought forth a son on the wrong side of the blanket.

Still, right or wrong side—and who am I to pull a doubtful upper lip?—I'll take you, Dad, for better or for worse. Heaven bless you, my dear old parent, if you're going to mean whisky and meat instead of a kick in the pants.

What perplexed him, however, in view of the revelation which met his very first attempt to mug up on facts, was the attitude of the godly respectable people whose decent faces had lit up at the sight of him; who had pressed money into his hand; who were obviously glowing with the desire that he should sit down with them and be feasted as Stevenson's son and prototype. Were they then, these uncompromising Scots, prepared to condone a lapse into sin for the sake of some baffling invisible grace in the sinner? They must have *known* their man was "childless". There it stood, plain as print could make it, defying every holy sanction.

No good worrying about the strangeness of this and the strangeness of that. How long had he sat there staring? The woman would be along at any moment wanting her precious books to lend them to other subscribers who had filled up forms—"witnessed by two pairsons of reputable poseetion".

He remembered that a girl was mentioned in that very letter at the end of Volume Four. Katie, was it? Have another look.

Kirstie, not Katie. Kirstie would do fine, as a name.

That settled, he read up the essential dates: Born 1850 in Edinburgh; died 1894 in Samoa. This was 1911, and he, Robert, was thirty-eight, and looked more. Be systematic: subtract thirty-eight from 1911, and where and when did you first fetch up? Robert, my lad, you fetched up in 1873. The author could have been a youngster round about twenty-two (Robert the Younger was beginning to enjoy the fun) when he fell from virtue. The next thing to do was to read the letters of that period, find out exactly where to pitch the wistful little romance of poor Kirstie and her boy-lover; then let Kirstie run away to England and hide her shame. All in good time she could die or abandon him—and he could then, at the age of say six or seven, be transplanted to the Orphanage Home for Destitute Children, where in reality he had been derelict since he was only a few days old. And his father (if that fitted in) sailed for the South Seas in—when was it?—without ever knowing he had a son alive. Robert intended to produce a few touching infant memories of how Kirstie (already established as a Highland lass, in his charlatan autobiography) had told him cot-side anecdotes of this debonair young father. Perhaps he could himself be persuaded to recall, by an effort, a slender stripling with bright dark eyes who had dashed down from the North at odd moments, knelt on the floor to play with the child; told him stories of pirates and treasure islands; brought him presents, if rich enough at that time to be able to afford journey and presents? All the circumstantial details could be ransacked out of the appropriate books. Good thing he had learnt to read, and liked it.

He had not felt so light-hearted for years as now, charted to set sail on a buccaneer expedition from the curious harbour of the Dumburnock Public Library. And though he tried to frighten himself into caution by interpreting his queer thrill as a premonition of disaster, it was merely a futile attempt at self-deception. For he *knew*: it was luck ahead, and disaster left far behind. . . . My face is my fortune, Sir, he said.

He opened the earlier of the two volumes.

"Ye'll kindly no' be humming ony tune in this building. Ye should hae mair conseederation to ithers."

Robert flashed old Sour-Face a grin, and read on in silence.

"Wull ye stop laughing and making a' that clatter. It's agin the rules."

Yes, Robert reflected, but how *you* would have laughed and made a clatter, old codger, if you were me and had found what I've just found. For one remark, so apt as to be absurd, had tickled him beyond control, in a letter from the young R.L.S. to his mother: "You shouldn't have had a tramp for a son."

"If ye canna read in silence, and wi'out banging on the table, ye'll hae to leave the library."

And wouldn't *you* have banged on the table, Mr. Beaky-Nose, if you were trying to pin down this hobo to a solid address and fix him there long enough to get yourself born? Holy Moses, you might as well try and hammer a nail through quicksilver.

"And noo I distinctly heard ye using a profane worrd. I willna' warn ye again."

And wouldn't *you* have used a profane word, my good hag, if you'd fished about in a dozen letters raving of the sunset and the hills and the dicky-birds, and not one line to narrow it down, such as: "had a glorious bean-o with my wench Kirstie, lying in the heather"?

Nevertheless, almost at once he had begun to find this fellow Stevenson congenial; conscious of a sense of warmth and well-being in his presence, even though the presence were no more than a handful of letters read seventeen years after the man was buried and cold. Here was surely another vagrant like himself, restless and indolent, with suddenly a mischievous glint in his comments on the respectable and respected burghers of his native city.

[26]

Robert was exasperated, however, at the continued omission—serious from his point of view—of any reference to a lovelorn heroine whom he could establish as his apocryphal mother. The exasperation was less with Stevenson than with Colvin, Sidney Colvin, who in the preface owned he was responsible for the choice of correspondence to be printed or left out. If a young man went with girls, why in heaven's name try to muffle it up? Robert had no patience with a scrupulous attitude when it stood in his way. Were those rows with Mr. Stevenson Senior only about religion and the choice of a profession? Why not include wenching, and give a poor devil the clue he needed to an . . . honest living? He knew about heavy fathers; at least, he had heard and read about them; if there had been constant trouble in the grave Edinburgh home over the rebel ways of an only child who refused to follow in the family tradition as a lighthouse-keeper—no, a lighthouse engineer— and jibbed at worship in kirk regularly every Sabbath, well, it could be logically assumed that father and son had likewise not seen eye to eye on that other more important matter that must have bubbled up, hot and ardent, during those early years, roughly from 1871 to 1875, when the letters were sparse, and long intervals stretched a sombre, impenetrable curtain in front of the truth.

Robert dared not make notes in case it might be remarked and brought up against him later on, when already successfully established as the prodigal son of Scotland's whiteheaded boy. ("It's varra odd, Inspector, but I distinctly saw him write down pieces from what he found in a book. Varra odd indeed, if he's what he says he is.") So he had to trust his memory for fluent acquaintance with places and persons involved in the early history of R.L.S.

Many of the letters were written to a Mrs. Sitwell. These he skipped for the present; they were irrelevant to the quest of a plausible birthday for himself: no full-blooded man would be likely to scribble pages about one woman to another. Plenty of letters to his mother as well as to Mrs. Sitwell, therefore the same objection; skip them too. To Charles Baxter, "college companion and life-long friend"— More

[27]

promising. Come now, my lad, surely you could have told Charles Baxter all about dear little Kirstie? In 1871 (travelling backwards through the pages) Louis had chucked his engineering job; (Quite right, if that's how he felt). Months wasted in Germany; not wasted for him, perhaps; seems to have had a high old time; but damn it, I'm no son of a German girl, so let's see what happens when he gets back to Edinburgh? Hell! Nothing. Nothing but the same old row with his father over religion. And in November 1873 he was off again to Mentone. Where's that? France? Again, no good; my mother was no French girl either, I'll be bound.

Once he thought to have discovered a letter fruitful in promise, all about the beauty of tall women . . . till they turned out to be some arty nonsense called the Elgin Marbles. No wonder that he swore aloud, focusing a neighbour's ire.

Rows with his father; and afterwards, long rambles out of the city to the coast or to the hills; nearly always in a mood for anything to prove his passionate revolt against the Puritans of his home town.

No letters at all between February and July of 1873? Why? That's a bit fishy, unless— Again Robert laughed aloud; again upset the apple-cart of Sour-Face and Beaky-Nose at the table. He laughed because he had at that moment decided when to be well and truly born, having whittled down the years and the months and the weeks to a date just before Christmas 1873. And no more argument, if you please. When I say I'm born, I'm *born*.

He was so absorbed in this fascinating accumulation of evidence, that he would have given the lie to anyone who might have pointed out that the affair between Kirstie and Louis was nothing but a fantasy of his own, and but for an accident of eyes or mouth or profile, he might equally well have declared that he was born of any Tom and any Bessie at any date, in any county of England, Scotland, Ireland or Wales.

Now that he had made mental notes of the first facts which he would need to produce, exhausted by unaccustomed effort, he stretched his legs and spread his arms with a mighty sigh. . . . Good to relax, be done with strict study and allow himself a bit of reading for the odd pleasure of it. What a bit of added luck that out of the ten million men whom he might have strikingly resembled, it should prove to be a kindred spirit, whom Robert would have relished on the spot, but as a boon companion, and father my foot! He could readily imagine picking up with a mate cheerful and unashamed who at the age of sixteen-and-a-half could petition in this vein:

Respected Paternal Relative,—I write to make a request of the most moderate nature. Every year I have cost you an enormous —nay, elephantine—sum of money for drugs and physician's fees, and the most expensive time of the twelve months was March.

But this year the biting Oriental blasts, the howling tempests, and the general ailments of the human race have been successfully braved by yours truly.

Does not this deserve remuneration?

I appeal to your charity, I appeal to your generosity, I appeal to your justice, I appeal to your accounts, I appeal, in fine, to your purse.

My sense of generosity forbids the receipt of more—my sense of justice forbids the receipt of less—than half-a-crown.—Greetings from, Sir, your most affectionate and needy son, R. STEVENSON.

Had they not been divided by seventeen years between death and today, here was the lean light-hearted boy whom he could imagine loping along beside him on his road, a careless truant from kirk and home and university, approving of Robert's hoax, while with shouts of laughter they plotted the gestures of their conspiracy. It was pleasant to be so sure that Louis (the familiar address seemed wholly natural) would undoubtedly have bade him go on with the game, and wished him good hunting.

A shame to be hobnobbing with his prospective parent over a fistful of letters, instead of more suitably over a pint of beer. If Louis were his fellow-tramp, would he be sitting now, an unwelcome visitor to the Public Library at Dumburnock, planning to annex this profitable progenitor? If wishes were horses . . . you still could not ride them North and South at the same time.

Unaware that his eyes were involuntarily rejecting any graver, more mature passages of the letters as useless to his special errand, he went on happily flipping over the pages. With increasing delight he noted how certain unsanctioned pleasures of truancy and holiday were apparently viewed favourably by Louis as well:

. . . I had intended to spend my life (or any leisure I might have from Piracy upon the high seas) as the leader of a great horde of irregular cavalry, devastating whole valleys. I can still, looking back, see myself in many favourite attitudes : signalling for a boat from my pirate ship with a pocket-handkerchief, I at the jetty end, and one or two of my bold blades keeping the crowd at bay ; or else turning in the saddle to look back at my whole command (some five thousand strong) following me at the hand-gallop up the road out of the burning valley : this last by moonlight.

. . . This pleasant middle age into whose port we are steering is quite to my fancy. I would cast anchor here, and go ashore for twenty years and see the manners of the place. . . . I spy a little bright café in one corner of the port, in front of which I now propose we should sit down. There is just enough of the bustle of the harbour and no more ; and the ships are close in, regarding us with stern-windows—the ships that bring deals from Norway and parrots from the Indies. Let us sit down here for twenty years, with a packet of tobacco and a drink, and talk of art and women. By-and-by, the whole city will sink, and the ships too, and the table, and we also ; but we shall have sat for twenty years and had a fine talk ; and by that time, who knows ? exhausted the subject.

The context might have perplexed him here and there, had he bothered about it. But he was content to browse, only partly understanding what was going on, until—

—An exultant whoop. And down went the book with a bang, as he half leapt from his chair. Immediately on this exhibition of outrageous behaviour, Beaky-Nose, Sour-Face, My Good Hag and Old Codger indignantly clamouring together, summoned the Librarian already hastening towards them. After several unavailing protests from Robert, who brazenly denied that his conduct had in any way been other than meek and conformable, the breaker of sanctuary found himself wrenched from literary research and banished into the street.

[30]

He did not care. A paragraph he had found, amazing proof of complete affinity in outlook, was worth all the subsequent fuss and hullabaloo:

I have the strangest repugnance for writing. . . . A paper called A Defence of Idlers (which is really a defence of R. L. S.) is in a good way.

Had he been a writer himself—a far-fetched notion—he could hardly imagine a more satisfying title nor a more appealing theme: "Defence of Idlers"; defence of all the Roberts who had been chidden innumerable times for loafing and laziness; bone lazy, his first schoolmaster at the Home had said; and that was right enough; bone lazy, and these bones incurable, for they had never yet been given a good enough reason to make it worth while to struggle against their natural inclination to decline work. How strange, then, to encounter now a champion of idleness, as a sort of buckshee blessing on his researches. "A Defence of Idlers"— So elated was Robert that he really minded very little, as he carelessly took the first road to lead him out of Dumburnock, that he had been ignominiously ejected from the Public Library. What had he to do with the municipal advantages offered to the smug and holy? Time now to make a start and trust to his own wits to fill in any blanks. No use, he reflected, stuffing your memory with a lot of facts and figures to make you go heavily and warily; that was never his style. All he still required was a cue where and how to find the man who should have the honour of being his first victim. Not in Dumburnock, certainly; in Dumburnock he had already blotted his copybook.

He struck north at random. The weather was warmer and a stray glimmer of sun burnished the puddles. Robert felt fine; fine and hungry too, but preferred to remain hungry for the present, rather than by mere common back-door and farmhouse cadging, lower his new exciting standard. Suddenly he wondered, still amused and in no way discouraged, whether what he proposed to do were against the law? "Rogues and vagabonds"— Oh, he knew all the patter of old: "no visible means of support"— Yes, but look here, if he could succeed in passing himself off as Stevenson's son, was that not a means of support? Then up jumped in his brain another jack-in-the-box phrase: "Obtaining money by false pretences" . . . Robert stopped still for a moment and mentally contemplated those unfriendly syllables: "by false pretences". Then laughed, shrugged his shoulders and walked on again.

He could see the roofs of a town, and beyond them a gunmetal streak of water, and it occurred to him that he might ask for the local schoolmaster and not waste time on the ignorant and unscholarly; he who had just spent over an hour in serious reading, library reading.

A schoolmaster in Scotland was apparently called a dominie. Robert put his question three or four times before he stumbled on a lad bright enough to understand and correct the foreigner:

"It's the dominie ye'll be wanting."

"Aye," Robert replied briefly, trusting he would not presently be expected to commit himself in this rough burry dialect. It would have been interesting to find out if the dominie were an elderly man, old enough to have met— The girl at the library had said: "This is Stevenson's ain country ye're in."

He would know, of course, if he had aimed right and hit his mark, directly the man looked at his face; know by whether he would stare in startled fashion, drag his visitor indoors, fetch out the dram of whisky, gaze brimming with sympathy at the poverty-stricken condition of a wayfarer with that voice, those eyes, that special smile, peculiar tilt of the head, line of the jaw. . . . He could not tell exactly where it lay till he had seen a decent portrait.

The dominie was at his midday meal. His servant was trying to push Robert backwards over the threshold, and Robert, still in his buoyant mood of "follow my star and I can't go wrong", was stoutly resisting, when Mr. Mackay himself came into the kitchen. To Robert's disgust he was young and unresponsive, and to judge by his pebble stare, might not even have heard of a Scots author who had written *Treasure Island*. In sheer mischief Robert was tempted to reply to the dominie's inhospitable: "Ye'd better be gone: I've no work to give ye," with a cool: "Wait till you're asked for work, you ill-read schoolmaster; and take a look meanwhile at 'A Defence of Idlers!'" But deciding that this would really not get him much further, and feeling hungrier every moment, he substituted a fluent mysterious tale of how he had brought a message from across the ocean— Yes, the Atlantic Ocean, and further than that, from right across on the Pacific coast—

"And from whom would that be?"

"From one who died years ago," spoke Robert, dreamy and according to plan. "But the message is not for you."

Mr. Mackay remarked drily that in that case he could see little sense in coming to disturb him.

"Who migh. be the man ye're seeking?"

The tramp put his hand to his head: "I've been ill, ill for months, and the name has gone. . . . When I try to remember, it's knocking at a locked door. No—wait—" He paused, rapidly improvising a portrait of any simple old customer most likely to swallow bunk delivered alive and leaping hot; there ought to be at least three or four of this type within a ten-mile radius. "I believe they told me he lived in a large house by himself, or at least with only one other elderly relation, who left him a good deal alone; not that he minds, always buried in his books. He has lived in the neighbourhood off and on for nearly thirty years. They say he's kind and generous and would never forget an old friend. Always dwelling on the past; sometimes he forgets his meals, with all this dwelling on the past. Goes for long rambles with his dog—not a savage dog," added Robert hastily, "a friendly little beast. The name of the house? No, I've forgotten that too. Surely," he went on, trying to shake a response out of this stolid plump instructor of youth, "surely you can help me? give me some sort of an idea where I'm to find him?" He added a hint pregnant with his dramatic identity: "I've never been here myself, but my face is my message, and the old man in the house will take it before I open my mouth."

"Then he'll be luckier than masel'," said the schoolmaster, "for you've opened your mouth enough, never have I met such a gabster, and still for the life of me I canna tell what it's all about, though I fancy the name ye say ye've forgotten must be Mr. Renfrew of Ard-Daraich. It does sound near enough, anyhow, and he the only recluse I can call to mind without a family, and a fine classical scholar— Ask him to show you his translation of Sophocles so far as it's gone," suggested the sardonic Mr. Mackay, "when ye've delivered this precious message that weighs so heavy on your mind." He pointed out a road running north-east through the town: "When ye think to have gone a matter of four miles, ask your way again. And that will do, for I have my pudding getting cold on my plate."

"I apologize for keeping you away from it." But before Robert finished his graceful speech and bow, the door was slammed in his face. "And pudding yourself!" he shouted back over his shoulder, furious with this flabby-faced dominie who had given him such a poor reception. Then, as usual, he recovered his temper and laughed at his own wrath. These slight set-backs were only part of the game; and after all, he had a clue, and by that much information was further on in his quest for any gullible old fellow with a strong sentimental admiration for his famous compatriot. Quite a useful notion, to sketch an outline and let someone who knew better fill in a name and address. "A message from the Pacific coast" was henceforth likely to become part of his equipment; "passed on from someone who died" . . . in a passionless voice bound to arrest attention; he need prepare no other preface beforehand for the elderly, scholarly, generous, and above all, simple-minded Mr. Malcolm Douglas Renfrew.

. . . "Na, na," said Mr. Renfrew, sorrowfully shaking his head, "it was my cousin ye hoped to find. They were boys at the University together, and at play-acting too, but that was later with Professor Fleeming Jenkin; ye'll have been told that story, how Louis got himself into sair trouble when he raised the curtain at the wrong moment of the Greek play; eh, dear, dear, how my cousin used to laugh about it; dead now, poor man, or I'd have sent ye on to him. I was not living in Edinburgh then, so I've nothing to tell ye but what others have passed on, and no doubt ye'll have heard a hundred times the trick played by that high-spirited young rascal?" He peered with kindly curious eyes through his silver-rimmed spectacles at the figure lounging back at ease in a deep leather armchair, long legs stretched to the blazing fire; peered at him as though it were the most normal thing in the world to be enjoying a quiet scholarly hour of reminiscence with a crony who happened to look like a tramp: hair shaggy, chin badly in need of a shave, boots burst open at the seams, no collar, coat threadbare and worn into holes. His speech, however, patched here and there with American slang or American stresses, showed traces of education; better still, he was confident, carrying his rags with an air. Mr. Renfrew continued to beam at him, finding nothing incongruous in his affiliation with several rows of handsome volumes, dark red with a white label, arranged on the shelves just behind his head: the complete Edinburgh edition. R.L.S. had been a wild enough young scamp in his student days, no stability, no sense of expedience; and this son of his returned to Scotland from half across the world, hardly gave an impression that the blood had been mixed with a gentler, cooler strain; but God in Heaven! what a likeness to that Nerli drawing, the one with the piratical, rakish look aslant, and the long lean neck. . . . No need with yon face to have visiting-cards printed. Visiting-cards! Again Mr. Renfrew chuckled. He was no society-man, and Robert, even without that extraordinary thunder-and-lightning announcement of his birth, was as welcome a visitor as any other during a stormy November week. He bade him make a stout meal of the sandwiches and beer at his elbow and not fash himself to talk any more until he had finished. And did he say he already knew the story of the Fleeming Jenkin theatricals?

[36]

Robert shook his head, his mouth full, his body pleasantly roasted.

Mr. Renfrew was delighted. "His friend Professor Fleeming Jenkin of the Univairsity, and I may tell you almost the only reputable friend he had in Edinburgh in those wild days, was fond of private theatricals, for his wife was a fine actress and he very proud of her. Louis took part in many of the plays, though not, mind ye, a leading part, but he enjoyed it. Once when they performed a Greek tragedy, they set him, Heaven knows why, at the side of the stage to be responsible for working the curtain; he had to touch a spring; one of those modern inventions. The end came and the curtain fell on a scene of great power and grief between two young Athenians. While the audience was applauding, these young actors, no doubt glad the play was over, did a joyful war-dance on the stage, and then flung themselves down on to opposite ends of a couch, their legs up and their feet meeting in the shape of an inverted 'V'. Young Stevenson could not resist it: he touched the spring; the curtain went up again. There was a roar of laughter from the audience at the tableau. Terrible it must have been for the two lads, who leapt to their feet just as the curtain fell once more. Professor Jenkin was in front and saw it all. Without a word he rose and went behind the scenes. Louis heard a voice behind him, cold as the Arctic wind, saying: 'Mr. Stevenson, I shall ask you to give me a few minutes in my room.' . . . And it was the talk of the city, my cousin vowed, for many days after, and the respectable folk would not have him in their houses—but that was for darker doings, not just a mischievous prank. Darker doings," he repeated slowly. "Aye well, his father kept him too strict. How many parents could have foreseen those noble years at the end. Now here ye sit in my armchair, and all this more than forty years ago— Or when did he say ye were born?"

The question was shot out so suddenly after the soothing drone of anecdote, that Robert was temporarily off his guard. Trying to visualize the few important dates he had learned by heart before he was chucked out of the library at Dumburnock, he replied promptly and (according to his own pre-arrangement) incorrectly: "1876."

Mr. Renfrew nodded again with a thoughtful air, and played with a paper-knife.

Robert had been stunned at the success, so far, of his second professional contact. In Mr. Malcolm Douglas Renfrew's well-stocked, well-warmed library, he sensed that the fat of the land awaited him. The old boy was sitting there with an air of childish expectancy; the time had obviously come to supply the bed-time story, add a new tale to the old Arabian Nights. . . .

So out came the mythical Highland lassie essential to his present existence; out came the brief romance of Kirstie. Brief, because Robert had decided not to make it last longer than one calendar month; he was less liable to commit mistakes within that enclosure. He staged it somewhere in the Pentland Hills, not too far from Edinburgh, and was well away and leading up to a fluent graphic picture of Kirstie's discovery of her shame, her renunciation and flight, when his host interrupted: "*When* did ye say it happened, this love-affair?"

"August," replied Robert, giving his pseudo-parents a nice warm month for it.

. . . But there had been an error somewhere; he could see that, directly the word had leapt from his mouth; and could only trust, in his mood of happy-go-lucky optimism, that when it came to light it would not prove irretrievable.

"In August 1875, if I'm not making a mistake, and I doubt I am—" Mr. Renfrew put out his hand for a volume which Robert recognized at once as one of the 1911 edition of the Letters. "In August of '75, R.L.S. was in France, at Barbizon with his cousin Bob and the artist colony. Yes, here we have it. . . . So taking it ye were born the following May—"

Robert immediately decided that it would be quicker and less trouble to change his mother, than to involve himself in an intricate addition and subtraction of dates: "I was coming to that," with a sad dignity that imitated an impoverished aristocratic Frenchman he had known in New

Orleans, and came ready to hand just when he required it. With the same consideration towards his present needs, the name of that cheeky little French-Canadian skirt who had ordered him to shave off his stubble beard, also shot into his mind. . . . And Mr. Renfrew never realized how brilliant a transition was effected from a Scots lass who jilted her lover, to a demure French maiden, Léonore, who consoled him not wisely but only too well, all in the space of one month.

"So your mother was a French demoiselle, and ye were born out there in France?"

"No, she ran away to England. Her father was a narrow-minded peasant; he would have beaten her." He did not care whether Léonore ran away northwards from France, or Kirstie southwards from Scotland, as long as he could get himself born in England, where as soon as possible he could slide from jeopardy into safer truth, and relate how he was brought up at a Home for Foundlings near Bristol. "You see, France was so far. In England he could come down and see her sometimes; see her—and me."

"Aye, but he spent a large part of his time in France after 1875."

And in a flash it came to Robert that here was where he had skidded: 1873, not 1876, had been the date he had originally chosen. If only he had remembered, he need not have brought in this Léonore at all; Léonore, he felt already, was superfluous, in spite of her trim figure, nut-brown complexion and black sloe eyes. Henceforth, until he passed on from Mr. Renfrew to his next victim, he might have to be a little Frencher than he knew how, for he had never been to France.

Slightly intoxicated with his own unsuspected powers of weaving romantic fiction, he let Léonore swiftly find an English husband and bear him a legitimate son; then she turned against the memory of a reckless, half-gay, half-melancholy Scottish stripling, and neglected and abandoned her first-born at an early age, with a callous shrug as to his ultimate fate amongst strangers. On some other occasion, perhaps, he might ginger up the tale with a spice of variety; recall two or three vivid little pictures of a boyish father sitting beside him on the floor playing at trains and soldiers; but not for Mr. Renfrew; no, *Sir*; he had spent time and imagination in abundance on Mr. Renfrew. Now to cut the cackle and get to the horses. You could not sit in a library for ever.

But Mr. Renfrew spoke first:

"And now what can I do for you? What sort of work may be to your taste?"

A fleeting grimace from Robert. Damn his bowels! Was the whole world crazy on this idea of work and work and work? Except one man who had written "A Defence of Idlers"?

Mr. Renfrew, who may or may not have been an acute psychologist, advised his visitor in an encouraging tone not to be too diffident. "I'm not asking for a list of your successes. Some men run up against trouble whatever they try to do; but ye're no fool, and if ye're tramping the roads, that may well be because ye've chopped and changed too often."

Robert sighed; chopped, yes; we're off to the woodshed, not a doubt of it.

"Ye canna humbug me," his tormentor went on, innocent of irony in that complacent reflection. "Ye came along here with the notion of asking me to help ye to a good job, even if ye had to use your birthright to bully me round to it."

"Can you call it a birthright?" Robert found no difficulty in producing a slight wince and an over-sensitive contraction of the brows.

"Grow another skin"; the advice was, however, kindly given. "And now, what can ye do, what have ye done, and what do ye like best of all ye've done?"

"War," Robert replied slowly, and, as it happened, truthfully. "Not that I cared for killing, but it's a man's life."

"Ravaging carcasses for loot?"

"You don't ravage all the time."

Mr. Renfrew's eyes twinkled and snapped: "Fought under Wellington, I presume?"

"Not quite. Wish I had. Boer War. Batman to a

cavalry captain who got killed during Dundonald's charge to relieve Ladysmith. A wonder I wasn't, flat under those thundering hooves."

"So ye're satisfied ye fought in a righteous cause?"

"No," said Robert briefly, rather cross that the conversation should have swerved so far from the congenial topic of supplying him with unearned increment. "No, the Boer War was *not* a righteous cause. Everybody knows that now, so where's the harm in saying it; maybe we'll fight our next war for a better reason."

"We varra near found ourselves in the middle of the next, a few days ago," remarked Mr. Renfrew, "when the German Emperor got to loggerheads with the French on the question of Morocco. Impairtinence of the man, sending his German squadron to Agadir to cut a fine dash before the world. Aye, it looked like war then; we sent a cruiser for him to know that if he didn't clear out—"

So that was it. Agadir. Robert had vaguely noticed the posters throbbing with portent.

"Your father was a soldier," said Mr. Renfrew in that sudden disconcerting way of his.

"Sure he was." Though surprised, Robert concealed the question-mark.

"D'ye mind what Barrie said of him: 'A soldier every inch'? 'Little Barrie', Stevenson wrote in one of his letters. I can see him now, at the great meeting Lord Rosebery called together here in Edinburgh in 1896 to discuss a memorial: little Barrie standing up wi' hands deep in his pockets and his shoulders hunched—" Mr. Renfrew sprang to his feet and in an instant became that writer, shy and yet oddly eloquent.

"'They were only soldiers in the ranks'—(that's the younger writers of the day) 'but they were proud to claim him as their leader, and when he called his muster-roll they would be found answering to their names, "Here, here, here." Stevenson was dead, but he still carried their flag, and because of him the most unworthy among them were a little more worthy, and the meanest of them a little less mean.' But wait, I'll find it for ye, and if ye're a writer yourself—" Mr. Renfrew might not have put forward that somewhat fantastic proposition had he been looking straight at Robert; but he was already half-way up a small ladder and running his fingers along a shelf in search of the book he needed, so accustomed probably to having an attentive man of letters in the armchair where a tramp now sat, that he took his audience for granted.

"Here it is, and 'twill warm your heart: 'They were only soldiers in the ranks—'"

Robert stopped him, not rudely, but a child of nature taking for granted that nobody would wish to repeat the same line twice over: "We've had that. That's where you began just now."

A little disconcerted, for the students or grave scholars who usually sat in that chair and listened, let him repeat himself three or four times, Mr. Renfrew returned aloft to that particular corner devoted to Stevenson; Robert should have more whether he desired it or not.

"Aye, poor laddie, he would like fine to have been a soldier. He and the little Osbourne boy, his stepson, used to play their war-game on the floor of the attic at Davos week after week. And they had a room set apart for it at Vailima, too, which they called the Soldier Room. Six hundred toy soldiers, and a whole campaign covering whole countries, and maybe his wife hadn't the heart to make him clear it up every evening as Cummy did when the little sick boy played at the Crimean War on his counterpane. But if ye're asking me for more— Wait while I find it. . . ."

Robert was not asking for more; but he had no option against such a desperado as a book addict on the spree. He was, however, warm and comfortable; he could stretch out his legs and toast his toes through his broken boots; now and then, screened by the armchair's back, he threw another log on the fire, while the busy cherub on the steps in a far corner of the room became more and more absorbed, pulling out book after book, until several tumbled from his too eager fingers and fell to the ground; here Mr. Renfrew joined them, scrambling down with another huge armful, and sitting on the floor completely surrounded by his darling volumes, reading a passage from one and then from the other with a running commentary and an uncanny instinct to find his way about: at least, it seemed uncanny to his hearer, half amused, somewhat impatient, but summing it up with his usual nonchalant appraisal: "Little Half-pint's bats!"

"Wait while I find it" was the phrase that by repetition seemed to reassure the old gentleman that he was not doing this for his own pleasure, but to provide the pleasantest entertainment for someone who had somehow got into the library.

"He had it strong and hot at last, out there in Samoa. Ye can tell from his letters the joy he took in helping the right side to win: the native king Mataafa; a rebel king, the Germans called him; ye ken the Germans governed the island then, and still do, though a better government and more justice than in Stevenson's day. They had cause to fear him, for though he didn't fight them with swords, he used every other weapon without fear for himself. Wait while I find it in his Vailima letters—no, I'm too early: it came little more than a year before the end:

We wait, with a kind of sighing impatience, for war to be declared, or to blow finally off, living in the meanwhile in a kind of children's hour of firelight and shadow and preposterous tales; the king seen at night galloping up our road upon unknown errands and covering his face as he passes our cook. . . .

Graham and I got into the saddle about one o'clock and off down to town. In town, there was nothing but rumours going. . . . Three hundred yards beyond is a second ford; and there—I came face to face with war. Under the trees on the further bank sat a picket of seven men with Winchesters; their faces bright, their eyes ardent. As we came up, they did not speak or move; only their eyes followed us. . . . So home, a little before six, in a dashing squall of rain, to a bowl of kava and dinner. But the impression on our minds was extraordinary; the sight of that picket at the ford, and those ardent, happy faces whirls in my head; the old aboriginal awoke in both of us and knickered like a stallion. . . .

He slammed down the book triumphantly. Robert had been nearly asleep; he roused himself, listened for a few moments, and then the soothing murmuration of Mr.

[43]

Renfrew's voice dropping lower and lower, telling tales to his books, reading aloud to his books, sent him off again. . . .

"Ye'll remember, I make no doubt, the numberless times he stresses the use of the sword in his work and in his letters; as if he loved the weapon itself as a blade of shining steel, not only a symbol. When he was a child of six and they gave him a toy sword many sizes too big for him, and then tried to swathe a shawl over it, he struggled at first, for by make-believe he was a giant fellow with a bearskin helmet in the Crimea. And someone made mock of the sword, so the wee lad spoke up, maybe out of a book they'd read him: 'The hilt is of gold and the scabbard of silver, and the child is well content.' Well content . . . he learnt that lesson bravely, and passed it on, when we wake to look for his example." This was not directed at Robert's slumbers, of which Mr. Renfrew was happily not aware, but as part of that oblivious monologue by which scholars living alone communicate their enthusiasms to the four walls of their hermitage. "Now where is it, what I am looking for?—his dedication of *Weir* to his wife—I know it by heart:

> . . . For who
> Burnished the sword, blew on the drowsy coal,
> Held still the target higher, chary of praise
> And prodigal of counsel—who but thou ?

A grand tribute but for the one line." Mr. Renfrew chuckled in mischievous relish. "'Chary of praise and prodigal of counsel!'—Women are like that, they canna help it and she was right to be chary of praise: a true man is glad not to have it all day long in his ain hoose—'Ye're wonderful' with no discreemination. She better than all the rest could see how his life was a fight and the adversaries strong. What did he write to Meredith? I expect ye're acquainted with the works of George Meredith?—they're none so bad," in parenthesis. "Wait while I find it: 'And the battle goes on—ill or well, is a trifle; so as it goes. I was made for a contest, and the Powers have so willed that my battlefield should be this dingy, inglorious one of the bed and the physic bottle. At least I have not failed, but I would have preferred a place of trumpetings and the open air over my head.'

And in another letter—" here followed a long-drawn-out pause while Mr. Renfrew for once hunted for something he could not find, and at last gave up with a sigh. "It's got the devil in it; I could have sworn it was in that volume; a shrewd remark and we'll see it come true again: 'Where there are traders, there will be ammunition'—he knew wars had their dairty patches. Once, feeling weary, he wrote that he'd like best, if he made a mucker, to end up in a revolution with his back set against the wall, and the lead pellets whiffed into him. And then somewhere else—" He flicked through several pages of another book: "'Here lies one who meant well, tried a little, failed much.' . . . Poor laddie, he had no conceit of himself. Folks should read his Christmas Sermon: '. . . The summons which calls a defeated soldier from the field: defeated, ay—but if there is still one inch of fight in his old spirit, undishonoured. The faith which sustained him in his life-long blindness and life-long disappointment will scarce even be required in this last formality of laying down his arms. Give him a march with his old bones—'"

Mr. Renfrew's voice rang out in a sonorous peal, waking Robert; who, however, accustomed to casual sleeping at odd times and in odd places and to casual disturbances of his sleep, did not resent it but was merely a little surprised to find that the monologue was still going on. "'—Give him a march with his old bones; there, out of the glorious sun-coloured earth, out of the day and the dust and the ecstasy—there goes another Faithful Failure!'

And what d'ye think of that? Is it no' a fine piece?"

"Fine," Robert echoed, ready to oblige, and even dimly aware that there was something that appealed to him in "the glorious sun-coloured earth" which he had taken for granted for so long.

"If ever a man had a soldier's funeral," Mr. Renfrew went on a little dreamily, laying down the Christmas Sermon, "it was that man whose bier the Samoan warriors carried shoulder-high up the steep and rugged mountain to the

peak, by the path they had hacked during the night he lay
dead in the hall of his house; while the native boys watched
sorrow-stricken beside him and chanted prayers for the dead,
and the chiefs filed past one by one, to say goodbye to their
chief, bringing precious gifts—'Alofa, Tusitala. . . . Farewell, teller of tales.' . . . And they left him alone up yonder,
high on Mount Vaea. But first the oldest chief stepped forward and tabooed the use of firearms on the hillside; for they
knew he had loved well the song of the birds, so leave them
undisturbed for ever to sing around his grave."

Robert listened fascinated. The fragment was tantalizing
and he longed to ask for more, but was aware just in time
that he would utterly destroy any chance of still bamboozling
the rich and simple-hearted old gentleman if he betrayed
that this was the first he had heard of the strange, romantic
burial-place of R.L.S. He made a mental note that he
might as well look it up if he ever found himself again
inside a Public Library.

"Agadir," mused Mr. Renfrew, returning to the present.
"That's blown over for a wee while, and we'll no' be fighting
the Germans. Ye remember what your father said about
our responsibility in the fall of Khartoum?"

Robert assumed a mien wistful and patient; and reminded
the old man that he had had little opportunity to remember
anything his father had said.

"Said? Come now, I mean wrote." And went on to
remark a little testily that he had taken it for granted that
an ardent son had devoured every line of the writings of
R.L.S.

"Never gave the fellow a second thought till I landed in
Scotland last week"—but this piece of honesty was left unspoken, for Robert was still hoping that their dithering
exchange of views on wars and letters would not last for
ever; he felt again, and even more strongly, that he had
had his bellyful. Very nice for Mr. Renfrew to have company and so forth, but company was not here for chopping
conversation—nor wood. He resolved on a bold move.

"If you're talking of a likeness more than skin deep," he
laughed, "I *am* like him in this, I too defend idlers with all

my heart. Fact, I'm a born idler by nature, as he was."

Mr. Renfrew stared. The flame of the fire leapt up and flung a ruddy light across the two faces: the scholar's chubby and incredulous; the other, the rogue's, dark and gaunt and mobile, relaxed into sublime unconsciousness that he had stepped into a very morass of blunder; ready to oblige with any quantity of light philosophy as long as he successfully dodged the curse of Adam. Then the flame died down again on the side nearest Mr. Renfrew, so that only his host's outburst of powerful indignation roused Robert to a sense that something had gone very badly wrong indeed. . . .

A few minutes later, he was inwardly shaken with sardonic laughter at the joke revealed: That of all outstanding traits he should just have pitched on idleness in the man whom he happened to resemble, when according to Mr. Renfrew—(Robert had to grant that Old Mutton-Chop was well up in his subject)—this very same man had been one of the most persistent and unflagging workers the world had ever known.

"A born idler by nature—*that* man ? who never spared himself, though his life, as his friends well knew, hung twisting on a spider's filament? He knew it too, but worked through fever and cough and hemorrhage and pain and sleepless nights and racking cares; when he had to lie motionless in a darkened room, his right arm strapped to his side, he learnt to write with his left hand; learnt the deaf and dumb language that he might go on dictating when he had to stay in bed, not allowed to speak a word for weeks. He worked when he crossed to America, an emigrant in the steerage, surrounded by noise and crying and other sick folk, as the *Devonia* plunged and staggered through the waves; and when the yacht *Casco* sped through a gale, he wrote with his pen spearing the ink-bottle, and his papers on the table thrown about as they lurched through a hurricane squall. He wrote and re-wrote and revised and destroyed and was only satisfied after he had hunted for the pairfect phrase and found it . . . though the cart of Byles the butcher, he said,

[47]

was evermore driving swiftly at his heels. He wrote in a white heat, yet careful as a monk toiling over an ancient missal, never satisfied to let the wrong word go out on a page till he had striven to make it the right one. *Idle?* When a story had been written during three days and three nights, he burnt it all and wrote it again rather than just tinker about with it as young men do today." The sneering scorn of Mr. Renfrew's voice on the word "tinker"! *"Idle?* He? That long grind behind him and the long cruel grind before him, till he fell dead there on the verandah. . . . Idle, ye said? working against sickness, never flinching, never daring to relax; with aching head, weary and torn by his cough, and working still; working through sciatica and writer's cramp— For mind, they were no picture-book ill-nesses that were on him all his life—"

"Put a sock in it," Robert murmured; but the corners of his mouth were still twitching with the concealed joke against himself; a joke he would have relished sharing with his prototype, for he could imagine no one else who would so keenly appreciate all the subtler points of his discomfiture. Compared with his previous contentment in a solitary exist-ence, he began to be exasperated by this new and unsub-stantial intrusion on his private life; this desire for Louis somewhere round, stimulating, resilient, uncritical; wickedly in sympathy with the whole racket and willing to come in on it . . . at this point Robert would like to have demanded of the man what the devil he meant by his ridiculous enthusiasm for hard labour, his desperate tenacity in sticking to it against odds?

But Mr. Renfrew had still not put a sock in it : "Surely," bouncing up and down in his chair, "knowing all this about him, ye could never have believed literally what he put down in that trifling essay ? and he not yet twenty-four when he composed it. Nay, you can be no son of his if ye've missed his indomitable purpose that would not, could not stop to lie aback awhile and to repose in the satisfaction of fame well and truly achieved."

Robert only heard one sentence of all these rolling periods: *"You can be no son of his!"* Deal with that quickly, or never set out on the quest again. It flashed through his mind that not only must the blunder be retrieved at all costs, but also that it was vital he should somehow earn enough—yes, earn it if there were no sweeter way—to *buy* those four volumes of Letters; buy and study them before venturing forth again as a pedlar of hocus-pocus. He had been over-confident, over-impudent, on insufficient data. These two urgencies, to lull Mr. Renfrew back again into benevolence, and to earn a sufficient sum to possess and read and master those darned Letters, could be united and dealt with by one brilliant burst of bluff.

He smiled gently at the wrathful old gentleman: "So you took me seriously? What's a poor devil to do when that happens? Get up and sling his hook, with a whining 'Thanks for your hospitality'?—No, I'm damned if I'll leave you to go on thinking for the rest of your days that I'm a born idler with a liking for idlers. That essay with its cock-a-snook title can feed a mood for an hour or two and that's all there is to it. Look, I'll prove how I meant damn-all of my lazy jabber. Look, I need a job, you've said it, and that's why I came to you. Make it tough, I don't care, I'll stick to it. I only want the chance—"

He was never to be sure how far he had allayed the suspicion of his patron by his *volte face*, but he was determined that the job, whatever it might turn out to be, should take him a long way off from here. He had queered his pitch and deserved what he got. These volumes of the Letters were his necessary stock-in-trade; and as a preliminary to abandoning work for ever and living a life of leisure as delicious as it was illegitimate, he could think of no better investment. So again he peremptorily demanded what Mr. Renfrew was prepared to do for him? And curbed his unruly tongue from adding that though to toil for a bare living was strictly against his principles, he was willing this once to overlook it.

A businesslike discussion followed. Robert continued to carry off matters with a high hand, taking over control of the dialogue in case it should again escape into questions perilous for one so lamentably unprepared. He made a brief (and truthful) inventory of what he had done and what he could do, including a few months on a sheep-farm in the West Country when he was a boy. So it was agreed that he should be sent to Gleann Bàn in Argyll to a distant cousin of Mr. Renfrew, who had a sheep-farm of several hundred acres of rough hilly land on the edge of a small loch; and had complained of a shortage of labour, now that the winter season was near, for the essential business of draining the slopes.

"Could ye do that?"

"Why not?" grimly.

"It's not what I call a soft job, and Charlie Fenwick's not what I call a soft man."

"I'd rather he wasn't. What will he pay?"

"What I tell him to, I've no doubt."

"And my fare?"

The old man chuckled. "Ye're in a hurry to fill your empty pockets. What's wrong with tramping the distance?"

"Can't afford it. I've been sick, and I'm on my beam ends."

"Yet ye're willing to spend the cold months out-of-doors wrestling with nature? It'll be heavy going."

He might have interpreted Robert's answering lift of the head as dauntless. Actually it arose from a swift calculation that two or three weeks' wages would probably be enough and a bit over, to purchase the Letters, and that would be the end of faithful service. The bit over was his fare south to Edinburgh. He had read enough to be aware that in and around this city might be the most promising market for his peculiar merchandise.

4

The bookseller's shop butted out at a corner from one of
the steep streets off the Canongate, running down from the
Castle. It was small enough to seem overcrowded by only
four or five customers. So Robert thrust his way towards the
shelves at the far end, and waited modestly until the owner
had leisure to attend to him. He could afford to appear
modest, for he was today no mendicant, but himself a
customer, arrogantly conscious of the money he had earned
by hard and honest labour during the past three weeks.
The farmer at Gleann Bàn had let him off nothing. Casual
labour was all very well, but when Charlie Fenwick took
on a vagrant, even sent by Cousin Renfrew, he preferred
to make sure the job was begun and finished by the same
hands. He and his old shepherd Macnair could look after
the flock, though this bumptious fellow appeared to think
he knew something about tending sheep. Perhaps he did,
but watching sheep quietly graze in meadows in the west
of England could hardly have ripened his experience of
sheep seeking rocky hill pasturage in Caledonia. So let
him try and use yon great draining-spade in the right way;
he'd find it not so easy as saying his prayers. Then, having
taught Robert what had to be done, and why, and how to
do it, he informed him he was welcome to a bed in the loft
above the byres, and board, but not a penny should he get
till his grim task was accomplished and the ditches dug to
carry away the danger-floods of rain, and later the melted
snows that would pour down and threaten to engulf the
farm buildings.

It took Robert just over three weeks. Fenwick was not
displeased with his fury of toil, though masked by scorn of
it except as means to an end; he paid him his £3, and told

him he might come back at the same season next year, if he liked; it would save the trouble of teaching an even worse fool how to dig in a zigzagging course, to control the stupendous rush of waters and prevent scouring which caused pot-holes into which the sheep might fall. The mockery in Robert's eyes gleamed brighter as he departed with his earnings. Come back to work? He? Likely, wasn't it? That infernal climate, soft and relaxing, had done his chest no good; he felt about twice as ill and brittle as when he undertook the job. And no energy left to hoof it even as far as Glasgow; luckily there was plenty of tin and to spare for the train from Arrochar. And what was left would buy the Letters; money now actually to be spent on the purpose to which it was originally dedicated; a unique event in Robert's life; therefore his sedate demeanour was jeopardized by the slight swagger in his walk, and a suggestion in the carriage of his head that his battered old tramp's hat supported a cock's feather stuck in at a confident angle.

He had already seen the 1911 edition of the Stevenson Letters displayed prominently in the window, so he did not bother to search for them; four volumes, priced at five shillings each. They were, so to speak, already his; already possessed by the man who could pay for them.

But on the shelves he lit upon *Robert Louis Stevenson, A Life Study in Criticism*, by H. Baildon. Had Robert remembered the probability of a portrait as the book's frontispiece, he would not have opened it so nonchalantly—

—For it opened at his own face.

It was a shock. He had obviously been prepared for a strong likeness of feature, but this was uncanny; this, instinct told him, was his very look: dark eyes slewed round to taunt some unknown person with a half smile, rakish, audacious; lean bare neck; high cheek-bones in a gaunt, piratical face. Gosh! No wonder they had stared thunderstruck when he appeared on the scene in Scotland, he and his moustache, as though a visitor had returned from another world. No wonder they had forked out good and plenty. Stared? He stared himself, by a sense of having been hailed by a spirit strongly akin to his own, suddenly understanding a little of what men had meant when they mourned for a mate sent to sail on different seas: "I kinda miss him, see?" And understanding, forfeited for ever an ample slice of his enviable independence.

The caption informed him this was a sketch for a portrait by Count Nerli. Robert ached to possess it, but to him there were more normal ways than *buying* it; purchase of a library hardly figured in his itinerary, beyond the Letters. The matter of transferring the portrait did not offer itself as an overwhelming problem; the sheet was loose; he was partly hidden from view where he stood in a dim corner with his back turned towards the shop where the stout elderly proprietress was busy with her other customers; a twitch of his fingers, and out it came. A shapeless pocket bulging with all the property he possessed in the world (the other pocket was torn too wide for use) could still hide a scrunched-up page. He slid it in and thrust it down—

"Can I interest you in any of my stock?"

Robert spun round, swayed, and dropped in a faint. He rolled over and over across the mounds of books stacked loosely on the floor, dragging some of them along with him. Then he lay still.

Miss Gibson too had received a shock when the stranger suddenly turned at her voice and she had caught a glimpse of his face. She had been too busy to notice him when he first came in, except a general impression that a seedy ragamuffin with his trousers tied up with string was hardly likely to prove a satisfactory customer; indeed, she was faintly surprised that he should have come in at all; his sort usually hung about outside. However, she was a practical woman, and all questions could wait. The shop was empty now; promptly and efficiently she applied the usual first-aid remedies, just as though her heart were not thumping like mad; the heart of an ardent young novice who had not dared hope for a vision, least of all while on lay duty. Yet Jane Gibson's business associates (she had hardly any personal friends in Edinburgh) would have described her as a woman with a good head on her square shoulders, a little brusque in manner, and no nonsense *at all*.

[53]

. . . Manifest nonsense for a tramp to push in just before closing-time, and be so absorbed in Baildon that he swooned like a Victorian maid at the sound of her voice. However, he was beginning to mutter and throw his arms around; next came a few incoherent phrases, rough as you might have expected them to be, lapsing into unintelligible slang, American slang as far as she could judge. And in the same idiom, he swore at her for pouring cold water over his face. . . .

Then he opened his eyes.

She had read about those eyes, oddly enough, in a recent copy of *The Bookman*: ". . . eyes of strange beauty . . . half alert, half sorrowful . . . there appeared to be a haunting sadness in their very brightness . . ."

Directly he caught sight of her, he laid his tongue on sentences of entirely educated and polite English; Robert was always remarkable for the swiftness of his power of transition to fit any circumstances and any company; a gift which so far had neither landed him into an honourable position in the Diplomatic Service nor brought him enormous wealth. It was useful, nevertheless.

The lady had been most kind, he said; and he had entered the shop to buy the four volumes of Stevenson's Letters, please; and would it be too much trouble for the lady to make them into a parcel? His childlike pride in his rôle of customer as, still sitting on the dusty floor, he held out the money for his purchases, exactly the right sum without asking, prompted her to pick up on the same conventional note and ask him with sarcastic courtesy if she might send the parcel to his private address?

"That's an awkward suggestion," murmured Robert; "I'd rather you hadn't made it."

"You've only just come to Edinburgh? You've nowhere to sleep tonight?" And she wished she did not know quite so clearly what she was going to say next. To invite a wastrel to accompany her home to her neat lodgings, sleep on the sitting-room sofa, share her supper?—Preposterous. Yet he was ill, and that was sincere enough; no amount of smarmy lies about his homeless condition could have been as effective as the way his bones stuck out, the big drops of sweat on his forehead, his skin clay-coloured, his breath short and difficult—

Besides, he had told no smarmy lies as yet; the usual patter and whine of the professional outcast was missing. And when he dropped out of American, he spoke an English like her own; they were both strangers in Scotland and it was her duty to do what she could to help him (only for tonight, of course).

And finally, she *had* to find out why he had bought that expensive set of Stevenson Letters directly after he had stolen the Stevenson portrait from the Baildon Life?

She compromised by giving her invitation roughly as a disciplinarian might issue an order. And forbade him to move while she went out and sent an urchin to fetch a cab, for it was sleeting. Then waited, leaning up against the jamb of the doorway, heedless of the sky's inclemency. For she sorely needed this breathing-space to view her world transfigured.

One more glance up towards the Castle before returning to her patient— Patient! this meek and muffled word, applied to Robert, was ridiculous. She laughed aloud, and as though triumphantly catching up her laughter and spreading it over the whole city, the Castle buglers sounded the nightly retreat. She could not ever remember hearing it before: "That's foolish. Of course I must have heard it every evening unless I left early."

A cab jolted along and pulled up at the corner; the side street was too steep for the horse, but the urchin tore up to demand his pennies.

Robert meanwhile had stumbled to his feet and seized his opportunity to open the first three volumes of the Letters and take a swift excited look at the frontispieces. But they yielded no such thrill as when a few minutes ago he saw the portrait that was now pushed to the bottom of his pocket. He was only to have that moment once again. As for these—

"R. L. Stevenson, aet 35 (I suppose thay mean 'at'); aet 40; aet 20."

"Aet twenty." A youth neatly dressed to have his photograph taken; arms folded; all the character chased from his face except submission to the ordeal of looking wise, thoughtful and older than his age.

"Aet thirty-five": good-tempered and natural enough; smiling, not handsome; the same coat; well, there was nothing remarkable in that; Robert too had worn the same coat for fifteen years and more; but here the lapels looked pushed up and rumpled as though the buttons were thrust through the wrong holes.

"Aet forty" interested Robert most of the three. Those brilliant eyes met his own with a sort of teasing challenge. "Yes, maybe he *has* got a look of me about the eyes!" Enough to amuse anybody, considering how the chance resemblance was going to be employed. But Robert did not care for a certain indefinable threat of a sermon in the pose of the figure leaning forward over an arm of the chair, the folded hands, the almost clerical collar. "I don't want any 'Dearly beloved brethren' from you, old son!"

Miss Gibson called: "Here's the cab!"

"O.K." Leaning on his stick, Robert managed to limp across the shop and join her at the door. She supported him down the slope.

"Hi, stop! You've forgotten my books."

She *had* forgotten them, but was pleased with him for his persistent memory. "Let me see, it was Lockhart's *Life of Scott*, wasn't it?" she teased him.

Robert slid her one of his brilliant, wicked looks: "You can throw that in for nothing if you want to; I shan't read it."

Miss Gibson deposited him in the cab as though he were a package himself, and a breakable one; then returned to the shop for the Letters. Which led to the discovery that she had not locked up. All her routine had been pulled awry tonight; just imagine leaving the premises open like that for anybody to get in and help themselves. "I must be mad."

And striving for a little compensating sanity, as for the second time she marched down to the waiting cab at the corner, she decided it was high time to ask that young man a few questions. Young man? Not so young. Mentally she placed him at about forty, or allowing a more haggard stamp on him from the life he must have led, perhaps thirty-six.

"Are you English? You don't talk like a Scot."

"Nor do you."

"My maternal grandfather, from whom I inherited the shop, was an Edinburgh man; my father was a Sassenach."

The word had no meaning for him; and she went on, still prodding: "Once or twice I took you for an American."

"Educated there, mostly. Worked over there, too, for the last eleven years."

"Worked?"

"On and off. You needn't judge by my clothes. I'll have a new outfit this time next week if I'm lucky."

"And are you lucky?"

"Look at me now," he laughed, "treated to a drive in a cab and supper with a lady: you're going to give me supper, aren't you? As well as a shake-down for the night?"

She nodded crossly.

It was a long cab drive and would eat up all her profit on selling him the Letters; they were not yet out of Princes Street.

Presently he said wearily: "Are we nearly home?"

And she repeated: "Nearly home."

It gave her a grim pleasure to reflect that her taciturn way of living, with no prying friends or landlady to drop in uninvited, might have been in deliberate preparation for what she knew, at the age of fifty-nine, was the most exciting evening of her life.

Just before the cab stopped at an unremarkable house in Comely Bank, she asked the question she had been fighting back since the moment he had swung round and faced her in the shop. "You're Stevenson's son, aren't you?"

And repeated it, for it sounded even more incredible put into words a second time: "You're a son of Robert Louis Stevenson, aren't you?"

"Yes."

[57]

Luck again. He had never dreamt of such a credulous victim, such a dead man's disciple, prepared by lonely idolatry and refusing to admit it. Not likely he would be deceived by her show of brisk sensible questions as from any lady to any tramp to whom for pity's sake she had given a lodging for the night.

"Eat up your supper first and talk afterwards. I can wait." Yes, she could just wait; and wait again while she washed up. He did not offer to help; really too spent and bankrupt in energy to do anything except sprawl in the armchair, with a huge steaming cup of coffee, and watch her going to and fro to the tiny kitchen, while with lazy amusement he silently got ready his story. It would have to be of the simplest variety; for though he now possessed the Letters with their prefaces, he had had no time to arrange anything nearer akin to the facts than when he had blundered so ridiculously three weeks ago with Mr. Renfrew over "A Defence of Idlers". So take no risks, and make as quick a transition as possible from fake to truth. Now then.

Miss Gibson drew up a hard chair to the opposite side of the fire, and sat inflexibly upright, clicking her knitting-needles. He observed her hands tremble, so that she had to keep on putting down the sock, to pretend the fire needed making up with shovel and poker . . . till at last she surrendered wholly to wonder, and remained on her knees, awkward and entranced, while he pitched her the tale, Number One Edition, Suitable for Beginners:

His mother was found collapsed by the roadside clutching a baby a few days old, near a small town in the South-West of England. She was taken to the Workhouse Infirmary, but exposure and under-nourishment had left her too weak to recover. Before she died, she let fall to the authorities his father's identity; and begged them never to try and communicate with him: it would be no good; he knew nothing about her plight; he was still a youngster; lived far away; had no money; owed her nothing. . . .

Robert ran swiftly over this bridge towards truth on the further shore, like a man hardly trusting his weight to the splintering wood. Now he was on firm ground again, and could go on telling her of his life as it had been in reality :

"So they handed me over to a Charity Home"— Queer, he noticed dispassionately as a stage producer from the back of the auditorium intent on whether a certain performance would get across, queer how your voice sounded exactly the same whether you were supported by firm ground below and could take long steady strides through the past, or whether you skimmed and balanced on a lie, and then over the ice to another lie, and one more, until you were safe again.

Miss Gibson helped to make it easy; though she liked to think herself independent of old-fashioned conventions, a woman engrossed in commerce who had little patience with the flippancies of life, nevertheless she got busy with the fire and poker, her head turned away from Robert, until the fallen girl was dead and buried, and the baby decently established at the Institute.

. . . At last and gruffly she asked: "When did they tell you?"

"When I was fifteen or thereabouts."

"What did you do?"

"Ran away."

The answer was unexpected; for she had meant: "What did you feel?" But Robert was not at all sure what, for future profit, he should have felt, so he selected action; and indeed, he *had* run away from the Home when he was fifteen, so why bother to invent?

"Weren't they kind to you?"

"Oh yes; only I was one of a hundred or more; you couldn't expect them to sing me lullabies; just another young scamp who had to be brought up to support himself by a steady trade."

And now it was Miss Gibson's turn to reveal a sense of humour. He thought her plain weather-beaten old face was rather jolly when she grinned at him like that.

"What 'steady' trade did they choose for you?"

Robert searched for something on which she could hardly put him immediately to the test. Farm work, of course.

[59]

The truth again. It was a perpetual surprise each time he discovered fiction to be unnecessary in his rôle:

"They tried me on a sheep-farm first, but I ran away."

"Didn't you like it? Did you run away to America?"

For she thought he sounded in a no-man's-land between education and unbelievable ignorance. On the former, she was able to give him praise in a schoolmarm voice at which he laughed, recognizing that she would not insult his supposed birthright by asking too bluntly where on earth he had picked up his schooling, considering his toes were through his boots? No harm, though, in continuing to tell of his career as it really had been, from the time he grew restless and impatient of toiling inland for no one's sake; got himself taken on as a cabin-boy; and after two or three voyages, fetched up at a small port on the islanded coast of New England; was left behind in hospital with a fractured leg, after a fall, and adopted by the kindly schoolmaster and his comfortable wife whose only son had been drowned. With them Robert had stayed for four years, and they had had much delight in him.

"Then that accounts for it," remarked Miss Gibson, who had returned to her chair and her knitting, furiously jealous of the schoolmaster's wife, but determined not to show it. Doubtless she had then died, and the old man had died, and had forgotten to provide for this poor fellow whom they had loved like a son.

"I can't bear unpractical people," she muttered. Aloud she enquired if his farming experience had come in useful, and gave him some crisp facts about sheep-farming in New England, picked up from one of the odd books over which she had browsed at the back of the shop when trade was quiet: *Shepherd o' Salisbury Plain*.

"Maybe," replied Robert, totally indifferent as to whether the folks of Maine alone of all the States in the eighteen-eighties, had made the mistake of leaving their sheep without a shepherd, to find their own pasturage among the high sunburnt ridges. "I ran away after four years."

"Again?" And Miss Gibson added with a tart edge on

her tongue: "You seem to make a habit of it. What didn't please you this time?"

Robert chuckled. "Shucks, I dunno. Got sick of it. Humdrum; too much of the Meeting-house; and the minister always droning on about our sins. I can't bear sermons. And seeing all the other chaps go off on voyages, and hearing them yarn when they got back as though I were a softie and a stay-at-home. Old Merrill wanted to train me to teach, so that I could take on the schoolhouse after he died. Can you see me?"

Oddly enough, she could, for a flying moment; the boys would have liked him, listened to him, and played no tricks. Still—he ran away.

Suddenly the question occurred to her which she might easily have put to him several hours ago, but even now it was difficult to say: "What's your name?" Or "What did they call you?" Or "What do you call yourself?" Sometimes with one of her less reputable customers she had had to go by a devious route to discover what should have been information volunteered; and if she had never walked delicately before, she walked with delicacy here:

"Did he, the schoolmaster, allow you to take his name too? Or"—she paused; his face was in shadow and she could not tell if he winced—"or have you preferred to keep the one that you . . . that they . . . that your mother . . ."

No good. She should not have started. There she floundered, hopelessly bogged. But God in Heaven, had the man no feelings? She could have sworn that inwardly he was laughing again, as he rescued her from the quaking black mud:

"Sure, I've had plenty of names, though my mother forgot to leave them written up on the workhouse slate. I expect *she* had plenty of names, too, but I don't know any of 'em. At the Home they'd a system for the waifs they picked up: depended whereabouts they came on the list: North, South, East, West; and the colours: Black, White, Green, Brown, Grey. We had a Scarlet too, but he got ragged too much; they dropped Scarlet after that. The trades: Smith, Baker, Butcher, Shepherd— Oh, I've forgotten the rest. A good many had their own names, anyhow; only I wasn't one. She . . ."

—And Miss Gibson understood "she" was the woman who had died so pitifully soon after giving him birth.

". . . She'd called me Robert; they stuck to that; I was Robert Black till I went to live with Mr. Merrill. And you're right—I hadn't dossed a night under his roof before they called me Merrill too. But I'm willing to take any name where I sleep, if it's to oblige," said shameless Robert, gazing straight at Miss Gibson.

But he had put her in a mood where she was not inclined to be lenient, for he had committed the unpardonable sin of ingratitude.

"And you've never been back once to the Merrills, or sent them a present, or even written to them thanking them for all they did for you during four whole years?"

Robert shrugged his shoulders, only slightly surprised at her indignation; he had met it before in others on the same count; and never attempted to explain or justify his code, as far as it went, or his lack of a code. Supposing *he* had been a schoolmaster in New England, and the Merrills had limped up to the porch, a pair of vagabonds, and he had taken them in and looked after them for four years or thereabouts; and then supposing they had walked out on him and had gone on to a different life, feeling quite a lot better for the change and rest; would he have expected *them* to write him an appreciative letter of thanks and go on writing every second Tuesday? Not he; he would have understood right enough that even if they had behaved pleasant and affectionate all the time, they might have sickened of the village and the humdrum life; always the same neighbours dropping in with gossip slow and kindly, or sharp and shrewish; bringing their herbal remedies for small ailments; clacking of an up-country wedding and their grandmother's funeral; gentle boasts of the glories of their ancestors in the mercantile marine, when women and children had gone long hazardous voyages in the gallant sailing-ships bound for the Orient from those little coastal towns now off the trading routes and quietly preoccupied with their own con-

cerns, content with only the deep-sea roar held in the huge
spiky shells that lay with other ocean trophies on the mantel-
piece. But Robert at twenty did not care for life heard
from the distance. He was by nature neither a potential
farmer nor, certainly, a potential schoolmaster.

Yet it would hardly be expedient to upset the old girl
enquiring into his autobiography, so he continued to build
up a career of mingled fact and fantasy, suppressing the
portions that he judged were not suitable for her understanding.

He told her, and she listened, not quite as Desdemona
might have listened to Othello but fascinated by the motley
ways men contrive to keep themselves alive, how he had
been a ship's hand on exotic voyages with exotic cargoes;
how a rich old Chinaman took a fancy to him, but yet again,
slippery as an eel, he could not be held. Boer War. Casual
labour driving a ramshackle car for a troupe of minstrel
entertainers across America. A period as a drummer (which
he had to explain to her was the same as a commercial
traveller); he did quite well at it, helped by his cool assurances and immunity to rebuffs, no less than his gift of the
gab. Pneumonia put a finish to that; and when recovered,
he slipped down the social rung from a commercial traveller
to peddling and hawking. Ill again and in hospital; his
neighbour in bed was a journalist, and when Robert could get
about, he too tried his hand at journalism. Little success
there. Better luck serving barbecue steaks at a filling-station
in the Middle West—till the owner got rid of him with harsh
words: "Not that I blame him," said Robert in handsome
tolerance. "But it should have been his wife he sent
packing, see? Or don't you?" A period of auto-wrecking
in California: "No, ma'am; not a crime; lawful; the old
cars brought to us we broke up for their spare parts or
for scrap-iron." Ill once more while working his passage
on a tramp steamer from Newfoundland bound for the
Clyde. . . . "And a spell of foul weather on the roads; a
job again on a sheep-farm over at Gleann Bàn. And—
here I am."

And Miss Gibson, who desired desperately to think well

of this man, for the magic of his dark lean mobile face, tried to forget how he had jarred her.

So she remarked stiffly: "If Mr. Merrill trained you to be a schoolmaster, you must have become acquainted with good literature while you were with him?"— Then plunged into the subject she had been longing to talk about, faltering on the brink, and the next moment in:

"Did you read all your—all Stevenson's books?"

Robert thought: "I might have known that was coming." And temporized with: "Mr. Merrill only had *Treasure Island*." And with some skill, he quickly invented a violent prejudice on the part of the poor innocent schoolmaster against all literature from the Old Country: "I'm wrong; he didn't even have *Treasure Island*; I read that while I was in the Home; they had quite a good collection of 'wisely selected fiction' given by 'interested friends'. One of the Board did start a 'forbidden fruit and product of the Devil' campaign to give us only Sermons, but luckily we had Mr. Gladstone on our side. Gosh! I'd forgotten from that day to this; old Gladstone sat up all night in bed reading *Treasure Island*, didn't he? And that was good enough for the rest of the Board. Yes, Sir. You'd have thought they'd have jibbed at Long John Silver; he didn't even come to a bad end. I do think bad men ought to come to a bad end, don't you, Miss Gibson?"

She remarked thoughtfully that one of them very nearly had, on the doorstep of an old bookshop on a sleety evening in Edinburgh. Robert liked her the better for the spirited reminder; folk should be able to hold their own.

"You've missed something by not reading *Kidnapped*," said Miss Gibson.

"Oh, but I have. I didn't know—" he pulled himself together. For: "I didn't know *Kidnapped* was by Stevenson" would hardly have created a happy impression from a pseudo-son of R.L.S. So: "—I didn't know women cared about that sort of book."

"You've got to care about Alan Breck, whether you're woman or man."

"*Alan Breck!*"

[64]

. . . They might have been close comrades for years, he and Miss Gibson, from the way they raced on together now, each eagerly breaking in on the other: Robert, his memory magically renewed, spouting of the fight in the Round-house of the "Covenant" with such relish, some of the words true and right, and some of his own, that Miss Gibson was compelled to go to her book-shelf and pull out the last volume from a uniform row bound in red, and bring it over, and find the page, and read aloud:

" . . . The wrestler dropped at last ; and Alan, leaping back to get his distance, ran upon the others like a bull, roaring as he went. They broke before him like water, turning, and running, and falling one against another in their haste. The sword in his hands flashed like quick-silver into the huddle of our fleeting enemies ; and at every flash there came the scream of a man hurt. I was still think-ing we were lost, when lo! they were all gone, and Alan was driving them along the deck as a sheep-dog chases sheep. . . .
The round-house was like a shambles ; three were dead inside, another lay in his death agony across the threshold ; and there were Alan and I victorious and unhurt. He came up to me with open arms. 'Come to my arms !' he cried, and embraced and kissed me hard upon both cheeks. 'David,' said he, 'I love you like a brother. . . .' "

Robert joined in on the next line:
" '—And oh, man,' he cried in a kind of ecstasy, 'am I no a bonny fighter?'" . . . as though a fight like that and a speech like that had often gone singing through his mind, to an invisible ally he would have liked always beside him: a mate staunch and honest as David, hot and fiery and brave as Alan Breck.

Delighted at his response, the first she had won from him, Miss Gibson cried: "Alan Breck figures in *Catriona* too. I'm getting the whole Swanston Edition as each volume appears, and *Kidnapped* is the most recent, so you'll be able to read them as they come out."

Then she stopped, aghast at what she had let slip. Twenty-five volumes, and only ten had been published. Was she mad, assuming he would stay until her Swanston Edition was complete? Sheer stark lunacy. Yet after all, Mrs. Merrill had adopted him. Yes, and look how he had treated

[65]

Mrs. Merrill. Besides, Mrs. Merrill had been Mrs. *and* Mr. Merrill.

Perhaps Providence was kind, and he had not heard? Troubled, she went on in a spate: "'Swanston' is even more appropriate than the Edinburgh or the Pentland Edition, don't you agree? Swanston meant so much to him, and to all of us. You'll see when we come to *St. Ives*. . . ."

We?—there she was, at it again. "I ought to be shut up," reflected Miss Gibson grimly. But she was relieved, when she looked across at him, to see him stifling a yawn, his lids dropped over his eyes.

Robert was pretending overwhelming sleepiness to conceal that he did not understand what was so appropriate about the word "Swanston"? The woman had spoken it like an incantation. "Swanston"? He had vaguely come across it in his rapid Free Library half-hour, and stretched his mind in vain to recall whether it were animal, vegetable or mineral? Place, person, house, or favourite dog? Until he had time to study the Letters properly and find out, he had better feign uncontrollable heaviness and let her take the hint.

Yet he still had a few yards of dangerous ground to negotiate before he could relax and be alone. Miss Gibson had taken *Kidnapped* back to the shelf above the desk.

" I hate keeping books behind glass doors," she murmured, "but we mustn't let the city smoke and the city dirt get to them. . . ."

And she lifted down and caressed a book bound in faded peacock blue, lettered in gold across the back : *A Child's Garden of Verses*; opened it; looked at the dedication and poem on the title-page as if she were brooding over a treasure :

To Alison Cunningham from her boy.

. . . From the sick child, now well and old,
Take, Nurse, the little book you hold.

"*So* well and *so* old?" Miss Gibson murmured, in tender mockery of an eternal optimist; then turned back to a front page blank of print, but a name was written on it in a small cramped bothered hand. . . . She glanced over her shoulder at the tattered rapscallion in the armchair. Should she show him now? Tomorrow? Ever?

"Look," in a queer tense voice, "this may interest you."

He took it, and flicked over a few pages.

Sleepy and unregenerate, his sole comment was: "We sure don't seem to have been the same sort of child in the same sort of garden."

Miss Gibson was a fair-minded woman. It would have been hardly surprising if a waif from a charitable institution had spoken with bitterness of the delicate child adored by nurse and parents and aunt, who had played his imaginative games with his cousins in the garden of Colinton Manse, or alone in the nursery of Heriot Row; nevertheless, she did not think she detected any bitterness in Robert's tone, only a laconic acceptance. He must have an exceptionally nice nature. And the conclusion was worth more than a thousand pounds to her at that moment.

"What have you found?" For he had paused at one of the poems:

> " When the grass was closely mown,
>   Walking on the lawn alone,
>   In the turf a hole I found
>   And hid a soldier underground.
>
>   Spring and daisies came apace ;
>   Grasses hide my hiding place ;
>   Grasses run like a green sea
>   O'er the lawn up to my knee.
>
>   Under grass alone he lies,
>   Looking up with leaden eyes,
>   Scarlet coat and pointed gun,
>   To the stars and to the sun.
>
>   When the grass is ripe like grain,
>   When the scythe is stoned again,
>   When the lawn is shaven clear,
>   Then my hole shall reappear.
>
>   I shall find him, never fear,
>   I shall find my grenadier. . . ."

He stopped as though he had had enough. And she waited for some illuminating comment. Thanks no doubt to Mr. Merrill, he read aloud not at all badly and as though he responded to something of the meaning.

"Loony kid," remarked Robert lightly; "why in heck did he want to bury his soldier?" And he repeated: "Loony!"

With truly frightful dignity, Miss Gibson was about to take the volume from his unworthy hands, but Robert, still idly toying with it, had by now discovered the autograph on the front page; and before it, a name scratched out with such vigour that it could no longer be deciphered:

For ▮▮▮▮▮▮
affectionately,
from Robert Louis Stevenson.

After "loony kid", Miss Gibson expected desecration of holy ground, but unpredictable as ever, Robert stared down hard at the page and said nothing.

Exultant once more, she reflected: "He's really moved." On what a see-saw had she been lifted and dipped since dusk this afternoon.

Interested he certainly was. It might come in useful to be familiar with the autograph of R.L.S., though for the moment Robert did not quite see why or when. He continued to scrutinize the genuine handwriting of an author whom for outrageous reasons he had adopted as his father. . . . This was again one of the moments when it occurred to him that he was making up stories about a man who had once actually been alive. As a sort of incantation he repeated under his breath: "Born 1850, died 1894."

("Come off it, sawny! Just a book you're holding, full of wishy-washy poetry scribbled to please elderly nannie-goats like Miss G. He can't have given it to *her* or she wouldn't have scratched out the name. Wonder if she pinched it?") With a twinkle of brotherhood, he looked up at her. No, he'd forgotten; not the class that pinched things; respectable to the marrow.

"Bought it in with a job lot?" he asked, guessing right.

"Yes; it happens three or four times in the life of a bookseller, that we retrieve some valuable treasure-trove by someone's ignorance or carelessness. I think, don't you, this must have been stolen originally? Perhaps the friend died to whom he had sent it, and some dishonest person saw their opportunity, and scratched out the name so as not to be traced."

"Dirty trick."

Robert bent closer. She was right, the signature was quite undecipherable. It occurred to him that here was an answer as to what use he might make of it; and he did not add in his mind "if it were mine". . . . Robert liked short cuts, even in his mental processes. Yes, he could pretend that the crossed-out name was his mother's; using an alternative version of his autobiography which he intended to produce as soon as he had more data: himself at the age of five or six remembering R.L.S. coming with gifts to see Kirstie and Kirstie's little boy. . . . Then he looked at the date: 1885. And asked Miss Gibson: "Was this when it was written?"

"Yes, it's a first edition, except for a few rare copies still called 'Penny Whistles'." With a true bibliograph's zeal and authentic information, she gave the history of the title she preferred: "When he first fixed on it, he ordered a design of many whistles crossed, for the title page. He could be happy for hours tootling on a tin whistle when he had to stay in bed."

"Nice for the other fellows trying to get some sleep."

Miss Gibson did not directly contradict his impression of Stevenson lodging with other Weary Willies and Tired Tims, which rose before him as a matter of course; instead, she drew a picture of Châlet la Solitude on a hill above the Mediterranean, and a man lying for weeks in a darkened room, all the day's radiance shut away, his right arm strapped to his side, forbidden to speak above a whisper, making up clear and joyous rhymes about children having fun out of doors.

. . . "Though he began to work on them in Scotland, before they came South."

"Call it work?"

"*Yes*," in a flash of temper. "And don't scoff at a job you know nothing about. You're one of those dunderheads who have to see the sweat roll down, before you can recognize a labouring man."

Robert laughed.

And she recovered her equanimity, and allowed that R.L.S. himself had got the idea of trying his hand at these Penny Whistles from idly picking up a Kate Greenaway Birthday Book for Children, with verses by Mrs. Sale Barker, which had been given to his mother in 1881: "These are rather nice rhymes," he had said, "and I don't think they'll be difficult." With professional pride she produced the identical little brown volume, square and dumpy, with the imprint in old-fashioned lettering: "London, Engraved and Printed at Raquet Court by Edmund Evans."

"Is that valuable too?" But he spoke from far away, for he was weighing dates in his mind, and came to the reluctant conclusion that after all the *Child's Garden* was no good to him as a touching corroboration of the boy and girl love-story; 1885 was much too late. Whether he chose to keep his fictitious mother alive for a few years after his birth or let her die at once, was nobody's business, as he rather oddly put it; but he must positively stick to a date for his own arrival into the world: 1873, or he would get into a most awful muddle; and even give rise to an unkind suspicion, if any of his future victims were to meet and compare notes, that he was fraudulent and a pretender.

Robert yawned, stretched, dropped the book, apologized, then yawned again thrice.

"Sorry, I don't seem able to keep my eyes open." And he flung himself on the slippery horse-hair sofa. "D'you mind if I say good-night? You're so stimulating, it's all been rather too much for me." He judged she could stand just that amount of butter, but no more.

"Don't go if you're not ready for bed," he added, sincerely, not aware that he was affronting the conventions: "I can sleep with anyone round; used to dossing twenty in a row."

But Miss Gibson was not disposed to make even two in a row; though with renewed compassion for the hard life he had led, she tucked him up with a thick rug, and brought him another pillow and a glass of hot milk. Having read about toughs of his calibre and their taste for raw spirits, she was surprised that he liked the milk and asked her if she had any more?— "But don't worry if you're short." He was looking suddenly so young, with his mouth milky and the pillow tugged down with both hands to support his cheek, that she made an incredible fool of herself and suggested leaving him a night-light?

Robert's hearty shout of laughter broke the illusion. She laughed in fellowship at her ludicrous notion, and heard him still softly laughing as she turned the gas right out, and groped her way towards the door which led to her bedroom.

Nevertheless, she could never think of him again as a "proper" tramp, sunk into slouching degradation; who might have drunk milk, certainly, in a ravenous, perpetually under-nourished condition, but who could never have spent an evening among books as she and Robert had just done to the satisfaction of both. This man may have slept on hard boards or on filthy mattresses on the cellar floors of a hundred lodging-houses for his ilk, bullied by authority and hedged in by rules that barely acknowledged these creatures as human; his condition betrayed that he had probably lived for weeks at a time on bread and margarine and tea; he might have assimilated, without shrinking, the habits of the ragged regiment and suffered their miseries as a matter of course, spoken their tongue, cursed with their curses, picked up cigarette-ends from the pavements as they did, and relished them; but he had not conformed; he limped, but he did not shuffle; he remained a "casual" who miraculously kept an incongruous air of being free to do as he chose; and if what he chose was to avoid work, wear broken boots, expose himself in all weathers, treat his benefactors with shocking ingratitude, take it for granted that you threw yourself down and slept without washing your face or saying your prayers, still he was no melancholy degenerate. Nor was Miss Gibson afterwards amazed to the extent she might have expected, that she should have quoted poetry to him (not that he had paid much attention; "Loony kid" he had said) and offered him the equivalent of a nursery fire-guard and a woolly bear to cuddle.

She was so dazed with happiness that she confidently expected that sleep would touch her at once; but perhaps that last too convivial moment had torn the web of drowsy enchantment which had formed since, hardly giving her an instant to see his face, he had tumbled in a faint at her feet.

Sleep had its obstinate mood and held off as though it would never consent to have salt sprinkled on its tail. Every minute she felt more and more wide-awake, her hearing alert and strained, her mind swinging like an intoxicated pendulum from one argument to another, justifying what she had done, to a surrounding chorus of: "You must be mad, Jane Gibson. Stark staring mad. A tramp in your sitting-room!" To most women of her age tramps belonged just beyond the threshold saying: "Thank you, Mum," wiping their mouth with the back of their hand, watched off the premises by a vigilant dog. "You must be *mad*, Jane Gibson!" And so she was—gloriously mad. At last she had done something worth while, co-ordinating her whole existence. . . .

Towards morning, exhausted by these hours of rich satisfaction after an austere diet of fifty-nine years, she fell heavily asleep.

She fell asleep a contented lunatic. She woke up late, sane and furious with herself; a down-to-earth mood. Her lurid deeds of the evening before had to be dealt with and rationalized while she washed and dressed and twisted her hair into a firm bun: "After all, the man was ill and needed a rest. Presently he'll be off, looking for a job. I'll give him some bread and cheese to take along and half a crown— no, a florin. No, half a crown, and that'll be the end of the matter."

It did not occur to her that he might have been off already and taken, so to speak, the sitting-room with him. That would certainly have been the end of the matter. But Robert bore out her opinion of him as a stationary object, for when she marched into the room, there he still lay stretched out on the horse-hair sofa, propped by two pillows (she had lent him hers, and missed it), hands clasped behind his head, and a sweet smile to greet her.

He asked her how she had slept, as though he were really interested in the answer. And far from ready to make a move, with or without bread-and-cheese and a florin, he was obviously waiting for her to get him his breakfast; that was as clear as if he had shouted it aloud.

Miss Gibson set her teeth, accepted this chastisement as a deserved comment on her folly, and without wasting energy on sparkling conversation, prepared excellent porridge and coffee and bread and butter for two, and slapped it down on the table.

"Smells good," said the tramp.

"Will you draw up your chair?" enquired Miss Gibson. "Or shall I bring your breakfast over to you?"

Robert never bothered with sarcasm. He replied that he would prefer her to bring it to him. And got it.

She remarked pointedly that she always had to make a good breakfast to sustain her for her day's hard work.

"And what are your plans? Do you know Edinburgh? No, I forgot, you said it was the first time you'd been to Scotland. Then will you be looking for a job in the city itself, or are you trying further afield?"

But Robert's "plans" were not in the plural; his plan was to spend the day indoors, as he hardly felt up to anything more strenuous: warm and recumbent, he would read his four volumes of the Stevenson Letters. He did not mind telling her now, as an item of interest, that his last three weeks of labour in the wind and driving rain, had been a tax on his rotten health, and was only undertaken for the purpose of making himself her legitimate customer in the shop. Though here at home, he added with another winning smile, he was no customer but her guest.

"You've given me such a splendid breakfast, I shan't want any lunch. In a day or two, I'll think of looking up

[73]

any of my famous father's friends who may be alive and handy." He paused. . . . And by some trick of telepathy, she saw swiftly appear and disappear between them, the Nerli drawing with its brilliant slanted scrutiny of a buccaneer summing up what danger lay in wait for him.

The buccaneer's prototype went on: "Expect I need a shave. I mustn't grow my beard again—now." The "now" was in a voice too low for her to hear. "But that can wait for a day or two, if you don't mind? And if I'm lucky, I'll get some clo' to go visiting, a bit more decent than these." He could take a chance on "if I'm lucky"; its significance was too obscure for Miss Gibson. "I expect I look an awful tramp," he finished; and stretched for one of the four bright red books on the floor beside him; with a certain childish cockiness, endearing were she in the mood to find it so, indicating that they were his own, paid for as any other bona fide customer would have paid.

Miss Gibson wondered if this were colossal effrontery or the natural innocence of a cherub? On the whole, she was inclined to think the former. Nor could she guess that it was characteristic of Robert, when he genuinely felt ill and aching in every bone, to rag more impudently than usual, as a sort of dare to illness, because he felt it a degradation that his body had not yet learnt expedience.

So she looked in vain for the dark melancholy Ishmael who had so thrilled her last night. Or was it she who had changed in the broad, too broad daylight? She came of an independent Spartan stock who did not laze and read in the morning; it was wrong; you sold books in the mornings and afternoons, for decent people to read at night. And if you were a man, even a wastrel, it was all out of order to have the woman go out wage-earning while you politely let her off getting you lunch.

In a towering rage she whisked away the breakfast things, washed them up, and banged them on the draining-board; too angry to do anything about removing last night's ashes from the fire, or relaying it, or tidying the sitting-room. Curtly, while skewering on her uncompromising felt hat, she told him where he might wash.

"Presently," called Robert from the sofa.

She snatched her old tweed cape from the peg in the hall, and without further speech stumped downstairs and out into the street.

She had already crossed the road and was hurrying for her tram, when a dreadful idea brought her to a halt.

Honest? Why, she knew the fellow was *not* honest; she had had ocular proof of it. And yet she had left him alone with a treasure; not merely a sentimental treasure, but a thing of value. . . . She recalled distinctly the thoughtful look in his eyes when he pored over the autographed page of *A Child's Garden of Verses* ; his inflexion when he asked: "Is this when it was written?" He was quite shrewd enough to know the value of first editions compared with later ones.

Miss Gibson marched straight back to the house and upstairs into the sitting-room, not to be held from her intention by any law of hospitality.

He looked up, but she did not even glance in his direction. Crossing to the bookshelves with the glass doors, she locked them, thrust the key into her handbag and strode out again. He heard the front door slam for the second time.

It was just as well she had not glanced in his direction, for if she had expected him to be outraged, she would have been bitterly disappointed at the amused gleam in his eyes as they watched her much too expressive movements.

He gave a long, low whistle: "Gosh, so she *did* see me pinch that photo, after all!"

5

Not many customers came to Miss Gibson during the day;
so as the hours dragged on, she had plenty of leisure to feel
less satisfied that on waking that morning, common sense
should have reclaimed her behaviour from lunacy. No doubt
she would have been a fool to have let an unknown tramp
remain alone in her lodgings with every well-oiled opportunity to walk off with an object of value, especially as she
had already seen with her own eyes that he was not a really
scrupulous character. Nevertheless, though law-abiding
citizens would certainly have approved of her return to make
sure the key was turned on the treasure, she could not,
though in anguish she tried, force herself to the same
approval. Wiser here to have been a fool than a wise woman.
Wiser to have lost the book, lost the substance, than to have
violated the spirit contained in that book and in all the range
along those unlocked shelves. The approval of law-abiding
citizens was of all tame rewards the tamest ; and suspicion
of all dingy qualities the least godlike. Yet she had behaved
like a suspicious law-abiding spinster, as an alternative to
abiding by her new impulsive self that had flamed up on a
sleety November evening, and turned the wet city and the
pouring gutters to shining fantasy.

Of course he would be gone by the time she returned
home; she had had a rare chance and lost it for ever. Re-
morse, rejecting that picture of a departing thief, which let
her off far too easily, presented instead a Chattertonian vision
of Robert lying half on, half off the horse-hair sofa, frozen
to death because she had not lit the fire before going
out. . . . What had been his last thoughts of a woman who
could only be kind, even for his father's sake, for a few
brief hours?

The empty bookshop became a torture-chamber. Striving to re-establish her self-respect, Miss Gibson told herself weakly that in his passion to offer constant hospitality, R.L.S. had meant it to embrace only his friends. But truth spoke in stern correction: His hospitality was for the stranger, the outcast, derelict, leper, beachcomber, drunkard, any down-and-out man, woman or child who happened his way.

In a final desperate attempt to harden herself against the unholy image of Robert Black—Robert Merrill—perhaps Robert Gibson—("I'm willing to take any name where I sleep, if it's to oblige")—she went deliberately to remove a certain volume from her shelves of new books and place it among her second-hand stock; for now that the frontispiece from Baildon's *Robert Louis Stevenson* was missing, its value was halved; surely no business woman, and she had always been a business woman, could readily forgive such an assault on her profits?

. . . She stood there holding the book, wondering by what paradox the missing page was its own appeal, and an appeal in the wrong direction?   For instead of incensing her against the robber, it melted her to a perilous tenderness. Would she have to get rid of her shop, sell it and set up some-where else in Edinburgh, to escape the persistent haunting of a tall bony figure in rags who swung round at her voice . . . to front her with the very face he had dared steal and scrunch into his pocket? Think of the insolence of the man when after that, he could buy four comparatively expensive volumes of the Letters and pay her for them with a lordly air, as though he had a magic to put all things right.

Even theft of her property.

Yet now she hated property. But for her autographed first edition of the *Child's Garden*, and her sudden absurd fury to protect it as a tangible possession, she could have gone home this evening and perhaps found Robert still there. Son of a "vanished Tusitala" . . . like a cord tautly strung through her mind, this echo vibrated: last signature to a last letter.

Tusitala vanished.   And the man who looked like his

son, said he was his son, and might indeed and indeed actually be his son—he would have vanished too.

("I can't abide yon woman. There was no call to be rude, for all that she hadna the book I wanted. She'll no' see me in her shop again.")

Miss Gibson decided to put up her shutters and return home an hour earlier than usual. At least in the vacancy of her own rooms she would not have to force herself to be polite to people with no intent to buy, but under the usual delusion that in bookshops you may stay for hours pottering round, asking questions, putting finger-marks all over the stock, and demanding a zealous attention for nothing, simply because it *is* a bookshop, and you are a woman, and people who keep bookshops are known to be gentle, abstracted, unbusinesslike and fond of company. So Miss Gibson defied the good salesmanship that only yesterday had been her pride; hating herself even more than she hated the law-abiding citizens of Edinburgh to whom from now onwards she belonged, since she had forfeited a wilder gayer fellowship.

She decided to walk home; the tram would be unbear-able with the memory of a jolting cab running parallel, and a voice, husky, laughing, saying with its alien lilt: ". . . if I'm lucky."

("And are you lucky?"

"Look at me now; treated to a drive in a cab and supper with a lady. . . . Are we nearly home?")

Home. How wearily he had asked.

Miss Gibson might have spared herself these red-hot stripes of castigation. Far from finding her rooms reproach-ful and empty, or full of corpses, they were full of Robert comfortably stretched on the sofa and greeting her with the cordial smile of a favourite nephew:

"I've got a good fire for you. It was touch and go; you left me a box with only one match."

[78]

❧ 6 ❧

What he had to do was to get his *facts*; get them clear and hard, without any sob-stuff; get them by heart so that his future benefactors would never be able to trip him up and shamefully expose him, as Mr. Renfrew so nearly had over that "Defence of Idlers" business. It was nice and quiet here; better than the Dumburnock Library where noisy talkative people kept on interrupting his studies. What a good thing the old camel went out to work. Tomorrow, if he felt strong enough—no use hurrying it—he too would go out. . . .

He took a preliminary glance through the four volumes of the Letters. They appeared to be divided into sections, each section with its preface. Today it was on these prefaces he would need to concentrate. His mistake last time had been to allow himself to be tempted and go jumping to and fro among the letters themselves, just because Stevenson's style to his intimates was gayer and easier to read and therefore more to his taste than Colvin's, whom he darkly suspected of being a scholar. Last time he had been too bent on getting himself duly born, and inventing a credible sort of romance to account for it. He hoped he had gained sense since that careless half-hour in the Dumburnock Library; for he was aware now that for his future campaign's success he must hammer out a brief outline of events straight through from beginning to end, in their right order. Not that he supposed for a moment that he would have to recite it to any of the mugs whom in his mind he already saw filing towards him in a haze of gold. But *he* must know, he, Robert Black, exactly where he was; Robert Black must keep a cool head, and could not do that if he were all the time struggling to remember; he recalled with satisfaction how Mr. Merrill had always praised his marvellous memory, while deploring his reluctance to use it.

That reluctance was on him now, yet he spurred himself to the initial effort, punched a rather prickly sofa cushion into the right shape to support his head, and picked up Volume One.

Robert Louis Stevenson. Born 13th November, 1850, at 8 Howard Place, Edinburgh. Christened Robert Lewis Balfour; later his father changed spelling of his name to Louis for dislike of a certain Edinburgh Lewis. Stevenson himself at eighteen dropped name Balfour.

His father, Thomas Stevenson, youngest son of Robert Stevenson who built Bell Rock Lighthouse; family of official engineers to Commissioners of Northern Lights. Strong, outspoken, but soft-hearted; sometimes stern and gloomy, then suddenly full of fun. His mother, Margaret Isabella, youngest daughter of Rev. Lewis Balfour of Colinton. Affectionate, weak on the chest, looked on the bright side of things.

Delicate only child just kept alive by care of his mother and his devoted nurse, Alison Cunningham.

1853. Parents moved to 1 Inverleith Terrace; in 1857 moved again to 17 Heriot Row, their Edinburgh home until Thomas Stevenson's death. As a boy spent a lot of time at manse of Colinton on Water of Leith. Had little regular schooling because of his ill-health. At a preparatory school for a time; later at Edinburgh Academy. Spent about a year in Germany, on Riviera and in Italy with his parents, then to school near London. Again left to join parents abroad; afterwards private school in Frederick Street, Edinburgh; tutors while travelling. Often went to Scottish health resorts such as Bridge of Allan, Dunoon, Rothesay, North Berwick, Lasswade and Peebles, and with father on his nearer professional journeys to the Scottish coasts and lighthouses. Love of wandering: ("If we *had* been related," mused Robert, "I'd have said that's where we took after each other.")   Life more settled, and they divided their time between Edinburgh and Swanston Cottage—

—Robert gave a whoop of recognition.   This was the Swanston which Miss Gibson had mentioned as though he should know all about it because it "meant so much" to Stevenson.   Now he knew whether it were animal, vegetable or mineral: it was a cottage in the Pentland Hills which Thomas Stevenson had rented from 1867 onwards.

Family hoped he would become a civil engineer like father and grandfather and uncles.   Edinburgh University for several winters.   Only attended these classes when he felt like it: ("I'm with him all the way, so far.")   Had an eager and interested mind and read like billy-o, English poetry, fiction, essays, French; particularly interested in Scottish history.   Walked a lot in the Pentlands, on shores of the Forth, and explored the low-down quarters of Edinburgh.   He says of himself that he spent much of his time "scraping acquaintance with all classes of men and womenkind".   His worried family thought this was idleness and a love of low company.   In spite of truancies, remained favourite pupil of professor of engineering, Fleeming Jenkin.

Robert grinned: here was another piece that linked up nicely; old Renfrew's story of the idle young devil who'd pulled up the curtain at the wrong moment in the Fleeming Jenkin theatricals.

Took pencil and notebook everywhere.   Wrote poems and stories.   Really did try for three years to prepare himself for family profession; went to Anstruther on coast of Fife, and to Wick to watch harbour work of father's firm.   Received Edinburgh Society of Arts silver medal for a paper on suggested improvement in light-house apparatus: ("Gosh, how in heck did he pull that off?")   Sea and out-of-door part of the job appealed to him, not dull office work with figures.

Always crazy on the sea, Robert could not for some little time break away from this section of the letters, to continue with his imposed task of learning only the bare outline of Stevenson's life from the prefaces.

The worst work I had was when David (Macdonald's eldest) and I took the charge ourselves. He remained in the lighter to tighten or slacken guys as we raised the pole towards the perpendicular, with two men. I was with four men in the boat. We dropped an anchor out a good bit, then tied a cord to the pole, took a turn round the sternmost thwart with it, and pulled on the anchor line. As the great, big, wet hawser came in it soaked you to the skin : I was the sternest (used, by way of variety, for sternmost) of the lot, and had to coil it—a work which involved, from *its* being so stiff and *your* being busy pulling with all your might, no little trouble and an extra ducking. We got it up ; and, just as we were going to sing ' Victory ' one of the guys slipped in, the pole tottered—went over on its side again like a shot, and behold the end of our labour.

Wrenching his attention back to dry land, Robert learnt that literature was thought a poor show by Stevenson's father. But the lad was allowed to give up engineering and read for the Bar. For the next few years he went to Law classes in the University.

Robert preferred "Kirstie" as his mother, to the hasty substitution of a little French girl, when he had blundered in his dates with the all-knowing Mr. Renfrew; so he seized with some excitement upon a description in one of the prefaces which appeared to give colour to his invention of the Kirstie legend:

The storms, which from time to time attacked him, of shivering repulsion from the climate and conditions of life in the city which he yet deeply and imaginatively loved, the moods of spiritual revolt against the harsh doctrines of the creed in which he had been brought up, and to which his parents were deeply, his father even passionately, attached ; the seasons of temptation to which he was exposed alike by temperament and circumstance, to seek solace among the crude allurements of the city streets.

Summer 1873. Went to stay at Cockfield Rectory in Suffolk. Met Mrs. Sitwell; also Sidney Colvin (later her husband). Both became Stevenson's lifelong friends. She helped him to believe in himself. Wrote her millions of letters. Continued to read for the Bar.

Rows with father etc. too much for his health. Specialist said lungs in danger and he must go South.   Mentone in France for six months, where wrote essays which Mrs. Sitwell and Mr. Colvin helped him get published.   Knocked around with two Russian ladies and their children. ("Wonder if they turn up again?   If they're not going to be important, I needn't bother with their names.")

1874.   Returned home via Paris.   Lived at Swanston and Edinburgh with his parents.   Things easier there. Went to see man called Henley in Edinburgh Infirmary. ("Looks as if *he* was important.")

Went to London; joined Savile Club; began to know some of London literary society.   Yachting trip in the Western Isles with his friend Sir Walter Simpson.

Scottish winter no good for his lungs—("No, nor for anyone else's, I'd say.")   In the spring stayed with his cousin R. A. M. Stevenson, among artists in Forest of Fontainebleau.   Returned to take his finals for Scottish Bar.   Passed exams.   Frightfully bucked.   Made effort to settle down to life of good little Edinburgh advocate, but soon chucked this.

France with Simpson to do a canoe trip; wrote a book about it later: *An Inland Voyage.*   Autumn at Grez and Barbizon with his cousin Bob and artists.   Met "his fate, the romance which decided his life".

Rightly supposing this meant that here Stevenson met his future wife, Robert searched ahead till in the next preface he found the actual date of the meeting to be 1876, and of the marriage 1880.   He repeated these dates several times until he had memorized them.   "Four years between?   A whole lot could happen in four years."

1877 in Edinburgh, London, Fontainebleau and Paris ("Wish he'd keep still sometimes!")   Autumn of 1878 went tramping through the Cevennes Mountains in France, and wrote *Travels with a Donkey.*

Robert skipped several pages till that name caught his eye again which he had noticed recur so often in the Contents that it had obviously better be included in his own mental

[83]

inventory: "They'd expect me to know about Henley"—that dim "they" as yet nameless and unspecified, who were presently to supply him so pleasantly and easily with all his needs.

Had a number of essays published, especially in *London Magazine* edited by Henley.

His first book, *An Inland Voyage*, published in 1878. (Robert twice repeated: "His first book, *An Inland Voyage*, published in 1878"—because people minded about people's first books.) *New Arabian Nights* in the *London Magazine*. Collaborated with Henley in plays; *Deacon Brodie* one of them.

("That's enough about his writing. Where's his romance got to? 'Mrs. Osbourne—' Here we are.") She went back home to America in 1878. 1879 let him know she was going to divorce her husband. She was ill too. Hoping that with a bit of luck he could marry her afterwards, made up his mind to go to California. Of course his father and friends would think this a pretty wild idea, considering his rotten health and his future and no money; so wouldn't take any help from any of them, but they couldn't budge him. He made the journey steerage to New York, and in the emigrant train across America to the coast.

Again Robert was jerked out of his commendably objective studies, into a warmer interest. He knew something from first-hand experience of steerage and emigrants, and reckoned that in the 'seventies, conditions would have been even rougher; besides, this Scottish boy, though he wasn't aware of it—they never are—had been coddled. ("He showed guts, though; didn't knuckle under; and the hardships of the journey must have been pretty fierce, if they damaged his health ever after.")

I was pretty nearly slain: my spirit lay down and kicked for three days; I was up at an Angora goat-ranche in the Santa Lucia Mountains, nursed by an old frontiersman, a mighty hunter of bears, and I scarcely slept, or ate, or thought for four days. Two nights I lay out under a tree in a sort of stupor, doing nothing but fetch water for myself and horse, light fire and make coffee, and all night awake hearing the goat-bells ringing and the tree-frogs singing when each new noise was enough to set me mad. Then the bear-hunter came round, pronounced me 'real sick', and ordered me up to the ranche.

Collapsed again at Monterey. Nearly a goner. Recovered. Lived cheap and worked hard.

Here, on the edge of the Pacific, Robert was in familiar surroundings. It amused him, reading these volumes in Miss Gibson's prim rooms, to compare the present with that first rum experience when munching one of Pop Ernest's abalone steaks at this very Monterey, and an old sailor at the same table was tantalized by his looks, his eyes especially, to a memory of someone. . . . Who?—oh, just someone.

Odd collection of friends seem to gather round Stevenson wherever he stayed. At Monterey, a little French doctor; the chap who kept the restaurant where he had his one good meal a day, played chess with him and talked his head off; François the baker and an Italian fisherman. Three months later, moved to San Francisco. Broke. Lived pretty grimly in a workman's lodging with next to no grub. Just managed to hang on and keep himself alive. Chopped his own wood on his own window-sill to make a fire. ("Where was *she* all this time?") Lonely and out at elbows. Any other man under the sun wouldn't have a laugh left in him, but this fellow would laugh in his tomb.

Robert, who had slipped among the letters again, became aware at this juncture that his thought had been subconsciously dictated by: "Sketch of my tomb follows", set up in odd spacing in the middle of a page:

Sketch of my tomb follows :—

ROBERT LOUIS STEVENSON

born 1850, of a family of engineers,
died   .   .   .   .

‘ Nitor aquis ’.
Home is the sailor, home from sea,
And the hunter home from the hill.

You, who pass this grave, put aside hatred ; love kindness ; be all services remembered in your heart and all offences pardoned ; and as you go down again among the living, let this be your question : can I make someone happier this day before I lie down to sleep ? Thus the dead man speaks to you from the dust : you will hear no more from him.

Who knows, Colvin, but I may thus be of more use when I am buried than ever when I was alive ? The more I think of it, the more earnestly do I desire this. I may perhaps try to write it better some day : but that is what I want in sense. The verses are from a beayootiful poem by me.

Helped to nurse landlady's dying child, and nearly died himself. Dragged back to life by doctor and Fanny. Married her when he was a bit better but still a bag of bones. They moved to deserted mining camp in Californian Coast range. *Silverado Squatters.* Letter headed Calistoga, Napa County. (“Yep, I should know it. Near where I broke my ankle unloading cargo at Vallejo.”)

News of serious illness and marriage reached Scotland. Pop cabled at last: “Count on £250 annually.” (“Must have been a relief after they'd cut him off for so long.”)

They asked him to bring his wife home. So came back to Edinburgh with Fanny and his young stepson Lloyd. Fanny went over big with his family, and were his pals glad to see him! Climate of Scotland foul for his health. (“Foul for mine, too!”) Off to Davos in Switzerland. Summer in the Scotch Highlands, and began *Treasure Island* to amuse the kid. Seems to have been fond of him; made him a toy printing-press when they went back to Davos, and they played those soldier games that old Renfrew carried on about. Fell sick. Took house near Marseilles (“Wait, where are we now? 1882.”) Writing *Prince Otto.* Hemorrhages, fever, nearly died. When better, Châlet at Hyères a stunning success; working hard (“didn't he just keep on! No wonder I looked a fool with Grandpa Renfrew!”). *Treasure*

Island published as a book; got a hundred guineas for it. Nearly off his head with so much jingling cash all in one swoop. ("Get that date by heart: 1883, *Treasure Island* published; long live Long John Silver!") Off to Nice on a binge with Charles Baxter and Henley—sounds like one hell of a good party. Nearly did for him, though; stinking hemorrhages.

Left South of France and came North. Father gave Fanny a house in Bournemouth ("he must have thought her pretty swell"). Stevenson called it Skerryvore after lighthouse built by his family. Health putrid during three years they lived there; nearly always in bed; often only allowed to whisper; had to write down what he wanted to say to friends and family. Doing plays with Henley. No go; had to give them up because he needed cash. Finished *Child's Garden of Verses*—("That's the precious book the old girl showed me last night and locked up this morning! Funny to have written those sort of baby rhymes each time when he was more than half a goner, at Hyères and Skerryvore.") Wrote *Kidnapped* 1886. Blow when his great friend, Fleeming Jenkin, died. Wrote *The Strange Case of Dr. Jekyll and Mr. Hyde*. Knock-out success in England and America— they even preached sermons about it ("Can you beat it!") Got all steamed up about Irish widow and daughter of a farmer guy called Curtin who got himself murdered. ("Needn't remember that; no importance.") Had to go to Edinburgh because his father was dying. Badly cut up about it. In 1887 decided to try climate of California on his lungs. Sailed on SS. *Ludgate Hill*, taking Fanny, Lloyd, his mother and their French servant, Valentine Roch.

Tremendous welcome in New York because of *Treasure Island*, *Kidnapped* and *The Strange Case of Dr. Jekyll and Mr. Hyde*. Found it pretty good to be famous; what a difference from last time when he arrived in the steerage. Then he got ill with too much fuss and flattery, and they sent him up into the Adirondacks, to Saranac. Bitter mountain air suited him a treat; able soon to

shovel snow, skate, etc. Rather fancied himself as a wild
man of the woods, in buffalo robe and leggings:

You should also see our back log when the thermometer goes (as
it does go) away-away below zero, till it can be seen no more by the
eye of man—not the thermometer, which is still perfectly visible,
but the mercury, which curls up into the bulb like a hibernating
bear.

Wife got sick; too high for her; went to California to see
her folks. He wrote *Master of Ballantrae* ("says Saranac
reminded him of Scotland"). Collaborated with Lloyd
Osbourne in *The Wrong Box*. Editors came chasing all
the way up to offer him the earth if he'd only write for
them alone. Lean days seemed to be over. Found it a
bit chilly and grey up in those hills:

We are all fit, and the place is very bleak and wintry, and up
to now has shown no such charms as Davos, but it is a place where
men eat and where the cattarh, catarrh (cattarrh, or cattarrhh)
appears to be unknown. I walk in my verandy in the snaw, sir,
looking down over one of those dabbled wintry landscapes that are
(to be frank) so chilly to the human bosom, and up at a grey, English
—nay, mehercle, Scottish—heaven ; and I think it pretty bleak.

("That's about how I felt at Gleann Bàn, and thankful
I'd no more than three weeks of it.") So when Editor of
Scribner's asked him to write articles about South Sea
Islands, decided on a tropical cruise in luxury yacht *Casco*,
and damn the expense:

(. . . An old dream of mine which actually seems to be coming
true, and I am sun-struck.)

So 1888 must have been the grandest year for him:

On June 15th the schooner yacht *Casco* will (weather and a jealous
providence permitting) steam through the Golden Gates for Honolulu, Tahiti, the Galapagos, Guayaquil.

First to the Marquesas; touched at some coral atolls
and on to Tahitian Islands. Felt like the cat's whiskers
whenever he was on board, though down with the old
fever once at Papeete. On to Tautira. Already making
friends with native chiefs and kings wherever they landed;
sworn brotherhood and all that. Honolulu by Christmas.

Paid off *Casco* and stayed there six months. Finished *Master of Ballantrae*. Sent his mother back to Scotland. Visited leper settlement at island of Molokai.

("Wonder how old he was by then? 1850 from 1889—must have been about thirty-nine.") Health now like any other man; able to walk and ride and swim, and take a hand when they ran into squalls. Eager to stay another year in the Pacific, but no more luxury yachts. Took passages for himself, Fanny and Lloyd on trading schooner *Equator*, to the Gilbert Islands :

The interest has been immense. Old King Tembinoka of Apemama, the Napoleon of the group, poet, tyrant, altogether a man of mark, gave me the woven corselets of his grandfather, his father and his uncle.

Then to Apia, capital of island of Upolu in Samoan group. Wrote to Charles Baxter:

I have bought 314½ acres of beautiful land in the bush behind Apia ; when we get the house built, the garden laid and the cattle in place, it will be something to fall back on for shelter and food. . . . We range from 600 to 1500 feet, have five streams, waterfalls, precipices, profound ravines, rich tablelands, fifty head of cattle on the ground (if any one could catch them), a great view of forest, sea, mountains, the warships in the haven :⁻really a noble place.

("Sounds all right to me!")

At Sydney, collected letters and made plans for going home to Scotland. Wrote and printed famous Open Letter in Defence of Father Damien. Laid low with a bad hemorrhage again. Told he would have to remain exile in tropics to have any chance of life. Cruise on trading steamer *Janet Nicholl* to get himself fit again. Gilbert Islands etc. Terrific gales; fire on ship; enjoyed it, but they nearly chucked all his writings overboard in a blazing trunk—Fanny saved them. Fanny always ill at sea and on mountain-tops; expect she didn't care for him to take risks with cannibals and lepers, but as long as he was well and happy, all this adventure stuff O.K. by her. ("That's what I call a wife—even if she did seem a bit bossy at times; maybe she had to be; looks as if he'd never stay quiet and treat himself like a sick man.")

Back to Sydney; then to his land in Samoa, where the woods were being cleared and a four-roomed wooden cottage built. ("He calls it 'a rough barrack'—bet it was if he said so.") He and Fanny started real pioneer work of clearing jungle and building proper house. Lloyd off to England to fetch furniture. Big house ready early in 1891. Called it Vailima (five streams). Family consisted of Fanny, Lloyd, Belle (his stepdaughter, older than Lloyd), her son Austin, and presently old Mrs. Stevenson. Native staff. Whole show like a feudal clan. Letters from all over the world. Lots of visitors—painters, writers, planters, traders. Soon became friend, adviser and judge to kings and chiefs of Samoan tribes. Stevenson at Vailima a gorgeous legend to friends at home. In spite of longing for Scotland, passionately interested in Samoan affairs. Always ready to help in local disputes and problems. Germany, America and England shared government of the islands, but Germany uppermost, and backed their chap Laupepa as king against rebel king, Mataafa. Stevenson dead nuts on Mataafa but did his damndest to keep 'em all from each other's throats.

("He certainly seems to have gotten himself well mixed up in any trouble that was round. . . .") Nearly deported several times for interference. ("Can't make head or tail of it. Why should I anyway? Nobody'll expect me to know all this when I get going.") Wasn't in his nature to sit pretty and do nothing when he saw injustice and treachery and bungling. ("I like him when he gets mad with the Government and lets himself rip.") They believed it would be a whole heap nicer to get rid of him, but he managed to hang on. Had a whale of a lot of influence all round: whites and natives, even the missionaries thought him a wise lad. Great friends with officers of British warship, H.M.S. *Curaçao*, stationed at Apia. They called the road to Vailima "the Curaçao track".

Worked good and plenty: *Catriona* (sequel to *Kidnapped*); *The Wreckers* and *The Ebb Tide* both with Lloyd Osbourne; *Island Nights Entertainment*. ("I guess that pretty well covers the first three years at Vailima.") Lived reckless and extravagant as he always did, chucked away all he earned; helped anyone who chose to ask, and often when they didn't. Endless strain on his health from grind of looking after his land and household, paying for damn well everything and fixing everybody's quarrels. Always kept cheerful at home, but now and then let off steam in his letters to Colvin; doesn't seem to be writing to Henley since—when? Can't remember; let's have a look at the index. Three times in 1887; once in August 1892; then no more.

War in Samoa. Mataafa banished: ("That means their side must have lost—damn shame!") Stevenson went storming down to look after and feed his Samoan pals badly treated in prison. When they were released, eight of their chiefs arrived at Vailima with their Talking-man, squatted round and said that in return for what he'd done for them, they wanted to make him a gift: a road joining Vailima to the public road ("Called Road of the Loving Hearts in one place; Road of Gratitude somewhere else.") Anyway it was opened in October, 1894. And here's what they put on the board they stuck up :

THE ROAD OF GRATITUDE

Considering the great love of Tusitala in his loving care of us in our distress in the prison, we have therefore prepared a splendid gift. It shall never be muddy, it shall endure for ever, this road we have dug.

I like that: *It shall never be muddy, it shall endure for ever, this road we have dug.*

Tusitala is what they called him, out there.

1894. Dangerously ill again from overwork; couldn't get a move-on with *St. Ives*, anyway. His friends Colvin and Charles Baxter let him know they were arranging Edinburgh Edition of his books so that he needn't worry about money and could let up work for a year or two. Stevenson delighted, but couldn't stop all the same; not he. Feeling pretty down about everything. Homesick and played out as an author. Took up idea of book he had started before and chucked, *Weir of Hermiston*. A winner. Racing along at top speed. Thought it might be his best. Never finished it. On the third of December, while feeling swell, suddenly burst a blood-vessel in the brain, and died in two hours.

Buried on top of Mount Vaea.

7

Odd to find herself in the position of a repentant prodigal, welcomed home by kind words and a prodigal fire, a glorious wasteful fire seldom seen by economy. But Miss Gibson was so glad she did not care. Suppose she had found a cold grate, and her visitor gone. By a miracle he had come, by a miracle remained; and the relief which settled on her soul was perhaps a sweeter emotion than any that had ever yet warmed her experience.

The blow lasted all the evening. It was a more intimate evening than the last; they knew each other now, trusted each other (thought Miss Gibson); and Robert felt stronger, though she would not allow him to help her get supper nor wash it up; and he acquiesced very easily in all the pleasanter aspects of being looked on as a guest. While she was busy, he swept a last-minute glance through his four volumes of the Letters, like a schoolboy before an examination. . . .

She noticed that on the whole he ate and drank sparingly; and when she returned to the fire, remarked on it; keeping to herself, however, her conventional idea that tramps (at the back-door) were perpetually ravenous, and, if thwarted, menacing.

"Yes, that used to worry Mis' Merrill, when I left half the rye drop-cakes she'd pile on my plate for supper. 'Never seen a lad for dreamin' so much and eatin' such a mite,' she'd say."

"Dreaming? Are you dreamy?"

"Great Jumping Jehoshophat, no! Not by day. Not such a sap. But I dream when I'm asleep and can't stop myself. Hell, do I have dreams!"

Miss Gibson was a little disappointed. A Robert who

roamed over sea and land, his eyes rapt and far away, dreaming splendour while awake, would have been more to her taste. But suddenly a resemblance clicked in her mind, and she was richly compensated:

"*He* used to dream more vividly than most people, and more strangely."

Robert nodded, fairly confident after a day's study, but unwilling to say more till she gave him further clues.

"You know his 'Chapter on Dreams'?"

Damn the woman! He had told her last night; was he obliged to do it twice over?

"I must be frank: I've read awfully little of R.L.S. You'll be shocked how little."

She nodded. At the Institution, naturally, he could only read what he was given. And during his four years of keener education with the schoolmaster of a New England village, his adopted parent had apparently harboured an absurd prejudice against English writers. Yet surely his natural curiosity, or call it pride, would have led Robert to discover more than *Treasure Island* and *Kidnapped*. That is, unless he were bitterly resentful at being born a—a— Even in the seclusion of her own mind, Miss Gibson's instinct for literature sought in vain to replace the blunt word, the shovel word, with a more delicate analogy.

"But *since* you ran away from the Merrills?"

Robert laughed. "Lady, have you a notion how we live once we're on the road? See here, we don't buy books; we don't go regular to the Library; and you'll be surprised, but folks don't lend us books; and if they did, they'd be too heavy in the pack. Whiles, we pick up a bit of print from the dump, and throw it on the next dump when we're done with it; but I just didn't happen to find a Stevenson. I made myself promises—" Robert turned on a quite attractive shyness for his next piece—"I used to think: 'Darned if I'm going to scuffle round reading a bit here and a bit there and a bit out o' the middle, and having to leave off for months maybe. One day, I'll read the lot straight through. One day I'll get among folks that knew him, and don't think me plumb crazy for caring.'"

"So *that*'s why you came to Scotland. I see now."

"Of course." And inwardly he blessed blind fortune for leading him to this excellent reason for the accident of his journey to a country where strangers stopped him to ask: *Are you Stevenson's son?*

There was a touch of involuntary drama in Miss Gibson's stride across to the bookshelves; she meant to fling open the glass doors and say: "Here you are; help yourself"— satisfying a man's long dream by all that prodigal wealth she had collected, perhaps for this, down all the years she had been a bookseller in Edinburgh.

It was sheer wicked luck she should have forgotten that the doors for once were locked.

Robert was a kind man, and lenient at moments. . . . While blushes mantled her cheeks, or rather while shame turned her a dull purple, and she groped for her handbag and dropped it twice, once shut and once open, and fumbled for the key which lay under her foot, he forbore to take any petty revenge or even betray that he knew exactly what was going on and why. Instead, he strolled to the window and exclaimed: "The lamps of Auld Reekie!" with appropriate comments on the view, taken straight out of the Letters he had been studying all day.

"Here," said Miss Gibson, a very subdued voice replacing the clarion tones by which she had intended to make him free of the kingdom, "here's something that might interest you. It isn't exactly a Life of Stevenson; it's a sort of Miscellany."

Robert took the scrap-book gingerly, not quite knowing what "a Miscellany" meant, nor whether it held pitfalls for him; it was obviously home-made; by Miss Gibson herself? or another devotee? Replying to his question in her most offhand manner, she told him that she had, since the death of Stevenson, snipped out or copied and stuck into this album any reference to him that specially took her fancy, any bit in the papers or poem or speech or portrait—

Robert had opened it at the portrait in front; and Miss Gibson, breathless with excitement, looked too:

"He was very young when that was taken: the period

when the poet James Whitcomb Riley called him 'the visionary boy'."

"How old did you say?"

"Twenty-two or three."

He did not feel the same leap of kinship that he had felt with the gay marauder whom he resembled so outrageously, but he made a mental note: "Here he is at the age when I'm going to have been born"; and it occurred to him that every now and then in his counterfeit fairy-tale he might effectively make room for one of these photos, tattered and stained, thrust down near the heart of poor little Kirstie and cherished by her until she died. . . .

Meanwhile, Miss Gibson was babbling of what other poets had written about R.L.S.: "There are some fine poems by Gosse, and Le Gallienne, and Robert Lynd, and Austin Dobson; they couldn't help pouring out their grief when he died. Oh, and Barrie, in 'Scotland's Lament':

> I've ha'en o' brawer sons a flow,
> My Walter mair renown could win,
> And he that followed at the plough,
> But Louis was my Benjamin."

She looked over his shoulder: "And that's a good poem by Robertson Nicoll:

> Let the weary body lie
>   Where he chose its grave,
> 'Neath the wide and starry sky,
>   By the Southern wave. . . .
> We shall find him when we seek him
>   In an older home,—
> By the hills and streams of childhood
>   'Tis his weird to roam."—

Miss Gibson broke off. "He once said a queer thing: 'To understand Stevenson, you must first have spat a little blood'."

Robert had had enough; but while in her present mood, he thought he had better give her her head; perhaps she would exhaust herself in one burst and then he need never listen again. He read aloud a line from an elegy by Richard Le Gallienne: "'Not while a boy still whistles on the earth—'"

"Go on," she encouraged him.

"He'd have liked that himself. Sort of young and careless, walking beside a brook, peeling a switch of hazel and thinking of islands and buried treasure and kidnapping—oh, and apples. But it goes on the same as all poetry:

> Not while a single human heart beats true,
> Not while Love lasts, and Honour, and the Brave,
> Has earth a grave,
> O well-beloved, for you ! "

She was surprised and pleased at his discrimination, and at his way of reading aloud, not ranting but neither as though "all poetry" were senseless doggerel. Somewhat surprised, too, that he had not picked out her own favourite lines from that poem:

> " Death ! why at last he finds his treasure isle,
> And he the pirate of its hidden hoard ;
> Life ! 'twas the ship he sailed to seek it in,
> And Death is but the pilot come aboard.

But don't you think that few of the poems are as vivid as the Henley sonnet?" Then at an impatient movement from Robert, she realized that she had slipped up again. ("Jane Gibson, you *must* try and remember that this poor fellow is only now on the quest for what you keep on assuming he knows.")

Though he had possession of the album, that was not likely to daunt her; she knew "Apparition" by heart:

> " There shines a brilliant and romantic grace,
> A spirit intense and rare, with trace on trace
> Of passion, impudence, and energy.
> Valiant in velvet, light in ragged luck—"

Robert repeated softly: "'light in ragged luck' . . ."

"It might stand for you."

"It might."

After a silence, Miss Gibson was again in spate: "Henley

was in the hospital infirmary when R.L.S. was first taken to see him. A huge fellow with a tangled red beard and hair, sitting up in bed in that dismal gaslit ward, and receiving visitors as though it were a king's palace, Louis said. There were two little boys, Willie and Roden, in bed in the same ward, playing at operations, at surgeon and patient; can you see them gradually leaving off their game and sitting upright staring with round eyes and scarlet cheeks to hear grown-up men talk of things that had nothing to do with being grown-up? One can imagine how those two buccaneers must have raced on about everything under the sun; penny plain and tuppence coloured; hardly more than youngsters themselves; both poor and almost unknown; both hot-blooded and full of hope; out to change the world if they could, as well as make their fortunes. Oh! I could go on for ever— it was one of the great friendships like David and Jonathan, Roland and Oliver, Damon and Pythias— Only it ended so tragically."

Robert mentally backed away from the long panorama implicit in the narrator's "for ever". He could well have borne to hear more, much more, of that first encounter between Henley and Stevenson, for though he had small use for Great Friendships, the world of guttering gas and workhouse infirmaries overlapped his own. Fine to have been one of those tousled little boys, flushed and breathless, getting a taste of pirate talk, Treasure Island talk, at its source. But he was already queerly reluctant to receive it via Miss Gibson. Not fair; she had had years of living amongst books, finding out all these lively, provocative stories which for him had only just started leaping out of the water like trout, one flash and gone again. Let her shut up and give him a chance to go out himself with rod and line.

In case she had another prudent spasm of locking up her favourite volumes, he took one more look at the portrait of the "visionary boy", and this time a curious surge of emotion swept over him, half mocking, half protective, as if for a kid brother: "Time he woke up! You bet life woke *him* up, and pretty roughly at that. Now if I'd been around— Rather wish I had." Deriding himself for the wish, for looking after romantic youths was hardly his line, he went on idly browsing from page to page. . . .

"Why are you smiling to yourself?" Miss Gibson asked.

"Nothing. Tell me some more. I mean," hastily, "give me some more to read."

Miss Gibson did not notice his amendment; she acknowledged in honesty a fair amount about herself, but not that given a fraction of a chance she was voluble beyond all checking; for when, until now, had she been given a chance? "I think you'd like the *Amateur Emigrant*."

Robert expressed some doubt on the subject; amateur emigrants were no treat to him, a professional.

She wondered at what stage she had lost his attention. Never had there been anyone so unpredictable, or, for her, so endlessly fascinating or as remote from her experience as Robert.

"'An Apology for Idlers'," Miss Gibson read out.

Here he instantly responded; not, as she expected, with interest, but paradoxically, as though she had accidentally hit on the one title which, for some reason obscure to her, would determine him to search no further. A phrase to describe his attitude sprang up at her from the page: "an arrogance of disregard that is truly staggering". Yet because she could never help reading on and on, as a drunkard, though he may resist a drink in the next room, falls for what happens to be on the table by his hand, she discovered an episode new even to her in all that prolific autobiography. Come now, this *had* to be shared with Robert:

"Once when I was groaning aloud with physical pain, a young gentleman came into the room and nonchalantly inquired if I had seen his bow and arrow. He made no account of my groans, which he accepted, as he had to accept so much else, as a piece of the inexplicable conduct of his elders ; and like a wise young gentleman, he would waste no wonder on the subject."

But this was Robert's very own way of accepting pain and the world's lack of concern with it. "You didn't expect the kid to stop and cry over him, or hold his head, did you? *He* didn't."

"Certainly not. Children are naturally callous. But

[99]

surely it showed a marvellous freedom from self-pity, a fine sense of proportion, that while in pain he should still not feel aggrieved, nor assume that the child might have stopped to show a little sympathy."

"Sympathy? Pity."

"It's the same thing."

"Not quite. You can't help being sick; but you can be ashamed of it, and glad for other folk to take no notice and get on with what they're doing."

"That," argued Miss Gibson stiffly, for she was not of those who found it easy to incorporate religion into her speech, "that would not have been Christ's way, to get on with what He was doing."

"By what I could pick out from all that preaching and purity at the Meeting-house, it wouldn't have been His way, either, to get all ruffled up with a kid for keeping after his bow and arrows. While you're sick, you're plain awful —think I don't know it? So for pity's sake—"

"There you are," interrupted Miss Gibson, triumphant, "you've said it yourself—'for pity's sake'."

"Then for pride's sake. But don't suppose I'll fall down and worship this hero of yours simply because he understood the rules, same as I do."

Miss Gibson shut the book with a bang. She was furious; puzzled too, that Robert should have spoken of "this hero of yours" in that detached tone; it was the first time since he had recovered consciousness in Miss Gibson's shop and practically in Miss Gibson's arms, that he had forgotten to keep the act going.

But as a blind rolls up of its own accord with a sharp click, darkness went luminous, and she saw in Robert's matter-of-fact refusal to praise what seemed to her an astonishing code of excellence, a clear proof that he was governed by the same code; a legatee of the same cheerful acquiescence in the perfect fairness of outlawry by pain; pain which must never impinge upon the lordly possessors of health at their normal pursuits.

Fool, then, to have been perplexed and angry! What more could she ask? Ten thousand who took off their hats to the king: but here, to honour her lodgings, one in ten thousand who took it for granted he need not do so, for he was of equal blood. No amount of taking thought could have settled the matter more favourably for a Pretender than this involuntary accent of non-worship. Miss Gibson was so elated that to steady herself and to bring down Pegasus to earth, she took with trembling hands from the Stevenson shelves a volume which she knew contained his quietest story: "This is my favourite of the shorter tales—'Will o' the Mill'. It might easily become your favourite, too. R.L.S. put all his creed and philosophy into it." She held out the book, and Robert, as seemed to be his aggravating habit, opened it in the wrong place:

"'To Lloyd Osbourne'," he read aloud, "'an American gentleman, in accordance with whose classic taste the following narrative has been designed, it is now'—"

Miss Gibson laughed. "Oh no, that's the dedication to *Treasure Island*; they're in the same volume, in this edition. You'll find a reproduction of the famous map at the beginning. He found Lloyd tinting it, and filled it in with make-believe names, and little curly ships and dolphins, and there's the inscription under the map too—

> Given by above J.F.E. Mr. W. Bones Maite of ye
> Walrus Savannah this twenty July 1754. W. B.
>
> Facsimile of chart latitude and longitude struck out by
> J. Hawkins."

Robert glowered down at the map of Treasure Island. Something about the whole matter, he could not tell what, was not altogether to his fancy. . . .

"I'd like you to read 'Will o' the Mill'," Miss Gibson urged, being tiresome. "The appearance of Death, when he and Will share a bottle of wine in the arbour—nobody could read it unmoved."

"Bet you *I* could," muttered Robert as she guided his reluctant hands to the right page and to the passage which ended the story. Like all enthusiasts, she was an ass to insist on his reading the end of a story, before he had had a chance of beginning it.

Something fell out on the floor from between the pages: a photograph torn from a magazine. Robert picked it up, looked at it . . . and burst out laughing.

"Sorry, ma'am, but gosh! didn't he just enjoy having that high and handsome picture taken! Maybe it was his mother arranged him for it. Wouldn't you think he was going out to rescue a whole handful of lives, just to say, noble and quiet: 'Don't thank me. I only did my duty.' Bet your sweet life this is the one he'd see got sent round to all his best girls."

If she had been furious with him before, she was wincing now. This was her favourite (except one) of all the numerous portraits; and now this tramp—every now and then Robert fell from grace and became "this tramp" again —had dared tease her about what was certainly a far-away gaze to beyond the horizon, a sort of dark and lustrous nobility. . . . Perhaps the photographer (or Mrs. Thomas Stevenson) *may* have arranged the drapery behind his client a little self-consciously. Still and with all that, it was a fine inspiring portrait or she would not have cut it out from that Memorial number; unfortunately she had forgotten having slipped it into this book. She determined then and there that however long he might stay with her —and at that moment she felt like slinging him out at once —Robert should *never* be allowed to see the portrait at the beginning of Methuen's 1899 two-volume edition of the Letters which she kept in her room on the table beside her bed. It was sheer luck that so far she had not produced it and said "Look . . ." taking for granted that first sight of it would be bound to give him that breathless moment which still, after looking a hundred times, it could give to her.

"Mind you," Robert went on, with great zest and relish, "I expect by the time Mr. Grainger the photographer sent them along, he was ready to pass them round as a good joke when his pals were feeling glum. Oh *boy*! look at my velvet coat, look at my wavy hair, look at the—"

She flashed out " *You*'d prefer the Nerli drawing, I've no doubt"— Then it rushed back into her mind that Robert had already preferred the Nerli drawing; indeed, more than preferred it.

. . . The ticking moments that followed were woefully embarrassing for her; though not at all for Robert. Yet though he was not likely to spare Miss Gibson over that absurd photograph she had kept pressed so lovingly between the pages of "Will o' the Mill", he now perceived she was flying signals of real distress, distress lest she should have hurt him by her impulsive reference to the stolen Nerli (as though he cared!). And again his essential kindness, as in the incident of the locked bookcase, went swiftly to the rescue by a change of subject:

"Remember how he said in one of his letters that his photos were all of a different man and all of them junk?— 'It's a lottery. The truth is, I've got no real appearance; a certain disreputable air is the one thing that my face presents; the rest change like water'—I haven't remembered it quite right."

She smiled, a little tremulous still, but thankful. Apparently he had not recognized the name of Nerli.

"All the same, you've got a phenomenal memory."

"Yes, ma'am. Mr. Merrill, he'd always say I'd two things that were outstanding—memory and idleness." And now he hoped he'd not used a word to release from her a long diatribe on the outstanding and terrifying capacity for work in the man who had written "A Defence for Idlers". He had had enough of that from Mr. Renfrew. To divert her from any such unnecessary admonition, he enquired, nodding towards a pile of heavy tomes, uniform, but not in the Swanston Edition: "What are those?"

"Those? Oh, those bound volumes of *Scribner's*. I picked them up cheap, and had no idea till I unpacked them in the shop, that they contained all the Stevenson essays which were first published in 1888. Then of course . . ." She had no need to go on and tell him with what triumph she had brought them home and added them to her collection.

"Here's one you'd enjoy. I'll read it to you," said Miss Gibson firmly. And Robert acquiesced, unaware as yet how that phrase of five simple words was in time to bore and exasperate him to the point of parting for ever from this generous, excellent woman.

She sat down on the arm of the chair under the lamp, restored to complete enjoyment of their homey evening among the books.

"Not a sermon?"

"Goodness, no; it's delightfully personal; about his life and the family life in Samoa during his last few years. He didn't write it himself, of course."

"Who did?"

"Lloyd and Isobel," replied Miss Gibson from the depths of the book, and forgetting that Robert was not already on terms of Christian names with this dear familiar group.

Her eye ran down the list of contents. "'Vailima Table-talk'; 'Home Life at Vailima'; 'Pola'—I always think that this funny little fellow, weeping because he had no sun-shadow of his beloved Tusitala, is even more poignant than the sombre tragedy of native warriors carrying the bier to its grave on the summit of the high mountain. Pola was a baby Samoan, a miniature dandy in light bronze, of the purest blood on the island; I won't read you the whole chapter now, only this touching little scene over the sun-shadow—

After Mr. Stevenson's death so many of his Samoan friends begged for his photograph that we sent to Sydney for a supply, which was soon exhausted. One afternoon Pola came in and remarked, in a very hurt and aggrieved manner, that he had been neglected in the way of photographs.

'But your father, the chief, has a large fine one.'

'True,' said Pola. 'But that is not mine. I have the box presented to me by your high-chief goodness. It has a little cover, and there I wish to put the sun-shadow of Tusitala, the beloved chief whom we all revere, but I more than the others, because he was the head of my clan.'

'To be sure,' I said, and looked about for a photograph. I found a picture cut from a weekly paper, one I remember that Mr. Stevenson himself had particularly disliked. He would have been pleased had he seen the scornful way Pola threw the picture on the floor.

' I will not have that ! ' he cried. ' It is pig-faced. It is not the shadow of our chief.' He leaned against the door and wept.

' I have nothing else, Pola,' I protested. ' Truly, if I had another picture of Tusitala I would give it to you.'

He brightened up at once. ' There is the one in the smoking-room,' he said ' where he walks back and forth. That pleases me, for it looks like him.' He referred to an oil painting of Mr. Stevenson by Sargent. I explained that I could not give him that. ' Then I will take the round one,' he said, ' of tin.' This last was the bronze bas-relief by St. Gaudens. I must have laughed involuntarily, for he went out deeply hurt. Hearing a strange noise in the hall an hour or so later, I opened the door, and discovered Pola lying on his face, weeping bitterly.

' What are you crying about ? ' I asked.

' The shadow, the shadow,' he sobbed. ' I want the sun-shadow of Tusitala.' "

At this point Robert coolly took the volume away from her. "Thanks. But I'd far rather read for myself what I want to, while you're gone in the daytime."

Miss Gibson was saved from being offended, by the implication contained in his words. So he was going to stay, and indefinitely? Only yesterday she would have been appalled; but now when it seemed pretty well established that Robert had no intention of quitting his comfortable quarters, she was glad to her very bones.

"I shan't have time to read it tomorrow. I mean to go and see Swanston and Colinton and Rullion Green and Glencorse."

"You won't be able to go to all these places in one day." And because convention prompted her that an invitation came better from the host than the guest, she added: "Of course you must stay on here as long as you want to."

"Why, sure. I may sometimes be off for a while, but I'll come back." For now he had so much data, it was time he used it. Miss Gibson's home would do as headquarters and inn, but you didn't pile up much on that, and he decided that on this particular racket, he would not take money from women.

The rest of the evening sped on in an atmosphere of amiability and congenial talk; and if either of them felt they were an incongruous pair linked in the strangest fashion, it was not Miss Gibson.

Nevertheless, when at last she said good-night and went to her room, she did not omit to pick up the first volume of the 1899 edition of the Letters, to hide it away from eyes that knew so well how to mock at enchantment. With the drawer already open, she had another look at the frontispiece: an enlargement of a snapshot that his stepson had managed to take by the grace of heaven, coming upon the man unawares. Yes, that is how it must have been; he could not have looked up from his writing suddenly like that, his expression startled yet half amused, and behind it something deeply searching, had he known beforehand that Lloyd was plotting at last to get a live photo.

A live Robert was walking up and down in the very next room; and she still felt his presence too fantastic to be true, till she heard him cough as the smoke of his last cigarette curled too far down into his lungs. So he too had rotten lungs, poor lad? His tread, now he knew himself alone and safe, was light and sure as an animal on grass. She visualized his feet and hands: They must once have been slim and long and elegantly shaped, though his glover and bootmaker could hardly have helped him to maintain that standard. Yes, all these items tallied and added up to a tremendous acceptance. . . . But could Robert's face, so shockingly like the Nerli portrait, bold, soulless and expedient, could it be in any way related to this portrait in front of her now, where the dissimilarity, not the likeness, was striking? For this face had the distinctive quality of a fighter for lost causes, never yet wholly beaten, that swept it further from Robert than was Samoa from Edinburgh.

Miss Gibson murmured: "Yet they're both of the same man. Jekyll—and Hyde."

8

The life of Miss Gibson covering the next few weeks became unrecognizable, even to herself. She was desperately unhappy, yet happier in her desperation than she had ever felt before. She had never been a religious woman, but now, paradoxically, her soul reminded her that she was forfeiting heaven every hour and every day. As for high principle and self-respect, they were the first two burnt-offerings to crawl in smoke along the ground and dissipate into shameful nothingness.

Robert was not with her all the time. Sometimes he disappeared for two or three days together. By mutual but unspoken consent, they kept to their formula of looking up anyone "who might be interested"; and indeed, she supplied him helpfully with suggestions of various people, their names and if possible their whereabouts, who might care to be visited by a son of R.L.S. "Think he'd be interested?" Robert would enquire nonchalantly; and: "I'm sure he would," from Miss Gibson.

She dared not define that "interested", nor ask him for a definition, for it was more than likely that their ideas on the subject would not run parallel, and that Robert's would depart from hers on a very peculiar curve.

He came back from these rounds in varying moods; often gay and confident, slinging down a handful of uncounted notes and coins on the table, insisting that his benevolent landlady should take them in fitful payment for board and lodging and fire. Returning from the shop, she curbed her vigorous step on the stairs, for the pleasure of hearing him fill her empty sitting-room with whistles and burst of unclassical song, and perhaps the jingle of money from his triumphant arrangement of copper and silver in little heaps on the table to attract her eye by their glitter directly she entered; the warmth of the prodigal fire he always built up enveloped her as she opened the door, and the warmth of his live presence, even before she saw his dark, sparkling eyes and quick smile of welcome.

But at other times he returned from his expeditions rueful and silent; never bad-tempered, but as though he were inwardly plaguing himself, taunting himself for some failure in achievement that his wit might well have avoided.

Achievement in what capacity? Here was trouble for Miss Gibson whenever she let her mind dwell on it, to speculate and wonder; for he did not choose to explain the money he brought back, though once he told her with apparent frankness that he took on light jobs kindly found for him by preference because he was the son of his father.

"I can't pretend to you or to myself I'd have got them otherwise," laughed Robert. "Expect I'm fairly unemployable, but of course I can chop wood and that sort of thing."

"Do you like wood-chopping?"

"Fine. I'd cry if I didn't get it."

Miss Gibson hoped wildly that none of this was falsehood, and that he did get given light jobs. No harm, surely, in using the pull of a true story to influence those who might not otherwise have cared to employ such a ramshackle candidate for work? Yet . . . she could not help suspecting him. He did not *look* like a man who came home tired from honest toil; nor did he produce any circumstantial evidence; and every now and then he bothered her by some odd question which left her unsatisfied, for she could not fit it in anywhere on her mental map of how she most desired Robert should be spending his days. When she handed him a suggestion of this person or that, near Edinburgh or further afield, she became gradually aware from the spacing of his returns, and some inadvertent comments he let fall on landscape, road or weather, that he never "looked up" that particular name at once, but went in an opposite direction; though making a mental note of it for use later on. Was it to avoid any possibility that she could keep tally on his movements or his doings? Half of her was clearly aware

that she could not decently countenance any of this euphem-
istic "visiting"; and she did more than countenance; her
helpful suggestions made of her a positive and guilty
accessory.

But what was she to do about it? Give him up to the
police? Unthinkable. Request him to remove himself
altogether? She remembered with a shudder the agony
of mind she had gone through during the day after his first
entrance, light in ragged luck; the day when she believed
that she had so insulted him that he would have walked
out on her. Again to risk losing the transfiguration of her
days into brilliance and fun by the mere presence of Robert
to share her enthusiasms, or more usually, from his royal
vantage, rag her quite unmercifully about them? return
to her stolid grey lump of daily life, the yeast withdrawn,
the bread not risen? No, she could not even bear to contemplate so severe a form of penance. She was a disciple,
and queer calls have sometimes been made on true disciples;
queer adjustments of code and creed and honesty.

Besides, she had a shrewd suspicion that now he would
laugh and just not go.

No choice, then, but to surrender to whatever Robert
chose to impose on her; and enjoy to the full the sensation
that she was no longer lonely.

One fine evening he had treated her to a square meal
at an inn he had discovered along the Firth waterside; and
told her an enchanting incident—"an old fellow who was
a kid at the time, passed it on to me"—of how young R.L.S.
and his cousin came canoeing to the island they could see
now from where they sat; an island humping to a duck-
house and a seal's rock; and how one of the group of little
boys encamped on the shore helped to haul the canoes to
land in the teeth of a gale, and countered Stevenson's:
"What other savages live upon this island?" with a cheeky:
"You must have forgotten your *Robinson Crusoe* or you
would know that it was the savages who came to the island
in canoes. There were no savages till you came." A reply
which had naturally delighted R.L.S., who often thereafter
through the happiest of summers used to take this hero-

worshipping "savage" on perilous adventure in a cockle-shell canoe, even as far as the isle of Inchmickery on a certain grand Sabbath-breaking occasion.

Robert was so exhilarated by the brisk wind and the small slapping waves, by cool draughts of beer and the sound of his own voice, that he walked home in hilarious spirits, chucking up silver coins from one hand to the other, that he might watch them glitter in the sharp moonlight as they twisted and fell. Small twinkling signals like these encouraged her to believe faithfully in his birthright; for Miss Gibson *knew* this was a trick he was subconsciously enjoying because he had read of someone who had enjoyed it before him, strolling out to Fairmilehead with his cousin Bob.

Always and by mutual consent they spoke of the man most in their thoughts, as a man in a fairy-tale and fable, with a name indeed, but not for mentioning.

Perhaps she was wronging him? perhaps he did work; he was generous and boyish and (sometimes) kind, so why might he not also be industrious and truthful? And he was not strong, poor fellow (so she went on stringing excuses together, plaiting them into a cloak to cover him), and he had had a hard life; and no man liked a woman asking questions all the time about what he did, how he fared, who employed him; least of all Robert, so debonair and independent; too independent, surely, to live on alms?

For her mental arguments became more and more fatuous, as the invisible opposition scored point after point against her.

*   *   *

During the first week of his stay he had contrived (contrived is an excellent word, so she repeated it to herself), he had *contrived* to procure some clothes second-hand in the Port of Geith: a fisherman's jersey, too broad in the shoulder for his emaciated frame, but warm and comfortable-looking, with a big red letter M on the chest; rough corduroy trousers and a pair of decent shoes.

He bought something else too. . . . Miss Gibson did not often feel the need of a stiff drink, but on the evening when

she came in and saw a man lolling in front of her fire, wearing a faded somewhat moth-eaten black velvet coat—

"Evening dress," remarked Robert, pretending not to
notice her emotion; "spotted it in the window of an old
clo' merchant. A bit fancy, but what's the odds? it'll do
to wear in the house."

Miss Gibson could not but perceive that he never wore
it, nor the jersey either, nor the corduroy trousers, nor
certainly his shapely shoes, when he went on his mysterious
round of calls; he put on his ragged outfit again, and
shivered; if those who received an appeal were at all
nostalgic about heroes dead and beyond their aid, no wonder
they felt a compulsion to come to the rescue; "*Look* at his
boots!"—yes, look at where the toes had burst the flapping
dingy leather, sodden with months of rain, worn thin by the
pitiless road. . . . It was when Miss Gibson saw him *not* wearing the clothes he had bought in the Port of Geith, that she
faced her own wickedness, and began that long manœuvring
to chase facts into shadowy corners where no strong light
could reach them; began on that "poor fellow" business;
began plaiting excuses to cover fear.

Yet it was strange that with all this going on within her,
she should still be so terribly happy.

*   *   *

"On the whole," reflected Robert, "I'm not doing too
badly."

Of course the moment would come when he was bound
to run dry of promising contacts in this part of Scotland;
but not yet; the old camel had a surprising knack of producing the names of potential victims. Very few had
personally known R.L.S., of course; nevertheless it was
gratifying (from the financial point of view) to find how
many were devoted to his works, proud of belonging to the
same nation; or more than anything and not for any specific
reason, queerly susceptible to some legend of magic he had
possessed, the potency not yet worn off. To cash in on
personal magic, someone else's, not your own, was really
as soft a way of earning a living as Robert had ever imag-

ined even in his most radiant dreams of a paradise for idlers. The Big Scoop had not yet come his way, though he was certain it would; it was merely a question of not letting himself be discouraged by those encounters when he had bad luck and failed to put it across. Meanwhile, he was saving a bit, spending a bit, using the old camel's library to mug up his stuff, giving her an occasional treat such as letting her come home after her day's honest work and see him in meditation at her fireside, a book in his hand, and wearing an old velvet coat. . . . That was a snapper rig, Robert mused, unholy mischief in his eyes; good and profitable, though it had cost him every penny of three bob.

He stuck to it that he would accept no money from Miss Gibson. She was a woman and a fool; there were enough fools who were men; let them fork out. As for the shelter of her rooms, he could easily have found others and not have to be bothered; but her R.L.S. library and her fund of relevant information, those could not be so easily replaced; therefore Robert kept her on as his headquarters over Christmas, and through January, and well on into February, when the snow was piled up in great dirty blocks that looked as though they would never melt on either side of the roads that led out from Edinburgh, when he trudged a pilgrim into the Pentland Hills; pilgrimage mixed with business.

*   *   *

"Do you know the hills behind Swanston?"

Miss Gibson nearly laughed. What a question—did she know Halkerside, Allermuir and Caerketton? So she did not ask: "Have you been?" but "How often have you been?"

Robert did not care to confess. The answer: "Too often to count," sounded rather silly. For these were only hills; he had known better and bigger hills; he had known mountains. To provoke her, he began to describe the Rockies; then, dismissing the Rockies as irrelevant, broke off and went back to the Pentlands: "Something about 'em when you stand in the garden and look up—"

"The garden? Swanston Cottage? How did you get in?"

"I got in," briefly. "There's a lot of snow on them now, but the slopes are green, and the white scars like waterfalls rushing down Caerketton—and the trickle of the burn, lonely and peaceful . . ." he paused, no adept as the boy of Swanston had been at seeing the hills of home when he was away, seeing them even more clearly across two oceans and a continent than when he had leant eagerly from his own window. . . . "The birds were swooping and complaining—those Scotch birds of yours; don't know their name?"

"Curlews," from English Miss Gibson; then she corrected herself: "Whaups. Crockett, of the Kailyard School of writers, dedicated a book to R.L.S. in those words: 'Where about the graves of the martyrs the whaups are crying,—his heart remembers how' and sent it to him in the South Seas. He had no reply for a long while, and I expect he kept on wishing he had never been so bold or so foolish as to send it. Then, and through a third person, the poem reached him. That must have been a moment! I know it by heart, of course."

Robert leant back, resigned.

" Blows the wind to-day, and the sun and the rain are flying,
    Blows the wind on the moor to-day and now,
  Where about the graves of the martyrs the whaups are crying,
    My heart remembers how !

  Grey recumbent tombs of the dead in desert places,
    Standing stones on the vacant wine-red moor,
  Hills of sheep, and the homes of the silent vanished races,
    And winds, austere and pure :

  Be it granted me to behold you again in dying,
    Hills of home ! and to hear again the call ;
  Hear about the graves of the martyrs the peewees crying,
    And hear no more at all."

"Wine-red'?" Robert repeated, savouring it. "That would be when the heather's out. I must come back to see it."

Her heart checked. He had said "come back". But surely he could not be going away? She did not realize

[113]

how it was impossible for Robert in February to think of himself still in the same place the following August. He did not contemplate removing himself from these snug quarters yet awhile, but automatically he thought and spoke in terms of "coming back" instead of "staying on".

"I've been to the Graves of the Martyrs," he boasted on a note of childlike pride. "At least, I've seen one, right up in the hills; lonely place."

"Was it where they buried a Covenanter who was killed in the battle at Rullion Green?"

"What's a Covenanter?"

Miss Gibson believed that she knew all about the Scottish Covenanters, and started off in grand style. . . . But then, as often happens, discovered that she did know for herself, but had nothing formulated to explain to someone else, unless it were to someone who knew almost as much as she did. She managed to give Robert a rather scrambling notion of the Covenanting Army who had fought so fiercely for their own Puritan creed, defending the Solemn League and Covenant against brutal repressions after the Restoration in 1660. She was aware of the *feeling* R.L.S. had had about these brave fanatics, ready to testify and die, not yielding one inch: a special feeling, induced no doubt in very early childhood by his nurse Alison Cunningham. "My Covenanting buckies," he had affectionately termed them somewhere. She remembered, too, how he had quoted a couplet from the tombstone of the two Covenanters buried in an oakwood beside a stream:

> We died, their furious rage to stay,
> Near to the kirk of Iron-gray.

But beyond this it was all a little lame and disjointed.

"R.L.S. intended to write a history of the Covenanters, but I expect," vaguely, " you have to be a Scot to appreciate them properly. A good deal of it happened in the Pentlands," and to conceal her ignorance, she fetched a book with illustrations of Swanston. Robert was attracted for a moment, as a child might be, seeing pictures of an actual place where he himself had recently stood and felt the reality of its green and brown enchantment. Then Miss Gibson made the mistake of trying to show him one special picture—"No, you're looking at the wrong one; here, in the view called 'Haymaking at Swanston'—you can see the scars on the side of Caerketton." Robert immediately lost all interest, ignored the reason for which Miss Gibson had fetched the book, and opened it elsewhere. At once he was punished, for in his swaggering arrogance he had been contemplating a visit to the firm of the Northern Lights in George Street; he had passed it several times, with its model of the Bell Rock Lighthouse gleaming white in a niche above the portico; so why not see if he could clean up on his story there as well as anywhere else? If his face and effrontery had taken him thus far, it would take him further; at every encounter his tale, glib and plausible, gained extra touches of verisimilitude: "I'm the goods, I simply can't go wrong"—and it was just now, at the height of bravado, that he gave up the whole idea of approaching the "Lighthouse Stevensons". For he had opened the book on a portrait of Thomas Stevenson, father of R.L.S. and inventor of the intermittent form of lighthouse lantern; and confronted by that handsome head with its inexorable features of rock and granite, the piercing eyes shrewdly summing him up from the page, Robert hastily decided: "I'm not his weight." He knew that Thomas Stevenson was long ago dead; nevertheless he could not quite shed his panic of finding him sitting there at the desk, ready to appraise and strip an impostor at a glance—"Well, my man, and what can I do for you, and who may ye be? or I should say, whom do ye want me to think ye are?" A pity to over-rate your powers of bluff, even by an adept in bluffing; exposure in the offices and by the head of the firm of Stevenson, whoever it might be now, would undoubtedly build into an excellent joke, but not quite the sort of joke that Robert could afford.

Quickly he turned to another page: "R.L.S.—Last Portrait": a tall sinewy man in white tropical clothes, his left hand thrust carelessly through the folds of a swathed sash; his eyes keenly surveying the world as though by

[115]

then he had learnt to sum it up kindly but shrewdly. "Looks mighty respectable," Robert mentally scoffed at the evidence of tie and boots, to conceal that a certain possibility of matured judgment latent in the portrait made him uneasy, in the same way that the pictured regard of Thomas Stevenson had just now caused him to mistrust his own plausible gifts.

"What are you thinking of?" Miss Gibson could not refrain from what was always a dangerous question.

"Respectability."

"An odd subject."

"Edinburgh's full of it. It always was. *He* could have told you, in 1873 . . . But now we're on a wall of St. Giles's Church, and all the respectable are mighty proud of us."

"It's a very fine Memorial." Miss Gibson felt impelled to defend the Burghers of Edinburgh and the purchase of St. Gaudens's medallion of a bronze man sitting up in bed with blankets over his knees, industriously scribbling.

"It sure is. Nothing against it. You'll pardon me if I say it reminds me just a mite of the photograph by your Mr. Grainger." He began to make up doggerel couplets, slangy stuff thrown at the greybeards of a city who had solemnly subscribed to do honour to their famous son in the very church where a rebellious young agnostic had once refused to worship, and nearly broken his father's heart.

" Did ever any chap turn out a crop of pictures stranger
  Than those which hang in the stoodio of honest Mr. Grainger ?

  Tell all the dames to stay outside for they're in horrid danger
  Of being fixed up as goddesses by the camera of Grainger.

  Other photographers may spit on his works, but each is a dog in
    the manger
  Fairly ate up with jealousy of the brilliant Mr. Grainger.

  Oh give me an afternoon alone and I would choose to range a-
  -Mong the packet of droopy toffs that's photographed by
    Grainger."

Miss Gibson recognized a mischievous parody on the jingles Stevenson had scribbled to Count Nerli, to beguile the boredom of being painted.

[116]

"I wish you'd stop picking out all the nonsense I copied into my Stevenson scrapbook, and let me advise you what you'd really enjoy of his work."

"Advise" was too schoolmarm for him. He shook his head: "I can find all I want, thanks, when you're out. Not but that it's always a pleasure to see you home again," he added politely.

"You're for ever reading the Letters."

"I like 'em best."

"How do you know? You've hardly touched the Works themselves."

"Looked at some of the outsides, dull as pews and pulpits: 'Vailima Prayers', 'Moral Emblems'—I've no use for preaching."

It was Miss Gibson's turn to score. She took down from the shelf her *Moral Emblems*, a battered second-hand copy in the Edinburgh Edition. "Have you looked *in*side?"

He shook his head. "Title's bad enough."

"My poor Robert, you've no sense of humour. But if the text is really too heavy for you—"

—And he saw it was a comic picture-book, with gaily callous verses on the opposite page.

> "The Abbot for a walk went out,
> A wealthy cleric, very stout,
> And Robin has that Abbot stuck
> As the red hunter spears the buck.
> The djavel or the javelin
> Has, you observe, gone bravely in,
> And you may hear that weapon whack
> Bang through the middle of his back.
> Hence we may learn that Abbots should
> Never go walking in a wood."

Robert laughed, and handsomely admitted he had been hasty in dismissing *Moral Emblems* as solemn stuff. The peaceful atmosphere was only broken when he happened to look back at the table of contents in the same volume: "On a New Form of Intermittent Light for Lighthouses", "On the Thermal Influence of Forests"—and was somewhat taken aback; just as he was settling down for a comfortable appreciation of this flippant fellow whom he had temporarily adopted as father, he was offered sober scholarship instead. It was difficult to explain such a transformation satisfactorily. "Expect he got someone else to write them," remarked Robert lightly.

Miss Gibson flared up, as he knew she would:

"You only admit one side of the most many-sided writer of the last hundred years. Do you know that *Dr. Jekyll and Mr. Hyde*, when it was first published, was used as the text of a sermon in St. Paul's, and then from pulpits all over England."

"Wal, there, that puts paid to Dr. Jekyll and Mr. what-did-you-call-him, as far as I'm concerned. It can go in with the Prayers and the Latin essays and all that geography-made-easy you've been trying to plant on me." He meant this, and in his mind drew a black line through the title, marking it off. Funny, though, how the old camel had not yet grasped what would be likely to lure him and what repel him, where her precious library was concerned.

When she was blessedly out of the way at the shop, he was left alone to browse; and by stubbornly avoiding her recommendations, he made some illuminating discoveries on his own. One of these seemed to throw a long narrow ray of light as though from the dusty wings of a proscenium, on what might have started Miss Gibson's adoration. It occurred in *Memories of Vailima*, which attracted him because it was on the man's life and not the author's literature:

Louis will never allow any jokes on the subject of ' wallflowers ' or old maids. He reduced me to tears describing a young girl dressing herself in ball finery and sitting the evening out with smiles, while her breast was filled with the crushing sense of failure.

He smiled, not cruelly but with a certain compassion for an arid past so remarkably unlike his own. A special consideration for old maids might easily have been the origin of her obsession. That irrepressible spring of kindness in Robert caused him to spare her from chaff on the subject; he would not even let her know that he had spotted it, but

[118]

for fear he might be growing sloppy, he was all the more merciless in attacking her on his other find in *Memories of Vailima*:

"See here, didn't you tell me 'Will o' the Mill' was his own creed and philosophy? You did? You should read more carefully, ma'am. Now listen; this is straight reporting by his stepdaughter, and she ought to know: '"Will o' the Mill" made a great impression upon Graham Balfour in his youth, and he declares that his character and life are moulded upon that story. Louis repudiated the tale altogether, and says that Will's sentiments upon life are cat's-meat.'"

"'Cat's-meat,'" Robert repeated in triumph. Then softly: "How do you stand up against that?"

Their evening skirmishes were always vigorous. "'. . . There were two dead combatants upon the field . . . and we tenderly carried off each other's corpses,'" she quoted, innocently pleased at the resemblance to the spirited warfare which with sound of trumpet and galloping hoofs had prevented the Stevenson marriage from falling into stagnation. And it was true there was some pretty hard hitting between Robert and his hostess. Miss Gibson knew her stuff better; she had had years of solitary intensive reading; but Robert had the nimbler tongue, and chivalry in him was only intermittent, a green patch here and there. Miss Gibson hoped she made up for her ostrich outlook (if it can be called an outlook) on Robert's secret activities, by refusing to give in over any argument on the actual matter contained in the books. He could draw her into a rage with the greatest of ease and enjoyment:

"I've been reading some of the shorter tales. They're fine, especially those you don't like so much."

"How can you possibly know which those are?"

"I'm a good guesser. For instance 'The Treasure of Franchard'. There's a whole lot to be learnt from that tale."

Miss Gibson could hardly believe her ears.

"Yep," he went on; "that ragamuffin they adopted, the French doctor and his wife, same as you kind of adopted me"— a muffled protest from Miss Gibson—"he was no end of a fool, that kid, to bring back the treasure once he'd got away with it."

"*Robert!*"

Robert looked innocent. "Isn't that what the author was trying to prove, that the boy was bats?"

"You can't—" she began, struggling for calm. But Robert burst out laughing; her face was too much for his gravity; and he conceded that it was a grand tale, though he stuck to that oddly oblique point of view that Jean-Marie was a fool in his honesty. He even submitted to letting her read portions of it aloud, for as he had previously read it to himself, he did not have to listen. Unluckily, Miss Gibson adored reading aloud; and living alone had not quenched this perpetual lust, but on the contrary, sharpened it. It would have been much nicer for her if Robert had never been taught to read for himself beyond the primer stage of a cat who sat on the mat.

After about twenty minutes of purgatory, a word caught Robert's inattentive ear: "What's ratio—ratiocinate?"

She looked it up in the dictionary: "'The act or process of deducing consequences from premises.'"

"'Premises'?"

Again Miss Gibson consulted the dictionary: "'A proposition antecedently assumed or laid down: the two propositions of a syllogism, called respectively major and minor, from which the conclusion is deduced: subject matter of a conveyance or deed as set forth in the beginning.' *Now* you understand"—which was paying off old scores with a vengeance.

But Robert looked so discouraged that she relented, and gave a slightly clearer definition of deducing consequences from premises, which he interpreted colloquially:

"Putting things right for yourself as you go along?"

"Yes, I suppose one may say that is the meaning." She wondered why he looked amused. Nothing, surely, in "ratiocination" to justify that dancing devil in his eyes? For how could she guess he had a mischievous idea that "putting things right for yourself as you go along" was exactly what Miss Gibson was doing, against her upright nature and all her principles, by keeping an idler and a parasite and tacitly allowing him to go round raising money by whatever doubtful means he chose, because she could not bear to send him away. "She believes who I am, but hates what I do. If she knew the truth, she'd hate what I am, but not care what I did." Ratiocination!

In their next fight, Miss Gibson was the winner.

He had brought in a bottle of Burgundy for their dinner; and Burgundy led her to the last moments in the life of R.L.S., acutely poignant as small events must be which herald tragedy, when he went down to the cellar to bring up a bottle of his favourite wine to make a celebration feast with the salad that was mixed and never eaten.

"I wonder what they did with that salad? If they sort of couldn't bring themselves to throw it away. . . ."

"It's strange you should say that. I've wondered too—" but she broke off, for fear he was at his usual flippancy, often unwelcome, but here unforgivable. Seeing she need not have feared and that he had been sincerely wondering, she rushed on too fast, taking an ell where she had barely been given half an inch. Robert fidgeted and scowled; not wanting to hear her plunge all over the sorrowful irony of those last hours of life at Vailima. He interrupted, jerked her back to Burgundy, and thence to a poet, rascal and vagrant, one Messer François Villon, declaring with enthusiasm that Stevenson's story *A Lodging for the Night* was more to his taste than any other; and drank a mocking toast to his companion, teasing her by a too apt analogy which put himself in the rôle of Villon and cast her as the old Seigneur who had sheltered the merry thief—a comparison not acceptable to Miss Gibson. She said with primness that she had only read the story once; a masterpiece, indeed, but horrible in its cool acceptance of the vileness of human nature.

"Too tough? I'll say you're right. Wait! I'll give you some of your own medicine," and he read aloud to Miss Gibson (who also resented the compulsion occasionally thrust on her to sit and listen) Villon's characteristic speech that ended the story:

"Villon was sensibly nettled under all this sermonising. 'You think I have no sense of honour!' he cried. 'I'm poor enough, God knows! It's hard to see rich people with their gloves, and you blowing in your hands. An empty belly is a bitter thing, although you speak so lightly of it. If you had had as many as I, perhaps you would change your tune. Any way I'm a thief—make the most of that—but I'm not a devil from hell, God strike me dead! I would have you to know I've an honour of my own, as good as yours, though I don't prate about it all day long, as if it was a God's miracle to have any. It seems quite natural to me; I keep it in its box till it's wanted. Why now, look you here, how long have I been in this room with you? Did you not tell me you were alone in the house? Look at your gold plate! You're strong, if you like, but you're old and unarmed, and I have my knife. What did I want but a jerk of the elbow and here would have been you with the cold steel in your bowels, and there would have been me, linking in the streets, with an armful of gold cups! Did you suppose I hadn't wit enough to see that? And I scorned the action. There are your damned goblets, as safe as in a church; there are you, with your heart ticking as good as new; and here am I, ready to go out again as poor as I came in, with my one white lie that you threw in my teeth! And you think I have no sense of honour— God strike me dead!'

The old man stretched out his right arm. 'I will tell you what you are,' he said. 'You are a rogue, my man, an impudent and a black-hearted rogue and vagabond. I have passed an hour with you. Oh! believe me, I feel myself disgraced! And you have eaten and drunk at my table. But now I am sick at your presence; the day has come, and the night-bird should be off to his roost. Will you go before, or after?'

'Which you please,' returned the poet, rising. 'I believe you to be strictly honourable.' He thoughtfully emptied his cup. 'I wish I could add you were intelligent,' he went on, knocking on his head with his knuckles. 'Age, age! the brains stiff and rheumatic.'

The old man preceded him from a point of self-respect; Villon following, whistling, with his thumbs in his girdle.

'God pity you,' said the lord of Brisetout at the door.

'Good-bye, papa,' returned Villon, with a yawn. 'Many thanks for the cold mutton.'

The door closed behind him. The dawn was breaking over the white roofs. A chill, uncomfortable morning ushered in the day. Villon stood and heartily stretched himself in the middle of the road.

'A very dull old gentleman,' he thought. 'I wonder what his goblets may be worth.'"

Robert slammed the book in triumph: "And cat's-meat to you again! You're always ramming down my throat that R.L.S. was a sort of mission-house preacher; reckon he had to do that sort of thing for his public when his exchequer was low, but I'm not taken in by it. He could never have understood Villon the way he does, unless he *was* Villon part of the time."

Miss Gibson was about to deny this heatedly; and being Miss Gibson, to kill her own point where she sought to establish it, with illustration from *Dr. Jekyll and Mr. Hyde*, that every man has within him a dual personality for good or for evil in perpetual conflict. But just then a more subtle weapon occurred to her by which Robert could be effectually vanquished; Stevenson's own essay on François Villon, proving how scornfully his judgment stripped away any glorious awards from a man who could live by robbery and murder and all mean debauchery.

"Oblige me by reading this, my dear Robert."

Robert obliged her.

" But Villon, who had not the courage to be poor with honesty, now whiningly implores our sympathy, now shows his teeth upon the dung-heap with an ugly snarl. He envies bitterly, envies passionately. Poverty, he protests, drives men to steal, as hunger makes the wolf sally from the forest. The poor, he goes on, will always have a carping word to say, or, if that outlet be denied, nourish rebellious thoughts. It is a calumny on the noble army of the poor. Thousands in a small way of life, ay, and even in the smallest, go through life with tenfold as much honour and dignity and peace of mind as the rich gluttons whose dainties and state-beds awakened Villon's covetous temper. And every morning's sun sees thousands who pass whistling to their toil. But Villon was the ' *mauvais pauvre* ' defined by Victor Hugo, and, in its English expression, so admirably stereotyped by Dickens. He was the first wicked *sans-culotte*. He is the man of genius with the moleskin cap. He is mighty pathetic and beseeching here in the street, but I would not go down a dark road with him for a large consideration."

He was disconcerted. More, he was stung and had little further to say. His fellow-vagrant had seriously let him down.

"Considering he was a bit of a lad himself when he was young, kicking up his heels in every rowdy tavern in Edinburgh, to pitch into this French gallowsbird for doing the same in Paris a few hundred years back, is humbug and cant; that is, cant if he meant it. I don't believe he did."

Miss Gibson remarked quietly: "You've got brains enough to tell if a man is passionately sincere or just amusing himself with his pen."

Robert shrugged his shoulders. "I'm not a writer, thank God. I've no reason to worry what they're at."

"You're a reader, and I should have said with a very special reason."

He swung round towards her, on the alert; then saw with relief that she referred to his quest from the spiritual and not the pecuniary point of view.

Brave with Burgundy, but far too deeply in earnest to see that she could not challenge this mountebank and hope to win, she went on: "You seem only to register the care-free element in R.L.S., and let your eyes instinctively skip the rest; I've said so before. No one knew more charmingly, more unselfishly how to bring gaiety, but to be amusing isn't everything, and the soul and body of his work lies well over the border-line from perpetual laughter. For instance, you were so full of that story you read of how his mother and aunt were driving down the High Street and lamenting his wild ways, and suddenly his aunt saw a disreputable rag-and-bones man walking along with a sack over his shoulder selling rabbit-skins—"

"You've got it wrong," Robert interrupted. "I didn't say a word about rabbit-skins; and I was told about the rag and bones, I didn't read it. He had to do something; he was hard up and his father kept him short of cash."

"Who told you?"

Robert hedged. It had been one of his most profitable visits, to an old Edinburgh lady who was "interested". "I thought it funny, didn't you? With them driving along so grand and respectable, and then seeing him. Bet he didn't care a tinker's cuss, either."

Miss Gibson did not say whether she thought it funny. Actually she did, but Robert was not to be encouraged. "But when I told you last night about the Samoan tribes who before going to war brought their valuables and money to Tusitala for him to look after, trusting him above all others, and asked him to accept the gift of a live turtle, all you did was to jeer at the turtle."

Robert defended himself: "I didn't jeer. An admirer on board ship asked him once if he would accept the gift of a Webster's dictionary, and he said 'I signified a manly willingness to accept anything as a gift.' That's not jeering, to remember his manly willingness. I'm a willing man myself."

"You! You can only react to what's visible; never to what lies between the lines. You couldn't see how wonderful it was that these warriors should have come to love and trust a foreigner of different race and colour who had come to live among them, enough to hand over without any qualms all they held most precious. They could only have done it through being sure by their instinct, as children are sure, that he loved them too and desired their well-being; and not from any political standpoint or from the necessity of being comfortable among them or even as raw material for his work; he loved them as human beings. Don't you think it's time you . . . forgot the turtle?"

"Hallelujah!" Robert intoned in the bass. "Let us pray!"

Miss Gibson quoted with malicious pleasure: "'Robert's voice is not strong but it's impressive.'"

"What's that?"

"When he was a little boy at school and liked declaiming pathetic poetry: 'A Soldier of the Legion lay Dying in Algiers', he was misguided enough to carry home his master's opinion of his voice, and his father never stopped roasting him about it: 'Robert's voice is not strong but it's impressive.' It never occurred to me before," Miss Gibson mused, "but I believe this is the only place I've ever noticed Stevenson himself or anyone else refer to him as 'Robert'."

The other Robert marvelled, not for the first time, at the authority and information of the old camel; and at how well she told the simplest anecdote, with neither too much nor too little emphasis on the point; yet how badly she read aloud from the printed page, as if her whole life depended on making her listener feel what she so unfortunately felt herself. To reward her now for getting the better of him, he faithfully promised to forget the turtle. Immediately throwing away her advantage, Miss Gibson picked up a small volume by H. J. Moors who in Stevenson's time had been a leading American trader in Apia; and started to recite a letter to him from Mataafa, the rebel king exiled after the Samoan War.

At the first sentence, Robert's hand shot out automatically; there was always the hope that she might pass over the volume to him; but not, apparently, when red wine was in her:

"I write this letter in ever-loving remembrance of the Chief Tusitala. It is impossible for my heart to forget the great love of this Chief. He loved me exceedingly. He was to me like a true father and a true brother. His advice to me to keep peace and good order in Samoa was excellent; it was very necessary that Samoa should not be fighting. His great love to me was even shown by the raiment that he gave for the keep of my body. I dearly love him, and the good wishes of my heart are ever with him. I greatly love his wife and Lloyd, their son. May the King who reigns in heaven receive this Chief in His eternal mansions!

This letter is ended, but my love towards his Excellency Tusitala will never end."

Miss Gibson felt that it must be possible to move Robert by what she herself had always found so moving, shake him out of his provoking nonchalance; yet by the time she had finished Mataafa's letter, she had almost forgotten motive and hearer. In her exalted mood she was out in Samoa on the island, seeing those hot-coloured scenes when the Road of the Loving Hearts was being made, axes swinging and voices lusty in song and joke as the trees crashed down. . . . "The Road of Gratitude" was what they had wanted to name it, Mataafa's warriors whom Stevenson had championed and tended during their year in prison, from the hour when he had flung himself down to Apia in a rage at the filthy conditions and the bad food allotted to them. Released, they pleaded to be allowed to build this road for him even before they returned to their own lands, though their country was poor and famine was threatening their homes, disorganized from the long want of husband and father. "They desired to build this road at their own cost and of their own free will because they were grateful. In his speech at the opening of the road, he said: 'I speak to those who are not too proud to work for gratitude.' You must read that magnificent speech—"

Robert knew what was coming.

"—I'll read you the conclusion and then I'm certain you won't be able to keep yourself from the rest. May I borrow your Volume Four of the Letters? I think it's at the back of Volume Four."

"Sure thing," Robert gave gentle permission, but without moving himself.

" Chiefs ! Our road is not built to last a thousand years, yet in a sense it is. When a road is once built, it is a strange thing how it collects traffic, how every year, as it goes on, more and more people are found to walk thereon and others are raised up to repair and perpetuate it and keep it alive ; so that perhaps even this road of ours may, from reparations to reparation, continue to exist and be useful hundreds and hundreds of years after we are mingled in the dust."

She could not be sure whether she had made a tremendous impression on Robert, or whether he were merely sleepy? his eyes were narrowed and he offered no comment whatever. So she determined to follow up this onslaught on his more serious side, by yet another flank attack. She searched for a few minutes in Volume Two—and then handed him the book, her finger jabbing at what she desired him to read.

"Must I ? It looks dull stuff."

"To please me," said Miss Gibson solemnly.

"Wouldn't it please you just as well if I finished my smoke

in peace, and we had another glass each, and said good-night?"

Miss Gibson remained obstinate. Robert sighed heavily, and ploughed his way through the letter she had indicated:

" Here is my problem. . The Curtin women are still miserable prisoners ; no one dare buy their farm of them, all the manhood of England and the world stands aghast before a threat of murder. (1) Now, my work can be done anywhere ; hence I can take up without loss a backgoing Irish farm, and live on, though not (as I had originally written) in it : First Reason. (2) If I should be killed, there are a good many who would feel it : writers are so much in the public eye, that a writer being murdered would attract attention, throw a bull's-eye light upon this cowardly business : Second Reason. (3) I am not unknown in the States, from which the funds come that pay for these brutalities : to some faint extent, my death (if I should be killed) would tell there · Third Reason. (4) *Nobody else is taking up this obvious and crying duty :* Fourth Reason. (5) I have a crazy health and may die at any moment, my life is of no purchase in an insurance office, it is the less account to husband of and the business of husbanding a life is dreary and demoralising : Fifth Reason.

I state these in no order, but as they occur to me. And I shall do the like with the objections.

First Objection : It will do no good ; you have seen Gordon die, and nobody minded ; nobody will mind if you die. This is plainly of the devil. Second Objection : You will not even be murdered, the climate will miserably kill you, you will strangle out in a rotten damp heat, in congestion, etc. Well, what then ? It changes nothing : the purpose is to brave crime ; let me brave it, for such time and to such an extent as God allows. Third Objection : The Curtin women are probably highly uninteresting females. I haven't a doubt of it. But the Government cannot, men will not, protect them. If I am the only one to see this public duty, it is to the public and the Right I should perform it—not to Mesdames Curtin. Fourth Objection—"

Four objections, and how many more? Ten on this page alone. Robert was beginning to feel faint with the effort of grinding all through this. Yet with Miss Gibson's eyes fixed on him, staring, avid to catch the effect of every line, he dared not skip a whole page and turn to the next; so he let his eyes move to and fro along the lines, moving them more ostentatiously (for Miss Gibson's benefit) than eyes usually move when reading, but letting them not take in the sense of a single word, for this was less tiring than the more intelligent process of really reading. It was now time to turn over, and near the top of the next page a phrase caught his eye and he stopped merely pretending:

"But I charge you this: if you see in this idea of mine the finger of duty, do not dissuade me. I am nearing forty, I begin to love my ease and my home and my habits, I never knew how much till this arose; do not falsely counsel me to put my head under the bed-clothes. . . .

He threw the book down with a scornful exclamation: "He's loony, same as when he was a kid: it's burying the tin soldier all over again, and expecting it to grow up as a rose-bush. These two women and their beastly old farm are nothing to him, nothing much to anybody that I can see—"

"You haven't understood—"

"If he had to fight, there were ten thousand worse things going on in the world before he need go and plant himself down at the end of nowhere for the sake of a couple of dreary hags, when the whole affair would be forgotten in a week. Great Jumping Jehosophat, I'd like to have heard what his missus had to say about it. What good did he suppose would come of it? Supposing everyone rushed about, and barged off to Ireland and shut themselves up in lonely farms. He was pretty sound in his ideas most of the time, with his hate of cant and phoney respectability, but these letters—I expect he was a bit delirious; they don't make *sense*."

"Aren't there finer things than sense?"

"Maybe; but they'd be sane things. Let him stay at home and write balderdash if he felt he had to, collect money and send it across to those women, and then think no more about it. Life's too short."

"His life *was* too short for all he felt he had to do," Miss Gibson acquiesced sadly enough. She was silent, trying to rearrange the torrent of eloquence rushing and foaming through her mind, into the sort of dispassionate arguments that might make some appeal to a soulless vagrant. It was somehow important to convince him, by these very intentions he thought so crazy, that Stevenson was right to maintain how responsibility lay on each individual man to be active in the cause for justice where injustice had been done, and if need be, die for it. The very fact that these women, as he said, were probably dreary hags, surely lifted the whole creed into that kingdom of the spirit familiar to Don Quixote and every other fighter for a lunatic cause unsupported by worldly sanity. "It would be no sacrifice to go forth and rescue Beauty in distress—" Miss Gibson, fumbling for forceful sentences, did manage to get her point across as far as that, and Robert took her up on it:

"—If you're sure to have a roll in the hay with her afterwards? That *is* so, and it's mighty creditable in you, ma'am, to have figured it out that way."

She gave in, unable to protect herself from confusion and a queer shame at the sight of him lounging there, one leg crossed and swinging over the other, surveying her with quizzical eyes discerned vaguely through the blue smoke that blurred him from view. What was she to *do* with this man, she thought in despair, a witness who desired to testify but was afraid.

At this juncture, Robert saved her any further trouble.

"You're not *going out*?" she cried in sheer dismay.

"'I like the fresh air and these stars and things.'"

He laughed at her look of sheer bewilderment. So for once the pupil had puzzled his instructress, had he? Good, and praise be to the devil or whoever gave him his excellent memory. Worth while to be hand-in-glove with Old Nick if he could prompt you at the needed instant with a quotation that would leave the old camel guessing; and not only guessing, but searching for several hours, if he knew anything about her.

"The fresh air and these stars and things" were a welcome

change. He had had a bellyful of evenings with Miss Gibson in a stuffy room with a big fire, talking about books. Old nostalgic cravings seized him for those lean and limping years when supperless he turned off the road, glad to fling himself down and sleep on a spread of straw in a draughty barn. Well—there were still barns and still straw; come to that, he had money in his pockets to jingle and spend. For a week or two at least, he could shift for himself, or if he were lucky, plant his story on another votary, this next time a male instead of romantic females spouting rhetoric to beat the band.

—He became aware that he had walked out on her in his velvet "evening" coat. Serve him right for pandering to sentimental photographs and nicknames. He would have to slip in and change tomorrow while she was at the shop. Sighing a little over the inconveniences that so swiftly attach themselves to gentlemen with a change of wardrobe, Robert strode out towards East Lothian and the Lammermuirs.

*　　*　　*

It was in those desolate small hours of the morning that are so far from being small that they swell huge out of all proportion, when a haggard Miss Gibson at last lit upon the source of his parting line. Volumes of her library lay scattered around her on the faded Turkey carpet, piled up on the horse-hair couch and on the mahogany table; several more sliding from her lap. It had been quite an exhausting search, with only one clue: that a master-craftsman who had loved the stars and knew how to celebrate his love, would never when writing in his own person so fumble for a phrase; therefore it must have been spoken by an inarticulate character deliberately invented for a tale or a novel.

It turned out to be a short story. Miss Gibson had not read "Providence and the Guitar" for many years, or she might have found the line sooner:

'One,' said Léon. 'Four hours till daylight. It is warm; it is starry; I have matches and tobacco. Do not let us exaggerate,

Elvira—the experience is positively charming. I feel a glow within me ; I am born again. This is the poetry of life.'

. . . The young man drew near in the twilight. He was a tall, powerful, gentlemanly fellow, with a somewhat puffy face, dressed in a grey tweed suit, with a deer-stalker hat of the same material ; and as he now came forward he carried a knapsack slung upon one arm.

' Are you camping out here too ? ' he asked, with a strong English accent. ' I'm not sorry for company.'

Léon explained their misadventure ; and the other told them that he was a Cambridge undergraduate on a walking tour, that he had run short of money, could no longer pay for his night's lodging, had already been camping out for two nights, and feared he should require to continue the same manœuvre for at least two nights more.

' Luckily, it's jolly weather,' he concluded.

' You hear that, Elvira,' said Léon. ' Madame Berthelini,' he went on, ' is ridiculously affected by this trifling occurrence. For my part, I find it romantic and far from uncomfortable ; or at least,' he added, shifting on the stone bench, ' not quite so uncomfortable as might have been expected. But pray be seated.'

' Yes,' said the undergraduate, sitting down, ' it's rather nice than otherwise when once you're used to it ; only it's devilish difficult to get washed. I like the fresh air and these stars and things.'

Her grandfather-clock in the corner struck four. Nearly five hours of wakefulness that mocking rascal had inflicted on her. Miss Gibson burst into tears. She was so tired, and her nerves were taut from the strain of close hunting through page after page; she was not used to Burgundy; she was not used to making tremendous eloquent speeches and see .her audience nonchalantly get up, stub out his cigarette on the antique mahogany coal-box and depart and not come back.

And not come back.

9

Miss Gibson was alone in the shop when Robert sauntered in about ten days later, with a malicious hope of creating a sensation. But whatever went on in her breast, she was fortunately able to control any outward signs, and to greet him with no more than a cool nod, much preoccupied with a parcel of new books.

"Anything fresh?"

"They're all fresh," replied Miss Gibson. "No, don't handle them; they're for sale, remember."

He looked so snubbed, like a small boy reprimanded for dirty hands, that she relented a little. "Here's Chatto and Windus's new edition of *Father Damien*, with a preface by Mrs Stevenson."

Robert checked an impulse to take it from her, and kept his hands stiffly down at his sides. "Are you bringing it home?" he enquired meekly; and Miss Gibson's pulses leapt. Home? So truancy had not been a success?

"This copy? No, it's been promised to a special client" (a fib, but Robert need not think that she existed merely to supply him with literature as well as with food, fire and forgiveness). "But I'll tell you about it this evening. Run along now and take a bath; I'm busy."

His reappearance had fallen a little flat, and Miss Gibson congratulated herself as he turned and walked despondently away: Handle him briskly, that's the way, she told herself; and it was true that Robert responded to skilful handling, only Miss Gibson so rarely could bring herself to achieve it.

After supper, it was he again who had to break through their politely superficial conversation:

"What about that book you had in the shop—Father something-or-other?"

"*Father Damien : An Open Letter to the Reverend Dr. Hyde of Honolulu*," she prompted him. "Surely you've come across the title?"

"Father Damien? Yes, I do remember he was mentioned in the letters. What was all the fuss about? Something to do with lepers, wasn't it?"

He expected his irreverence would cause her to flap about like an agitated fish on a slab; but during his absence Miss Gibson had recovered her forfeited poise and dignity. "Yes, something to do with lepers."

She did not offer to read it to him, though in his submissive mood he might have put up with even that formidable ordeal; but told him instead the story of how Stevenson had visited the island of Molokai shortly after the death of the priest who had lived there for sixteen years turning it from an unbearable hell into a place of suffering indeed, but made endurable by his labours.

"R.L.S. flamed out in his defence, and wrote and had published this open letter, so that everybody might know of the sacrifice of Father Damien who had gone to work among the lepers, and contracted leprosy himself. He was only human, so perhaps now and then, as the Rev. Mr. Hyde had suggested, he had found human solace in that desolate plague-ridden island of those cast off from mankind."

Robert suppressed a yawn at the boring whang-whang of fervent oratory in her voice. "Who opened the open letter and what was in it?"

"Whips and scorpions."

He raised his eyebrows and drawled: "Is that so?"

"It's no use my describing it if you've never had the curiosity to look it up for yourself—" Miss Gibson did a touch of whips and scorpions across his indifference. "It was conceived in the same spirit of wrath as driving the money-changers out of the Temple, and with the same disregard of consequences; for the Rev. Mr. Hyde could easily have prosecuted him for libel and might have won the suit too, and that would have meant financial ruin to Stevenson and the loss of all he had; though he had qualified for the Bar himself, he had all his life a childish fear of the law, so it was an especially courageous thing for him to run full tilt against it. He did ask his family if he were to publish the letter, for he felt they had a right to say; it concerned them more than himself whether their life of hazard and insecurity should have to begin all over again? but of course they declared unanimously that he was to go ahead with it. So now Father Damien is remembered twice over, for his work and for Stevenson's defence of his work."

She waited for Robert's almost inevitable "Loony!" But he only said "Good fighting!" which was distinctly better.

"Was that the story in the new preface you said his missus had written?"

"No, all I've just told you is public property and can be found in any biography. This incident which Fanny relates *is* new: It happened when the yacht *Casco* was at anchor at some tropical island on their voyage, and they had been paddling in the warm lagoon and catching bright little fish and having a glorious time: different from his former invalid life when he had had to remain indoors 'like a weevil in a biscuit'. Then they flung themselves down on the hot sand and lit cigarettes and lazed and were perfectly happy—till Fanny said 'There's a native behind that tree. He seems to want to speak to us.' Stevenson beckoned to the man, who slowly approached, accepted the cigarette offered him, lit it and squatted down beside them. After a few puffs he handed it back to the donor to finish, as was the polite custom in those islands. Fanny watched in horror . . . two fingers of the man's hand were eaten away with leprosy. She stifled a cry, wondering if Louis had seen it too? wondering what he would do?

"'You came to this island on the mission ship?' the native probably asked; and Stevenson may have replied, serenely puffing at the cigarette:

"'No, and for a very good reason: I shouldn't have been allowed to smoke.'

"'Ah, yes; I have seen you are one who smokes with love.'

"After a little desultory talk, he took leave of them. Stevenson waited till he was out of sight and hearing, and then flung away the remains of that nightmare cigarette:

[135]

"'Well—I didn't smoke *that* one with love.'

"'You *saw*? Then why didn't you—'

"'I couldn't refuse it. He's had enough to bear already without mortifying him any further.'

"'What will you do if—if—'

"'If I catch leprosy? Oh, we'll go and live on Molokai and carry on Father Damien's work—while we can.'"

Robert was silent. He screwed out the glowing end of his own cigarette with some consideration in an ash-tray as Miss Gibson preferred him to do, instead of chucking it wherever was handiest. Her narrative style, penny plain, was surprisingly quiet and effective; with that knowledge of detail and character as though she herself had been there and could claim authority for adding this or that in a dialogue which might not have been on any printed page.

"He took a lot for granted," Robert remarked at last in a matter-of-fact tone.

"From his wife? Yes, he exacted courage from those surrounding him, simply because it didn't occur to him there could be two ways of looking at it. He may have felt that otherwise they'd have loved not him, but a different sort of man leading a different sort of life by completely different standards."

Robert felt it was time he asserted himself against this strangely new aspect of the old camel, or he would have to start respecting her; and that would be a nuisance. So he remarked: "We've been talking for hours; d'you know what time it is?" spoken with a touch of reproach, as if he were the sober father and disciplinarian of an unruly household, and Miss Gibson a whole handful of his rebel sons and daughters who had reeled home after days and nights of dissipation and refused to retire to their beds at a decent hour. His hostess, still informed by wisdom, said no more of Father Damien, but took the hint and left him.

She half expected that by listening intently, she would just catch the soft opening click of the door of her bookcase. But she was disappointed; Robert had decided to thwart her; he would read *Father Damien*, but not till her business removed her altogether from the premises; for he did not

[136]

wish to be aware that beyond the cheap graining of the door was a woman who might be saying to herself in triumph: "At last I've lured him into reading something really serious. Shall I peep in presently, and ask him if he doesn't think it splendid?"

She managed never to ask him: "Have you read it and isn't it splendid?" though by every other maddening trick she soon reverted to her old self. It was just as well for her that she was able to make this one exception, for her head would have been bitten off; Robert had lost his nonchalant good-humour; a very grave loss from his point of view. Miss Gibson exasperated him more than ever, for his spontaneous return after desertion had inspired her with altogether too much confidence. She interpreted it, poor woman, as a sign of how much he had grown to love his cosy little home with her in Edinburgh, his regular meals and hot baths, their nice chats almost every evening; she imagined that now he had again taken sample of his old roving ways and obviously disliked them, she need fear no more: he had given them up for good; and no wonder, poor fellow; a tramp's existence in winter and in Scotland could be neither agreeable nor healthy. And Robert had an ugly-sounding cough which in its romantic reminiscence gave her a queer glow. . . . Had he been a rough broad-chested navvy, then she might have walked up her own stairs every evening in trepidation lest the "call of the wild" had again seized hold of him, as in those husky books that her male customers were always demanding. But Robert was now her property and protégé; he had gone and come back. This was his Safety Corner.

And no one to warn her that Safety Corner, that whimsical abode, had never been so precariously exposed.

She had given him a latch-key so that he should be free to let himself in and out. He accepted it as a matter of convenience, yet with a secret naïf pleasure over his unlikely reincarnation: "Look, I'm a cove that has a latch-key!" But lately, instead of inflating him with a sense of greater liberty, paradoxically it began to irk him as a symbol of restraint; to be entrusted with a latch-key by the old camel

any old camel) presupposed domesticity, home, affection—
"I *won't* be trusted!" He could break in, couldn't he,
whenever he needed to get in?

It only needed her suggestion that he should let himself
be photographed, to touch the spring of catastrophe. She
introduced the subject playfully:

"Robert, when's your birthday?"

The question was lacking in tact, to a gentleman born
obscurely in the workhouse. True, he was supposed to
know the date within a week or two; nevertheless "birthday", brightly spoken, lumbered on to his jumping nerves
with the hoofs of a rhinoceros.

"Why?" grimly; "want to give me a present?"

"On the contrary, I'll stand you a visit to the photographer
for your birthday, and then *you* can give *me* a present."

"Pola!" Robert mocked her. "Bothering me for my
'sun-shadow' before I'm even dead."

She was delighted. It was obvious, she thought, that her
request had flattered him; that like all men, even tramps,
he was vain of his appearance. Like all men—and like one
man.

She had never been further from a clever guess. The
whole notion had scared him; coming from Miss Gibson it
insinuated more horrid family ties, and fell into the same
category as latch-keys. A photograph neatly framed and
put to hang on the wall, perhaps, like that infernal Grainger
portrait she was so keen on. . . . Was she getting too soft
about him?

And it had police associations, linked up with a recent
somewhat sinister interview just before he came back to
her, when he had barely escaped from a night in the cells
and "further enquiry". A photograph? The law welcomed
photographs.

So he declared brazenly that thanks very much all the
same, but the only photograph of himself *he* needed was by
Mr. Nerli.

And that was the first time he had come out into the open
over that shy little incident; not only tacitly confessing that
he had stolen it, but that he damn well intended to keep it.

He met her startled gaze as though daring her to deny the impudent casuistry that he had a right to that particular likeness.

What *is* the matter with him this morning? Miss Gibson mildly speculated on her way to the shop; as someone about to be involved in a landslide might be sorry they had inadvertently dislodged a pebble.

*   *   *

For reading *Father Damien* had queerly shaken him; he felt robbed of his invisible mate, quick-witted and brazen and audacious; the very prototype of his own virtues (such as they were; some might have called them vices); a mate who would have been tickled to death at his cheerful cheating masquerade. Only gradually, as from the lessening tremors after an earthquake, did he assemble enough poise to front the world and Miss Gibson.

It was not the Letter's revelation of agony among the lepers which stamped itself on his mind. He had seen too much of humanity in its dark spots, its patches of squalor, wretchedness and disease, to be moved to such depths as the Edinburgh boy who had been nursed and sheltered tenderly through his childhood. No, but it was a shock that any man could think so little of his own ruin when charging to the rescue; feel so loyal a passion on behalf of another human being; and at the same time regulate the energy of passion so as to use it to its full value. Robert had seen how men, defending their own advantage against unfair attack, would fly into rages, and squander what might have been their force and helpfulness by stammering and spluttering, by confused oaths and incoherent counter-accusations. From the vindication of Father Damien he gathered, however, that it was only in self-defence that eloquence destroyed itself; in a crusade, passion could function dispassionately as the pistons of an engine, strong and tireless and perfectly controlled. Not being in close touch with the higher administration of justice, it did not occur to Robert that the defence of Father Damien owed something to the author's legal training; and that he had brilliantly conducted the case, as a counsel, determined to thrust home shame where it belonged, would marshal his arguments in closely linked file and formation, and only let passion seem to overcome lucidity when it was a help, not a hindrance, that it should do so.

If nothing spoken can ever again be unspoken, it is equally a dead certainty that nothing once read can ever be unread; whether you will or not, it may remain in possession of that perverse and infinitesimal portion of your memory until you die.

So curse Miss Gibson for telling the story of the cigarette and leper's hand, so that he was falsely and insidiously led to the book without in the least knowing what he was in for! It was a disgrace for such a hardened reader to expose a soft-shelled new-born innocent like himself. From this injured point of view, he veered round to a cross denial that he would ever have read anything just to please auntie; no, nor from the slightest interest or curiosity on his own behalf: his real motive—and stick to it!—was from expedience, to add it to his repertory. For perhaps the old camel was on the right tack for the wrong reason when she kept on and on that he was not paying enough attention to the *serious* writings of R.L.S. Could that be why he had not been doing so well lately on his round of calls?

Yet he did no better afterwards; gained nothing.

Forget it, he told himself impatiently. But he was as impotent to forget certain haunting passages, as to forget that his name was Robert:

I imagine you to be one of those persons who talk with cheerfulness of that place which oxen and wainropes could not drag you to behold. . . . Had you been there, it is my belief that nature would have triumphed even in you; and as the boat drew but a little nearer, and you beheld the stairs crowded with abominable deformations of our common manhood, and saw yourself landing in the midst of such a population as only now and then surrounds us in the horror of a nightmare—what a haggard eye you would have rolled over your reluctant shoulder towards the house on Beretania Street! Had you gone on; had you found every fourth face a blot upon the landscape; had you visited the hospital and seen the butt ends of human beings lying there almost unrecognisable, but still breathing, still thinking, still remembering ; you would have felt it was (even today) a pitiful place to visit and a hell to dwell in. It is not the fear of possible infection. That seems a little thing when compared with the pain, the pity, and the disgust of the visitor's surroundings, and the atmosphere of affliction, disease, and physical disgrace in which he breathes. I do not think I am a man more than usually timid ; but I never recall the days and nights I spent upon the island promontory (eight days and seven nights), without heartfelt thankfulness that I am somewhere else. . . . And observe : that which I saw and suffered from was a settlement purged, bettered, beautified ; the new village built, the hospital and the Bishop-Home excellently arranged ; the sisters, the doctor, and the missionaries, all indefatigable in their noble tasks. It was a different place when Damien came there and made his great renunciation, and slept that first night under a tree amidst his rotting brethren ; alone with pestilence ; and looking forward (with what courage, with what pitiful sinkings of dread, God only knows) to a lifetime of dressing sores and stumps. . . . Lastly, no doctor or nurse is called upon to enter once for all the doors of that gehenna ; they do not say farewell, they need not abandon hope, on its sad threshold ; they but go for a time to their high calling, and can look forward as they go to relief, to recreation, and to rest. But Damien shut-to with his own hand the doors of his own sepulchre.

Damien was *dirty*.
He was. Think of the poor lepers annoyed with this dirty comrade ! But the clean Dr. Hyde was at his food in a fine house. . . . There is not a clean cup or towel in the Bishop-Home, but dirty Damien washed it.

. . . You had a father : suppose this tale were about him, and some informant brought it to you, proof in hand. . . . Well, the man who tried to do what Damien did, is my father, and the father of all who love goodness ; and he was your father too, if God had given you grace to see it.

These last lines with "Father" repeated and repeated again, beat through Robert's brain like an incantation ; perhaps from an obscure longing, buried fathoms deep, to be using the word familiarly and every day, like other children.

He tried to tell himself that all this blasted nonsense had nothing to do with him, and to exorcise it by a hard bout of study among the rest of Miss Gibson's collection, on the savage silent excuse that he might as well make final use of it, for he would not be here much longer; the material available to him in the neighbourhood of Edinburgh was running short and difficult, like a tricky tide. And moreover he had felt unsafe since the police had begun to notice his activities.

But some mocking demon now led him persistently to what he had missed before. Wherever he opened them, these books played traitor. His luck was dead out. Seeking for reassurance, he could only rummage out more and more evidence to confirm his dark suspicions that the gay sceptic whose image he had built up in his own image was in fact considerably nearer to what had been God's rather more complete idea of a man.

> . . . 'Fiaali'i, you have confessed that you stole the cooked pigs, the taro, the palusamis, the breadfruit, and fish that fell to Vailima's portion at yesterday's feast. Your wish to eat was greater than your wish to be a gentleman. You have shown a bad heart and your sin is a great one, not alone for the pigs which count as naught, but because you have been false to your family. . . . It is easy to say that you are sorry, that you wish you were dead : but that is no answer. We have lost far more than a dozen baskets of fruit ; we have lost our trust in you, which used to be so great, our confidence in your loyalty and high-chiefness.'

This was no damn good to him, either. Then he noticed the name Fleeming Jenkin on the back of a book, and it was unusual enough to touch a spring of association with an incident Mr. Renfrew had related, concerning a lively young rebel who had upset the solemnity of an Edinburgh audience watching theatricals in the Professor's house, by raising the curtain at the wrong moment. If the rest of Stevenson's *Memoir of Fleeming Jenkin* were in the same vein—

He opened it at random at page 124, and saw the word "amusement". In search of this promised "amusement", Robert skipped half a page about Fleeming and his plan for Sanitary Associations :

> . . . His schoolmates bantered him when he began to broach his scheme ; so did I at first, and he took the banter as he always did with enjoyment, until he suddenly posed me with the question : And now do you see any other jokes to make ? Well, then,' said

he, 'that's all right. I wanted you to have your fun out first; now we can be serious.'

"Not if I know it!" Disappointed, Robert tried again:

. . . 'Yes,' said he, 'I'm afraid that *is* a bad man.' And then looking at me shrewdly : 'I wonder if it isn't a very unfortunate thing for you to have met him.' I showed him radiantly how it was the world we must know, the world as it was, not a world expurgated, and prettified with optimistic rainbows. 'Yes, yes,' said he ; 'but this badness is such an easy, lazy explanation. Won't you be tempted to use it, instead of trying to understand people ? '

It was strange that after this, Robert should have gone on searching at all for something more palatable to his present humour. Especially did he wonder afterwards why he paused again at a page which hinted a resemblance to the hated New England sermons of his boyhood:

I remember taking his advice on some point of conduct. 'Now,' he said, 'how do you suppose Christ would have advised you ? ' and when I had answered that he would not have counselled me anything unkind or cowardly, 'No,' he said, with one of his shrewd strokes at the weakness of his hearer, 'nor anything amusing.'

Why did they keep on jabbing at him? He hunted furiously for a title to break this exasperating spell of wrong selection, and restore him to the sunny pages which had originally beguiled him into a false feeling of fellowship. *The Life of Robert Louis Stevenson* by Graham Balfour— somewhere surely in two large volumes he would strike stories to remove the bad impression created by Father Damien and Fleeming Jenkin.

. . . the two Stevenson cousins, about this time, in one of their visits to Paris, an experience which Louis afterwards transferred to the pages of *The Wrecker*. 'Stennis', it may be explained, was the nearest approach to their name possible to Barbizon, and accordingly it was as Stennis *ainé* and Stennis *frère* that the pair were always known.

The two Stennises had come from London, it appeared, a week before with nothing but greatcoats and toothbrushes. It was expensive, to be sure, for every time you had to comb your hair a barber must be paid, and every time you changed your linen one shirt must be bought and another thrown away ; but anything was

better, argued these young gentlemen, than to be the slaves of
haversacks. ' A fellow has to get rid gradually of all material
attachments : that was manhood,' said they ; ' and as long as you
were bound down to anything—house, umbrella, or portmanteau—
you were still tethered by the umbilical cord.'

Setting aside that unknown quantity, the umbilical cord,
this was much better. Confidence returned, only to be
smashed again at his next encounter with a really gay
episode in the *Life of Robert Louis Stevenson*:

In the first week in May Stevenson was attacked with the most
violent and dangerous hemorrhage he ever experienced. It occurred
late at night, but in a moment his wife was by his side. Being
choked with the flow of blood and unable to speak, he made signs
to her for a paper and pencil, and wrote in a neat firm hand, ' Don't
be frightened ; if this is death, it is an easy one.' Mrs. Stevenson
had always a small bottle of ergotin and a minim glass in readiness ;
these she brought in order to administer the prescribed quantity.
Seeing her alarm, he took bottle and glass away from her, measured
the dose correctly with a perfectly steady hand, and gave the things
back to her with a reassuring smile.

If this was death . . . Looking along the shelves, he was
struck by the terrific output achieved before Stevenson's
death at forty-four. "I've plenty of time," Robert muttered,
not specifying time for what, but to prevent his mind from
prowling on the outskirts of some disturbing comparison.
Though where and why he should have imagined such
comparison might arise—

And then it struck him that were he Stevenson, he had
already bitten deeply into his frightening grant of only
forty-four years, and could not take careless reckoning of
thirty-odd years still to come, of the usual man's usual span.
Were he Robert Louis Stevenson, he had only another six
years to go.

*   *   *

The last straw to break his back was supplied by the old
camel. Miss Gibson had been worrying about his cough:
"You're to take this, Robert, three times a day after meals;
it's excellent stuff. Now mind, I shall know if you've for-

[144]

gotten, by the number of doses left." She yammered on a little longer about the chemist belonging to the homeopathic school, and how he had cured his grandmother's cough with this very prescription; implying that what was right for the chemist's grandmother could not go far wrong on Robert. Then she hurried away, arch and benevolent, leaving him with the bottle of mixture in one hand, a dessert-spoon in the other. . . . He need not have feared that his gift for profanity was getting rusty.

"Three times a day after meals." That settled it. He had no further use for an existence presupposing three meals a day by which to regulate a chemist's grandmother's homeopathic remedy. To state that he was out of his element was putting it mildly. Only one remedy for him: escape.

Escape to the South, to a warm climate, to the Mediterranean. What was he doing up North where grey winter sleeted on and on, stubborn not to mark off the end of February from the beginning of March by any border of brightness?

Escape.

Nevertheless, he was determined that wherever he journeyed, he would never return to the chopper and saw, but persist in his unique method of *not* earning his bread. "I'm afraid," Mr. Merrill used to say, sadly shaking his frosty pow, "I'm right down afraid, son, of where your easy-going nature may lead you." And in spite of Mr. Merrill's prayerful wrestling with the Almighty on behalf of an adopted child, "easy going" had remained Robert's congenial motto, and easy going had brought him to his present pastures of sweet juicy grass. He marvelled now that those who equally disliked being cumbered and beset by the necessity of earning a living, should not have solved it as he himself had solved it. Nearly everybody, he argued, looked like *someone*; and if only they would take the trouble to find out what great man or other they resembled, they would surely find many victims glad and willing to be gulled in a foolish enough cause. Let them construct a good lie, stick to it resourcefully, and rake in what it would bring: "It's an answer to prayer"—and Robert did not reflect that if this were so, it would be a very odd answer to an even odder prayer.

He had finished with Scotland; the ground was sour. He owed it no grudge for that. The ground had yielded, to abandon metaphor, £22; twenty-two "jingling, tingling, golden, minted quid"; talk about Treasure Island! He kept his wealth in a tobacco-tin rammed down among some ragged odds and ends of property, at the bottom of an old knapsack. Robert had felt, like the Stennis cousins, that he was seriously imperilling his lightfoot freedom when he bought this strong though battered knapsack; but his loose torn pockets would not hold any more; that was the worst of forsaking a nomad existence; and presently, what with velvet coats and jerseys and a change of trousers and shoes, and belles-lettres (four volumes), he anticipated having to degrade himself yet further by travelling in a train; there was a swelling of sad pride in the thought. . . . A phrase "I must give myself time to pack" had only just entered Robert's vocabulary.

*   *   *

The first time she had reminded him, after supper: "Take your cough mixture, Robert," he replied, looking at her steadily:

"I've had my three doses already today." And somehow she had not the courage to argue that unless he had been constantly having meals, he was hardly giving the homeopathic grandmother of the chemist a proper chance to assert herself.

The next time, he made exactly the same answer—"I've had my three doses already today."

"After meals?" Miss Gibson asked.

"Sure thing. After meals. Before *and* after."

"Robert!"

"Yes, ma'am?"

She was soon to lose heart, but not quite yet. She waited two days. His cough continued extremely troublesome.

"Robert, are you taking your medicine regularly three times a day?"

"*Five* times a day," said Robert, with the air of a seraph unassailable in virtue.

"That's foolish if you're making it up, and excessive if it's true."

"Five times a day," repeated Robert. "After meals. Five meals."

Her gaze went to the sideboard. There sat the bottle, virgin as when she had brought it in.

*　　*　　*

Do you know where the road crosses the burn under Glencorse Church ? Go there, and say a prayer for me : moriturus salutat. See that it's a sunny day ; I would like it to be a Sunday ; and stand on the right-hand bank just where the road goes down into the water, and shut your eyes, and if I don't appear to you—

Robert could have kicked himself the whole way back to Edinburgh. *Of course* he had not expected anything to happen; *of course* he had only followed the instructions as a joke because he happened to be along that very road and remembered the letter; or if he had looked it up before starting out that fine Sunday morning, their first sunny day for weeks, whose business was that but his own? And what sort of a credulous unworldly ass would for one single instant imagine that behind closed eyelids and set to the ripple of the burn running under the road, a man would have hailed him, slight unspeakably, with dark bright laughing eyes; hailed him with familiar affection as though they had been careless mates at sea, on the tramp, at the tavern; and maybe they would have swung along together for a few paces—

—Before he opened his eyes. The sun had gone in and a little empty wind blown up. Robert covered the miles home scoffing at a superstition, wishing men would not write letters, wishing he had never come to Scotland with its vacant moors and snow still bitten into the slopes of Halkerside and Allermuir, even in March, when in Arizona you would already be searching for a patch of shade and lie there

[147]

supine till evening brought coolness. From cursing himself and cursing Scotland's weather, he began to curse the old camel for selling him those four volumes of letters, as well as egging him on to read *Father Damien*, solely for her own wanton sense of fun.

"Stand on the right-hand bank just where the road goes down into the water"—

Being, therefore, in that wilful mood where one had rather make things worse for oneself than better, to scratch up irritability rather than soothe it (at least let him have legitimate cause to swear) he asked Miss Gibson casually through the open door while she was getting supper:

"Do you know where the road crosses the burn under Glencorse Church?"

She dropped a bowl and it broke and the broth ran out over the floor of the tiny kitchen. Nor did she stop to wipe up the mess, but came in and stood beside him, breathing hard, her eyes welling with awful sympathy. She did all the wrong things; she laid a hand on his arm; she said:

"Oh, Robert, did *you* try it too?"

Too? Damn and damn and damn. Why had he let fall one word that could ever affiliate him with Miss Gibson? He burst into jarring scornful laughter. And Miss Gibson, who had shrunk back in amazement from his blistering glare, the words of understanding still unspoken on her lips, breathed a sigh of relief; though it was relief mixed with bewilderment, for what was there to laugh about? or what cause for hate, a moment before?

"Directly I came across the letter, I just knew you'd have tried out that conjuring trick. Gosh, I can imagine you with your eyes all screwed up, waiting for some phoney jack-in-the-box vision to jump over the bank!"

She turned away. There was nothing to answer. Robert could catch a glimpse of her beyond the door, gathering up the broken bits of the soup-bowl.

To despise the woman for her fatuity and be secretly linked to her by an equally fatuous moment, it was unbearable, it was bloody hell.

At supper his good temper seemed to be restored; and

Miss Gibson, though her hand still trembled, basked in the lighter atmosphere. "I know him through and through. It's all over quickly and he never sulks or bears a grudge."

He never did. But a couple of weeks later he was off.

Perhaps now she did know him through and through: he never remained in one place for an instant longer than it suited him; he never cared whom he hurt by going; he never let himself become humanly attached to man or woman; he never said goodbye, nor, certainly, thank you for what you've done for me. He was free and self-sufficient and quite detached. She could not even comfort herself by saying: "Presently he'll begin to miss me," or "He'll miss his comfortable home." Fundamentally, Robert did not care if he were comfortable or not; he enjoyed it for a while, put up with it for a while longer, then shook himself and vanished, impenitent to the end. A graceless rogue.

She had not put any faith in his gratitude, remembering always how he had treated the Merrills; and more, how that blank spot in him had never even realized that the Merrills could or should have been treated otherwise after loving him like a son for four years. Four years to her three months. Nevertheless, realizing all this, she still reeled from the shock of discovering that her illusion of their jolly companionship which had felt to her so robust and rewarding had meant to him just nothing at all, a cobweb floating from a beam.

She did not suppose this time that he would return, that it was a matter of ten days' suspense and there he would be, grinning at her from the door of the shop, not doubting his welcome nor asking her to pardon him (for what did he want with forgiveness?). For this time he had taken his possessions. It gave her a little shock that one could involuntarily think of Robert with possessions, but it was a fact that he had acquired a few things. Acquired how?— No, better leave that alone.

And now all that blaze and enchantment which Robert

had brought into her life dissolved into mist, and nothing was left of R.L.S. but an autograph on the fly-leaf of a book of verses.

She went slowly to the bookcase, pulled open the glass doors. . . .

10

Reading in trains, from a well-bound volume of belles-
lettres, was a new experience for Robert. In a corner seat
facing the engine, his feet comfortably resting on the vacant
place opposite, he looked up several times with affection at
his knapsack which had been placed on the rack by a porter.
And that, too, was a new experience. The porter had carried
it the full length of the platform, trudging three paces ahead
of Robert, who kept his hands in his pockets and mooched
grandly along carrying nothing at all. He gave the hireling
sixpence. All these were expensive items in a style of opulent
living which until now had included neither porters nor tips,
though two or three times before, chiefly in America and
South Africa, he had travelled by truck and train; one was
to the jail of the nearest town in the Middle West, which
hardly counted as a voluntary trip.

Never had it been in such grandeur as this.

He wore the sailor's jersey and corduroy trousers bought
second-hand in the Port of Geith; yet somewhat dimmed
the glory of his array by his unspeakably filthy old overcoat,
tattered and dingy; for this museum-piece could not find
room in his luggage; and Robert would never have parted
from it; combined with his hacking cough, it was a most
valuable "property". He also cherished tenderly and for
the same wicked reason, a weather-stained felt hat with a
torn brim and barely a crown; it had been tossed jauntily
on to the rack beside his knapsack.

The nervous old gentleman shrinking into the far corner
went on trying to accustom his fascinated stare to Robert's
boots; cracked shapeless objects with the naked toes pro-
truding; tramp's boots, worn defiantly because they were

not his only choice; a pair of almost new shoes was reposing in his knapsack; incongruous that a professional hiker should have been tempted to buy shoes that he "saved for best"; perhaps they were a symbol that his bona fide tramping days were over. With a better pair packed, a worse pair inevitably represented wilful dressing-up; apart from profit, his present peculiar relish in dressing-up was not to look pretty nor to look funny nor even to look important, but a declaration of nonconformity; an assumption that he could wear what he pleased, and outstripping vanity's desire to be looked at, *not* be looked at. No, not by any old codgers in railway carriages. Robert was quite ready to be affable to a fellow-traveller who was also, no doubt, a two-pairs-for-his-feet man, and like himself, a man who could pay for tickets and porters and antimacassars spread voluptuously behind the head. He might have been highly entertained to know that at any moment he was expected to pull out some short bludgeoning weapon from his dilapidated pockets, and repeatedly hit the other over the temples; even more entertained had he guessed that the old codger was memorizing the exact position of the alarm-cord. . . . "Just time to spring for it, if he moves!"

Nevertheless, after an hour of considerable tension, the nervous old gentleman's fears subsided, and he began to wish he knew what Robert was reading with such close attention? Dangerous to ask, of course; but it tantalized him that the book should look so decorous and well bound, so totally at variance with the rest of that dreadful creature's appearance; indeed, one would hardly have expected him to be able to read at all.

He edged a little nearer, putting his life in jeopardy for the sake of one glimpse at the print. Letters? Impossible!

. . . While my hand is in I must tell you a story. . . . I was very young, very green, and very shy. There came one day to lunch at the house two very formidable old ladies—or one very formidable, and the other what you please. At table I was exceedingly funny, and entertained the company with tales of geese and bubbly-jocks. I was great in the expression of my terror for these bipeds, and suddenly this horrid, severe, and eminently matronly old lady put up a pair of gold eyeglasses, looked at me awhile in silence, and then pronounced in a clangorous voice her verdict, ' You give me very much the effect of a coward, Mr. Stevenson ! ' I had very nearly left two vices behind me at Glenogil—fishing and jesting at table. And of one thing you may be very sure, my lips were no more opened at that meal. . . .

No doubt you're ill, and unco ill, I believe ; . . . if you are at all like me—and I tell myself you are very like me—be sure there is only one thing good for you, and that is the sea in hot climates. Mount, sir, into ' a little frigot ' of 5000 tons or so, and steer peremptorily for the tropics ; and what if the ancient mariner, who guides your frigot, should startle the silence of the ocean with the cry of land ho !—say, when the day is dawning—and you should see the turquoise mountain tops of Upolu coming hand over fist above the horizon ? . . .

I tell you frankly, you had better come soon. I am sair failed a'ready ; and what I may be if you continue to dally, I dread to conceive. I may be speechless ; already, or at least for a month or so, I'm little better than a teetoller—I beg pardon, a teetotaller. It is not exactly physical, for I am in good health, working four or five hours a day in my plantation, and intending to ride a paper-chase next Sunday—ay, man, that's a fact, and I havena had the hert to breathe it to my mother yet—the obligation's poleetical, for I am trying every means to live well with my German neighbours. . . .

. . . I'll put in a word when I get home again, to tell you whether I'm killed or not. ' Accident in the (Paper) Hunting Field ; death of a notorious author. We deeply regret to announce the death of the most unpopular man in Samoa, who broke his neck at the descent of Magiagi, from the misconduct of his little raving lunatic of an old beast of a pony. It is proposed to commemorate the incident by the erection of a suitable pile . . . ' Muckle they cared about Tusitala when they had him.' . . . He was beautiful as the day, but his day is gone done ! And perhaps, as he was maybe gettin' a wee thing fly-blawn, it's nane too shune. . . .

The whole head is useless, and the whole sitting part painful : reason, the recent paper-chase.

> There was racing and chasing in Vailele Plantation,
>   And vastly we enjoyed it,
> But, alas ! for the state of my foundation,
>   For it wholly has destroyed it.

Come, my mind is looking up. The above is wholly impromptu —
On oath,   TUSITALA.

Robert laughed aloud, laid the book down and fell into a reverie, his eyes fixed on the flying landscape as it darkened

[153]

and glimmered beyond the window. The lights had not yet been turned up in the compartment, and presently, to the old gentleman's horror, that fantastic silhouette over in the far corner began softly to whistle and to croon snatches of obscene songs. . . . Robert was accustomed to do this, hoofing for mile after mile along unfriendly roads at night; he kept himself company that way, and was quite unaware that trains, so to speak, were different, and that to a harmless fellow-traveller he had become a figure in a tottering night-mare. It was not a corridor train, so that when it slid to a stop, the old gentleman dared not take advantage to change his carriage, for fear the tramp in the corner should prove touchy. If only someone else would get in.

A band of rowdy youths scampered along the platform and paused outside, tugging at the door-handle and swearing because it was locked. Robert frowned in fastidious dis-couragement; like any maiden lady on a journey, he now preferred to remain immune from nasty noisy company; and those fellows sounded as though they didn't know how to behave. He was relieved when they rushed on again. The well-behaved old codger in the corner, on the contrary, had entirely won his approval; as the train started, Robert grinned at him in a friendly way and offered him a cigarette he had rolled with grimy flexible fingers: "Here, Whiskers, have one?"

The nervous old gentleman nearly died. Mutely he shook his head.

"Don't smoke? Bad for the beating heart?"

Had he said bursting heart, he would have been nearer the mark.

"Are you, may I ask—" (flatter the monster; keep him good-tempered) — "are you going South on —er— business?"

"In a sort of way. Esau's business."

"Wh— What?"

(Gosh, old Merrill would have jumped for joy to hear me remember some of his Scripture twaddle. . . . Must look up old Merrill one day.) Aloud, Robert expanded his theme: "Got to see a fellow, several fellows, about a mess of pottage."

"In-*deed*?" (a tramp would have been bad enough, or a lunatic. But *both*—) "In—ah—London?"

"I'll break my journey in London. Then I'm for France."

"I'll break my journey in London" sounded good; he had heard it used by the toffs, though in an existence of broken journeys it had meant little to him until now. He intended in France to continue replenishing his exchequer by "looking up some of my father's friends who might be interested".

Could he perhaps consider the nervous old gentleman, professionally speaking, as a victim to be bled? Then he dismissed the idea; it was a pity to waste the chance, but you owed a certain propriety towards your fellow-travellers in trains. Anyhow, it was only opportunity postponed; using the letters as his guide-books, he would surely light upon luck again round the forest of Fontainebleau or down on the Mediterranean coast. But in London, so Miss Gibson had said, dwelt the author to whom that jolly intimate letter was written which he had been reading just now, about paper-chasing and severe old ladies. There had been other letters to the same author; quite a handful, and on the same note of an elder brother confiding in one not at all behind him in wit and understanding. The letters were sped between Samoa and Scotland; Miss Gibson had waxed quite sentimental on the friendship, quoting and reading aloud from the younger man's memoirs:

.   " Vailima was the one spot on earth I had any great craving to visit, but . . . in the meantime that happened which put an end for ever to my scheme of travel. I shall never go up the Road of Loving Hearts now, on ' a wonderful clear night of stars,' to meet the man coming towards me on a horse. It is still a wonderful clear night of stars, but the road is empty. So I never saw the dear king of us all."

Robert had thereupon expressed an opinion that often it was much more tragic when people did meet than when they didn't, and in answer she had spoken a mouthful more.

Every bit of information came in useful if you waited long enough; so he decided then and there while in London to pay a visit to the author, who sounded the sort of boy with pockets full of toffee for an Ishmael carrying off his forlorn condition with that peculiar smile, gay yet wistful. . . . Robert did a rehearsal smile on the nervous old gentleman—who jumped out of his skin lest this should presage an attack by bludgeon. Hoping to avert trouble by more chat, he pulled forth an old-fashioned hunter watch on a gold cable round his middle; then regretted the rash act, for was it his fancy that the villain's dark eyes were fixed upon it with an acquisitive glare? "We're already an hour late," he quavered. "Your friends whom you were going to see —about a messuage, I think you said?—will they meet you at Euston?"

Robert's wistful smile relaxed into natural amusement: "No, I don't think they'll be at the station."

Well, R.L.S. himself had first gone to America as an almost penniless emigrant. In spite of having told Miss Gibson that he disliked amateurs, during the course of his four months' stay at Comely Bank, Robert had taken down and read *The Amateur Emigrant* and *Across the Plains*, at first with a professional's scornful curiosity to see how a rich and sheltered young gentleman had indeed managed when forced into real hardship, or whether perhaps he had not magnified a bit of discomfort? Presently he would have been glad to apologize for his doubts on the matter. There was one passage . . .

Monday.—It was, if I remember rightly, five o'clock when we were all signalled to be present at the Ferry Depot of the railroad. . . .

I followed the porters into a long shed reaching downhill from West Street to the river. It was dark, the wind blew clean through it from end to end ; and here I found a great block of passengers and baggage, hundreds of one and tons of the other. I feel I shall have a difficulty to make myself believed ; and certainly the scene must have been exceptional, for it was too dangerous for daily repetition. It was a tight jam ; there was no fair way through the mingled mass of brute and living obstruction. Into the upper skirts of the crowd, porters, infuriated by hurry and overwork, clove their way with shouts. I may say that we stood like sheep, and that the porters charged among us like so many maddened sheep-dogs ; and I believe these men were no longer answerable for their acts. It mattered not what they were carrying, for they drove straight

into the press, and when they could get no farther, blindly dis-
charged their barrowful. With my own hand, for instance, I saved
the life of a child as it sat upon its mother's knee, she sitting on a
box ; and since I heard of one accident, I must suppose that there
were many similar interpositions in the course of the evening. It
will give some idea of the state of mind to which we were reduced
if I tell you that neither the porter nor the mother of the child
paid the least attention to my act. It was not till some time after
that I understood what I had done myself, for to ward off heavy
boxes seemed at the moment a natural incident of human life.
Cold, wet, clamour, dead opposition to progress, such as one encounters in an evil dream, had utterly daunted the spirits. We had
accepted this purgatory as a child accepts the conditions of the
world.

The landing at Jersey was done in a stampede. I had a fixed
sense of calamity, and to judge by conduct, the same persuasion
was common to us all. A panic selfishness, like that produced by
fear, presided over the disorder of our landing. People pushed, and
elbowed, and ran, their families following how they could. Children fell, and were picked up to be rewarded by a blow. One
child, who had lost her parents, screamed steadily and with increasing shrillness, as though verging towards a fit ; an official kept
her by him, but no one else seemed so much as to remark her
distress ; and I am ashamed to say that I ran among the rest.

And the second time he had gone as a famous writer,
only eight years later, the population had turned out to
give him an ovation at the docks of New York.

"The two pilots who went out to meet the boat had got
nicknamed Jekyll and Hyde," Miss Gibson related with her
proprietorial air of one who had ably arranged the whole
thing. "That's the sort of involuntary tribute which pro-
claims louder than reviews and new editions, that a writer
has really arrived."

"Yep. Who were the two blokes?"

"What two blokes? Jekyll and Hyde? Surely, Robert,
you've read it by now? Don't you remember how a whole
sermon was preached about it at St. Paul's, and over all
England, and then it got pirated in America and sold tens
of thousands. One night when his mind was overburdened
with debts and responsibilities—'my work still moving with
a desperate slowness—as a child might fill a sandbag with
its little handfuls' . . . he fell asleep and got the idea from
his Brownies—"

[157]

"*What* Brownies?" he asked in some apprehension; for the woman had a positive mania for rubbing his nose into an aspect of R.L.S. which he had determined to ignore.

"In his essay on Dreams——"

"Don't read essays. Or sermons, come to that."

"*Jekyll and Hyde*," she lumbered on, "was an allegory, not a sermon. The sermons were inspired *by* the allegory."

"Don't read allegories." Robert heaved himself up, went out, and stayed away four days. He cleaned up well on that trip. In fact, if Miss Gibson had not goaded him into leaving her till she had cooled off prosing about this Jekyll and Hyde, he might not have afforded this train journey now, hobnobbing on lordly terms with nervous whiskery old gentlemen. So that everything worked out for the best.

*   *   *

The author sat on a settle in the cave of the fireplace, one foot tucked under him, smoking a huge pipe disproportionate to his size, coughing and staring into the burning logs. He was trying to think of a new play. The only idea that would come to him was a sentence with nothing round it, as a tiny Hebridean island is seen through a Scotch sea-mist: "*Do you think the dead ought to come back?*" But can you make a play out of that? He had pilfered a new notebook, too, in wanton excess of what he allowed himself, which ought to have inspired him as it often did; but just this afternoon he felt perversely more inclined for the scribbled entries in one that was chockful and done for; yet so much warmer, so much more human than the white pages that had not yet had the chill taken off, like a bedroom when you arrive at an hotel in winter. So sighing a little, he got up and fetched out a pile of notebooks dating back a great many years, and started flicking them through, and halted at random on this fragment from 1896 headed "*Play*", on a dream about a dead friend:

"*In house belonging to T. I saw signs of foul play, curious servant, etc. Heard jeering laughs. Vague feeling that this man was personating T. to get his effects. . . .*"

Can I do anything with that? he wondered crossly and sadly. Could he do anything with anything? This was one of his doubting hours, though he was a very famous and very successful author who coughed a great deal and was often alone. But that was because he said he liked to be alone, and acted the determined recluse with such conviction that his friends believed him (alternately with not believing him). And it happened that this particular murky afternoon, the fog rising from the river even as high as his third-floor windows, coincided with a time when they were all believing him together.

The air was dull brown, his room was brown, and his thoughts felt very brown indeed, without a dash of colour; as for his cough, it was the brownest part of all.

The butler came in, a short cheerful North-countryman. The author raised one eyebrow, a trick of his which amused little boys up to the age of seven and then quite suddenly stopped amusing them; as he had a large number of friends up to the age of seven and after, he had plenty of opportunity for stumbling up against the moment when they first looked coldly at his performing eyebrow, with the remark: "You've done that before; do something else now."

His butler answered the eyebrow: "A man outside says he must see you, sir."

"What sort of a man?"

"Well, sir, I'd have said a tramp if he didn't seem so cocksure."

"Tramp's clothes?"

"Terrible, sir; hardly hold together; toes coming through his boots. And yet somehow, can't think why, but I don't believe he's footed it that far; not today, at any rate; doesn't seem tired enough."

"How far?"

"Scotland, sir. That's what he says."

"Give a name?"

"No, he wouldn't give a name. Got nothing to sell, either, not even matches nor bootlaces."

"Pity. I might have bought a box of matches."

"You do certainly use up a lot, sir."

[159]

"But I never see anyone without a name. Go and tell him."

The servant went, closing the door behind him. Presently he returned.

"What now?"

"Pretends he was sent, sir."

"Who does he pretend gave him the introduction?"

"A Mr. Stephenson, he says."

"What Stephenson? There are dozens."

The manservant went out again; this time he forgot to close the door.

"Well?"

"He says from a Mr. R. L. Stephenson."

The author replied in a perfectly matter-of-fact tone:

"That's odd, considering Mr. R. L. Stevenson died fourteen years ago."

"I thought so myself, sir."

. . . "Not so odd, is it, after all?" Robert had sauntered in, and stood waiting for the usual stare, the usual start of surprise, the usual agitated question.

The butler took a step forward towards the intruder; the tramp was emaciated, and he himself the stocky type; it should be easy, if required, to throw him out, pitch him downstairs and into the street. But his master shook his head and signed to him to go.

Robert's spirits rose. A vision of coins jingled musically in the air . . . he had no doubt but that in a few minutes they would materialize into his pockets. No, he had forgotten, the pockets of his property garment were full of holes; but the tobacco-tin lay safely at the bottom of his knapsack deposited in the station left-luggage office. You can't achieve the proper results from paying calls when accompanied by a change of boots, four volumes of Letters, a warm jersey and an elegant second-hand pair of trousers.

The author looked at Robert, who remained perfectly nonchalant and at ease. That was why he was here, for inspection. And on the brink of a big clean-up; he felt it in his bones.

After a long pause: "Distant relation?"

"His son."

Until this moment, Robert had never been compelled to make the dramatic assertion himself; only to assent when others made it. But "distant relation" my foot! What cash lay in that? So he repeated:

"His son."

But from Poker-face absolutely no reaction. Not even anger. Not even: "Get out! You're a fraud!" Only a gentle:

"Is that why you chose to say he had sent you?"

"He might have, in a way."

"Yet I shouldn't wonder if you'd never set eyes on him?"

"I haven't." (And expedience just kept him from adding an impudent "Nor have you.")

Robert had scored, and enjoyed a brief triumph. For variety's sake, he produced a mother, on this occasion the demure French maiden—what was her name? Marianne? —who had run away from her French peasant father—or run away *to* him—how had he previously invented it for Mr. Renfrew of Ard-Daraich? Then it struck him that he need not stretch his brains to make the stories tally; why should he? If the author and Mr. Renfrew happened to be acquainted enough to compare version one and version two, that would be such fantastic bad luck that he might as well take ship for South America without further ado. Half-way through his legend, "Marianne" slipped back into Léonore, his original choice: Robert did not notice till just too late; only a trifle disconcerted, he had to elaborate and turn his French mother into enamoured twin French sisters, one following hard on the heels, so to speak, of the other.

—A pause after Léonore had come to England and duly died in childbirth.

"And what do you suppose I can do for you?"

"My cough's cruel bad," Robert's voice ran up the scale till it cracked on a childish piteous note which would have made any of his hobo companions goggle in surprise; but lately he was beginning to feel himself a genuinely pathetic case in a hard world. "I'd pneumonia at the beginning of the winter, and can't get rid of it in this lousy climate. If I'd my fare to the South of France where you can get into the sun and soak in it, that's all I'm asking" (more and more of the professional whine). "'Tisn't much; just my fare; give a poor devil a chance—" He was overtaken by a paroxysm of coughing: unluckily for the effect of this, so was the author, and at the same time. They both coughed, with streaming eyes.

Robert hated him. This interview kept on inexplicably twisting the wrong way, and he felt he had not done himself justice (considering his talents), nor attracted special attention in a special sort of way (considering his special line of attraction); you don't plod doggedly through four volumes of letters, to produce no better than a common mendicant patter, to say nothing of enduring further education out of the mouth of Miss Gibson. Weariness at the mere thought of Miss Gibson reminded him of the value of apt quotation where other methods, audacity and pathos, appeared to have had as yet little effect against a blank surface; so he repeated "Get into the *sun*"—and tacked on a remark from a letter once written to this very same Poker-face: "You take the boat at San Francisco, and then my place is the second to the left.'"

(Now then, smile or sob, blast you! Turn on the sentimental lay about an island in the Pacific and how you never went after all except in your dreams. I've given you your cue, I can't do more.)

The author responded in Robert's least favourite way. He did not throw himself face downwards on the rug, burst into tears, and immediately endow this stranger, half loafer half angel, with a home and all his worldly goods. No, he puffed thoughtfully at his huge bull-dog pipe, remaining a little absent-minded, with that melancholy air of wishing he had not been born and was ready to die at any moment, and then murmured:

"So I presume you've come to me for a job?"

This to Robert, at his present conceited stage, was to be viewed only as a taunt, a wilful insult. He forgot himself, all his selves, and especially the self which used to be a good loser.

"Thanks, boss. But you can find another man to chop your bloody wood."

The author betrayed by a lifted eyebrow that he was just faintly astonished.

"We don't do it on the premises."

His weariness yet held enough rebuke to show Robert that he was well on the wrong track. He tried too late to cancel his flash of temper, ingratiate himself on the note of "Look here, as man to man" . . . going on to confess, frank and proud and simple, how you felt if you longed to work, longed above all for independence, winced at the bare idea of charity, but kept on being thrust back on it by your damnable health.

None of this rang quite true; his touch was not what it was in the early days of Edinburgh and Miss Gibson. Then it had been stimulating as well as profitable; amusing even when he was detected. Then it had been easy going. Recently the game had lost its kick; he wanted it to be over quickly and the cash safe in his tin box; he kept on getting angry and did not quite know with whom; angry unless fate sent him the rapid success he considered due to his bright claim.

Offer *him* a job? My God!

His abrupt transitions to insolence and back to boyish pathos had indeed cut no ice; the author decided the fellow was a liar and an impostor. Yet still disturbed by those haunting looks, and because the whole fantastic scene had caught at his interest and entangled it, he resolved on a mischievous test: without replying to all that sickening rigmarole about "the only thing I care for is to be well enough to do a job of work decently", he wandered into his bedroom . . . and reappeared with a framed photograph, personally inscribed to him "from Tusitala". This he handed to the so-called son of Tusitala. . . . And waited for the reaction: an outburst of super-bunkum, of romantic mummery.

Yet as a test, it failed; he was puzzled at Robert's long

[163]

intense look at the photograph: "Yes, that's how I remember him . . ." and then no more said. For it sounded spontaneous, and not part of a clever impersonation.

And indeed, it seemed to Robert himself at the new encounter with the man in the photograph (encounters that became increasingly exciting) that he could *almost* imagine he had seen him in this very attitude: narrowed laughing eyes, head thrown back and fingers clasped round a knee carelessly crossed over the other, an air at once alert and quizzical as though he were perfectly able to cope with whatever might walk in at the door, even a cheapjack peddling a trumped-up story that began with a cry of "Daddy". . . .

But this of course was nonsense, to set up a photograph taken in 1890 in Australia as nearer akin to a father he might have vividly remembered, than the "visionary boy" gazing so seriously from the 1873 photograph. Pack of nonsense, to pick and choose among "sun-shadows" when none had any concern with him whatsoever except to bring in the dibs.

While all this went racing through his brain, his host was crouched upon the settle by the fire, apparently not aware of him at all. Yet he was watching him pretty shrewdly, not quite as certain as before that the tramp was wholly a charlatan. "*That's* how I remember him. . . ." What could it possibly mean? Was truth at the core of this rotten apple?

R.L.S. at forty. . . . This lean arrogant gipsy looked as though he were himself not far off from that age.

In silence the author held out his hand for the photograph to be returned.

A boy of eleven marched into the room and turned a couple of somersaults to show that he was of an antic disposition, before reminding his guardian that he was sworn to drive him home in a hansom that evening after a lobster dinner, whatever anyone might say. He had dropped into the kitchen to see the lobster and make sure nothing had been forgotten and all was satisfactory: "And Rollo's already bought you a birthday present in case he'd spent all you gave him yesterday by June, it was 8½d. and I think he ought to have bought the larger size but still I expect you can make

[164]

quite small notes in it. I promised him I wouldn't tell you what it was. I've got you a torch only you'll have to buy another battery, Rollo and me nearly finished this one doing flashes from the street up through people's windows; it dances on the wall like Tinker Bell, you know, and bothers them if they can't see what it is. And now what are we going to do till supper? By the way, I've told them it's no good bringing in a glass of milk because it's not what I'll drink with the lobster. How do you do," to Robert, shaking hands with grave courtesy, "I didn't spot you at first. How jolly for you that they let you wear that coat even with the pockets all torn; they never let me. Are you staying with my guardian?"

Robert grinned, guessing that the author had ejaculated "God forbid" under his breath:

"I'm not quite sure," he replied, giving the question his full attention. "From the look of things, I'm staying another five minutes or a week. Torches are A 1, but a binnacle lamp's even more fun if you can get hold of one. A binnacle is where they keep the compass of a ship," he answered the boy's look of enquiry.

"Have you been to sea? Are you a sailor? You don't," frankly, "look like one."

"On and off; when I was at school I lived on a small island off the coast of Maine where they used to send out the whalers."

"Whalers? You mean you *caught* whales—the Jonah kind?"

"Well, no, we boys didn't catch 'em, didn't go far enough North; and besides, by then they'd stopped whaling from there. But we often caught mackerel when they were striking in the bay."

"And did you use what you just said, a bubbicle lamp when you went on the sea at nights?"—he turned eagerly to his guardian: "Please could you give me one for my birthday, as I'm giving you a torch for yours."

Suddenly the author became quite a different person. Robert never knew what had worked the charm . . . that they were all three of them comfortably sprawling round the

fire, drinking luscious hot chocolate and eating buttered
crumpets, while the eldest of the trio read aloud to them
about the exploits of a gang of boys in Scotland who called
themselves the Lantern-Bearers:

" Towards the end of September, when school-time was drawing
near and the nights were already black, we would begin to sally
from our respective villas, each equipped with a tin bull's-eye
lantern. The thing was so well known that it had worn a rut in
the commerce of Great Britain ; and the grocers, about the due
time, began to garnish their windows with our particular brand of
luminary. We wore them buckled to the waist upon a cricket belt,
and over them, such was the rigour of the game, a buttoned top-
coat. They smelled noisomely of blistered tin ; they never burned
aright, though they would always burn our fingers ; their use was
naught ; the pleasure of them merely fanciful ; and yet a boy
with a bull's-eye under his top-coat asked for nothing more. The
fishermen used lanterns about their boats, and it was from them,
I suppose, that we had got the hint ; but theirs were not bull's-eyes,
nor did we ever play at being fishermen. The police carried them
at their belts, and we had plainly copied them in that ; yet we did
not pretend to be policemen. Burglars, indeed, we may have had
some haunting thoughts of ; and we had certainly an eye to past
ages when lanterns were more common, and to certain story-books
in which we had found them to figure very largely. But take it
for all in all, the pleasure of the thing was substantive ; and to be
a boy with a bull's-eye under his top-coat was good enough for us.
    When two of these asses met, there would be an anxious ' Have
you got your lantern ? ' and a gratified ' Yes ! ' That was the
shibboleth, and very needful too ; for, as it was the rule to keep
our glory contained, none could recognise a lantern-bearer, unless
(like the pole-cat) by the smell. Four or five would sometimes
climb into the belly of a ten-man lugger, with nothing but the
thwarts above them—for the cabin was usually locked ; or choose
out some hollow of the links where the wind might whistle overhead. There the coats would be unbuttoned and the bull's-eyes
discovered ; and in the chequering glimmer, under the huge
windy hall of the night, and cheered by a rich steam of toasting
tinware, these fortunate young gentlemen would crouch together
in the cold sand of the links or on the scaly bilges of the fishing-
boat, and delight themselves with inappropriate talk. . . . But the
talk, at any rate, was but a condiment ; and these gatherings themselves only accident in the career of the lantern-bearer. The
essence of this bliss was to walk by yourself in the black night ;
the slide shut, the top-coat buttoned ; not a ray escaping, whether
to conduct your footsteps or to make your glory public ; a mere
pillar of darkness in the dark ; and all the while, deep down in the

privacy of your fool's heart, to know you had a bull's-eye at your belt, and to exult and sing over the knowledge."

Unlike (for instance) Miss Gibson, the author did not exact hard-breathing attention from his hearers while he read aloud; and for that very reason they were able to eat and drink at ease, and interrupt, and look over his shoulder; and in the latter part, the boy snatched the book once or twice and did the more dramatic bits again himself—"Have you got your lanterns?" . . . though he was not nearly such a good actor as the author, who when he buttoned an imaginary top-coat closely over an imaginary cricket belt and a tin bull's-eye lantern hooked on to it, and crept out of the house down to the hollow in the links under the huge windy hall of the night, played his part with such mingled relish and trepidation that surely the very smell of "rich toasting tin-wear" drifted into the sober sitting-room of a celebrity's residence in London W.C., in 1912. Had he shown himself for one moment aware that he was "playing with the children", Robert might well have been bored and exasperated, or worse, embarrassed by the silly performance; but he felt that the odd little chap had not meant to impress them with his acting; meant only to read them a fragment from *Random Memories* of Robert Louis Stevenson. That it seemed he might at any moment be sallying forth into the night, giving pass-word and answer when he met a companion conspirator, climbing into the belly of a ten-man lugger and there crouching in the scaly bilges, was, maybe, a wholly involuntary tribute to a fellow-author.

Next, when they had smelt enough toasting tin-wear, and eaten enough crumpets dripping with melted butter and strawberry jam, he seized Billy's hands and wiped them and sent him to fetch another book from the shelves, called *Moral Emblems*. Robert, feeling perfectly comfortable by now and as though somehow he had walked into the right place, gave a shout of recognition: "'The Abbot for a walk went out'". . . . The author chuckled and added: "'A wealthy cleric very stout'"— They did the rest in chorus. Billy, still hunting for the volume, gave them a look over his shoulder to indicate that he thought them mad but nice

[167]

to be with; and when shown the picture illustrating the
Abbot with a javelin stuck through his back, thought it jolly
good, considering. He liked even better his own choice,
and read it aloud twice at the top of his voice with special
emphasis on the last two lines:

> " . . . And he will spoil his evening toddy
> By dwelling on that mangled body."

Then they listened fascinated to the grim and bloody
story of *Robin and Ben* : or, *The Pirate and the Apothecary*,
and admired the spirited illustrations.

> " Come, lend me an attentive ear
> A startling moral tale to hear,
> Of Pirate Rob and Chemist Ben,
> And different destinies of men. . . .
>
> Together but unlike they grew ;
> Robin was tough, and through and through
> Bold, inconsiderate, and manly,
> Like some historic Bruce or Stanley.
> Ben had a mean and servile soul,
> He robbed not, though he often stole ;
> He sang on Sunday in the choir,
> And tamely capped the passing Squire. . . .
>
> The master of a trading dandy
> Hires Robin for a go of brandy ;
> And all the happy hills of Rome
> Vanish beyond the fields of foam.
>
> Ben, meanwhile, like a tin reflector,
> Attended on the worthy rector ;
> Opened his eyes and held his breath,
> And flattered to the point of death ;
> And was at last, by that good fairy,
> Apprenticed to the Apothecary. . . .
>
> At length, from years of anxious toil,
> Bold Robin seeks his native soil . . .
>
> Strange, when a man so great and good
> Once more in his home-country stood,
> Strange that the sordid clowns should show
> A dull desire to have him go.
> His clinging breeks, his tarry hat,
> The way he swore, the way he spat,

A certain quality of manner,
Alarming like the pirate's banner—
Something that did not seem to suit all—
Something, O call it bluff, not brutal—
Something at least, howe'er it's called,
Made Robin generally black-balled.

His soul was wounded ; proud and glum,
Alone he sat and swigged his rum,
And took a great distaste to men
Till he encountered Chemist Ben. . . .

Ben told the tale of his indentures,
And Rob narrated his adventures.
Last, as the point of greatest weight,
The pair contrasted their estate.
And Robin, like a boastful sailor,
Despised the other for a tailor.

' See,' he remarked, ' with envy see
A man with such a fist as me !
Bearded and ringed, and big, and brown,
I sit and toss the stingo down.
Hear the gold jingle in my bag—
All won beneath the Jolly Flag ! '

Ben moralised and shook his head :
' You wanderers earn and eat your bread.
The foe is found, beats or is beaten,
And either how, the wage is eaten.
And after all your pully-hauly
Your proceeds look uncommon small-ly.
You had done better here to tarry,
Apprentice to the Apothecary.
The silent pirates of the shore
Eat and sleep soft, and pocket more
Than any red, robustious ranger
Who picks his farthings hot from danger.
You clank your guineas on the board ;
Mine are with several bankers stored.
You reckon riches on your digits,
You dash in chase of Sals and Bridgets,
You drink and risk delirium tremens,
Your whole estate a common seaman's !
Regard your friend and school companion,
Soon to be wed to Miss Trevanion
(Smooth, honourable, fat and flowery,
With Heaven knows how much land in dowry) . . .

I had no gold, no marble quarry,
I was a poor apothecary,
Yet here I stand, at thirty-eight,
A man of an assured estate.'

' Well,' answered Robin—' well, and how ? '

The smiling chemist tapped his brow.
' Rob,' he replied, ' this throbbing brain
Still worked and hankered after gain ;
By day and night, to work my will,
It pounded like a powder mill ;
And marking how the world went round
A theory of theft it found.
Here is the key to right and wrong :
Steal little but steal all day long.'

—And that's enough of that," said the author.

"I *say*, you never showed me that book before. Did you write it yourself and draw the drawings ?" for Billy knew, having a guardian in the profession, that books happened by grim achievement, and did not grow on trees. "Didn't you? Well, who did? Does he come here?"

The author shook his head and answered doubtfully: "I'm not exactly sure if Lloyd wrote any of *Robin and Ben*; he was only twelve at the time; but it was his printing-press, and he helped engrave the pictures."

"Who's Lloyd? And who did he help?"

"His stepfather. They printed ninety copies of *Moral Emblems* and sold them for sixpence each; then another ninety with some new poems and pictures for ninepence; but that was rather expensive, don't you think?"

Billy agreed; ninepence was ninepence, threepence too much. His guardian then sent him to fetch another book which Robert at once recognized, though giving no sign, as a volume of Letters akin to those he had left in his own knapsack.

"Look, Billy! here's the programme of Lloyd's first adventure with his own printing-press before his stepfather came into it at all, though I've got a sort of idea that he wrote all the Opinions of the Press."

"I'd like a printing press," Billy announced promptly,

"and then you could write all the opinions of the press for me, couldn't you?   Like these."

NOTICE

To-day is published by S. L. Osbourne & Co.

ILLUSTRATED

BLACK CANYON,

or

WILD ADVENTURES IN THE FAR WEST.

An

Instructive and amusing Tale written by
Samuel Lloyd Osbourne

Price 6d.

OPINIONS OF THE PRESS

Although *Black Canyon* is rather shorter than ordinary for that kind of story, it is an excellent work.   We cordially recommend it to our readers.—*Weekly Messenger.*

S. L. Osbourne's new work (*Black Canyon*) is splendidly illustrated.   In the story, the characters are bold and striking.   It reflects the highest honour on its writer.—*Morning Call.*

A very remarkable work.   Every page produces an effect.   The end is as singular as the beginning.   I never saw such a work before.—*R. L. Stevenson.*

"Know it by heart," said Robert gruffly and somewhat untruthfully, when Billy held out the open book towards him.   The author threw him a quick appraising glance . . . and then left him to listen or not as he pleased, while he told Billy how Stevenson had one day come to the firm of S. L. Osbourne and Co. with a manuscript under his arm, which with deep humility he begged to submit to the Editor in the hope that it might be good enough to be published.   It proved an enormous best seller and actually brought in three francs royalties on the very first edition.

"Three shillings?"

"Nearly."

"But didn't Lloyd's stepfather get more than that for

[171]

his own books, to have been so pleased about three francs?"

The author smiled, but left the question unanswered, and went on instead to satisfy Billy with a further account of how the two became ambitious and thought how splendid it would be to have pictures, and of their first frightful struggles over the illustrations carved on fretwood with a small saw, and mounted on a wooden block to raise it to the level of the type; of the choking excitement, only to be dashed when the impression came out unequal: "Then the woman of their party saved them from double suicide by a really bright suggestion, considering she was born feminine and inferior; she suggested they should build it up with cigarette papers."

"Go on; go on; was it all right?"

Three boys of varying ages had been sprawling on the floor, stuffing crumpets and eagerly talking of the pastimes of another boy; the ringleader of them all, long ago dead. But now, like the ten little niggers of the rhyme, one had dropped out; one had been gathered back to the body of a scowling impatient man in tramp's clothing. And so there were only two. Two? perhaps not; for the author, aware of Robert's change of mood, did not wholly succeed in regaining the magic of complete and childlike concentration on the subject in hand. In fact, though he still held Billy's interest by a vivid account of the elaborate tin-soldier campaigns played on the floor of an attic at Davos, he depended largely for liveliness on extracts he read aloud of War Correspondence from Stevenson's Note-book, not mere juvenile nonsense, but a brilliant satire on some of the minor war reporting of that period; spirited slanging matches to bring into the room the panorama of those mimic armies, led and manœuvred by General Osbourne and General Stevenson through the imaginary countries of Scarlet, Glendarule, Sandusky, Mar, Tahema and Savannah.

" Glendarule Times. *Editorial Comment.*—General Stevenson may, or may not, be a capable commander. It would be unjust to pronounce in the meantime. . . . Some shrewd, but perhaps too hopeful, critics perceive a deep policy in the inactivity of our troops about Sandusky, and believe that Stevenson is luring on the cautious Osbourne to his ruin. We will hope so . . . but the situation to the west and centre wears a different complexion ; there his steady, well-combined advance, carrying all before him, contrasts most favourably with the timid and divided counsels of our Stevensons, Piffles and Pottys.

YALLOBALLY RECORD.—That incompetent shuffler, Genera Osbourne, has again put his foot into it. . . . How long is this dis-organisation to go on ? How long is that bloated bondholder to go prancing round on horse-back, wall-eyed and muddle-headed, while his men are starved and butchered, and the forces of this great country are at the mercy of clever rogues like Potty, or respectable mediocrities like Stevenson ?

YALLOBALLY RECORD.—We have never concealed our opinion that Osbourne was a bummer and a scallywag ; but the entire collapse of his campaign beats the worst that we imagined possible. . . . The infamous Osbourne is shaking in his spectacles at Savannah. He was roundly taken to task by a public-spirited reporter, and babbled meaningless excuses ; he did not know, he said, that the force now falling in on us at Yolo was so large. It was his business to know. What is he paid for ? . . . If we were to die to-morrow, the word ' Osbourne ' would be found engraved backside foremost on our hearts. . . .

Sandusky. Noon. Great gloom here. As every one predicted, Stevenson has already lost 600 men in the marshes at the mouth of the Sandusky, men simply sacrificed. His wilful conduct in not mounting the river, following his melancholy defeat before Mar, and his long and fatal hesitation as to the Armies of the West and Centre, fill up the measure of his incapacity. . . .

NOTE.—General Napoleon. His real name was Clamborough. A characteristic anecdote is told of the surrender. ' General,' said Napoleon to his captor, ' you have to-day immortalised your name.' ' Sir,' returned Stevenson, whose brutality of manner was already proverbial, ' if you had taken as much trouble to direct your army as your tailor to make your clothes, our positions might have been reversed.' . . .

YALLOBALLY RECORD. . . . Savannah is under fire ; that will teach Osbourne to skulk in cities instead of going to the front with the poor devils whom he butchers by his ignorance and starves with his peculations. What we want to know is, when is Osbourne to be shot ?

NOTE.—General Osbourne's perfect sincerity is doubtful. He must have known that Green was hopelessly short of ammunition. ' Unfortunate ', as an epithet describing the collapse of the

Army of the Centre, is perhaps without parallel in military criticism. It was not unfortunate, it was ruinous. Stevenson was a man
of uneven character, whom his own successes rendered timid ;
this timidity it was that delayed the end. . . .''

"Playing at soldiers like a bally kid! Had he never been
anywhere near a real sizeable war?"

Robert's scornful ejaculation grated across contentment
like a saw. Billy stared at him round-eyed; then asked
simply and without any notion of a come-back in repartee:

"Have *you*?"

"Fought the Boers."

This was good enough for Billy, who instantly demanded
not stories, but anecdotes of personal experiences ; these
Robert supplied in his most off-hand manner, which presently
rose to a flamboyant boasting style, as though with every
word he were defying the silent little author who had gone
back to his pipe and his seat on the settle; and through him,
to scoff cruelly at an invalid who had so desperately wanted
to be a soldier.

On a brief impulse the author had included the tatter-
demalion in his tenderer mood. Tenderness now was
ebbing faster than the river tide. Convinced that after all
the fellow was an impostor, he waited for a pause and decided
in the meantime exactly how he could cause him to expose
himself and take to his heels of his own accord. Any clever
trick was legitimate to clinch the matter without involving
Billy in a brawl. These bold braggarts beat it fast enough
directly they realized the police might be called in.

As though mysteriously aware of what was pending,
Robert's memories of the Boer War gradually lost their
vigour. . . . "That'll do, kid."

A small mournful voice spoke from the middle of a cloud
of smoke. "There were warriors and battles in Samoa too,
you know. They thought quite a lot of the High Chief
Tusitala."

Robert muttered something indistinguishable. Serve
him right; now he would have to listen to endless chronicles
of what Stevenson had done in the cause of Mataafa the
Rebel King, and against the unjust German rule in the

islands, before he got a chance to bring back the deeply interesting subject of a little financial assistance for himself: a contribution towards his fare to the South of France. Indeed, he seemed to have stayed in this room too long, and to have drifted leagues and oceans away from the primary intention of his call.

Nevertheless, it was not he but the author who unexpectedly ripped up the interview. Abandoning Samoan wars, he waved with his huge pipe towards some strips of tattooed native bark hung on the brown wall: "He sent me those from Vailima." Then, in the listless manner of one who could hardly be less interested: "I might give ye one—" keenly from under heavy eyelids he watched for Robert's face to fall at the offer—"I might give ye one as a farewell present, a wee memento of your visit here."

This, he was positive, would bring from the beggar-man an equivalent of a London cabman's disgusted: "'ere, what's the good of this to me?"—A strip of native bark when he wanted hard unsentimental money!

The contrary happened ; the scowl disappeared : the thin dark face lit up with eagerness and gratitude . . . and Robert held out his hand for the bark.

The author found himself in somewhat of a hole. Naturally he had not the slightest intention of parting from any portion of the present from a dead friend. It had seemed an ironic certainty that he would not be called upon to fulfil the rash offer. "Nay, I was joking. I can't give away what was given to me; he would no' have liked that. But hark, I'll give ye a pound instead." For whoever he might be, this vagrant, a strip of native bark could be of no value to him; he could not even sell it, for who would believe its authenticity? And as a seaside souvenir it would form a most bulky and inconvenient part of his luggage. Twenty shillings was a large sum to be squandering on the lying fellow, but it could not be helped; the trick had not quite worked out to plan; they very rarely did; the author was resigned to that.

Robert did not want a pound. Not now any more. He would far rather have possessed that strip of bark sent from

Vailima. That had been freely given him; people had no right to give presents and then withdraw them again. "Damn it, money's not everything!" Besides, had he *asked* for money?—(he had forgotten that plaintive little attempt to wheedle his fare to the South of France). A queer conviction thrust its way through his rage, that R.L.S. himself would never have treated even an impostor so ungenerously; R.L.S. would have played ball, and been mightily tickled; or honestly indignant from the very start, refusing to be hoodwinked by any lies, good or bad.

"What's the use of a pound to me? You can keep your stingy pound. Twenty quid's what I need if I'm to live till the summer, and that's not too much from a rich man. They're always the ones that don't like to part, oh no, not even for the son of a dead pal. *Twenty pounds*."

"You've gone just a bittie too far," murmured the author without moving; but glad Billy had wandered out of the room some minutes before, in search of the swifter pleasures to be found with a lenient staff in the kitchen.

"Clear out, and ye can be thankful I dinna communicate with the police. Should I hear of this game again, I will. Bear that in mind." He was not at all sure if this firm treatment would lead to threats and violence, or to a return of the former cadging note which he had liked so little.

But Robert did neither. He stared for a moment . . . then the hard anger died from his eyes, and the usual expression came back, half mocking, half strangely sorrowful.

"Thanks for my good tea," he said in flippant farewell. "Those crumpets were fine; reminded me of waffles and maple syrup way back in the States. Look in and have some with me if you should be passing. So long, Sonny-boy."

He swaggered out.

On his way downstairs he met a well-dressed gentleman coming up, obviously on his way to visit the author. There was barely room for the two to pass without one giving way to the other, and Robert was in no mood to efface himself. Nor, as it happened, was Clinton Bagot, critic and essayist, a man of character. Pushing rudely past him, Robert knocked his cane out of his hands and it went clattering to

[176]

the next landing. Robert raced on down, kicked the malacca with its silver knob out of his way, and a moment later the front door banged behind him.

"Thank you," remarked Clinton Bagot to the empty air. And retrieved his stick, laboriously making the extra journey.

He entered his friend's study, with a reproachful: "Look here, I've known tramps that are all sweetness and light, but I didn't care for the specimen I met just now on the stairs. Who was he, and how much did he get out of you?"

11

"That's mine, over there."

But Robert need not have been so emphatic in reclaiming
a dilapidated knapsack from the left-luggage office; no one
would have been likely to dispute the ownership. He felt
for the hard shape of the tobacco-tin, reassured himself, and
reflected crossly that he had acquired nothing further to put
in, and was now no richer than before he dumped his
luggage. His luck was still out; and judged by the mishap
of the last few hours, London was not a happy hunting-
ground; so give it a miss. Smarting from his recent unac-
countable lapse into real anger when he should have remained
wistful, hungry, ill and lovable, his instinct of self-preserva-
tion decided to hate London instead of himself. Anyhow,
here was no safe grazing for him after Mister Too-Clever-
to-Live had let fall that threat about the police.

He ran over in his mind the sequence of his adopted
father's travels: Scotland, England, France— That's right,
he would get himself to France; though not by any luxury
journey as from Edinburgh to London (you do that once
only, for the sensation) nor by working his passage; for
lately he had conceived a powerful aversion from the
strenuous way of life imposed on Adam. Water was cheaper
than land; he settled to get across by cargo-boat from the
docks of London; familiar with the ropes, he knew that a
few shillings pressed into the palm of the right man, a few
drinks poured down the right throat, would cover his transit.

From a French Channel port, he used again this same
language common to all men to get him to his destination.
His destination? The decision as to where the quest should
begin involved a certain amount of hard thinking. He

glanced at one of the Colvin prefaces to the Letters for a pointer to the right period and the special places that might repay visiting. The woods of Fontainebleau, haunt of artists in the 'seventies? Paris? The Cevennes? Barbizon and Grez— Now what occurrence which somehow displeased him, was linked with Grez, in the life of R.L.S.? He turned a few pages:

> I have been three days at a place called Grez, a pretty and very melancholy village on the plain. A low bridge of many arches choked with poplars and willows innumerable ; and about it all such an atmosphere of sadness and slackness, one could do nothing but get into the boat and out of it again, and yawn for bedtime.

Nothing to displease him in that. Dull spot, Grez, unlikely to yield a rich harvest. Barbizon would do for a start; after Barbizon, push on South for places of further association, Mentone and Hyères. Surely on the shores of the Mediterranean were many villas of the rich foreigner in France; and surely some of these were literate and might already have settled there a long while ago; Robert did a rapid mental calculation: 1882 was the Hyères period; hm— thirty years; rather too long for memory, but not for legend; and the Stevenson vogue was rampant once more since this 1911 edition of the Letters had apparently sold so well. Come to think of it, he usually did better with the sentimentalists who had read and vaguely loved R.L.S. without ever having known him, than with those in more disconcerting possession of the facts from personal encounter.

Journey South, therefore; yet no harm in seeing first what traces might be left of the summers spent at Barbizon.

At Barbizon, Robert again failed to strike oil; also he had forgotten to allow for distresses dating from the Tower of Babel; on his peculiar errand, fluency was all; and though in two or three cases he was received affably enough, he was unable to explain in French with the necessary dignity and pathos that he was no ordinary beggar, but, so to speak, an up-to-date version of Bonnie Prince Charlie.

He walked on to Montigny, which had an air of charming affluence. The occupants of these villas might, he thought, respond more impulsively to a tattered appeal than to his prettier toilet of seaman's jersey, corduroy trousers and velvet jacket. So concealed by a clump of bushes on the river bank of a well-tended garden, he changed, hid his knapsack, and limping a little in case any tender-hearted soul was watching him from the open window, advanced up the path between neat little statues on pedestals, towards what would probably be the drawing-room; no more back entrances for him; an educated Monsieur or Madame with a knowledge of English was his first requisite.

The *salon*, dainty and artificial with its miniatures and brocades and small gilt chairs, was empty. Robert strayed in, looked round appraising the value of what he saw, thought most of it a poor catch ; and not waiting for someone to come in and offer him a seat, sank down of his own accord on the chaise-longue, looking extraordinarily unlike Madame Recamier. He put his feet up, put them down again in case the owner should be odd enough to object, and was pleased to note that lying on the table beside him were quite a number of books that promised somebody in the villa had literary tastes. R.L.S. had been round in this neighbourhood quite a lot; with a bit of luck, (luck for Robert) he might conceivably have left a deathless name behind him. The first three that he inspected proved to be French poetry. A fourth was lying open and revealed that the inside cover was printed with facsimiles of letters overlapping; nearly all English letters; but that was not the miracle which made Robert grip the book in sudden tense excitement; one strip of letter was *in a writing he knew*; a writing that had autographed Miss Gibson's precious copy of *A Child's Garden of Verses*:

To Will H. Low: Damned bad lines in return for a beautiful book.

> Youth now flees on feathered foot,
> Faint and fainter sounds the flute ;
> Rarer songs of Gods.
> And still,
> Somewhere on the sunny hill,
> On along the winding stream,
> Through the willows, flits a dream ;

Flits but shows a smiling face,
Flees but with so quaint a grace,
None can choose to stay at home
All must follow—all must roam.

This is—

Robert gave up till the last couplet. The scrawl was too
tiny and difficult;

Life is gone, but life was gay :
We have come the primrose way !

R. L. S.

A long amused whistle. "Well, well, hit it in one. Oil
at last!" He began to turn the pages. The book was called
A Chronicle of Friendships 1873-1900 by Will H. Low. "A
Chronicle of Friendships" conveyed nothing, but the dates
were all right. On an inner page was written a pleasant
inscription from the author to some French gentleman of
Barbizon who, it seems, had shown hospitality to Mr. Low
long ago. Robert began to skip, hunting eagerly for names
he knew, relevant to his current professional career.

Embarrassment of riches ! The names "Stevenson"
and "Louis" occurred so often that it might have been
better for Robert to have taken the book away and read it
at his leisure. Unluckily, he thought that all time was his
leisure. Grez appeared after all to be the place which Louis
most frequented. Several pages about the local wine
(piquette)—and then an anecdote which confirmed his idea
that Grez might be a rewarding soil:

. . . The youngest of the strangers, Lloyd Osbourne, then a boy
of eight or ten, was the playmate of these children, and, as his
vocabulary in their tongue was limited, he once announced the
capture of a minnow in a convenient mixture of the two languages.
Returning there a few years ago, a grown man of thirty odd, and
making his identity known, he was at once greeted : ' Mon Dieu !
how you have grown, so you are *le petit feesh* ? '

Good. The air of Grez apparently made for long and
grateful memory. But Lloyd Osbourne? How did *he* come
to be a kid there? Yes, of course, it was in this neighbourhood (was it in Grez itself?) that according to Colvin, R.L.S.

had his first encounter with Fanny Osbourne, fell for her like a ton of bricks, and later on hitched up with her. Later still, at some Swiss mountain place, he had sat on the floor with Lloyd, playing with toy printing-presses and toy soldiers. . . . Robert was not yet free from the smart left on his vanity by that ill-fated London visit when too much talk of the boy called Lloyd had caused him so inexplicably to lose his temper, scoff and shout and demand £20. Now he skipped another handful of pages, saw the name Lloyd again, muttered "Hell!", tried to escape it, and was caught by the talisman word "photograph":

> The best of his photographs is the one not over-well reproduced in the first volume of the Letters, which was a veritable ' snapshot ', taken by Lloyd Osbourne who, then of school-boy age, was playing with a camera, and calling on Stevenson to look up, caught him unawares.

"That must have been the one out of the book in the Free Library that some swine pinched before I could see it."
He read on:

> There was another taken by a professional photographer, which we charged him with secretly loving and sending to all the young women who wrote to express their admiration of his work ; ' a fine, chicken-hearted presentment of a young poet ' he owned it to be, half confessing to this weakness, in which he was wholly abetted by his mother, with whom it was a favourite picture. . . .

—Madame, coming placidly downstairs from her boudoir to see if *la bonne* had yet returned from the market, suddenly stood still, her hand pressed to her heart. She had heard a great rejoicing bellow of laughter, lusty male laughter, affronting her from the *salon* which she knew to be empty. The shock was severe; but though a tiny delicate woman, Madame was braver than a lion. She did not stay to call for help, but marched in. A vagabond, a scarecrow of a man, tall and lean, was standing in *her* room, on her carpet, by her table, a book in his hand. "Qu'est-ce que vous faites ici? Qui vous a permis? Mon Dieu! quel toupet!" Rushing up to him, she snatched the volume:

one which had been sent to her father and therefore, though she could not read it, a veritable treasure of the house.

"All right, all right. No need to be so darned careful. What makes you think I'd have pinched it?" So spoke injured innocence, checked in his hearty enjoyment at so unexpectedly learning that Stevenson's mother and Miss Gibson had both favoured the same noble aspect of their hero.

But Madame could not understand him, nor he her. Drawn up to her full height, five feet two-and-a-half inches, she stood before Robert quivering with wrath, and pointed magnificently to the door—"Sale individu! Fichez-moi le camp!"

To her immense surprise, Robert shrugged his shoulders, and not hurrying, strolled out the same way as he had come in.

It was obvious to him that nothing could be gained from staying where people were all uneducated and had no means of understanding the beautiful romantic fiction of his parentage. He had not been going to do Marianne-Léonore here, but on the contrary, little Kirstie, the forsaken Highland lassie. . . . Look what they'd missed by being too hasty.

Madame was puzzled yet proud that this ferocious housebreaker, robber, murderer, should obey so meekly the mere suggestion of her pointed finger. As she could hardly guess that Robert's whole motive for paying a call was instantly annulled by his selected host or hostess not understanding the profoundly interesting lies he had to tell them, she attributed his departure to her own power to strike terror: "Quand même c'est inoui!" . . . For the rest of that day, she went about her duties smiling.

No luck in London, no luck in Barbizon or Montigny. Yet instead of going South at once, Robert found himself curiously impelled to discover Grez, though it was already linked in his mind with that boy of the soldier games and the printing-press: "le petit feesh".

And at Grez, though according to *A Chronicle of Friend-*

ships they were gifted with super-normal memories, he did not attempt to cash in on the past. He mooched along for a little way under the bridge and by the river . . . then threw himself on the grass and moodily watched a grey-beard busy with an overturned boat. The old man caught his stare, nodded to him, and went on caulking and tarring. On an impulse, Robert shot out the name Stevenson. It brought no recognition. No, of course not; Louis and Bob were known here as Stennis. He tried that: "Stennis! Stennis!"

The old boy paused in his job, straightened his back and slowly reacted: "Comment? Eh oui, oui . . . je me souviens. . . . Stennis . . . les deux messieurs Americains. Ils étaient drôles, ces deux-là! . . ." and so on, from a slow trickle to a flood.

These were valuable items of biography collecting from behind memory's rusty doors, but might just as well have been the alphabet. Irritably Robert shook his head, and departed in search of an *auberge* where the wine was cheap. He slaked his thirst, bought some bread and sausage, and a trifle appeased by good living at a price not too hard on his unaugmented capital, returned to the river's brink and sprawled and munched and went on watching the old boatman. . . .

"Stennis!" he shouted at intervals, no doubt with a vain hope that by the surprising processes of time, French might turn to English.

And the next day he returned to the same spot and sat and looked on while the old man worked. "Stennis" he said every now and then, but with diminishing hope. The boatman eyed Robert with curiosity, shaking his head, perplexed at the curious foreigner whose clothes spoke the international language of the down-and-out, yet who had apparently endless leisure to sit and watch another man toil. Robert stared back at this locked repository. He too was puzzled, but at himself. Why not leave the barren neighbourhood? What possible benefit could come from lying here beyond the bridge at Grez, eating black bread and sausage and watching an industrious dotard apply tar

to an overturned boat in the grass? True, the weather was
fine; and true, the smell of tar wet and glistening in the
sun vaguely soothed his disturbed soul (disturbed, he was
sure, by too much reading in Edinburgh), not so much by
reminder of his own road-mending days, as by giving him
pleasant assurance that now he was eating bread and garlic
sausage without doing any road-mending at all. A Defence
of Idlers!—As though idlers needed defending; young
Stevenson himself had been an idler during those summers
spent among artists who at least painted. So cat's-meat to
the sermons of industry perpetually preached by Mr.
Renfrew of Ard-Daraich and Miss Gibson of Edinburgh
and Mr. Merrill of New England.

A curé, black and dumpy against the green and gold of
early spring, waddled along the path. He stopped by the
old boatman, one of his flock, and spoke a few benevolent
sentences. The boatman, tired of Robert, tired of "Stennis"
as a one-sided topic of conversation, immediately engaged
Monsieur le Curé as an interpreter: "You, mon père, who
are so learned to speak Latin and all the tongues of the
world—" and then poured out a torrent of recollection
concerning two cousins, foreigners, one tall and fair, one
small and dark. . . . "It was thirty years ago, more, but ma
foi, such games they had, especially the tall thin young
man, un vrai squelette, yet nearly always laughing; and
he and la petite madame so devoted; she bien vive, très
brunette; every summer she come back to Grez with her
gosse, and shortly afterwards the tall young man would
arrive, and then the piquette that was drunk, the laughter,
the dips in the river, the racing in canoes, the standing
naked in tubs launched on the water and guided with
paddles till the craft overturned: yes, and once for some
bêtise they loaded their sabots with pebbles, and the laughing and shouting and applause and a prize for the winner!
And it did not seem that they did this only to amuse le
petit Sum, no; though the little Sum was the friend in
particular of the blonde Stennis, and the two so happy
together one would think they were boys of the same
age."

The fount of memory dried up with a few repetitions of what he had already told; and the old boatman returned to his task, while Monsieur le Curé translated the story into hesitant English for the benefit of a tramp lying on his back in the grass, hands clasped behind his head, staring up at him, staring and staring. . . . Mon Dieu, one meets with strange riddles, and none stranger, thought the little priest, than this vagabond's passionate, frowning interest in a story—enfin, hardly even a story, a few fleeting pictures— of what had happened here at Grez, when he himself would have been surely a little ragged boy in a country far away from the rivers of France.

"Sum?"

"Oui, oui, Sum, as it might be the uncle of all your America. Resembling John Bool ze Englishman."

"Uncle *Sam*," muttered Robert. Sam was a name common in America. Could Sam have become Lloyd? Of course! it came back to him now how the old camel had aired her professional knowledge by talking of the original *Treasure Island* dedication to "S.L.O., an American gentleman. . . ." The little coloured pictures thus called up were unnecessarily vivid . . . a canoe shooting down the river at a furious pace, paddles splashing and flashing in the sun; a little boy and a tall man, both half naked and very wet, standing up and calling. . . . Then the canoe overturned. . . . A great shout of laughter: "Say, Lou, *we* won, didn't we? even if we turned over twice." "You bet we did, Sam. Bob's a mile behind. Race you to the bank!" . . . The river was again empty and silent.

Robert got up abruptly and strode away. The curé and the old boatman gazed after him, bewildered. "Il est rigolo, ce type-là. Il reviendra demain comme d'habitude."

But Robert did not return tomorrow. He left Grez and went to Paris. For the moment his mood was for a city. And in Paris he could easily use the same technique as two or three times in Edinburgh: go round to the bookshops, preferably where they sold English as well as French books, and linger at the shelves pretending to search for some volume they would not be likely to have, till maybe a wise bookseller or a scholar customer would notice that provocative resemblance to an author dead eighteen years ago. Or he could even start the idea in their heads by enquiring for a book by that author. Not buy it—gosh, no! never such a fool again as to use up even twenty precious sous on a second-hand book. The phrase "living on capital" had acquired significance for Robert. Once he had bought four volumes and paid twenty shillings. He had had to work for those twenty shillings. Well—it might end in his having to work again if he didn't take darned good care of what he had left.

But no Miss Gibson materialized in the bookshops of Paris; and luck was still dead against him as it had been at Barbizon, Montigny, London. Yet he stubbornly refused to allow that the claim could have petered out already, all treasure drained. Treasure—Treasure Island—"To Lloyd Osbourne. . . .' Hell! He was conscious of a mounting fury at being perpetually reminded of the existence of that infernal kid.

Then in one night, Paris turned from spring back to raw winter; the streets muffled and sheeted with snow; the wind like knives thrust down your throat, up your nostrils, into the very crevices of your aching bones. Robert cursed himself for letting this ice-trap close on him unawares just as he was planning to foot it by easy stages southwards to the shore of the Mediterranean. Tramp it? Not likely, in this freezing wind. Not as tough as he used to be. Give it forty-eight hours, and then if the squalls continued, it would have to be by train or truck; slip down, maybe, to the railway line at night and hide among the cattle; they'd keep him warm; share their food. Anyhow, get away. White Paris was medieval, sinister, where before it had been no more than a town failing to provide loot. Grey Paris looked threatening as though the gaunt wolves might lope down at any moment with starving jaws . . . Robert fancied he heard their advancing howls; then imagination turned another crooked corner and listened in horror to the rattling of the gallows. . . .

Wolves? Gallows? "You're bats!" he growled; and flung the blame to where it belonged: to the poet Villon in *A Lodging for the Night*, with theft and murder up every silent street.

As though to unnerve him further, after a fit of violent coughing he spat on the crunched snow, and spat red. *"To understand Stevenson you must first have spat a little blood."* . . . God damn it, was he haunted, possessed of a daemon, that all these stray tags dogged his memory wherever he went and whatever happened?

Neither frightened nor self-pitying now, his immediate reaction was inflation of all his plans till they became insolent and grandiose. No confounded cattle-trucks for him; that had been a darned silly idea, to lie for hours among hairy legs and hoofs, deafened by grunts and squeals, trampled half to death. But they didn't care about that, did they? the callous station officials who would issue no tickets, not even those due to an invalid gentleman like himself, unless paid for in money.

His mentality was in a curious state of confusion, yet he could not accurately place his grievance: the freezing weather? Miss Gibson's library? The implacable French book-vendors who had not once put their hands generously in their pockets to reward him for a tale he had had no chance of telling? An old boatman? A French curé? A man and a little boy eating crumpets that dripped with butter, in a dark panelled room in London where strips of native bark hung on the walls? A man and a little boy in Davos . . . they squatted on the floor and played with a toy printing-press. . . . On the river at Grez they raced, shouting and laughing and standing up in canoes, half naked and joyous in the sunshine. . . .

And here was he listening to the gallows rattle, listening for the avid wolves to steal in past the city walls. Here was he with the queer thick taste of blood in his mouth, the unholy taste of blood. And actually having to pay his own train fare to Marseilles.

*   *   *

For some obscure reason not wholly understood by himself unless he had been unnerved by a sequence of undeserved

[188]

failure, he took no steps, once he reached Provence, to "look up old friends of my dad who might be interested". Living was cheap; the days were hot and the nights warm; so that he was able to return to a loafing existence not unlike his happiest periods in California and Arizona when after a spell of reluctant work he had relaxed in the sun, and where dimes and nickels had gone as far as dollars in the winter. Here and now, a sou was as good as a florin; he swallowed plenty of crude cheerful wine which had been stamped from the local vineyards of the autumn before, and he ate enormous quantities of fruit, and risotto, and salads flavoured with garlic and fennel, and goat cheeses; he slept out carelessly where the air was pungent with the smell of herbs, wild myrtle and wild mint crushed by his careless body; and woke to see a single admonitory cypress higher up the mountain, dark and grave and solitary among the cool-coloured olive trees, and chestnuts and acacias broken into young green flame.

And so he gradually healed. This life in the soft air agreed with him and he spat no more blood. His pallor gave way to a Romany, tan; his cough departed; his sleep was sound and free from angry dreams. Nor was he oppressed by restlessness, but sat quietly at a table outside any small estaminet, as he passed up and down the hills and through the villages which decorated the coast from Marseilles to St. Raphael like an eleventh-century Book of Hours; not letting it irk him any longer that he could not brag to whomever happened to be sharing the same table splashed with sun filtered through the lime-trees overhead; but content to watch them at bowls, listen to the loud tones of their wrangling or good-fellowship, and feel detached, sleepy and benevolent: even on occasions stand them a bock or accept a glassful of rough wine from their carafe; hardly caring that he spent a little more every day from his dwindling stock in the tobacco-tin. He did not walk much during the fierce heat of the day; but for three or four hours at sunset and under the flashing pointed stars, covered the ground with long strides, or splashed his way from grey rock to rock wrinkled and flat in the river-bed of a lyric valley of rose laurels, with no very clear idea of his motive in moving along that coast, nor to what end?

For already he had left Hyères far behind; though at Hyères in the region surrounding Châlet la Solitude he might well have discovered among the owners of opulent gardens and villas some welcoming soil for the planting of a good sturdy bush of lies; it was barely twenty-nine years since Stevenson had lived there. Yet in Robert's curious state of animal well-being, curiosity flourished no more than expedience; and the energy which had inspired him towards graceless pilgrimage to the hills at Swanston, to Portobello and Grantham and Colinton and Rullion Green, had now deserted him. He had not even bothered to visit the outside of the Châlet, but kept on the shore road through the aromatic sea-meadows where the jonquils were nearly over, promising himself vaguely that some time if he returned that way, he would climb up and have a look at the tiny dwelling with its glorious garden, coloured like a fairy-story, where R.L.S. had been happy in his first home with Fanny.

Robert did not resent Fanny. He had noticed that the few letters addressed to her, scattered among the multitudinous letters of the four volumes, were oddly matter-of-fact compared with the boy's early adoration for Mrs. Sitwell; but fairness and shrewd judgment led him to feel the difference: "She was his missus; he didn't *have* to write her a whole heap about love!" So he summed it up in homely terms of the tramp species with whom he seemed again wholly to belong.

Only in one essential had his nature become alien to theirs: he had formed an odd habit of reading, and could not shake it off. In California, when he had lain lazily under trees, or on beaches of the Pacific, he had felt free as a matter of course to do nothing; aware of two reasonable states of being: either asleep, or awake and idle; perhaps a third state, half awake, when you watched your fellow men, gazed at the sky and the clouds, vaguely noted the drift of smoke from a far-off steamer or the sliding flight of a bird. . . . Never, never had you said to yourself "Where's my book?" or been thwarted by the lack of it. Yet now this abominable habit had him by the throat: "Where's my book?"—and luckily or unluckily he always *had* a book; four, bought and paid for.

So all along the Côte des Maures and the Esterel and the lower slopes of the Alpes Maritimes, Robert read the Letters; opening them at random. And as a horrid warning to vagabonds of the road never to let this insinuating habit take possession of them, he gradually lost contentment again, and the Midi ceased to be a Garden of Eden. . . .

Fantastically, it was a procession of children that now rose up from the pages and beset him; crowds of children; as many children as ever followed the Pied Piper; children of all nations, clamouring and laughing . . . children to torment him by the same sort of freakish, malicious trick as in Edinburgh, whenever he opened the Letters and whenever he least wanted to encounter it, he found nothing but what Miss Gibson had called "the serious side of R.L.S." By this new bewitchment, the printed pages might have been suddenly emptied of all other topics but children. Curse the writer for a sentimentalist! As though he had not had enough of Lloyd: Lloyd and Treasure Island, Lloyd and his toy printing-press, Lloyd and the soldier games, Lloyd in canoes? And in Volume Four, when Lloyd was grown up, Austin came to Vailima. And along this very coast at Mentone, a much younger Louis was enchanted by Nelitchka, the little Russian girl; and in Edinburgh, Tommy Murphy was lost and Louis found him and carried him about all day; and in the hospital infirmary, Roden and Willie sat up in bed, round-eyed, listening to pirate stories; and years afterwards, a string of mischievous letters to Tomarcher—yes, he bothered to write them letters, these kids who couldn't even read them; and he played croquet with the leper children at Molokai; and wrote more letters to the Children in the Cellar, whoever they might have been, pages and pages; and he gave away his birthday to a child, Annie Ide; and nursed the landlady's little girl in San Francisco, getting ill himself with grief, and nearly dying after she died.

. . . More and more children, endlessly thronging and clattering; not only in the Letters, now, but remembered from hearsay: that boy who was taken canoeing on an Odyssey for two, among the islands on the Firth of Forth; Pola the faithful little native boy, grave warrior in miniature, trotting daily to open the gates of Vailima for a tall man on horseback, with the salutation "Sleep and long life! A blessing on your journey—" and the reply: "Sleep, long life! A blessing on the house."

DEAR TOMARCHER,—This is a pretty state of things! seven o'clock and no word of breakfast! And I was awake a good deal last night, for it was full moon, and they had made a great fire of cocoa-nut husks down by the sea, and as we have no blinds or shutters, this kept my room very bright. And then the rats had a wedding or a school-feast under my bed. And then I woke early, and I have nothing to read except Virgil's *Aeneid*, which is not good fun on an empty stomach, and a Latin dictionary, which is good for naught, and by some humorous accident, your dear papa's article on Skerryvore. And I read the whole of that, and very impudent it is, but you must not tell your dear papa I said so, or it might come to a battle in which you might lose either a dear papa or a valued correspondent, or both, which would be prodigal. And still no breakfast; so I said ' Let's write to Tomarcher.'

. . . It looked like a house in a fairy-tale, and just beyond we must ford a river, and there we saw the inhabitants.

Just in the mouth of the river, where it met the sea waves, they were ducking and bathing and screaming together like a covey of birds: seven or eight little naked brown boys and girls as happy as the day was long; and on the banks of the stream beside them, real toys—toy ships, full rigged, and with their sails set, though they were lying in the dust on their beam ends. And then I knew for sure they were all children in a fairy-story, living alone together in that lonely house with the only toys in all the island; and that I had myself driven, in my four-wheeled gig, into a corner of the fairy-story, and the question was, should I get out again? But it was all right; I guess only one of the wheels of the gig had got into the fairy-story; and the next jolt the whole thing vanished, and we drove on in our sea-side forest as before, and I have the

[192]

honour to be Tomarcher's valued correspondent, TERIITERA, which he has previously known as

Robert Louis Stevenson.

. . . I like children better every day, I think, and most other things less. . . .

My landlord and landlady's little four-year-old child is dying in the house ; and O, what he has suffered ! It has really affected my health. O never, never any family for me ! I am cured of that. . . .

. . . But you must not suppose that Austin does nothing but build forts and walk among the woods and swim in the rivers. On the contrary, he is sometimes a very busy and useful fellow ; and I think the little girls in the cellar would have admired him very nearly as much as he admired himself if they had seen him setting off on horseback with his hand on his hip and his pockets full of letters and orders, at the head of quite a procession of huge white cart-horses with pack-saddles, and big brown native men with nothing on but gaudy kilts. Mighty well he managed all his commissions ; and those who saw him ordering and eating his single-handed luncheon in the queer little Chinese restaurant on the beach declare he looked as if the place, and the town, and the whole archipelago belonged to him. But I am not going to let you suppose that this great gentleman at the head of all his horses and his men, like the King of France in the old rhyme, would be thought much of a dandy on the streets of London. On the contrary, if he could be seen there with his dirty white cap, and his faded purple shirt, and his little brown breeks that do not reach his knees, and the bare shanks below, and the bare feet stuck in the stirrup leathers, for he is not quite long enough to reach the irons, I am afraid the little boys and girls in your part of the town might feel very much inclined to give him a penny in charity. So you see that a very, very big man in one place might seem very small potatoes in another. . . .

. . . Austin came back from school last week, which made a great time for the Amanuensis, you may be sure. Then on Saturday, the *Curaçoa* came in—same commission, with all our old friends ; and on Sunday, as already mentioned, Austin and I went down to service and had lunch afterwards in the wardroom. The officers were awfully nice to Austin ; they are the most amiable ship in the world ; and after lunch we had a paper handed round on which we were to guess, and sign our guess, of the number of leaves on the pine-apple ; I never saw this game before, but it seems it is much practised in the Queen's Navee. When all have betted, one of the party begins to strip the pine-apple head, and the person whose guess is furthest out has to pay for the sherry. My equanimity was disturbed by shouts of *The American Commodore*, and I found that Austin had entered and lost about a bottle of sherry ! He turned with great composure and addressed me. ' I am afraid I must look to you, Uncle Louis. . . .'

Over and over again, Robert slammed the book down; hurled it violently away from him into the long grass, as though it had been a snake to inject poison. Over and over again, he vowed he would read no more. His mounting exasperation caused him even to scowl on the live Gallic youngsters with black sloe eyes and brown skins, scampering and shrilly screaming up and down the steep cobbled streets and across the *Place* . . . till the sight of them goaded him to drain his glass too hastily and stride away on to the road in vain search of a childless village where he could sit and linger and let drowsiness descend. But it was hot and glaring and dusty on the road; and if he turned aside, sweating, to fling himself down under an umbrella-pine where the shadow was thick and cool, after the first few moments of relief . . . he began to itch again for a book to read. And he had only these bloody books. And these books had only these bloody pages telling about children, bloody children all the bloody time: "*Kids is what is the matter with me. . . . Children are too good to be true.*"

Robert had worked himself into such a state that he came near to praying for anything that would shatter this absurd compulsion to read. Because his mood was far from prayer, he sent out a challenge instead, to whatever tricky gleeful fiends were responsible for the spell (fiends undoubtedly lost to all sense of what was really funny): Let him now open any of the four books at just one letter, however dull, which did not make mention of a child. There, that was the challenge. He did not care if the letter were literary or whether it let itself go on scenery or in denunciation of some point of morals or conduct; though in the past he had naturally skipped these . . . and his recent experiences had paid him out.

He shut his eyes, groped for one of the books, opened it, hardly dared look. . . .

The letter at one glance presented that sober solid appearance which presupposed a scholarly subject rather than kids. "To W. Craibe Angus", and an explanation by Colvin:

The late Mr. Craibe Angus of Glasgow was one of the chief organisers of the Burns Exhibition in that city, and had proposed to send out to Samoa a precious copy of the *Jolly Beggars* to receive the autograph of R. L. S. and be returned for the purpose of that exhibition. The line quoted, ' But still our hearts are true,' etc., should, it appears, run, ' But still the blood is strong, the heart is Highland.' The author of the *Canadian Boat Song* which opens thus was Hugh, twelfth Earl of Eglinton. The first quotation is of course from Burns.

"Of course," Robert agreed warmly. He was already liking W. Craibe Angus quite a lot; the sort of man to whom one didn't write wishy-wash and bilge-water about kids. . . .

. . . the anchor is weighed long ago, I have said my last farewell to the hills and the heather and the lynns: like Leyden, I have gone into far lands to die, not stayed like Burns to mingle in the end with Scottish soil. I shall not even return like Scott for the last scene. Burns Exhibitions are all over. 'Tis a far cry to Lochow from tropical Vailima.

> ' But still our hearts are true, our hearts are Highland,
>   And we in dreams behold the Hebrides.'

When your hand is in, will you remember our poor Edinburgh Robin. Burns alone has been just to his promise; follow Burns, he knew best, he knew whence he drew fire—from the poor, white-faced, drunken, vicious boy that raved himself to death in the Edinburgh madhouse. Surely there is more to be gleaned about Fergusson, and surely it is high time the task was set about. I may tell you (because your poet is not dead) something of how I feel; we are three Robins who have touched the Scots lyre this last century. Well, the one is the world's; he did it, he came off, he is for ever; but I and the other—ah! what bonds we have—born in the same city; both sickly, both pestered, one nearly to madness, one to the madhouse, with a damnatory creed; both seeing the stars and the dawn, and wearing shoe-leather on the same ancient stones, under the same pends, down the same closes, where our common ancestors clashed in their armour, rusty or bright. And the old Robin, who was before Burns and the flood, died in his acute painful youth, and left the models of the great things that were to come; and the new, who came after, outlived his green-sickness, and has faintly tried to parody the finished work. If you will collect the strays of Robin Fergusson, fish for material, collect any last re-echoing of gossip, command me to do what you prefer: anything, so that another monument (after Burns) be set up to my unhappy predecessor on the causey of Auld Reekie. You will never know, nor will any man, how deep this feeling is: I believe Fergusson lives in me. I do, but tell it not in Gath; every man has these fanciful superstitions, coming going, but yet enduring; only most men are so wise (or the poet in them so dead) that they keep their follies for themselves.—I am, yours very truly,

ROBERT LOUIS STEVENSON.'

Exultant at having won his challenge and broken the spell, Robert closed the book gently, laid it down beside him in the grass, clasped his hands behind his head, and lay there, dreamy and at peace. Nothing was left of his urgent irritable need to be for ever reading; why, he would hardly give a rap if he never saw another book; this delicious liberty was good enough for any man. Through the still golden air a cricket chirped like mad, and tree frogs further down the slope chanted a hoarse benediction on all sunset idlers.

He mused, perfectly happy, on the letter he had just read: "*I have said my last farewell to the hills and the heather and the lynns.*" . . . Funny how any man on a tropical island could have gone on and on being homesick for Auld Reekie— "As far as I'm concerned he can have Scotland, every bit of it; sleet and wind and rain; yes, and London too, and Paris. I'm where I want to be; I'm all right. I'm in luck again—

Every man has these fanciful superstitions! . . . Maybe that stunt with the book just now was superstitious; but it worked, you can't deny that, man! It worked a treat."

That clump of eucalyptus over there, pewter trunks, red and silver leaves hanging ragged against the distant weave of the sea's silk, reminded him of California. "Can't remember, did we have—? Hullo, what's that?" A bird flew by and vanished; its body was a flash of striped black and white, a crest of orange feathers sprang erect from its head— Gosh! Then a little breeze stirred a spicy scent of broom out of the bush that grew in brilliant spikes down the path by the grey old Roman bridge. The sun dipped behind the ridge. "New moon tonight.... Read too much, and you miss all that. 'I like the fresh air and these stars and things.'" Robert laughed aloud. "He wasn't far wrong!" Then it struck him that to quote was a woman's habit, an old-camel habit, say what you like! Rueful and a little ashamed, he underlined it as another argument to prove the evil consequences of reading.

"'*We are three Robins who have touched the Scots lyre this last century*'— Not Robert; *Robin*, that's what my father would have called me. He liked Robin."

... The thought passed idly as any other. Two or three more, too trivial for the mind's recording, followed it—

—Before he was jerked back on a lasso flung with diabolical skill from his own mind:

"That's what my father would have called me." How long had he believed himself to be the son of R.L.S., and been glad to believe it?

Perhaps by believing it himself, he lost his knack of peddling the dope successfully? Odd that while to him, too, it had been still a falsehood, it should have been so easy to impose falsehood upon fools; and that the instant he began to put faith in it, they should have lost faith in him. No moral in that, by God!

"'*We are three Robins*'" . . . Then a flash of sudden lightning; but lightning which remained behind, and by its painful brilliance let him de-code the unbearable truth:

So this was why he could not bear all those children running through the letters; robber children, usurpers of his place; children who had had what should have been his; he, Robert, swaggering, boosting himself up with delusions of toughness, hooding the one obvious fact that he was *jealous*; a damned donkey braying jealousy of them all: Austin, Pola, Tomarcher, Annie Ide, Nelitchka, even of the little leper children. . . . Jealous, above all, of Lloyd.

So this was why he had suddenly stopped enjoying the fun and lost his temper, while the author was telling him and Billy about the toy printing-press and about the soldier games played on the floor at Davos.

This was why he had growled and snarled at the dedication of *Treasure Island*.

This was why—the instances multiplied painfully—why he had bought a velvet coat at the Port of Geith; not to ingratiate himself further with Miss Gibson, but because he somehow liked wearing it.

The blazing ray of truth moved on, and licked another spot raw. So this was why he had been so fiercely disappointed at an offer of money, twenty silver shillings, instead of being given an unwieldy, valueless piece of bark.

And this was why—

Robert squared up to his final acknowledgment. Not because it was a first edition to sell, nor a stage "property" to exploit, but because he longed to possess the few words written on the fly-leaf—this was why he had stolen Miss Gibson's autographed copy of *A Child's Garden of Verses*.

⧽ 12 ⧼

You're Stevenson's son, aren't you?

Yes.

No, if you keep on with the lie, and exploit the lie and cash in on the lie. No son of mine.

What d'you mean, arguing like a fool? It isn't nearly such a lie as it was before; in fact, it's hardly a lie at all. It's *true*. I don't have to have proof.

That won't fish up a nickel from the shallowest pocket, my lad. Plenty of softies around, but none soft enough to fork out for what *you* say *you* know to be true. . . . Unless you have your story ready.

Robert was beginning to hate this second Robert who had the cheek to argue with him, scoff at him, upset him, just as he was feeling so happy in his amazing discovery. Mean, to get him all churned up again.

My story ready? What story?

Gold-digger's story. The pretty fable of your birth. Kirstie. . . . How she told the workhouse people who was the father of her child, and then died, wistful and forlorn, leaving a baby only a few days old to be brought up in a Charity Home. Or . . . sometimes she lived on for a few struggling years, and *he*, Scotland's rebel boy, came down and played tin soldier games with his little son, squatting on the floor together and—

Hold your infernal jaw, shouted Robert. Then (better propitiate him): Look here—

Yes?

—Look here, he wouldn't have grudged it to me. He'd have shouted with laughter at seeing me in such a stew about nothing at all. We'd have talked it over, man to man, not like the usual father and son always afraid to be honest and human with each other—

Oh, I wouldn't use the word "honest", honestly I wouldn't. Nor "honour", either, if I were you.

You're not me.

Sure?

Suddenly Robert decided to veer right round and come up on the same side as that other mocking devil of a Robert, and see how he liked that? see if that would silence him?

You're dead right. He'd have slung me out for this racket. But that doesn't make me any less his son.

The scoffer had no more to say. Good. Dished the conceited swine!

. . . But presently an idea stole in from a source Robert could not identify. No thundered text from the pulpit, no dark symbolical cypress pointing bleakly upwards in admonition. An idea spoken not to coerce, but so far from coercion that it might almost have been dropped offhand:

If you go on with the racket, you're *not* his son. You couldn't be. Don't you see you'll have proved you're not? He might have fathered knavery, but never that sort of a knave.

The conflict went on, tearing him apart; giving him no rest day or night, eating and drinking, walking as though he were pursued, stretched under the trees as though he were on the rack. His defiant periods were the most bearable; they seemed a degree more positive than the others, and certainly fitted him more easily, as a coat he had worn often before:

Are you Stevenson's son? Yes, by thunder I am. And I'll buttress it up with good, rich, plausible lies, when my chance of a Big Scoop comes along. And it's coming all right.

Plenty to be done with money if you can rake in enough: "*Wealth is only useful for two things : a yacht and a string quartette. For these two I will sell my soul.*" You don't intend to go on spitting blood all your silly life, do you? If it's T.B., it's T.B. in an early stage; cure it, as he did, by a trip to the South Seas; and mind you, do it in style: a private yacht, a Silver Ship passing through the Golden Gates of 'Frisco, with sails spread and a crew to command; I'll not be cargo again for any filthy old cargo-boats! Get cured in the sun, and find your girl; and have a son, a healthy son, a son of your own; call him Louis: teach him all the fun of the fair; make up for it that way round— and sucks to all of them!

And stop playing the fool with a mincing conscience; stop having dreams of an elegant birthright you can't see or touch, munch or swallow or take to bed with you. Accept your mess of potage. It's not a lie, I tell you, except that as pious men judge "knowing", you don't know. You're sure, but you don't know. Well then, act as though you *are* sure and *do* know.

Ratiocination. Remember the word? "*Making things right for yourself as you go along.*"

Robert again retorted triumphantly with another quotation: "*God himself hates a hanger-back.*" Reward at last for sticking to your books. Let's take to reading again and see what else we can find to gag that Old Sober-sides, Truth:

. . . I have finally bade adieu to inheriting any money. I must learn to live by my own pen or something. I promised my father (as I think it was entirely his right, and mind you, it was on no prompting from him, nor has he any notion how serious the words were for me) that I shall never use a farthing of his money unless I am a Christian. . . . I said to him that I should reckon any person a thief who would use another's money in such circumstance. And he said fervently,

' And a damned thief, too ' . . .
I shall not let myself starve, of course ; but beyond that, must try to be an honest man.

. . . This money irks me, one feels it more than when living at home. However, if I have health, I am in a fair way to make a bit of a livelihood for myself. Now please don't take this up wrong ; don't suppose I am thinking of the transaction between you and me ; I think of the transaction between me and mankind. I think of all this money wasted in keeping up a structure that may never be worth it—all this good money sent after bad.

I think now, this 5th or 6th of April 1875, that I can see my future life. I think it will run stiller and stiller year by year, a very quiet, desultorily studious existence. If God only gives me tolerable health, I think now I shall be very happy : work and science calm the mind, and stop gnawing in the brain ; and as I am glad to say that I do now recognise that I shall never be a great man, I may set myself peacefully on a smaller journey, not without hope of coming to the inn before nightfall.

. . . We had a dreadful overhauling of my conduct as a son the other night ; and my wife stripped me of my illusions and made me admit I had been a detestable bad one. Of one thing in particular she convicted me in my own eyes : I mean, a most unkind reticence, which hung on me then, and I confess still hangs on me now, when I try to assure you that I do love you.—Ever your bad son,

ROBERT LOUIS STEVENSON.

He would never have listened to any Archangel with a Sword stuff; not he; not Robert; but these scraps torn out of a man's life fell and piled up round his raging fever like a blessing of snowflakes which did not melt. Not only extracts from letters that he chanced on now in his search for further support, but reinforcements for the other side that were hardly even relevant; arguments which he remembered from what he had read against his will in Edinburgh; the terrific thunder-and-lightning judgment on the Samoan boy who had stolen a pig: "*You have shown a bad heart. We have lost our trust in you, our confidence in your loyalty and high-chiefness.*"

He had been forced to put up with something like this from old Merrill; but he'd never taken it to heart from old Merrill, not damned likely, no more than from the Archangel Michael! He'd only take it from a man who, like his very self, had wanted to do a thing and done it, and then wanted to do it just as much—and ruefully not done it. . . . Without putting it right for himself as he went along.

No good in fighting, was it, against your father, when he was that kind of a father? nonchalant, tender, amused, sorrowful; justified in authority because he was also a man acquainted with temptation.

Passionate integrity, passionate vindication of the need to work— All very well; but Robert did not agree with either of these; there was no quality in his nature to respond of its own accord. Left alone, he could be quite happy idling, playing at pitch-and-toss with the truth.

Then what was biting him?

Pride, perhaps, in acknowledging for the first time that someone had the right to discipline him, who yet was not an employer, a policeman, a minister.

Here's where you stop being a rebel, as you have already ceased to be a derelict walking alone and swanking your refusal to be pitied. Learn with wonder that the inconvenience of not being able to have it both ways is a stone wall reality: for if you long to believe you have indeed found a father, and can only believe it by proving a likeness that goes deeper than merely a piratical portrait, then, impostor, if you go on with your seductive profitable game, that will be where you yourself have flatly refused to testify.

The second Robert, Robert the Devil, made one more attempt at slick compromise:

Wait till you're broke again, good little boy. Then you'll feel differently; then you'll divide all this into believing it when it suits you, or not caring a tinker's curse whether you believe it or not. Depends on your pocket!

No to that. He could not be satisfied, now, with anything less than full affiliation. Ever your bad son.

13

"Look out for that fellow."

Clinton Bagot pointed to a tramp who had just passed the café where he and Marcus Powell were sitting outside at a table for their apéritif. It was one of those incredibly brilliant days towards the end of June when any figure at all striking or grotesque seems to be picked out as a moving black silhouette in the strong golden air, all its eccentricities sharply exaggerated, instead of merged, as they are in England, into the gentle landscape and the quiet weather.

Marcus turned just a little too late to see the man's face. He had already limped by.

"Poor devil," he remarked casually. There were many vagrants in the motley procession he idly watched year after year from tables outside cafés all along the coast; and though this tramp was loaded down more heavily than they usually were, an odd assortment bursting out of his knapsack or slung over his shoulder, yet his ragged trousers, horrible old slouch hat, torn and sleeveless shirt, and boots that were barely threaded together, the separate parts flapping on the road as he plodded along, provided nothing to justify Bagot's sudden alert note of warning.

"Not such a poor devil as he looks. Don't waste your pity. He's one of those plausible swindlers who make a good thing out of pretending to be somebody else. You didn't happen to see his face, did you? He pitches a tale that he's a son of Robert Louis Stevenson. There *is* a likeness, nothing to get excited about, to one or two of the portraits reproduced *ad nauseum*; long untidy hair—that's easily managed. But some people simply can't keep their generosity in check when a lazy impostor arrives on the doorstep; I believe they actually enjoy being cheated out of their money."

Marcus Powell remarked critically that from the back view of him, this particular impostor hardly looked as though he had raked in enough for a decent pair of trousers; and certainly no fortune.

"My dear fellow, his rig-out's an essential part of the game. You don't get the species out here as we do at home; at least, I expect you do, but it's a different kind: the Latin beggar is frankly a beggar and doesn't try to persuade you that he's a nephew of Napoleon or the grandson of Voltaire, or any little fancy bits like that. As it happens, I met this rogue on the stairs coming down from Jamie's flat, blazing with temper because he hadn't been able to squeeze anything out of him. I'm a tolerant man, but this attempt, according to Jamie, was crude enough to be insulting: the rascal traded on his likeness, cool as you please; did all the worn-out clichés of a beggar's stock-in-trade: bad cough, lost his job, pretending that his fare to the South of France might just save his life—"

His host reminded him that he had better hurry up and order another apéritif, as they would have to get back to the villa in good time for an early dinner; Bagot was taking the night-train to Paris. "And to be perfectly fair, I don't see what you've got to grumble about this mountebank pretending he wanted his fare to the South of France. Here he *is* in the South of France, all quite in order. He's probably the soul of truth and integrity." But Marcus was only lazily contesting the point. He did not really care whether Bagot's mountebank were honest or wicked, except that on general principle he would have preferred him to be wicked; it was less boring.

Bagot thought it over. "But I wonder what he's doing down here?"

"He might find some victims if he looks long enough. Hyères isn't very far away; let me see, it must be about twenty-five years or more since R.L.S. left there. So there could be some English or even French people who might remember and fork out for the sake of *Treasure Island* and *Jekyll and Hyde*."

"Yourself included," suggested Bagot. "He's sure to come to you when he hears about your collection of first editions and so forth. He obviously picks bookish men, especially if they're rich."

"But he didn't succeed with Jamie, who's both bookish and rich; romantic, too, when he's in the mood. But perhaps he wasn't in the mood?"

"I'll tell you something odd that puzzled Jamie; in fact at one point he was very nearly diddled into parting with a discreet sum; quite a trifle had made him reconsider whether perhaps after all the man might be genuine, or think himself genuine; it's the same thing."

Marcus was prepared to debate this abstract point on general grounds, but decided he would prefer to hear what had been this one odd contradiction in the behaviour of the tramp who had passed between them and the sea ten minutes ago. The vagaries of human beings happened to be among the few things that could rouse him out of an almost despairing listlessness; for he was only twenty-nine, had plenty of money, a beautiful villa with gardens that blazed in tropical hues level with the Mediterranean; but he was also utterly uncreative, no family surrounding him, and suffered from the sort of heart which obliged him to live here as quietly as possible without exercise or agitation; a poor state of affairs, which left him for everyday enjoyment only the spectacle of human nature, weak or wicked, caught in the sticky web of self-delusion.

"Well, go on, Bagot, what was the incident that made Jamie doubtful?"

"Just this: he wanted to clinch matters by making the fellow give himself away as an impostor, so he offered him 'as a wee souvenir' a strip of tree bark; you know, native stuff R.L.S. had sent him; he has them hanging on the wall."

Marcus laughed: "Yes, I can imagine the 'wee souvenir' touch. And his mistake was in expecting the man to spit at his gift for not being money."

[206]

Bagot looked at him curiously: "How did you know?"

"Smelt it in the air. Besides, you spoke of 'just one thing' that baffled Jamie in the interview."

"Queer the way you guess these things."

"I'm not a magician; when I'm told there's something unlikely to come, I guess at the most unlikely, and so win this marvellous reputation. Did Jamie let him walk off with half a South Sea Island tree over his shoulder?"

"Naturally not; he said he was joking, and offered him a quid instead. The man lost his temper, wouldn't accept the quid, turned insolent and demanded twenty, so Jamie sent him packing. But—"

"But—?" for Bagot had paused.

"He seemed to Jamie really upset, over not getting that bit of bark."

Marcus Powell's attention had at last been attracted: "He sounds original, your swindler. I hope he does look me up at the villa. I shall offer him the left leg of my Hermes and then tell him he can't have it, and see what happens."

He paid for their apéritifs, and they rose from the table and began to stroll along the sea-road towards St. Maxim.

"By his rigid covenant with integrity, how R.L.S. would have hated being roped in as an essential part of a begging story. All the graves of Rullion Green giving up their dead! All the same, it was quite a good choice, even leaving out the chance resemblance; the Stevenson idolatry was at its height during the decade that followed his death, but I imagine it's still fairly prevalent if your pal chooses wisely at what houses to pay calls."

"You needn't call him *my* pal. I arrived just too late to kick him downstairs; nothing would have given me greater pleasure."

"Nonsense; you'd have received him with Welcome on the doormat."

"I'm an hospitable man, but if you think I hang out flags and spread a banquet for every fraudulent relation of every second-rate writer—"

Marcus was delighted; he had remembered from a book of critical essays that Clinton Bagot was in the opposing

[207]

camp from the Stevensonian zealots, and had hoped to draw blood. "I'm not sure," he remarked coolly, "that a first-rate mind ever dismisses any other as second-rate. Doesn't it take a third-rate mind to use precisely that expression? And a character who compels more respect, not less, as you know him better, *must* have some quality too indestructible to be dismissed as flimsy and second-rate. I mean as well as his charm."

Bagot rose like a covey of partridges put up by the beater. "I'm a mild man, but if there's one word that sickens me it's 'charm': his engaging way of burning holes with his cigarettes in everybody's sheets and they kissed him for it and kept the hole all their lives. Acts of Kindness and Friendship's Hand—"

"Acts of Kindness and Friendship's Hand may be fulsome on a Christmas card, but more men have died for want of them than by enemy guns."

Unconvinced, Bagot went on muttering: "The infernal charm of R.L.S. would have floated a battleship."

"I should say his detractors had allowed themselves to be led by his charm just as easily as the hero-worshippers, only in the opposite direction. They deny him his due simply because his personality—not his writing, mind—lacked those austere lines which they've come to associate, rightly or wrongly, with good work."

"We deny him his due because his exuberant fancy ran to voluminous blue cloaks with buckles, and red sashes and an embroidered fez—"

"In his early twenties. And haven't you missed out an astonishing quantity of what went on beneath the fez?"

"I know you too well, Marcus: you've turned devil's advocate. Your brain happens to be working keenly this evening, and it's your last chance to goad me into a temper before I leave; but you're just as capable as I am of condemning Stevenson for his egoism and childish vanity."

"Sir Willoughby Patterne? Sentimental Tommy?"

"There you are!" Bagot rose to the bait—or the pair of baits. "You've owned up to it."

"My dear fellow, but have you ever heard of an egoist,

a sentimentalist, who owned up to it himself? Yet Stevenson told Meredith and Barrie too, ruefully enough, that they'd drawn these very characters from him. And Meredith replied that Sir Willoughby Patterne was universal. They all are. You're the Egoist and I'm Sentimental Tommy." A smothered protest from Bagot. "Very well then, *I'm* the Egoist and *you're* Sentimental Tommy."

"Not fair," Bagot complained. "You've been mugging up your subject."

"Now could I have guessed beforehand that a vagabond who was a living portrait of Stevenson was going to pass along the promenade at St. Raphael. No, Bagot, I maintain that the supercilious critics who could give R.L.S. a dressing-down for his vanity in dressing up, ignored that a man in bed in a strange city—"

"How you leap about! What city?"

"New York—gaily holding a reception, wearing an ink-stained old blanket with a hole cut in the middle for his head, had hardly chosen a way of enhancing his giddy attraction and sex-appeal. Besides, it was a convention of the period to dress up careless. Besides, when you're constantly ill, you wear what's easy and loose and comes nearest to hand; constant visits to the tailor and shirtmaker presuppose constant good health. Besides, in the miraculous intervals of finding yourself well again, you're likely to choose not conventional town clothes, but clothes in nostalgic imitation of the healthy swashbucklers; subconsciously hoping, perhaps, that in these you may snatch a little of their virility for yourself."

"Did he *want* to be virile? He'd have lost a good deal of his appeal as the Beloved Invalid—"

For the first time, Marcus showed himself genuinely impatient: "If you weren't so disgustingly robust, my dear Bagot, you'd have found out the unpalatable truth that physical frailty is rarely 'appeal' if it lasts longer than a fortnight. And his lasted over forty years. He was *not* the sort of invalid for ever shedding a softly radiant influence from his patient couch; in fact, his eagerness for getting himself into trouble again always led him to hurl his unrepentant body into the obstacle race long before it was ready.''

"All the same, he had the luck to look romantic and lean and delicate, and cashed in on it: 'valiant in velvet' and so forth, just as *you* have the luck to look saturnine and bad-tempered.''

"That's where you're wrong again. He could equally well have looked saturnine and bad-tempered, with that long, gaunt face and melancholy eyes; thin men always can. The point is that, unlike me, he never *was* bad-tempered; his temper was hot and strong, but that's different. As for hero-worship, do you know the derivation of the word 'worship'?''

"No," replied Bagot crossly. "Do you?"

They had reached the Château by now, and went straight out on to the terrace where dinner had been laid within the suave sound of the sea lapping at the foot of the shallow flight of marble steps. At the far end of the terrace a grassy path wound down between the tall pewter trunks of a clump of eucalyptus, to a private swimming-pool. As many of the English colony on the Riviera were wont to say a little crossly: "Old Marcus does himself well."

"It comes from the Old Saxon 'weordhscipe', meaning simply 'worth-while'; and needn't necessarily attach itself to altars."

Bagot banged his fist on the table. "That's what I complain of. I'm a patient man—"

"The qualities and quantities of man you think you are!" murmured Marcus.

"—But these disciples who rush about killing an author's reputation and dignity by grossly overestimating what their hero is worth—"

Marcus interrupted: "I don't condemn hero-worship; I condemn myself instead for being incapable of it. Dispassionately, I admire Stevenson. He fights with a clean blade and he fights what should be fought."

"Why the present tense?"

"At a guess, and allowing for an inevitable slump and recovery, the present tense is right. I prophesy for him the lively vagaries of perennial banishment and perpetual recall. And if, as your colleagues are so fretfully complaining lately, he never forgets himself in his Letters, at least he wholly forgets himself in his battles. But you know, it's not even true about the Letters."

"They're bursting full of himself. You can't deny it; turn up any page—"

"And equally bursting with energy and concern and good-will towards and about and on behalf of others; the traffic runs both ways. The man happens to be alive, that's all there is to it; not merely seven-eighths alive or three-quarters alive, but with every tingling drop of his blood."

"Blood and bones! Skull and crossbones! Pieces of eight!— Oh, let's all be little boys and play at pirates!"

"That's only a facet. Like his father who perfected the intermittent form of revolving light, he's brilliant and sombre in turn; at one moment an adventurous boy with a huge gusto for the Jolly Roger, and the next a stern Covenanter on a lean quest for responsibility, a quest that never ended. No, Bagot, I refuse to take part in these tedious de-coronations, this modern tendency to strip every king of his royal attributes, merely because you're irritated with his little disciples for calling him king. To convince you that anyone's worth while, the reading public should remain sitting, turn away their heads with studied indifference, and sneer. But that's not the normal way to show enthusiasm."

"For you of all people to defend the 'normal way' of the reading public— When you write your memoirs, I suggest for a title: 'Me of All People'."

A bitterness sounded in Marcus's rejoinder: "I can't write, as you know. Therefore I don't. Therefore I shall never expose myself." After a pause, he went on: "You're such a town-crier, Bagot, with your wearisome repetition of all the conventional indictments: he's second-rate, he's romantic, he's histrionic, a poseur, an egoist; he's so full of *charm*. . . . Stevenson's charm and popularity, as you might have noticed from the evidence that has since poured in, did at least succeed in making people happy—no, not merely at chance encounters; **the** evidence always came from the group among whom he lived. And you must admit, Bagot, we must all admit that that's the supreme and final test: not only to make a swift tight-rope passage across the abyss, but a tight-rope passage that you have to repeat every day and all day, until the hour of your death. Some of this adoration that worries you so much may have come from people who met him only once, but for most of it you can take a cross-section at random: his step-children, usually a difficult conquest and a difficult loyalty, but he achieved the first and kept the second without effort. His Samoan body-servant Sosimo, who would let no one else fold his dead master's hands; 'body-servant'—the term implies one who has more chance than most, of closely scrutinizing the hours most vulnerable in man; his daily getting up and lying down; no man is a hero to his valet— but R.L.S. stood the test and laid the saying flat. His French servant from Hyères; the frontiersman and his wife who looked after him at Saranac; his sister-in-law, a sedate little person from Indiana; his university professors; his doctors everywhere; missionaries of all denominations; French artists; tavern riff-raff; native kings and warrior chiefs; a group of chattering little leper children; his fellow-passengers in the steerage of the *Devonia*—he was a natural democrat. You notice what a solid, down-to-earth, representative assembly they form? not mainly a fanciful rabble of poets and novelists, of neurotic disciples mingling their tears with drunken hiccoughs; though the beachcombers are there as well, the tramps and the down-and-outs. We can take his nurse and mother and father and wife for granted, I suppose, and his cousins and friends, though it doesn't always follow: my old nurse detested me, and my cousins cried when they heard I was coming to tea. But you can't so easily dismiss his popularity with the spruce officers from a British warship, and with the mixed crew of a trading schooner battling through South Sea squalls—"

"Do for heaven's sake spare me any more of this ten-page catalogue, Marcus. You're laying it on with a trowel. Magic is easy."

"But not *sustained* magic; that's too difficult for most of us; certainly too difficult for me."

"I suspect more and more that the chief reason why you admire him is that he compares favourably with yourself."

The other man said nothing. A curse of his nature and therefore of his existence was a lucidity not only of outlook but in-look. So having piled up his defence mainly to provoke Bagot, he did now for a swift disconcerting moment visualize himself as the black Anti-type of the man whom he had been defending; and felt he could in future view himself with rather less of his usual equanimity, measured against a definite figure who had lived and died triumphantly his opposite.

His companion, still chaffing him, remarked: "Certainly no one in their senses could accuse you of being a 'seraph in chocolate'."

"He wasn't altogether a seraph, either. Nobody could be, with his strong ironic streak: always after the sweet, he offers us the olive. And don't quote Henley's 'assassin' review to me."

"'Assassin' is a terrible word; it should never have been used; Henley's attack was exasperated by the 'official' biography; it wasn't originally meant as an attack on R.L.S. himself."

"It read very much like one," Marcus commented drily. "But you know the article far better than I do; I remember now, you were one of 'Henley's Young Men'. My head is bloody, certainly, but never for one single moment have I been deluded into believing myself Master of my Fate."

"It's true that Stevenson was the gentler soul—"

"Especially when he wrote *Father Damien*," drawled Marcus. "Yet I concede that Henley's rage was no more, after all, than a passionate longing for his 'riotous intrepid scornful Stevenson' . . .

> We have been friends, Lewis and you and I,
> (How good it sounds, ' Lewis and you and I ! ')

the young Louis as against the R.L.S. who didn't belong to

[213]

him any more, who hadn't belonged to him for so many years."

Clinton Bagot had warmed up since Henley figured in the argument. He quoted:

> " . . . our Lewis then,
> Now the whole world's—"

"Typical of that bluff male thing, a sense of possession: Henley didn't mind Louis' mother, Louis' friends; he didn't mind Baxter to whom that poem was written (it was Baxter, wasn't it?), Colvin, Bob; he wasn't jealous: jealousy resents sharing with anyone and everyone. But it was after Fanny took over, that he chose to repudiate every Louis except the youth whom he had loved when they were young and wild and did good work together: 'O, we that were dear, we are all too near with the thick of the world between us.' . . . Not the clear space of the world, as a lesser poet might have written; Henley *felt* it to be dense and opaque and impenetrable. How Stevenson must have been wrung, out in Samoa, when he read that; wasn't it about then that he wrote once more to Henley?"

"Yes. But Henley never answered."

"Henley never gave way. I'm always inclined to feel that stories about friends who quarrel are far more tragic than of lovers; lovers are bound to quarrel; it freshens them up—or ends it. But friends unreconciled, with the thick of the world between them . . ." he was silent. And Bagot wondered whether he had been given a glimpse of what might have helped to twist this uncreative man into so wry a shape.

When Marcus spoke again, it was from a more objective angle: "We can't, surely, take Henley's extreme views as a cool, steady, unbiased indictment of the idolators and their golden-glory view of Stevenson. Henley himself was just as picturesque; a roaring, lusty, yellow-bearded, crippled lion of a man; just as vulnerable, too, for a romantic attack if anyone had chosen to make it. One gathers that he had more pain than Stevenson, but was less physically threadbare; he didn't suffer from exhaustion and was

[214]

therefore merciless in exhausting others; Colvin swears to that as a fact. Stevenson never ceased to celebrate life, not only as it came but as it went; a joyful communicant; but his body was painfully brittle. And Fanny's was the constant predicament of wives who are compelled to guard a husband's health at the expense of his freedom. I've heard Chesterton on the subject; he knew, none better, that they don't enjoy the rôle."

"Your unusual eloquence—"

"I assure you, Bagot, I haven't thought about Stevenson for years. Our recent glimpse of a rogue's back, or rather, your tale of a rogue has set me off. Stevenson is just the man I'd have liked to have staying with me here to chase away boredom; he'd have been a delectable guest; but that would be for his company, not as a famous writer. You see, I don't care for his writing."

Bagot was startled. "You *don't*? Why?"

"His style, to begin with. That 'rapt fastidious pen' which Le Gallienne praises; a style built with hard ceaseless striving doesn't appeal to me; too economical, too astringent, the flesh too ruthlessly carved away from the bones; I repudiate a whole feast of skull and skeleton, however salutary. If he were still anywhere around, he would be sick as mud to have his name draped with romantic association when he held so strongly that what should matter was to combine a lean and flexible style with an exciting story. I like *The Master of Ballantrae* best of them all; the Master is the devil incarnate. I enjoy him and respect his talents."

"You would," pointedly. "You're his twin brother."

"Thanks for the compliment. Stevenson is strangely at his best when he writes of villains: Pew, Silver, Huish— and foremost, James Durie of Ballantrae."

"And Hyde; I mean Damien's Hyde, not *Mr.* Hyde."

"Mr. Hyde too. He's a far livelier creation than Jekyll. That often puzzled me, why Jekyll the Good emerged so weak and unattractive. Unless Stevenson was being devastatingly cynical, as he was in *A Child's Garden of Verses*."

For a moment, Bagot's mouth was too full of *aubergines*

farcies to do more than splutter at this astounding statement.

"Two or three times," added Marcus, quietly pleased. Disappointing to have set out to be sensational, if your companion had failed to react.

"Cynical?" Bagot was able to exclaim at last; "in the *Child's Garden*? Pretty-pretty, chocolate-box, innocent cherubs at play! *Cynical?*"

Still smiling, Marcus got up, strolled indoors and fetched a small volume bound in faded peacock-blue and gold.

"First edition?"

"Yes, but unluckily not autographed. I've no Stevenson autograph. Now unless you'd rather wait until after dinner, have the goodness to read 'System'." He handed Bagot the book, open. "And after that, 'Foreign Children'. I've put a fork to mark the page."

"Aloud? With actions?" asked Bagot, elaborately sarcastic. "'Evewy night my pwayers I say'—"

Marcus took the book away from him, and in tones carefully level and free from expression read:

> "Every night my prayers I say,
> And get my dinner every day;
> And every day that I've been good,
> I get an orange after food."

"I shall be sick," interrupted Bagot.

"You probably will, but not from any abstract reasons.

> The child that is not clean and neat,
> With lots of toys and things to eat,
> He is a naughty child, I'm sure—
> Or else his dear papa is poor.

A dash after the smug sentiments of the first seven lines divides them from the conclusion ironically insinuated in the last line. A quantity of meaning can be contained in a dash, unless too frequently employed. For that poem, Bagot, was intended for adults, not for children. No grown-up man in his senses would have called a poem 'System' if it were for children, who wouldn't even understand the word. System—is that a title to plant in a child's garden? You can't persuade me that he's not drawing adult attention, with some bitterness, to the fact that it's perfectly easy to be clean and neat, 'with lots of toys and things to eat', if you happen to have a rich father; that's the 'system' which, according to the writer's passionate sense of fairness, needed a deuce of a lot of altering. And now here's 'Foreign Children' if you can bear to hear it?"

"I'm still your guest," Bagot replied in a resigned way, but convinced in spite of himself that Marcus was right in his discovery of Stevenson's irony in an unexpected place.

> " Little Indian, Sioux or Crow,
> Little frosty Eskimo,
> Little Turk or Japanee,
> O, don't you wish that you were me ?
>
> You have seen the scarlet trees
> And the lions over seas ;
> You have eaten ostrich eggs,
> And turned the turtles off their legs.
>
> Such a life is very fine,
> But it's not so nice as mine :
> You must often, as you trod,
> Have wearied *not* to be abroad.
>
> You have curious things to eat,
> I am fed on proper meat ;
> You must dwell beyond the foam,
> But I am fed and live at home."

"What is the lesson therein contained?" asked Bagot, trying to choose with discrimination between a ripe Brie and a luscious Camembert offered him, while his glass was filled up with a Châteauneuf du Pape of the 1899 vintage.

"The lesson of that, again conveyed through one of those smug infants you complain about, is, I should say, a disguised plea for international brotherhood; a caustic suggestion to the British white man that other nations and other colours may be not as aware of their own abject inferiority as might have been supposed by the British white man. 'You have curious things to eat, I am fed on proper meat.' Well, Bagot, where was the writer's tongue? in his cheek?"

"In his cheek," Clinton Bagot ceded the point. "I never

[217]

thought, Marcus, that I should live to eat my dinner while you read to me out of *A Child's Garden of Verses*." He chuckled at a sudden idea: "Imagine the respectable church-going leddies of Edinburgh reading 'System' to their off-spring as a bed-time treat."

"And seeing no wickedness. Because the graceless young reprobate of the 'seventies has had his shaggy edges trimmed to a decorous appearance of death and immortality, and all he wrote is safe and good."

The ancient Italian butler appeared on the terrace to announce that according to the chauffeur, il Signor Bahgo should be starting for the station.

* * *

Marcus Powell anticipated that the impostor being in the neighbourhood was bound within a few days to visit the most distinguished patron of belles-lettres along that stretch of coast; a patron, that is, with money enough to seem like an attractive victim. With that measured eagerness which was his nearest approach to enthusiasm, he looked forward to the interview, and was disappointed when the next three days failed to produce this relief from the accursed boredom which rolled towards him, and then clung like a fog. He had come to look on it as his positive right to be entertained, having no creative gift or talents by which to entertain himself in solitude; too active a brain to vegetate, and too corrosive to enjoy meditation. All the more was he disappointed when a guest, or call it entertainer, who was due to arrive on the very day Bagot left, sent a *petit bleu* from Paris to say she was detained permanently by her husband. Marcus had a theory that the axiom of the devil finding some mischief still for idle hands to do, was spoken in sadness by the devil himself reproaching his own hands for beginning to twitch.

At last he decided to go in search of the vagrant, and if he found him, lay himself open as a new and promising innocent. After drawing a blank in two or three villages, he thought of St. Tropez as a probable place: that type often had a fancy to lodge and eat on a harbour-side, perhaps from some instinct of rapid escape by water. Passing the more luxurious cafés, he at last caught sight of the man partially hidden behind a barricade of masts and sails, sitting at a table outside a cheap estaminet where the smells were thickest; and wolfing coarse black bread and sausage; his nomad baggage dumped beside him. Marcus strolled up to the table and asked courteously if he might occupy a vacant chair? Robert glanced up quickly at the English tongue, grinned at the request, for the other few tables were mostly empty, and said: "Sure thing."

Marcus sat down. He was perfectly aware he had already, as though inadvertently, given away that he had a special interest in a man with those special looks; deliberately given it away to hurry on the performance; for he longed to hear the technique, and then see how a pretender would meet exposure? He hoped that the fellow would be clever and impudent and not whine.

But Robert talked about the weather. And about the regional food and drink. And of local flora and fauna. Marcus could not grasp if this were to lead up to the announcement of who he was and what he desired; if so, it was an exceptionally long-drawn-out preamble. At last, impatient for his treat, Marcus commented diffidently on his companion's resemblance to a certain famous Scottish writer. Had anyone ever mentioned it to him?

"Think I'm like him?" asked Robert. "Lots of folk have said so."

"And you're no relation?"

"Oh yes. His son."

Marcus went through all the proper motions of surprise and gratification which he supposed would burst forth from one of the brigade of weordhscipers condemned by Clinton Bagot.

Robert had demolished his roll and sausage, tilted the remains of his beer down his throat, and wished aloud, frankly as a child, that he could have more of all three; but he said it neither to Marcus nor to the waiter, but, as it were, into space. Taking it as a corollary to his astonishing disclosures, Marcus deduced the preliminaries must be nearly over, and went more warily; remarking that though he had sat down here himself, it was because, seeing Robert, he had desired his better acquaintance; not on account of the excellence of the fare nor the service. Should they, therefore, move to a more high-class restaurant?

Robert shook his head; "Nearly down to my last franc again. Last week I sold my jersey, and I'm eating it now. It was a jolly fine jersey," sighed Robert, mourning for his garment. "Not new when I got it, but warm and comfortable. Quite whole too, not even patched. Oh well—" The threnody was over. "My corduroys will have to go next; I said to myself 'Robert, my lad, it doesn't do to be fond of your trousers—get rid of 'em.'"

Marcus was duly respectful. "Quite," he agreed; "gazelles and trousers: 'but when they grow to know me well and love me, they are sure to die'. And yours, if I may say so, look as though they have loved you in a most moving fashion."

"Oh, I won't sell these I'm wearing. I've got two pairs."

"No man can want more," Marcus agreed. "But on the other hand, no man can want less; it would be a shameful mark against civilization if you had to sell them: so, please, you must allow me to be your banker and tide you over the present crisis."

Robert's mobile face showed a variety of conflicting expressions. Marcus waited. If he had been surprised before, that Robert had had the wisdom to bide his time and not boldly ask for that which experience taught him was occasionally offered spontaneously, he was even more perplexed, now a pigeon had fluttered tame on to the table, that the grasp was not more instant and ruthless. Could it possibly be latent pride holding the man back? Robert's next words sounded like it:

"Mean you'll give me money for charity? Or because you believe I'm Stevenson's son?"

A subtle psychologist, and paying keen attention to the handling of this fascinating interview, the rich man nevertheless made a blunder: "Charity? Certainly not. It's an honour to be of some little use to a man of the same blood as R.L.S."

"Sorry," said Robert, firm though regretful.

"Sorry?"

"Can't accept it. Thanks for the offer."

If Marcus had been bewildered, he was now utterly lost. No amount of speculation would fit the extraordinary assembly of facts. According to Bagot's evidence, here was one of the tribe of begging impostors going his rounds like a hawker peddling his birth, and on the strength of those looks, probably doing well out of it. Again according to Bagot, he had been furious in the past when thwarted in his desire to make a touch; and this would have been a pretty considerable touch; he had not even had to call at the door for it; surely "let me be your banker" must have sounded like the sweetest music? Then he had acknowledged frankly that he was on his beam ends, and made no secret of the R.L.S. racket. That was strange too: he threw out "his son" as though he believed it himself. What was the game? It looked more complicated with every move: "Do you mean you'll give me money for charity or because I'm Stevenson's son?" What would have happened if he had replied "for charity"?

It had been months or even years since Marcus had been levered so thoroughly out of his boredom; presented with a human problem as tantalizing and as obscure. The fellow might be a bastard or an impostor—or both; that could not matter less; what mattered was to keep him under observation; a police phrase; but no policeman could have been more in need of Robert than Marcus, exhausted by the frequency of days on which nothing happened. But he realized by his recent error that care would have to be taken to lure this quite improbable creature into the conventional behaviour of a recognized swindler:

"Are you staying long in this part of the coast?"

"Never know from one day to another. It suits my health."

"Forgive me if I again seem impertinent, but you look to me as if that indeed needed consideration."

"I'd a bad bout of pneumonia last Fall; it must have got at my lungs." And Robert went on to add with mournful pride: "Couple of months ago, during a blizzard in Paris, I spat blood. Not, mind you, that it's a thing I'd ever mention."

Robert's notion of never mentioning, corroborated Marcus's belief that here was an entertainer of rare value whom he could not allow to slip through his fingers. Careful this time to couch his invitation in terms of impersonal hospitality, he invited Ragged Robin to come and stay with him for a while. And in case acceptance should still hang on a question of whether it were issued in charity or for the reason which apparently for the present had been abandoned, forestalled all these fine shades of delicacy, by a harangue on the text of "Who am I that I should have abundance of food and empty rooms in my home, when I have done so little to deserve it?" From here, Marcus switched back to a simple, friendly manner: "I'd be glad to do this for anyone who's ill and needs a rest. I've a dicky heart myself, so I understand." And wound up by assuring Robert that he or any less fortunate brother would be doing him a favour by lulling the clamour of an over-burdened conscience. He dared not scrutinize Robert for the effect of this high-faluting parade, so hoped for the best as he wound up by a pathetic sketch of his solitary existence; with no family of his own except an uncle, a retired colonel of the conventional type; and as lonely men sometimes do, how he had taken an odd fancy to Robert and would be deeply disappointed if their acquaintance had to end brusquely here and now, at a table by the harbour of St. Tropez.

"I *think* that's all right," said Robert slowly, after a tussle with a code of ethics which were still a bit new and stiff in his mind, and needed limbering up. For surely it entered under the heading of "hospitality"—"Yes, I think that's all right," he repeated with more confidence; and rattled down a few coins to pay for his insufficient déjeuner. Then he heaved his knapsack over one shoulder, slung his uninviting overcoat over the other, and not aware that he had once again negotiated a ticklish corner in ratiocination (and negotiated it wrong), announced himself ready.

His host suggested they should walk as far as the road and there pick up a fiacre; and Robert graciously intimated that that would do him fine; one ankle was blistered and swollen with a poisoned mosquito bite, so that tramping in the literal sense could be written off.

He was not as puzzled by Marcus, as Marcus by him. A tactful bloke, Robert deemed him, or he would have attempted to pay for the rough meal; and Robert was determined to accept no money; hospitality was different. When Marcus first revealed himself so near the sucker of all his dreams, the struggle was agony; beads of cold sweat had sprung to his forehead . . . before a refusal marked his first entrance into good on the positive side. So far, since his decision to give up the racket, he had faithfully abstained from lying or soliciting on a lie; yet until this rich mug walking along beside him had unwittingly tempted him with a pocketful, he had not actually been given a chance to say no. And by God, it hurt; not because he was greedy, but because money would have staved off that dreaded moment when (once he had sold and eaten his corduroys) he would have to work or starve. Toil and slavery—why in hell's name did a poor devil who had done no harm have to be arrested and marched off by these two spectral policemen?

Still, it had ended well. Odd little cove, his host; and from the point of view of legitimate prey, so alluring; even after the victory of righteousness, Robert longed to proceed with the game—art for art's sake—and then give back whatever he had extracted.

However, better not, just in case one did *not* give it back.

"Damn!" exclaimed Marcus, using his own methods to settle yet one more point which was contradicting Bagot's version of the tramp's impersonation: ("long untidy hair—that's easily managed"). "Damn, I walked in to St. Tropez on purpose to get my hair cut. Too late now; it'll have to wait. You've been wiser, I see."

Robert nodded. "I can't stick the feeling of a lot of hair

tumbling all down my neck in this heat." And it was a fact that some of his jersey money had just gone to the St. Tropez barber.

Marcus leant back . . . smiling at the absent Bagot.

Only one of the Château staff was about when they alighted; a French *femme de chambre*; and she merely caught a distant glimpse of the original appearance of Robert, and was ever afterwards disbelieved by the rest. For Marcus had caused the driver of the fiacre to draw up at a side gate of the garden. "Je crois bien," cried the old man; and added to himself that, ma foi, you never knew what a mad English milord would permit to sit beside him, and always with an air of je m'en fiche de tout le monde. But no doubt in this case it was to settle a wager.

Marcus would not really have minded whom his ragged guest had encountered, nor supposed that Robert, who like most rogues of the more amusing cut, had the effrontery of Old Nick himself, could not have carried it off with perfect sangfroid. But it happened that his Italian valet, Giuseppe, though an excellent man at his job, was not of the genus known on the stage and in fiction as "imperturbable"; and matters would therefore be easier all round if poor Giuseppe did not have to betray his lack of the essential imperturbability.

Two of the spare rooms were in a pavilion, and had their own entrance. As nonchalant as though he had been all his life accustomed to playing host to the Roberts of this world, Marcus showed him the bathroom adjoining his bedroom, and told him he would find everything there that he was likely to want: "But if not, ring. You'll be cooler and more comfortable in the sort of clothes we wear more or less all the time during the summer, so I'll bring you over some flannels and a thin shirt; oh, and a pair of espadrilles."

Robert looked puzzled, and Marcus held out his foot in a coarse white rope-soled sandal. Robert did not think much of them. "Don't bother about those; lend me some socks— some clean socks," he amended; "but you'd be surprised, I've got a pair of very decent shoes in my knapsack; and my corduroys," Robert went on; "and my father's letters in four volumes; I bought them." He paused for wonder and applause. "—*And* a velvet coat. I bought that too, second-hand; it's in quite good condition except where the moths got at it in a few places while it was in the shop; they don't take enough care in these shops. But Miss Gibs—a lady I used to know very well, said if the moths finished nibbling holes in it once, they wouldn't come back. What do you think?"

Marcus gave this theory his gravest consideration. "I'm no lepidopterist, but it sounds logical, and I suppose moths *are* logical. Well then, between us we seem to have provided everything you need, so may I take these away?" He picked up, managing not to do it gingerly, Robert's antique specimens of hat and overcoat and boots which had just been kicked off with a sigh of relief: lying there, they looked as though they had a distinct life of their own, incompatible with the parquet floor and delicate powder-blue rugs.

"No," Robert replied fiercely, defending his own property—or properties, Bagot would have said. "I'm not going to have them thrown on any muck-heap, even if you think them fit for nothing else."

Many men would not have understood Robert's outburst; or else have supposed it was rooted in sentimentality; but Marcus had an evilly-shaped little key to some (though not all) of this tramp's erratic psychology; and in this instance it fitted the lock: Robert did not want to be parted irrevocably from his piteous begging accessories in case the tenuous fabric of his present fortune should suddenly give way. It would indeed be difficult to replace in a hurry garments like those. So Marcus expressed himself courteously towards Robert's apprehension, saying they were certainly not going on any muck-heap, Robert could make his mind easy about that. Nor was he (in answer to a further look of sultry suspicion) at all ashamed of his visitor's possessions; but as man to man, servants were a little inclined to judge by outward appearances; and these trousers and boots and so forth, though answering their purpose excellently, were perhaps slightly unusual—

"Stow it!" Robert by that time had gone into the

bathroom. "Here you are," and the trousers came flying through the open door. "I know what I looked like, and what gents wear for the Rivvyairah summer season. Take 'em all away if you like, only I won't have 'em destroyed." He was not nearly as clear as Marcus over his reasons for not wishing them to be destroyed; for having vowed himself to a life without beggary, and moreover, recently proved that he could stand a severe test, it was outside his present range of vision that he would ever again be standing in deliberate and pictorial destitution, playing his old rôle in a dialogue that had begun to ring familiar (You're Stevenson's son, aren't you? Yes. . . .)

"I'll put them away somewhere very carefully," Marcus promised him. "You've only to say the word if you want them back again."

"No bloody fear!" Robert sang out, quite cheerful again; and then a loud splash. Marcus chuckled. Thinking he might as well provide against a tiresome explanation to any of the servants should he chance to meet them on his way across the loggia and upstairs, he hunted round softly for a receptacle for the boots, the hat, the overcoat and the trousers: finally he pulled off a drawn-thread pillow-case, and using it as a bag, slung his odd burden over his shoulder and departed, looking forward to a stimulating evening.

His friend the Abbé Ducros was expected for dinner. Marcus saw no reason to put him off.

*   *   *

"Gosh, I'll say you've got a lot of books."

A lean, handsome man in his late thirties sauntered into the Château library, and looked round him with an air that was appreciative but free from envy; an air which comes when one has no desire for the property oneself, but is not scornful of others for enjoying it.

Marcus silently summed up that Robert was getting acclimatized to the idea that books might be important. As for his appearance, he wondered whether it had occurred to him that by haphazard of climate and borrowing, he was wearing very much the same as R.L.S. himself during his

Vailima days in the South Seas. "'Faultlessly attired in spotless white'," he murmured.

"What?"

"You should say 'who'; I was referring to the perpetual hero of the lady novelist."

His guest shrugged his shoulders, and began browsing round the room. Marcus laid down the volume he had been reading and his paper-knife, and watched him. A bull in a rich field of buttercups; no, not a bull; the fellow moved too gracefully; a jaguar.

"Why d'you keep half of them locked up?" Robert asked, after shaking several glass-fronted doors. "Reminds me of Miss Gibs—a lady I used to know very well."

"You're always remembering Miss Gibbs, aren't you? Your fiancée?"

"My—?"

"Sweetheart?"

"Nope, she wasn't my sweetheart, but she had books. Though not nearly as many as you. Go in for them in a big way, don't you?"

"Yes, first editions and rare editions and autographed copies. Hadn't you heard of my Collection? It's quite well known."

Robert shook his head. He had discovered that the books on the open shelves that covered the walls were ranged in alphabetical order, and was already hunting among the S's, so his reply was absent-minded.

"Wouldn't have been likely to: don't know much of the language, though I've picked up a bit. But the lads I meet don't talk to me about collections of books."

Marcus then finally dismissed Bagot's notion that Robert had been making special enquiries as to a good deposit for his bundle of lies; his never-heard-of-you attitude was unflattering and would have been plainly impolitic.

Suddenly Robert hailed a book with an uncontrolled exclamation of delight: "*Jee*-hoshaphat!"

"Found something?" Marcus got up and sauntered towards him, curiosity alert.

It was one of two volumes that he had pulled out, in the

same binding with a dull cream label. Marcus glanced at the title of the one which remained on the shelf : *Robert Louis Stevenson. Letters to His Family and Friends.* The 1899 edition; he remembered it contained the only really fine existing portrait of R.L.S., seated at a writing-table and glancing up, taken unawares by Lloyd Osbourne.

But he was amazed at the effect on Robert, who had turned white as though he were confronted with—what? A spook? Lazarus risen from the grave? A stern archangel with a drawn sword? A policeman? (There surely had been moments in Robert's career when the sight of a policeman would have had as visible a reaction on him!)

Not, certainly, as though confronted by his own reflection in a mirror; this portrait was wholly unlike him in every way. And now Marcus had the final answer to the question tantalizing him almost beyond endurance: Robert *did* believe in his own claim to be Stevenson's son.

Yet had he always believed it, even in the past while making a lucrative business out of his Book-of-the-Words? and if so, why had he now ceased to cash in? As for this present emotional response which he could barely conceal— damn it, the man must have seen plenty of photographs; they were his stock-in-trade. Then what had moved him so terribly? What was it all about?

"Well?" asked Marcus, after the silence had been stretched far too taut to be natural. "Rather good, isn't it, for an enlarged snap? at least, I suppose it was a snap-shot; they're often the best, especially with such a mobile subject. Hadn't you seen that one before?"

Robert shook his head. He had received a shock quite distinct in character from his first amazement in Miss Gibson's shop in Edinburgh, when he had happened on the startling resemblance between himself and the Nerli portrait still crumpled at the bottom of his knapsack. Because this face did not resemble him at all. Could there be two distinct men, one like him and one so unlike, and an apparatus to stamp them both on to paper, labelled with the same name?

. . . He came out of his reverie to hear Marcus repeat: "Hadn't you seen that one before?"

PORTRAIT OF STEVENSON FROM A PHOTOGRAPH BY
MR. LLOYD OSBOURNE, REPRODUCED AS FRONTISPIECE TO
VOL. I OF THE METHUEN 1899 EDITION OF THE LETTERS.

"No. I've had this book between my hands, but it was in a Public Library, and some swine had pinched the picture."

"Dear, dear," Marcus clucked his tongue sympathetically. "People like that shouldn't be admitted."

Robert slowly closed the book and put it back. He remembered that he was no longer in a Free Library, devastated by dishonest people. He was staying here, and as this was not among the locked-up books, could come in at any moment and look again and again. For he had fallen in love, though for reasons entirely the opposite from those of Narcissus; and with his new-born love was mixed something of a child's flinching fear of being accused by a dark penetrating gaze that divided right from wrong by bare sword-judgment, leaving more flexible distinctions for the use of those not brought up in the covenanting tradition.

Then the awe passed, recalling that he was now a *good* Robert, his honour burnished and bright to behold, accepting hospitality only, and not one sou in hard cash.

"The lady you once knew, Miss Gibbs who wasn't your fiancée and who had a good many books but not as many as mine—didn't she have this edition of the Letters?"

Robert was unconscious of the volumes Miss Gibson had succeeded in keeping from him all the months he was with her, locked in a drawer of her bedroom; though as it happened, she need not have feared his mockery. He did not correct Marcus's notion of the name: perhaps the same obscure instinct which had prompted him to keep his tramp's disreputable clothes, equally warned him that it might be all the better if his two benefactors, the old and the new, did not enter into intimate correspondence.

"No, she was getting the Swanston Edition, but they hadn't finished coming out yet." His eyes went roaming along the shelves. He delighted Marcus by his incongruous technical interest in the various editions of R.L.S. "You haven't any of the Swanston lot?—they're quite decent; not very handy, though, for slipping in one's pocket."

"That's a pity," gravely from Marcus. ("Now where on on earth has he picked up his booksellers' jargon?")

"Wouldn't you rather have had 'em all bound the same?

Here are a couple—no, three volumes called the Pentland? Why, that amounts to almost the same as the Swanston; Swanston Cottage is *in* the Pentlands, you know. I've been there; walked on those hills, looked up at 'em from the garden. . . . There are white scars zigzagging down the side of Caerketton, just as he said." Robert went on questing: "I hadn't heard of a Thistle Edition."

"American."

"Oh, I see." He read a few titles: "*The Master of Ballantrae*, *Weir of Hermiston*—oh, no, it's in the Edinburgh. *A Child's Garden*—why, that's the same as—" Robert stopped. He had been going to say "mine". But Marcus had no chance to press him to finish the sentence, as fortunately for Robert, the Abbé Ducros was announced.

Marcus greeted him in English, knowing that the priest was almost bi-lingual; a beautiful little man with thick silvery hair and a youthful complexion. "I don't think you've met Robert before? Robert, this is my very good friend the Abbé Ducros, who most fortunately for you—for both of us," Marcus corrected himself politely, "can speak our language much more fluently than we can speak his, and certainly more correctly than we speak our own."

"Pleased to meet you," said Robert.

"I too am delighted. I have been twice to America. They make me so welcome, your countrymen. In fact, that is the charming phrase they always use and mean, when we say merci—'You're welcome.'"

Glasses of white vermouth were handed round. And presently dinner was announced, and the odd trio went out on to the terrace that lay between an orange-grove just above and the flight of steps down to the sea.

Marcus sent a mischievous thought towards Clinton Bagot who three evenings ago had been sitting in the very chair now occupied by Robert, and reading aloud with an effort to discredit Marcus: "Evewy night my pwayers I say . . ." He would be saying something besides his prayers if he could see what was taking place beneath the sedate routine of the Château.

Conversation at first was almost entirely between Marcus

and the Abbé. Robert barely heard them; he was still obsessed by the portrait he had just seen. Following his first wild leap of pride that he should be the son of a man who could look like this, came a mood of terrible humility; and Robert as a rule was not given to humility. It was a sharp corrective to the swagger induced by evidence of the Nerli portrait: he could himself look like a buccaneer, yes, that was easy, a buccaneer wary in his sidelong scrutiny of any approaching danger, yet more or less amused at himself for caring one way or the other. But not easy at all, directly his prototype by some intangible translation became a different finer character, with that deep tenderness for mankind which understood all and forgave all because it identified itself with all. Yet while the unconscious repudiation humiliated Robert, his blood was strangely stirred, as it had been stirred and excited when he had heard of the reckless crusade in defence of Father Damien. For here was a portrait of the Crusader.

Two men, not one; Robert, and the second too far removed for any hope of kinship. Two men, not one . . . two . . . one . . . Robert had a confused memory that the tale was vaguely familiar. Abruptly he broke into the conversation:

"See here," shyly, "isn't there a story anywhere, I sort of seem to remember, about two men, one good and the other bad, fighting it out in one body? fighting over which is going to get the whip hand?"

The Abbé smiled at him and quoted:

" For that which I do I allow not : for what I would, that do I not ; but what I hate that do I.
For I know that in me (that is, in my flesh) dwelleth no good thing : for to will is present with me ; but how to perform that which is good I find not."

Marcus, who had been on the verge of quite a different reply to Robert's question, checked himself and retired into his spectator's box. He sensed that something was happening relevant to the problem he had under dissection:

"Is that what Monsieur meant?" asked the Abbé, benevolent to the silent visitor from America whom he found oddly sympathetic, and perhaps in some unknown way a little touching too, and in need of what secret support could be given without transgressing any law of courtesy to his host. Like most men of his calling and experience, he was fully aware, not so much that he was dining with an atheist, which did not disturb him in the slightest, but that Marcus Powell was an exceptionally bad lot, spiritually speaking, and therefore (still spiritually speaking) in a poverty-stricken state that might have more urgent need of his liberality at any moment, than his friends settled in the Faith. Certainly Marcus's appeal was not nearly as transparent as that of the man who with apparent simplicity that concealed guile, had been introduced as "Robert" and no more; though neither was "Robert" aware that he might have need of anyone's services; he too was probably a bad lot, and no doubt visualized himself as Independence Day incarnate. Nevertheless, the priest answered the worried look fixed on him across the table, as though he were indulgently giving information to a very nice child: "You were thinking of those verses, Monsieur, were you not?"

"Dunno," said Robert. "The Bible, isn't it? I lived with a holy schoolmaster once who was always chucking sermons and bits of the Bible at me, but I didn't pay attention; too damn dull. Sorry," he added hastily, in case any special apology was due to the strip of purple silk showing beneath the Abbé's dog-collar.

"Yes, it is from the Epistle to the Romans, chapter 7:

Now if I do that I would not, it is no more I that do it, but sin that dwelleth in me.
I find then a law, that, when I would do good, evil is present with me.
But I see another law in my members, warring against the law of my mind, and bringing me into captivity to the law of sin which is in my members.

There, Monsieur, are your two men, the good and the bad, who are fighting in one body."

Robert thanked him and speedily lost all interest; for this had a religious cadence, this was Mr. Merrill and the New England minister, and perhaps even the beginning of

a long sermon. Better, therefore, to change the subject.
He remained unsatisfied that it could account for the yarn
he dimly recollected.

Leaving the other two to drink their coffee, Marcus slipped
away on a slight pretext. He had to do a trifle of research
in the library; not academic, but in that region which he
found so peculiarly delectable, of studying the human race
in their folly and their struggles to extricate themselves
from folly.

It took him some time, hunting through the pages of the
Index to the Letters, before he discovered what he wanted;
Dr. Jekyll and Mr. Hyde was listed neither under J or D,
but to provoke him, under Strange Case of. No, not in
Volume One. Anything about it in Volume Two ? On
the very first page of Colvin's preface it was mentioned:

> . . . *Jekyll and Hyde*, after threatening for the first week or two
> to fall flat, in no long time caught the attention of all classes of
> readers, was quoted from a hundred pulpits. . . .

Then what he sought should be in the very next batch
of letters. Almost at once he was rewarded: a letter to J. A.
Symonds, dated from Skerryvore, Bournemouth, Spring
1886:

> . . . Jekyll is a dreadful thing, I own ; but the only thing I feel
> dreadful about is that damned old business of the war in the members.
> This time it came out ; I hope it will stay in, in future. . . .

So he was right; here it was: "that damned old business
of the war in the members". "But I see another law in
my members, warring against the law of my mind, and
bringing me into captivity to the law of sin which is in my
members." No doubt but that Stevenson, a grandson of the
Manse and piously edified in his early childhood by Cummy's
reading from the Old and New Testaments, had had his
theme of Jekyll and Hyde originally inspired by that Seventh
Chapter of St. Paul. Deacon Brodie came into it, of course;
respectable cabinet-maker by day, Edinburgh gangster by
night, and the story might never have been written at that
particular moment but for the writer's helpful private

[233]

battalion of Brownies on night shift. Nevertheless, by quoting St. Paul, the Abbé had put the clue into Robert's hand; clue that would have led him straight from his vaguely remembered notion of some yarn about "two men fighting it out in one body", to the letter that would have told him what the yarn was and who had written it.

Where, by the way, Marcus ruminated, if he knew nothing of *Jekyll and Hyde*, had he drawn his "sort of notion" that there had been a yarn on those lines? And having drawn it, why had he left it unsolved? One could only guess the answers to both questions, but they were neatly coupled. Robert had bought the four volumes of Letters, so presumably he had studied them, essential no doubt to his recent career as a professional swindler. He must have assimilated, subconsciously, a Jekyll and Hyde flavour from references in the Letters. Then if the theme tantalized him (and his question to the Abbé had shown it did) why had he not come closer? read it instead of shying it away? Again the small section of mystery was cleared of fog, when Marcus recalled that fragment of autobiography revealed just now across the dinner-table by Robert's only too candid: "The Bible, isn't it? I lived with a holy schoolmaster once who was always chucking sermons and bits of the Bible at me, but I didn't pay attention; too damn dull." *Jekyll and Hyde* had first become popularized from the pulpit; assume that that piece of information had reached Robert, perhaps from Our Miss Gibbs—"a lady I used to know very well"—or perhaps from Colvin's preface, the association would be with sermons, which as a boy in New England he had definitely decided were not for him.

Therefore Robert had never read *The Strange Case of Dr. Jekyll and Mr. Hyde*.

Marcus drew a long breath, hardly able to credit the strangeness of this even stranger case. Robert might have left out all the rest of Stevenson's works and it would not have been any phenomenon of chance, nor indeed have made much difference to the situation. But that he should have skipped *Jekyll and Hyde* while in his own soul he himself was working out the very conflict between Jekyll and Hyde, nor have the satisfaction of knowing who had been before him in the matter, that was a device which Marcus could not have bettered had he been the only Inventor.

Half smiling, he threw himself down in the armchair to let possibility and outcome have full play in his mind. It really was almost too good to be true, in his own unholy realm of ecstasy. Delicate sport indeed, and a complete answer to the riddle of what Robert was about, accepting and then not accepting money, exploiting his story and refusing to exploit it,agreeing to stay at the Château if he were invited in hospitality, but not as the son of R.L.S.: his two selves in conflict and Jekyll at present in the ascendant. . . .

"That can't be for long," murmured Marcus. Yet whether the reign of Robert the Good were to be long or short, he would have to be kept at the Château till it had worked out to one solution or the other. Unaware that he himself, by his characteristic way of placing his bet, could have provided ironic amusement to another Marcus looking on, Marcus backed Hyde: call it 51-49. Exciting odds against a triumph for integrity. Hyde might have several reverses before he reached his final victory. Until then, no more boredom.

One day, when he had sucked the thing dry, when he was sick of the fellow, he would give himself the additional pleasure of handing him *Jekyll and Hyde* to read, with a warm recommendation: "I think you'll like this," and watch the reaction and relish it, miss not one tremor. . . . Then kick him out.

Not yet, my soul, not yet. . . .

Marcus strolled across the room, put back the Letters; abstracted *The Strange Case of Dr. Jekyll and Mr. Hyde* from further along the shelf, found the corroborative passage he sought: "And it chanced that the direction of my scientific studies . . . shed a strong light on this perennial war among my members"—

And still smiling, Marcus carefully hid the book behind some tomes of Greek drama in the original. He was not superstitious, and it was therefore somewhat of a mystery why he should have felt that all the fun of the fair—from his point of view—depended on Robert *not* reading *Jekyll and Hyde* till the perfectly appointed moment.

It's a godsend, Marcus told himself, with the same quaint notion of what God might or might not send, as Robert when he had said: "It's an answer to prayer."

14

"Hallo!"

Robert was in the swimming-pool. He turned on his back and shaded his eyes with a wet hand from the dazzling sun, so that he could have a good look at the apparition who had said "Hallo".

"Are you Marcus's Latest?" asked the apparition, lightly impertinent.

"Latest what?"

"Latest performing seal?"

Robert saw no reason to reply. He began swimming in the opposite direction, to where the water from the pool splashed down into a long tank of lilies before it rolled a little further into the sea.

"You can come back," laughed Brenda Dale-Carrington, throwing off a sophisticated bathing-wrap. "Anyhow you can't get far away from me, because I'm coming in. We haven't got a pool up at our own villa, worse luck." She dived neatly in at the deep end. And Robert walked out at the shallow end and seated himself on the steps.

"For the love of Mike," protested Brenda, "I'm not infectious, am I? Isn't there enough room for the two of us? It's a *big* swimming-pool."

"I've seen a bigger."

"Oh? Where?"

"Pacific Ocean," laconically.

But Brenda had been to China, so she was not impressed. She was, however, considerably impressed by the appearance (in bathing-trunks) of Marcus's latest "performing seal". A bit on the lean side; his long sinewy brown legs, especially, seemed as though they would go on for ever. And not young. But his face—my hat, *yes*! Brenda was very glad that curiosity had brought her over uninvited, and that she had come straight down to the pool at the end of the garden instead of calling politely first at the Château to enquire for her host. Not exactly handsome, either, this brown animal; she had been wrong to call him a seal; seals were plump and sleek, and Marcus's Latest was distinctly neither of these. She could not remember ever having seen such an unusual face, gaunt and mobile and exciting, with that sort of wicked watching expression, sidelong, as though he would think nothing of first pouncing and then robbing you of your purse.

"I'm only just back from Paris," she chattered; "and then last night I found them all talking about you, so I said I'll be over there like billy-o— Oh, you needn't scowl so furiously; we're used to Marcus, down here; none of us ever know what he's going to bring in next. Poor lamb, he simply *wilts* when he hasn't got something new and fascinating and eccentric to keep him occupied. I'm one of his regular troupe, so although you've made up your mind to hate me, you'll see me quite often if you're staying long. Are you?"

It was the same question that young Billy had asked; and the answer now might have been the answer then: "From the look of things, either five minutes or a month"; but he had liked Billy; and thought Brenda a pest and a headache, to say the least of it, and in spite of her exquisite figure sparsely clad; for she was a woman who prided herself on daring the conventions and darting well ahead of her period. Dispassionately he ran his eye over her, from pink bare feet to pretty apple-green bathing-cap matching her scanty costume in apple-green and black. If she were his host's property, he wished Marcus joy of her; if not, Robert might, he thought, consider the offer (for no doubt but that already under all the coquetry, the offer had been made)—and then chuck her away.

"Where do you come from?" she asked. "Sometimes you sound American and sometimes you don't."

"Sometimes I *am* American and sometimes I'm not."

"Hallo! not shy of me any more?"

"Never was."

"Well then," she teased, "if you never was, why did you climb out directly poor little innocent me plunged in?"

"It's a funny thing," said Robert, maintaining his poise without the slightest difficulty, "but I like bathing by myself."

"All on your ownsome?"

"Yep," he mocked; "all on my ownsome."

"They tell me you're never out of the water."

"I've got nearly forty years' dirt to wash off. Who's 'they'?"

"Rumour," mysteriously; "rumour with a hundred painted tongues."

"Too bad!"

"—Look, there's a dragonfly. Watch me chase it."

Robert did not watch her; and she did not chase it for long.

"I'm coming out."

He shifted along the sun-hot marble seat, allowing her plenty of room to run up the steps without brushing too close. If and when he wanted to feel a woman's flesh tingling and satiny against his own, he could always get over to the port of St. Tropez— No, he hadn't any cash. Never mind—(the thoughts went racing on oblivious of Brenda)—he had often managed well enough without. And it was true that his debonair take-it-or-leave-it style, in which a caressing voice draped a threat of brutal treatment, formed an irresistible challenge to female curiosity. Take-it-or-leave-it; they almost never left it.

Infernal nuisance, all the same, being planted down here in luxury and without cash, in spite of the three or four meals a day cooked by an experienced chef. If only you could bear off half those meals and sell 'em round the corner, there'd still be enough left and nothing wasted.

"What are you thinking of? I shall call you the absent-minded beggar." She was unfortunate; the last word was no favourite of Robert's. "And that reminds me, what *am* I to call you?"

"My suffering aunt!" he burst out, "do you have to call me anything?"

The Hon. Brenda Dale-Carrington had had her fill, in the past, of suave and adoring suitors. She had even had two husbands, for she was not quite as young as she appeared. "He'd be a marvellous lover," she reflected; stimulating and dangerous and quite different from the usual Riviera male.

"I wonder where Marcus—oh, Marcus, you startled me! How you slither round."

"I see you've introduced yourselves."

"Not exactly," laughed Brenda; "in fact, not at all. Your guest," a slightly mocking inflexion, "doesn't know who I am, and I'm afraid, Marcus, he doesn't care; I haven't clicked. But I'm eaten up with curiosity to know who *he* is? We've talked about seals and swimming-pools, but no visiting-cards exchanged. I'm beginning to suspect," she added musingly, "that he hasn't got one."

"Nor have you, dear, in that costume," Marcus skilfully flicked her into her place. "Robert, this is Mrs. Dale-Carrington; I imagine you'll be calling her Brenda fairly soon." He purposely performed the introduction in irregular order, to give himself a moment to think up a name for Robert. So far, the servants had called him Signor Roberto. And there had been no letters nor telegrams. Then he had a mischievous inspiration: "Sir Robert Faulconbridge," formally presenting Robert to Brenda.

Robert looked bewildered, but Brenda's eyes danced; she was swift to take a point; moreover, she was far from illiterate:

"Faulconbridge? A descendant of the Plantagenets?"
Marcus smiled, well pleased with her.

> " Madam, by chance but not by truth ; what though ?
>   . . . Near or far off, well won is still well shot,
>   And I am I, howe'er I was begot."

"You seem to know *King John* pretty well?"
"Yes, I played the Bastard in my last term at school. I wasn't very good; not enough panache. This fellow," with

a nod towards Robert glancing from one to the other, completely bewildered by the shuttlecock of their dialogue, "this fellow would be better."

"Far better," Brenda agreed. "Does he claim to be the son of Cœur-de-Lion?"

"Not so far out"; Marcus spoke more sincerely now.

Out of their rapid flippancy, Robert salvaged the word "father", of late significant to his ear as a white stone in a heap of black.

"*Who* did you just say was my father?"

"The Lion-heart," Marcus translated courteously.

And: "I'm always going to call you Faulconbridge," laughed Brenda.

"Thanks, I'd as soon remain a performing seal." With no more conventional farewell, Robert picked up his shoes and walked off, up the marble stairs and over the close grass to the pavilion. The two left by the swimming-pool watched his sure-footed exit.

"Marcus, what's really his name?"

"Angel-face, I haven't a notion! Nor, I imagine, has he. He tells me he was born in the workhouse and brought up in a Charity Home."

"A love-child, I gather by your subtle information borrowed from Shakespeare. And Cœur-de-Lion—?"

"He claims to be the son of Robert Louis Stevenson."

Brenda thought it over: "Might be. There's a likeness to those endless portraits that poured into every paper and magazine when he died; I was quite an infant, of course."

"Baby Brenda!"

She passed that. "Attractive enough, your new find; he needs fattening—"

"For you?"

"Maybe. I rather fancy that disreputable don't-care fashion of shaking me off; it puts an edge on it."

*   *   *

"Demoralizing" was hardly a word in Robert's vocabulary. Nor, had he known it, would he have applied it to life at the Château. Nevertheless, his independence had been locked away by Marcus like an armful of ragged old clothes, and instead he was given agreeable access to the art of luxurious living. Apart from that, he never for one moment felt free, for Marcus took pleasure in literal interpretation of Robert's refusal of hard cash at their first encounter; on a basis of liberal hospitality, he might have everything else; for as Marcus never ceased to remind him (though never in direct speech) that was how his guest had desired it, and a good host never forgets.

But at this stage of his patchwork existence, Robert found it more difficult to do without money than during all the years when he had wanted it only for food, and when food instead of money would have done as well. Now he *had* food, gourmet's food, connoisseur's drink; and only money would have satisfied his less tangible craving for freedom; less tangible, and now more precious. In the old salty days he had been often enough happy while hungry; now he was never hungry; yet a queer discomfort was always getting in the way of careless happiness.

Had he forfeited his easy-going, by coming to stay with Marcus so as to delay the evil of going to work? He had kept to the letter of a certain vow not to cash in on his birthright, but tampered perhaps with the spirit; and easy-going was having its revenge.

Besides, on the side of gay banditry, he missed the fun he used to have during his early months in Edinburgh, planning his dangerous calls on those who might be "interested", gambling on the results, doubling and twisting to save himself by his wits when the interview suddenly took an unforeseen turn against him. Impudence was an asset then; but here at the Château it rather occurred to him, while retaining his outward swagger, that he had better not be too impudent with Marcus Powell; "He's my host," thought Robert with a touch of desperation, seeking to justify fear by reasons of formal courtesy learnt long ago from Mrs. Merrill; fear which sprang from the experience of moving about in a perpetual spotlight for the edification of a stage-manager far more astute than himself.

For Robert was just beginning to suffer from the shadeless

torment of being too well understood, and understood without kindness. It felt like having no eyelashes.

Marcus was delighted to see him getting so restless. How soon, he wondered, would honesty fail again?

*   *   *

Summer went on. The heat did not disturb either of them; Marcus was used to a semi-tropical climate; and Robert throve on it. The dim rooms were cooled by the whirr of fans; fountains splashed in the garden so near the lapping of the tideless sea that their tinkle seemed as faintly superfluous as the swimming-pool coveted by Brenda and her set; the men at the Château wore less and less, till in their immunity from any outside gaze, they went practically naked. The white wine was delicately chilled, and ice clinked in the cocktails; the meals tasted like a chef's dream of what another no less sophisticated Cordon Bleu might cook for him in Paradise. No one did anything in the least strenuous except the staff of elderly Italian servants, and they only when well out of sight of *i signori*. Robert, of course, was one of the *signori*; one of the lords who while his moment lasted, had inherited the earth. Marcus had let fall to Amadeo in the most natural manner, that "il Signor Roberto" was an Englishman of anonymous rank and title; and—"by the way, I forgot to mention it before" —the name in which letters, telegrams and 'phone calls might be expected, was Faulconbridge.

The letters, telegrams and 'phone calls were not overwhelming in their number, but the Hon. Brenda Dale-Carrington lent a little weight to the idea by always asking for Robert by that name. So from il Signor Roberto of the first few days, he merged into Milor' Falcone; as near as they could get it. Robert scowled heavily every time he was thus addressed, even though he did not know what it meant.

—Until Brenda told him.

Told him, and precipitated a crisis. Told him in a mood of sweet revenge, because he did not respond to her wooing. This had very rarely happened to Brenda, so why should

[243]

the snubbing have come from Robert of all people? a nobody, or at best, a very strange sort of somebody, his background revealed to her by a fascinating series of glimpses. That Robert, therefore, should have the insolence to make her feel she had no attraction for him whatsoever, was a humiliation Brenda could hardly be expected to accept with meekness. Making the swimming-pool (and the performing seal) her ostensible excuses for preferring the Château to her own home, she was for ever coming over, going through what Marcus recognized with amusement as her whole bag of tricks; a formidable range; now plaguing Robert, now soft and seductive, now mysterious or wistful or forlorn or provocative, a grand lady or a little girl. . . . Surely, considering the very superior fabric in texture and gloss of the coat she was trailing in the sun to dazzle a tramp, it was highly peculiar that the tramp should remain undazzled.

To Robert she was no more than a skirt; and not even a skirt he wanted, or probably he would have seen to the matter in the first half-hour they were left alone. Marcus often did leave them alone. But when they were a trio, he and Brenda would have a picnic of literary allusion, and mostly at Robert's expense; though to do them justice, they could not altogether help themselves—for they had been brought up on books; whereas Robert's one great bout of reading since coming to Scotland had been somewhat circumscribed in author and subject.

Once when they were lazing on the terrace and Brenda was thinking crossly that Robert grew handsomer every day, she asked Marcus whether he were going to continue for an indefinite time his rôle of Shakespearean Lord to the tinker Christopher Sly? of Caliph Haroun al Raschid to a needy Abou Hassan?

But because the key was missing to the context of these characters who seemed so familiar to Brenda and Marcus, Robert had to let the banter pass to and fro across him; for by some chance when the three were together he always seemed unenjoyably placed between them. He could not help noticing that Brenda and Marcus were deriving exquisite enjoyment from these examples of high life having some sort of complicated joke at the expense of low life; and that the exquisite enjoyment was pointed at him.

"You're in a classic tradition, Marcus," laughed Brenda; "*your* Abou Hassan, *your* Christopher Sly, was also brought into sumptuous surroundings while he was drunk or asleep, and—"

"No, to be fair, he was neither; were you, Robert?"

"When?" Robert tried to keep his tone light and free from exasperation; "I've been drunk and asleep often enough."

But they preferred to tease without enlightening him, and Brenda went on: "I ought to have been here for the Arabian Nights scene, when Abou Hassan awoke to find bevies of slaves and dancing-girls and beautiful concubines provided for him, with no idea how this ravishing phantasmagoria had come to pass."

"Yes, you came in late on your cue, Cluster of Pearls."

("Cluster of cat's-meat," muttered Robert crossly.)

They had passed on, in the same spirit of secret relish, of mustard un-tempered by cress, to another incident; and this time, neither of them relying on memory, Amadeo was summoned to fetch a Shakespeare, that Marcus could read aloud the fragment which appeared to them so mysteriously apt:

" Sirs, I will practise on this drunken man.
What think you, if he were convey'd to bed,
Wrapped in sweet clothes, rings put upon his fingers,
A most delicious banquet by his bed,
And brave attendants near him when he wakes,
Would not the beggar then forget himself ? "

"Oh, *shut* your silly mouths!" thought Robert, more and more exasperated by the maddening couple in whose company fate had thrown him by some trick. . . . Some *trick*? . . . Trick played on Christopher Sly, a poor tinker, for the whim of a passing nobleman.

But he could get no sense out of them: now it was the French king Louis XI: a fable of what he had done to a certain ragamuffin ballad-monger, François Villon, making him for a short spell Grand Constable of France. Robert sat up

with a jerk at a name he knew. He remembered Stevenson's
story called *A Lodging for the Night*, and how he had tried
to goad Miss Gibson and her puritan conscience by medium
of that swaggering, unrepentant thief; and how she had
flung him from his seat of triumph by letting him know
Stevenson's more real opinion of Villon and his like; more
real because it was in an essay, not a story. He had not
wished to recall that particular rage, but it had fastened on
to his memory like fangs:

Villon had not the courage to be poor with honesty. He whines
for our sympathy . . . or snarls at us from the dung-heap. . . . He is
pathetic enough when you meet him, but I would not go down a
dark road with him for any large lump sum. . . .

—Something of the sort. How just like these two, to
insult his presence by dragging in François Villon. But he
kept his mouth shut; there would be more rippling derision
if they knew him to be familiar with the name.

"And what happened to Villon when the King grew
tired of the fantasy?" And Marcus added thoughtfully:
"They do, you know. The real Villon had to swing for his
sins, but we needn't go in for truth and realism here— Not
yet." He smiled sweetly at Robert, who found this ill-bred
gallows chatter supremely unattractive. Then Marcus
strolled indoors, having had enough, for the moment, of
baiting an animal only half tamed.

Brenda was delighted; and even ascribed to tact in him
what had been merely boredom. Mistaking herself once
again and once too often for Cluster of Pearls, she gave
Robert to understand that if he chose to invite her to the
cool shade of his deserted pavilion, now, while the sun
blazed from a Mediterranean sky, she was his for the asking.
Robert, his voice slouching offensively from lack of eagerness, replied with an equivalent of: "Later on, perhaps,"
or "Some other day, if I'm not too busy."

Snub direct. Worse, a blow in the face.

Suffering from the ignominy of being so cavalierly treated
by a nameless beggar-man, she vowed nevertheless he should
not have the satisfaction of seeing it, the dirty swine; so she

puzzled him with a laconic: "Just as you please, Faulconbridge; let's call it off till Tuesday week" . . . and began
humming the little tune of a nursery-rhyme, while she considered how she could viciously attack him where it would
hurt most.

Unluckily for Robert, he at once gave her the opportunity.

His impatience had increased over all these silly stories
they had been thrusting on him while perforce he stood
stock still, a scarecrow for anybody's old hat and coat.
Tinkers and balladmongers and—

"Who the devil *is* this Faulconbridge? And why the
hell do you both think it so damn funny every time you say
the name?"

Ah, Brenda ruminated, why indeed? "Shall we pace up
and down in yonder shady orange-grove, Robert darling,
while I do inform thee for thy better understanding?"

"Suits me," growled Robert.

She waited until they were a little way from the Château,
and her bare feet trod softly on the grass kept green by
indefatigable spraying. Then she began: "You see,
Faulconbridge was a bastard . . . too. You'll find him actually
described as such in the dramatis personae of Shakespeare's
King John, and referred to right through the text as 'the
Bastard'; they weren't squeamish in those days; and, in
fact, we're not squeamish now; but thirty or forty years
ago of course it was different; you would have to have been
kept dark, then."

But Robert had only just recognized the word. In the
society to which he had been most accustomed, the riff-raff
of America's Pacific coast, "bastard" was used frequently,
but as a term of abuse and with a drawled "a": "You
bahstard!" That was why he had failed to pick it up when
it was first presented with a short "a", during the swift
exchange of dialogue between Brenda and Marcus at the
swimming-pool nearly three months ago. "Yes, I played
the Bastard in my last term at school." But it had been an
educated pronunciation; literary, not literal. . . .

The dark colour rushed into his face. He was beyond
blood-heat, not with shame but with rage. So *that* was what

they meant, the brazen pair of them, each time they had accosted him, mocking his ignorance?

Brenda had brought him to the far end of the grassy terrace by now, where it was secluded. His "pavilion" was near at hand. . . . Not much like the darker dives of San Francisco or Sydney, but it would serve.

* * *

"To R. A. M. Stevenson, Vailima, June 17th, 1894." . . . A letter written less than six months before he died. Queer that the date and hour of his death, each time Robert thought of them, could still give him a pang, as though it need not have happened, should not have happened without his knowing, wherever he might have been. And again, as was now his habit, he did that swift subconscious calculation bringing his own age roughly to about twenty-one when this letter to Bob had been written. He had remembered seeing somewhere in the Letters a page which he had skipped several times, but which now he read with passionate interest, for it was about names, names in the family. . . .

You may be interested to hear how the family inquiries go. It is now quite certain that we are a second-rate lot, and came out of Cunningham or Clydesdale, therefore *British* folk ; so that you are Cymry on both sides, and I Cymry and Pict. We may have fought with King Arthur and known Merlin. The first of the family, Stevenson of Stevenson, was quite a great party, and dates back to the wars of Edward First. The last male heir of Stevenson of Stevenson died 1670, £220. 10s. to the bad, from drink. . . . From which of any number of dozen little families in Cunningham we should derive, God knows ! Of course, it doesn't matter a hundred years hence, an argument fatal to all human enterprise, industry or pleasure. And to me it will be a deadly disappointment if I cannot roll this stone away ! One generation might be nothing, but it is my present object of desire, and we are so near it ! There is a man in the same parish called Constantine ; if I could only trace to him, I could take you far afield by that one talisman of the strange name of Constantine. . . .

. . . I wish to trace my ancestors a thousand years, if I trace them by gallowses. It is not love, not pride, not admiration ; it is an expansion of identity intimately pleasing, and wholly uncritical ; I can expend myself in the person of an inglorious ancestor with perfect comfort; or a disgraced, if I could find one. I suppose, perhaps, it is more to me who am childless.

"*It is more to me who am childless*"— Impatiently Robert pushed away the book. What was the use? Were there not a million Roberts born every year in England and Scotland? His mother might as well have named him Tom, Dick or Harry, Edward or John, as his sole means of identification, before she died in the workhouse and left her brat without a surname, to be christene at random in a charity home. He was furious with her, as a couple of hours ago he had been furious with Brenda. *Women!* Just there to muck up a man's whole existence and then make game of the result. If only his mother had had the sense to give him a name which would at least have provided a clue, the slenderest confirmation; a name he could hitch on to something, like (for instance) Constantine.

Yet why in thunder should she have called him Constantine? From being fed up with the whole world, Robert was now fed up with himself into the bargain. Making up all that sentimental bilge; caring about it, too; caring about poppycock, inventing a whole lot of twaddle to ease a spot in his brain that burnt and smarted. . . .

"'*Of course, it doesn't matter a hundred years hence.*'"

It doesn't matter *now*. Not one solitary damn. Robert pitched the book away, stood up, stretched himself and yawned, musing untenderly on Brenda and Marcus. The latter would have been interested to note that Robert's expression was further from angelic than it had yet been since he arrived to occupy this charming room with its parquet floor and powder-blue rugs, cut off from the rest of the Château. . . . Whistling, he went into his magnificent adjoining bathroom and turned on the taps without waiting for Amadeo to come over in about an hour and do it for him, no doubt lest Milord Falcone should overtire himself.

* * *

From that day, Marcus noticed a lethal change in Robert: a swifter descent to the place where bad men go. And this,

[249]

in Marcus's language, was all to the good. Not that his guest (who had already been longer at the villa than most of his performing seals) wrapped himself in sulks and sable glooms. On the contrary, he now displayed a sort of depraved cheerfulness which, had Marcus been on the side of his moral welfare, might have aroused apprehension instead of delight. Really, in his present mood Robert would have been a boon to Satan himself.

One evening at the end of an almost tropical August, he had been cooling himself by drifting indolently in the sea; he seemed to prefer it nowadays to the swimming-pool; Marcus watched him, and by natural transition wondered why Brenda had not been down to visit them since Robert had reacted so fiercely to their dual chaffing act about Abou Hassan and Christopher Sly and François Villon? He had meant to ask Brenda how the scene had developed after he left them alone; instead, he now asked Robert, who, streaming water, had just climbed out and sat down beside him, suggesting that a drink of something less salty would not come amiss; he did not exactly say "Get it for me", nor did Marcus exactly reply with "Get it yourself, you pampered hound". Both remarks were implicit, hung in the air for an instant, and then melted away without any loss of good-humour.

"We haven't seen our Brenda lately, have we?"

"No, she hasn't been down."

"Don't you miss her?"

"Me?" And Robert added conversationally: "*That* silly bitch!"

"She was, wasn't she!"

"Hallo!" surprised. "You too? I mean, is that how you feel about her? I thought you and she were great pals."

"Pals," Marcus ruminated; "what's pals?"

"You were always slinging poetry at each other."

"Dear Robert, that's not pals. You call it 'mates' in your profession, don't you?"

"We call it lots of things," laughed Robert, who had enjoyed his bathe and was not in a touchy temper; indeed, he had not been on edge since he had drastically rid himself of Brenda and made one or two other adjustments in his outlook that left him much more comfortable than he had been all the long summer.

"Have you ever had a pal, Robert?"

Robert shook his head. Not likely he would confide in Marcus that curious sensation which had been his for a little while, of company on the road; a Scot with features not unlike his own, who had laughed at his impudent villainies and encouraged him in his imposture. . . . Rather a forlorn feeling, since this congenial spirit had deserted him. Better talk about something else: Brenda, for instance.

"She stayed away once before for a few weeks," announced Marcus carelessly; "soon after I'd first met her. And then started coming back again, pretending the swimming-pool allured her, so I never mentioned . . . a certain incident."

Robert grinned: "Sure, that's the best way." So in this one respect he and Marcus had also been "mates"; Marcus, too, had been Brenda's lover. And mighty little love about either of them, thought Robert.

Queer, how tonight he did not quite possess the theatre of his own thoughts, but let strolling players enter unbidden; it was not as though he were in a particularly sanctified state; on the contrary, very much of this world and not the next; alive to all advantages and glad of it. Soon, very soon, he intended to touch his host for quite a bit. . . .

—Suddenly Marcus noticed with a thrill that Robert had allowed his hair to grow too long.

Here at last was gratifying evidence that Hyde was well in the ascendant. He had suspected it, but welcomed such a tangible proof that the charlatan was deliberately preparing to set out again on his monstrous errands; that he had wearied of goodness, come to the end of effort. He had held temptation at arm's-length for several months; this time it was not likely that there should be any disappointing swing-back; Robert's tone was confident, his eyes twinkling and glowing in anticipation of a swift dramatic raid on the victim nearest at hand. Marcus had not quite made up his mind yet how he would respond; it would probably depend on the rogue's technique; already it was written down that the partial good of Jekyll was ultimately to be crushed and vanquished and absorbed by the whole wickedness of Hyde. Marcus found it perplexing that when Stevenson conceived and wrote his famous allegory, he should have directed the outcome to be that way round. The moral was certainly as effective, by showing the strength and horror of evil once it begins to conquer open territory; yet was it involuntary, to have presented the moral inside-out? Jekyll was too weak and composite to gain the victory; good in him was not a positive force, as evil with Hyde; good—was it not mostly maintained for the sake of its appearance among his friends, Utterson and Lanyon, and his prestige in his own sight as in theirs? Even while he was Jekyll, he was sorely tempted by the lusty pleasures of Hyde; but never did Hyde hanker after the purer airs that Jekyll breathed. Jekyll, in fact, and probably rejecting all the craft and labour spent upon him, Jekyll, if ever intended as a worth-while opponent to Hyde, was one of the writer's failures.

Why? The answer plainly lay in Robert, lounging naked on the steps beside him, smoking a cigarette and happily planning wickedness; evidence that the diabolical triumph of Hyde in the book tallied with the triumph of Hyde in the disreputable human soul. The contest had been a ding-dong affair: on the one hand, the living influence of a dead R.L.S. who had so incomparably worked out his own destiny; on the other, the strong strain of original sin in Robert, who was idle as R.L.S. had been in his youth (or as ten million others, if it should be that R.L.S. were not his progenitor, after all). But Stevenson had been saved for the side of the angels by the recognition of man's responsibility, since the Fall, to strive and toil, well or sick, to keep a family. Robert had no such saviour in his bones; and was moreover cheerfully ready to cadge, lie, rob, steal, employ every flexible trick and evasion, to dodge any encounter with honest work.

Of how much of the drama was Robert himself aware? Well, why not find out? A Machiavelli at improvisation,

Marcus consulted Robert on a problem apparently bothering a friend of his, a writer:

"I ran into him today at St. Raphael. He's set out to do a novel on that very theme—didn't I once hear you ask Abbé Ducros about it?—of two men, good and bad, shut up in one body, each struggling for ultimate mastery. He can't make up his mind on a determining last chapter: on which would better sharpen the moral, to let the good man win, or the bad?"

"It depends," Robert replied slowly. He was not looking towards Marcus, but straight out to the horizon. Though there was nothing at all striking in his comment (anyone could say "it depends") Marcus turned his head sharply to see what had happened to Robert during the silence when neither had been speaking their thoughts to the other. . . .

Robert went on quietly, even dreamily, but in the manner of one who spoke with authority: "It depends on whether this man who's writing the book is a good chap or a bad chap himself? Oh, I know he's bound to be both, but which is it deep down where he's *real*?"

"Good," answered Marcus, a little breathless at what was so far from the reaction he had expected.

"Then it doesn't matter what we may say he *should* do, he'll *have* to let the bad side win."

"The bad side? Why?"

"Don't you see, he'd know all about that fight because he'd have had it in himself. It's got to come out of oneself or one doesn't know the first thing about it; and when your trade's writing, I suppose you have to use what you pull out from inside. If the real part of him is a decent chap, he couldn't swank: 'Look, this is me, and I'm swell and the devils don't have a look in!' He'd think instead: 'I'm pretty bloody awful, and the bit of me that's good—God, you can hardly see it, it's so weak and small and mixed up with the rest. I don't much like owning up to this, even in a book that I expect nobody will read, but I've got to because it's my job to make it true; and maybe if I do own up that I'm 99 per cent. strong and bad inside me, maybe if I'm honest and show this clear enough'— Gosh, I don't know.

. . . But you couldn't be good inside, and write a book saying you *are* good inside."

Marcus stared; uttered a long low whistle; then, with an attempt to recover his ironic poise: "Metaphysical Robert!" he remarked.

Robert said nothing, too exhausted to be drawn; he felt as though virtue had gone out of him.

So for a while they sat in silence, their figures blurred by the falling blue of a Mediterranean dusk. Marcus was shaken out of his usual philosophic acceptance of the vagaries of human beings, by this wholly unforeseen burst of inspiration from Robert. Not that the actual words were eloquent; the pentecostal spirit had descended on him, but his tongue had stumbled to express his meaning. Yet the sudden illumination of a point which had often puzzled Marcus himself (when he had bothered to think of it) as to why Jekyll should have been so hopelessly inadequate either as a personality or an abstract expression of the good in man—that was amazing. Marcus did not care for Robert to know how impressed he had been; so he said aloud: "Poor Robert . . . 'the reed that grows nevermore again as a reed with the reeds on the river'."

And still Robert did not speak. Marcus was queerly uneasy.

"I'm going in again," said Robert at last, without rancour; indeed, as though he hardly knew Marcus were there. And he slid down into the water, warm as milk and only just rippled by the moonlight, as though he longed to be newly washed. . . .

Marcus lit a cigarette, and pondered.

He was convinced that the tramp had found the key to the riddle, and that Jekyll's impotence resolved itself into Stevenson's essential humility; confirmed by that obviously autobiographical confession:

Jekyll is a dreadful thing, I own; but the only thing I feel dreadful about is that damned old business of the war in the members. This time it came out; I hope it will stay in, in future.

This was no cant, but sincere self-searching that could not

[254]

allow the good within oneself to be anything but frail and
tenuous and ineffective compared with the devil's potency.
The writer could, when it came to presenting the conflict,
successfully visualize for his readers' benefit the brutality
of the Hyde in him, but he had been barely able to believe
in his own spiritual power to combat it; he could not externalize Jekyll with any conviction. . . . We should like him
less, thought Marcus, if he could.

Yet how R.L.S. would have marvelled had he known how
the good in him, the god in him, carelessly and unconsciously
displayed in the way he had felt compelled to live his life,
had smashed through the barriers of time and space; and
here in Robert, given battle to Hyde and vanquished him.

Vanquished him temporarily. Marcus sensed that Robert's
Hyde had only been thrown out during the last half-hour,
and would reappear.

Possessed— Yes, that was the answer. The man had
spoken as though he were bravely possessed.

Marcus did not believe in psychic influence nor in a future
world. Therefore he did not say to himself that Robert had
spoken with tongues not his own; but argued that it might
have been by mental legacy which only occasionally mani-
fested itself, as the physical likeness was also only occasionally true (supposing Robert really were whom he believed
himself to be); or it could be accounted for by Robert's
brain, almost virginal of education, cramming itself for a
peculiar reason, a fantastic reason, entirely with the works
of one man, and especially with his personal letters, and
getting drunk on them.

Marcus gave a little sigh of satisfaction at having settled
that. He did not care for perplexity as his companion, even
for a short time.

But now what was to be done? He had no intention of
putting up with another long period of Jekyll and nobility,
with the stained-glass atmosphere of the Château recurring
just when he had decided that his boredom was to be en-
livened by a fine exhibition of Hyde in action. So he mused
how he could bring back Hyde?

Money. Robert disliked being short of ready cash; Marcus

had noticed that the lack of it chafed him, not from greed, but because without money he could not feel free.

By the time Robert drew himself up out of the sea, apparently quite his normal self again, his body sparkling with tiny points of phosphorescence, Marcus had his little plan:

"Robert, have I ever spoken to you of Madame de Beaupré?"

"Don't think so. Has she ever been here?"

"No. She's a very old lady and rarely leaves her villa at Roquebrune. I think you ought to go over and see her."

"Me? Why? I don't want to go over and see her."

"She used to live at Hyères when her husband was alive," said Marcus, choosing his words with care and letting them out casually; "let me see, she must have been there from 1883 onwards."

"Oh?" Robert picked up Marcus's cigarette-case from beside him on the step and helped himself.

The other went on: "She's a rich old lady and very generous; gives a lot to the poor; intelligent about books, though rather simple in every worldly way; bi-lingual: French and English are exactly the same to her. Come now, Robert," with a sudden change of tone, as his companion showed no quiver of response (and few people could appear more stolid than Robert when he chose), "you know perfectly well what I'm driving at, so why pretend? Madame de Beaupré must have known Robert Louis Stevenson; known him well; in fact, now I come to think of it, I've heard her speak of him. She lived at Hyères all through the time he was at Châlet la Solitude. These personal contacts must be getting fewer and rarer with every year; and she could, I'm sure, tell you a lot about him. She might even ask you to stay with her for a few days; you'd be very comfortable. Why don't you drive over tomorrow? I won't hamper you with my presence."

Robert shook his head. He remained perfectly amiable, but said he was not fond of visiting.

"Yet you graciously consented to abide with me, didn't you?"

This shook Robert. Marcus had meant that it should; he did not care to have his suggestions meet with a rebuff, nor for Robert to withstand steadfastly the temptation to go forth and make three succulent bites of a rich and silly old lady who had known R.L.S. at Hyères.

"But you said then, when you asked me—you said it was hospitality. You said it had nothing to do with *him*."

"Yer wouldn't deceive a pore feller, would yer, Mister? Yer wouldn't be so crool 'ard, and you a toff?" Marcus burlesqued the inflexion of a much-maligned tramp whining for coppers.

Robert pitched his cigarette into the sea. "I don't think I'll go and see her, all the same," he replied; and, Marcus had to admit, not without a certain dignity.

❧ 15 ❧

Yet still Robert did not go. He remained on at the Château as Marcus's bankrupt guest; and because he knew well and clearly that this was dangerous, lingering between two regions of "ought" and "ought not", and because ratiocination had ceased to console or even to function, his temper gradually deteriorated during the weeks which followed on the devil tempting him with the rosy prospect of gradually exploiting all the rich and silly old ladies in all the villas on the Mediterranean. Amadeo, using a characteristic Italian phrase "Quello ti vuol' bene", had translated it for Milord Falcone's benefit: "that one wishes well towards you". He was not speaking of Marcus; but Robert by now had begun to identify Marcus as one who was *not* wishing well towards him.

The intensely hot weather broke early that year, before the end of October; broke into torrential rain and cutting winds. It was incredible in that Château of all perfection where none of the mechanism of comfort was visible, that for once the *chauffage centrale* should have broken down. Amadeo nearly cut his throat over what miseries *i poveri signori* had to endure during the four or five days while it was being repaired. Robert went about with a martyred expression, huddled into his velvet coat; closed any window that he found open, and shivered by the wood-fires that were quite inadequate to heat these lofty rooms and corridors with their paved or parquet floors. He found his sweetest solace in constant hot baths; the delight of plunging himself into cool water, sea or swimming-pool when the weather was hot, gave way to the equal delight of turning a tap to achieve the tingle and glow and then the delicious languor while sitting on the broad edge of the bath draped in folds of the softest towelling also warmed on the rail (for the heating system had not broken down in the guest's annexe). These were facilities that the vagabond could not endure to forgo. Following his new accursed habit of moving round with baggage, of being unable to lie quietly without fidgeting for something to read, Robert was now also a slave to water, h. & c.

So he did not go away, and he knew he should.

"Have you got a cold?" he asked Marcus one evening, darkly suspicious.

"I may have. There are unmistakable signs. Thank you for enquiring."

Robert drew his chair further away.

"Afraid of catching it, dear Robert?"

"Well, one does catch colds, doesn't one, if one has to be with someone who's got one?"

Instead of being fascinated at the sight of the ex-tramp in the process of pampering himself, Marcus, not feeling very well, enquired sarcastically what Robert would wish him to do about it? "I hate the thought of such a delicate flower exposed to infection."

"Oh, it's all right: I expect you'll stop up in your room till you're better?"

"I had not thought of doing so; but if for your precious sake you feel I might be spreading germs—"

"Keep your wool on," Robert advised him. Somewhat sententiously, he went on to relate an anecdote that he had heard in Edinburgh from sources unspecified (what a bore Our Miss Gibbs must have been, reflected Marcus with a sigh); an anecdote of how R.L.S. had been peculiarly susceptible to colds on account of his bad chest and lungs and spitting blood, and how his missus insisted that colds *could* be caught from other people who had a cold already, though all the doctors told her she was wrong and that colds could only be caught from cold weather, but she stuck to it that colds were catching and wouldn't let any of his friends with colds come near him till their colds were better so as to save

[259]

him from catching a cold, which they should have thought of, but they didn't in the way that people with colds—

"Would you mind *not* repeating that word 'cold' again," snapped Marcus, losing even an outward show of urbanity.

"All right, all right. Keep your wool on. I only said that colds—"

"And that's the second time you've told me to keep my wool on. I'm in no danger of losing my wool; but yours, dear Robert, if you'll excuse me for pointing it out, is literally in need of clipping."

"And how do you expect a fellow—" Robert flashed out, then stopped, his mind in something of a muddle. How did that mean devil expect him to get his hair cut when he had no money at all to pay for a barber's attention? On the other hand, he knew pretty well that though this had embarrassed him during the first two or three months of his stay at the Château while he was still Robert the Good, now even if he had the wherewithal, his hair would remain long and unkempt, tossed back and falling over his velvet coat-collar.

But he went on brooding over having no ready money.

*　　*　　*

On an afternoon nearly two weeks later, the weather still cold and inclement for a Southern autumn, they met in the library, both of them weak and irritable from *la grippe*, a most enervating illness. Marcus had already been downstairs for a few hours on the previous day; elaborately keeping his distance, he made many apologies for the inconvenience his infectious germ might have caused a visitor. He guessed at once from Robert's glinting eyes and manner of response that he had decided honour and decency might now go overboard. From their first encounter on the harbour at St. Tropez and ever since, Marcus had wondered what technique this professional cheapjack would choose to employ when finally he forgot his vow and openly solicited a payment in hard cash. This hour brought the reward of patience.

"See here," Robert began, belying his tough intention

[260]

by a frank and boyish manner, "feel like giving a fellow a present for his birthday?"

"What fellow, Robert? and when is his birthday?"

Still frank and boyish, Robert threw back his head and laughed. "*You* know well enough. It's my birthday today, October 27th."

"Your birthday?"

"Yes. It isn't a date I make much fuss of as a rule, but somehow just this year . . ." Robert let heartiness subside into the wistful orphan whom mummy and daddy used to load with gifts and birthday-cake and a party, but now there was no one.

Marcus sighed. "I wish you'd told me before. I really ought not to go out in this biting wind."

"Don't you go out, you haven't quite got rid of your 'flu, I can hear that. Gosh, I'm sorry."

"Sympathy is sweet," murmured Marcus.

"—And as to shops, no need to worry; I'm not proud. A hundred-franc note will meet the case."

Into his voice had crept that professional wheedling note that would turn to a whine or abuse if he were refused, as it had with the author in London. Marcus was enchanted. He had not dared hope that Robert would deliver himself so fully into the hands of the enemy.

That very morning Amadeo had privately consulted him as to certain small but mounting sums which he had laid out on behalf of Milord Falcone: should he present his little account to the latter? Twice before, he had presented accounts to Marcus for various necessities in replenishing Robert's wardrobe, and his employer paid them without comment. The major-domo's intuition had told him that Robert was not quite as other guests who had signed their names in the visitors' book of the Château; there had been no lavish tips discreetly slid into his hand; no casual requests to get this or that, and: "I'll settle with you later." The whole proceeding of Robert's stay with no luggage and no visible means of support was not as perplexing to Amadeo as it would have been were *il signore* not given to these capricious hospitalities to enliven monotony. Others of the performing-seal species had not usually been in such a condition of stark poverty; anyhow, these had been charmingly financed by their host—till their rather abrupt departures. Sometimes his "seal" visitors were only temporarily embarrassed, so that Amadeo, the soul of tact, always waited before taking the accounts to Marcus in case they should spontaneously offer to settle up for themselves. But Milord Falcone gave no signs of either expecting or receiving remittances from his own country, and indeed, seemed to take it for granted that his changes of shirt, socks, pyjamas, handkerchiefs and so forth appeared in the pavilion as part of the mechanism of the Château, perhaps his host's second-best (only Marcus's second-best were the natural perquisites of Giuseppe's unemployable but dandified younger brother). Therefore it was better that Milord Falcone's wardrobe should be bought and paid for. It was probable that Milord had not quite understood the fine shades of what was natural outlay from the Château household, and what custom and etiquette decreed should be paid for by the visitor himself. The only cash he had deliberately borrowed from Amadeo (and that not recently) had been trifling moneys to have his hair cut.

Amadeo had had no doubt but that Marcus would immediately settle this third little account; to his bewilderment and almost horror, *il signore* had behaved as though influenza were rendering him obtuse, and instructed him to take it to Robert for settlement.

Marcus's pleasure in what had transpired was sharpened by having lately grown to dislike Robert with all his heart.

"A hundred francs? You can't really suppose I'd insult you by recognizing your birthday in such a crude fashion? Don't you remember how you snubbed me when we first met at St. Tropez and I was tactless enough to suggest a loan ?"

Robert barely suppressed a blasphemous word.

"No, no, my dear fellow. I realized then that you were sensitive on this point and respected you for it; I've respected you ever since. We'll find something to please you in the Château," added Marcus, as though struck by an idea bright enough to satisfy both of them. He rose and went over to his locked bookcases, where the autographed copies and the rare and first editions were kept. And for the second time that morning, Robert was reminded of Miss Gibson. The first time had been the present situation reversed, when she had playfully asked him the date of his birthday so that she might send him to have his photograph taken. Strange how certain unpleasant moments cropped up again and again, with twists and differences: The author in London had offered him a present instead of money, but Robert's anger had been when the strip of native bark was withdrawn and a quid hastily substituted; then, in his absurd frame of mind, the gift seemed desirable, and the money of no importance; but absurdity had to stop somewhere; it was going to stop here and now, with Marcus coming towards him benignly smiling and holding out a book:

"I wouldn't give this to everybody, but *you* have special claims. Many, many happy returns, my dear Robert. You confessed once, I believe, that you had never read either *The Ebb-Tide* or *Weir of Hermiston*; in the Pentland Edition they're bound together. *The Ebb-Tide*, you know, like *The Wrecker* and *The Wrong Box*, was written in most happy collaboration with Lloyd Osbourne"—(telling Robert why this particular book had been picked out for him; clever Marcus had scented jealousy!). "I do hope, my dear fellow, that your delicacy will not again prevent you accepting it?"

Pulling out his fountain-pen, always finding all the minor accessories he needed without fumbling, a trait essentially Marcus, he inscribed it: "To my dear friend Faulconbridge"—

—And lashed Robert into a fury. He had never relished that particular morsel of wit from either Marcus or Brenda, though he might himself fluently have used Shakespeare's term descriptive of Faulconbridge, as more tender choosers say "son" or "love-child".

"—On the never-to-be-forgotten occasion of his birthday,

October—" Marcus paused. "October 27th . . . are you
sure that's the right date?"

The book was proffered, and Robert put it aside, yet even
at that moment touching it gently, not hurling it from him
as he might have done had it been by another author. And
demanded with cold insolence, as though carrying on a
conversation which had not as yet taken place:

"A hundred francs or five hundred francs, they're no good
to me, after all. I want my fare to California, and I expect
that'll be quite a bit more. This climate's better than Scotland, but it isn't hot enough; I can't run any risks; look
how it's been this last three weeks. You'll be glad to be
rid of me and— God, I'll be glad to be quit of you and your
ways; you've no right, considering who I am, to make me
a laughing-stock by sending your bloody ervants to ask me
for cash."

Robert had been shocked as well as amazed that morning,
when Amadeo, using all possible courtesy, had obeyed Marcus,
outraging what was done in the best country-house circles.
When he had bluntly questioned the butler why just these
items and not others had to be paid for, Amadeo assured
him that the others *had* been paid for at stated intervals by
il Signore Powell, but this time—

Robert had some trouble in extracting just what had
transpired . . . this time.

"Playing your filthy cat-and-mouse games with me! Hand
over my fare to California— It's the least you can do!"

Marcus scrutinized him with mellow satisfaction: Hyde
true to Hyde at last.

He picked out another book: "A few choice extracts from
Beggars by Robert Louis Stevenson. Listen, Robert:

. . . the rant and cant of the staled beggar stirs in us a shudder of
disgust. . . . The beggar lives by his knowledge of the average man.
He knows what he is about. . . . This trade can scarce be called an
imposition ; it has been so blown upon with exposures ; it flaunts
its fraudulence so nakedly. . . . Are there, then, we may be asked,
no genuine beggars ? And the answer is, Not one. My old soldier
was a humbug like the rest ; his ragged boots were, in the stage
phrase, properties. . . ."

Marcus's peculiar inflexion of the phrases: "*it flaunts its*

[264]

fraudulence so nakedly . . . his ragged boots were, in the stage phrase, properties" told Robert that more was behind this brilliant selection than even the desire to see him wince at Stevenson's opinion of beggars in general.

"How long have you known?" roughly.

"Known? Known what?"

"That I used to—"

"—Make up a plausible story of lies and go round cashing in on it? Surely, Robert, even you can't have supposed that in me you had met the perfect dupe? I was aware even before I went to look for you at St. Tropez that you were an unsuccessful impostor."

Robert's mind raced backwards over events. "Then . . . when you told me to go and see that old lady who'd lived along the coast at the same time as he'd lived there—"

"I was interested when you refused to go. What was your motive for such saintly behaviour? A hope of proving yourself an honest son of an honest man? And what good would that do you, when all's said and done? You haven't a hope of swinging yourself clear of the racket; you may struggle, your eyes fixed on nobler things, but presently and over and over again, you'll flounder back into the morass. *Foredoomed*, Robert, that's the word. Till at last you'll stop plaguing yourself about fathers, and make yourself at home in the trough among other swine not so full of cant about saving their immortal souls. That is, unless meanwhile you've lost confidence in your not highly original way of earning a livelihood? How terrible—you may now have to exist by hard work. For I'm not going to keep you any longer as an embodiment of love-in-idleness; you're not amusing enough."

Robert was no match for such an opponent. Every word that Marcus said undermined his resolution. Yet making a tremendous effort to testify, he declared defiantly that during the weeks after he had made up his mind to give up swindling and to work like other men, he was happier than he had ever been before or since.

"Yes, Robert, because you were doing no more than *think* about work; the life contemplative, one might say.

[265]

Actually to do it and go on doing it, will prove a rather more difficult matter. And you're not as tough as you were, are you? One gets out of the way of chopping wood."

Boasting like mad, Robert reeled off a list of all his past trades, ending with a statement which he threw in for colour and weight: "And what's more, I helped build the Panama Canal."

"It's so modest of you to call it 'helped', when you might simply have said 'I built the Panama Canal'."

Robert could brag no more; his power to resist was being rapidly drained away; inwardly (as Marcus well knew) he was not feeling too bold at the prospect of physical work—of building canals single-handed or otherwise; he was still terribly weak and shaky from his bout of influenza.

So what was he to do, except—

"I'm afraid it's too late for that." Again showing demoniac inspiration in divining the ignoble expedient which had sprung into Robert's mind, Marcus rang the bell and told Amadeo to have the car brought round; Armando the chauffeur was also down with influenza, but he would drive it himself.

"Is it wise, Signore?"

"Oh yes, I shall be all right. I'm only going as far as Roquebrune." Although he was talking to Amadeo, the significance of the direction was meant for Robert.

"Roquebrune" with all its implications was enough. Robert knew that he would not be given another chance to call on the old lady who had lived at Hyères in 1883 and was so generous and so silly and so interested in authors. And Marcus would not only warn her, but every possible victim along the coast.

Bolting from honest work? but his bolt-holes were being stopped. Stripped of all independence, all defiance, Robert was seized by a childlike fit of panic at being left alone in the villa to think . . . to think of all Marcus had been saying to him.

"Take me with you," he pleaded. "I won't ask her for money, I swear I won't. I won't ask for anything, but maybe she'd tell me things she remembered about—"

Marcus laughed in his face. "Tell you about a man who can have no concern with you? Stop pretending. Until you pestered me for money, you might possibly have been his son. . . . But on form, even you yourself can hardly believe that, now."

*　　*　　*

Whizzing along the bends of the Corniche Road, Marcus reflected that the beastly weather was just right for turning out an orphan to fend for himself in the cold cruel world. And when he warned all his friends and acquaintances not to give one single franc to this impostor, he could pretend that he himself had only just discovered the fraud practised upon his credulous good heart. It was an added pleasure to reflect that Robert had sold his warm jersey: doubtless the corduroy trousers and perhaps the velvet coat would have to go next; or would it be the shoes before the velvet coat?

But it would be a pity that Robert should get chucked out before he had read *Dr. Jekyll and Mr. Hyde.*

Marcus smiled in anticipation . . . "Yes, I'll give it to him this very evening, when I get home."

Robert drove the small car himself when he went to visit
Madame de Beaupré at Roquebrune.

He could not congratulate himself as the active cause of
Marcus being killed, admirable though that exploit would
have been. The Hispano had been smashed to bits in the
accident, and workmen were still engaged in clearing up
the débris when Robert, without a tremor of nerves or com-
punction, paused just long enough to enquire whether he
could get by, or if it were really necessary to obey the board
displayed further back ordering a détour by the upper
Corniche?

Since the first moment of awe on hearing of the catastrophe, Robert had with one bound reached the top of the
world. And even then, awe was mainly for his own stupendous luck, contrasting his present state of creamy well-being
with the condition of raw misery in which Marcus had left
him; more than raw; skinned for ever of all joyous response
to life and the day's light; humiliated, huddled, sick and
done for. Foredoomed, Marcus had called him with relish,
no notion that he was himself the one foredoomed, with less
than an hour to live when he set out on the cruel errand
intended to deprive Robert of every dishonest means of
subsistence. If he had started in a more kindly spirit
(Robert reflected) he might have been alive now.

Released as though by a miracle. It was grand to be a
favourite—he did not bother to specify of whom. During
that awful evening when he was left alone at the Château,
while Marcus sped away in his car to put Madame de
Beaupré on her guard, he had adhered desperately to the
illusion, born of the wish, that he was still a lucky person:
It was *not*, he kept on and on telling himself, it was *not* a

horribly unlucky coincidence that the very man whom he had met on the stairs in London, had spotted him down here in the South of France, so that Marcus could be warned beforehand; on the contrary, that this should have happened once and once only during the perilous masquerade which had begun nearly a year ago, was a clear proof of his marvellous good luck. Think of it, in all the time he was in Scotland, not a single disastrous encounter between his victims chancing to meet and compare notes. "Of course I'm lucky! Of course I am!" In his panic Robert kept on repeating it to ward off blacker panic. . . .

Till they rang up from the gendarmerie to inform Amadeo of what terrible thing had occurred.

The news caused a sensation; yet it revealed how painfully solitary was Marcus Powell's existence. No intimate sorrowing friends came forward to take charge; and the formal expressions and tokens of sympathy—to whom should they have been sent? Perhaps poor old Amadeo was the most upset; he wept a little as he stood holding the receiver with a shaking hand, listening to Monsieur le Commissaire officially informing him that there must be an inquest, though apparently no one was to blame: "You say your employer had been ill? Manifestly he should not have been allowed to drive, especially in the *crépuscule*." They asked the butler a few natural questions: Who was staying at the Château? Did he know the address of the nearest relatives, in France or England? If so, these must be informed at once. And the lawyer was Monsieur Caillou of Toulon? Ah, a pity, le Commissaire happened to know that he was not at his offices, but had gone to Brussels on business.

So Robert accepted and in fact encouraged the curious prevailing notion that he was now and vaguely till further notice, king of the castle, or at least lord and master of the Château. Neither knowing nor caring what might happen next, he continued to take joy in his release; a gipsy dwelling in marble halls; a merry urchin playing in a sunny garden at some bold extravagant game which, measured by his own absorption, was to last all day and for ever, immune from care for the future; for he was innocent of any aspect of legal or social procedure demanding that a mere visitor, though with no specified date of departure, should yet depart at once from a house of mourning (even discounting that your late host threw you out, as his last act on earth). When you are in the mood to feel that you have inherited the whole solar system, you are hardly likely to have meek scruples over the mere inheritance of a perfectly furnished château on the Rivvyairah and a trained staff of servants to carry out all your whims. The staff, indeed, though puzzled by the length of Robert's stay (not even the most eccentric of Monsieur's visitors had remained as long) were also inclined to believe Milord Falcone's own valuation of himself as a sort of missing heir; inclined, that is, to believe in it for the present, and for lack of anyone with the authority to contradict. When the uncle should arrive, *lo zio del signore*, then doubtless matters would arrange themselves differently. Meanwhile, Italians having an indolent capacity for living from day to day, they found it less strenuous to believe than to clarify and express their doubts; and behaved quite respectfully. Certainly there was a faint memory that Milord Falcone's original appearance had been unconventional; a wild legend which had been spread by la Bianca, of a man in rags, limping, dirty and without luggage, who was shepherded by *il signore* into the pavilion, to emerge clean and fair, and clad in *il signore's* white flannels. And a further sense of perplexity and botherment spread over the ensuing weeks, that Milord's wardrobe, his lack of luggage and correspondence, was not quite what it should be. *Mà!* a monosyllable to cover all, when accompanied by a characteristic shrug, an inflexion expressive of race philosophy which lay in letting the eccentric, sentimental English be as eccentric as they pleased without interference or protest from the practical realism of the South.

Moreover, and apart from all that, Robert had achieved popularity, especially in his present mood; he was wicked but charming, and his wickedness did not affect the staff at the Château.

As a schoolboy who has been let off from punishment is

inclined to believe his holiday will continue indefinitely, Robert wondered, when he woke from an excellent and dreamless night after the funeral, what fun he could have? Where begin an active career on what Marcus would not have sanctioned? The answer came promptly: visit Madame de Beaupré. You never know, the old lady might be the next to die, before Robert had had a chance to cash in; damn it, he was comfortable enough, but he still lacked ready money; Marcus had been too inconsiderate to leave behind him a blank signed cheque. Besides, had it not been Marcus himself who had first tempted him to go along the coast and pay a call on Madame de Beaupré.

Some silly scruples, he could hardly remember their origin, had interposed at the time to prevent him from falling in with this congenial suggestion. And then before you knew where you were, Marcus had turned sour on it.

And who looks a fool now? Marcus, whose clumsy driving was still congesting the road to Roquebrune with a wrecked motor-car? Or Robert, impenitent and debonair?

He laughs best who is alive to laugh. Driving a shade more carefully as he passed the fatal spot, Robert broke into heartless, ribald song, as was his habit when happy; by association, he sang a chorus of the minstrel troupe whom he had driven all over the Middle-West and Western States of America, many years ago. Funny, he had not sat at the wheel of a car since then.

He quenched his monstrous gaiety as, after enquiring the way, he ran up from the coast towards Madame de Beaupré's villa a little way inland at Roquebrune; and put on a decorous air more in keeping with his semi-mourning garments; he looked taller and leaner than ever in the borrowed black trousers and black tie produced by Amadeo for the funeral the day before; his black velvet coat appeared somewhat threadbare and shiny where the brilliant autumn sunshine fell on it.

"A close friend of the late Mr. Marcus Powell." That was how he had himself announced; adding that he had a message he could only deliver personally. So of course the old lady consented to see him. Approaching her with his subdued air shaded into sorrow as he brought forth Marcus's name, Robert took care not to notice her near-sighted scrutiny of his face . . . and then the long troubled look through her lorgnons, as though to make sure that she really saw what she fancied she had seen: "Mon Dieu, c'est un revenant!" she murmured, dropping her lorgnons and crossing herself in a state of considerable agitation. Robert did not know that "revenant" meant a ghost, a man who has come back again, but he was already convinced that here he had struck a full rich gush of oil. Gravely he explained that Marcus's last wish had been to bring him, Robert, to see her; and how he had refused.

"But why, mon ami?" she quavered. "You would have been sure of a good welcome."

He hesitated; then broke in with his strong suit: impulsive candour, warranted especially successful with all those over eighty:

"Yes, that was just why. *Please* understand, I was afraid you might think, when you saw me . . . that I wanted you to give me . . . a present. If I hadn't looked the way I do . . . but a man can't help his face; and anyhow," he lifted his head proudly, "I reckon I wouldn't have it different."

("And that's a fact," he added under his breath.)

There had been little need to plead for understanding; Madame de Beaupré, though equally senile in two languages, could still be enchanted by such motives of purest delicacy, and Robert was able to continue his tale with the ease of sliding down banisters.

Directly he heard of the tragedy, how he blamed himself for refusing his friend's last wish! He felt that the best reparation would be to carry it out belatedly. So here he was, a penitent seeking pardon. And moreover, it struck him she would be glad to hear that Marcus was thinking of her and on his way to see her when he met his untimely death. At which Madame de Beaupré produced a lace-edged handkerchief; and Robert, sighing heavily, walked over to the window to conquer his emotion. And stood looking out, till she should oblige him with his next cue.

He was left to stand looking out for so long that he began

to wonder on what pretext he would ever be able to turn round again, and was finally compelled to do so of his own accord. Another burst of boyish impetuosity which very old ladies cannot resist, landed him straight on the significant subject. In his callous frame of mind, which he chose to regard, oddly, as being in his "right mind", it only interested him for its potential gain, and not in the least for itself. He was, however, pleased to find that in spite of his recent six months' sojourn in the rarefied atmosphere of truth, he had not forgotten the knack, or more grandly speaking, the technique of his real vocation:

"You used to live at Ee-air, didn't you?" carefully remembering Marcus's pronunciation of a place which while he had only seen it as a heading to some of the Letters, he had pronounced "High Ears". "Can you, w-w-will you"—(enter an artistic stammer)—"I mean, would you m-m-mind telling me anything you can remember . . . about him?"

Bashfulness was the ticket and no need for names; those glasses stuck up on a gold stick had done their job all right.

And Madame de Beaupré began to ramble; she rambled to and fro; and she rambled all round Hyères and the 1880's ; and Robert hung on her words, cursing the ancient parrot for not being a more direct raconteuse. But she did ramble to Châlet la Solitude in due course, and warming up, scooped out a really quite vivid recollection of R.L.S. receiving a hundred guineas from his publisher for *Treasure Island*; and how, unspoilt, he had exulted in such a huge sum and rushed about telling everyone, inviting them to exult with him. Translating freely into her own idiom:

"'You cannot for yourself know how ashamed I have often felt,' he confided in me, for I was *sympatique*, *vous savez*; 'a big strong man, to lie in bed not able to work and earn enough to keep my wife and family. Now I need not write for help to my father; that above all is why I rejoice. I could sing and whistle all day but it would not be *comme il faut*.'

"That was his little joke," Madame de Beaupré explained. "*Il était si gentil*, *bon comme du pain*, and he did not care ever for what was *comme il faut*. And even so, French society received him and loved him and for his sake wished that the hundred louis d'ors could have been a thousand. Ah, he called himself a big strong man, but that was from his valiant heart; his body was that of a suffering child who, seeing his comrades more active, will attempt too much and then have to lie there broken."

The spurt of memory diffused itself again into vague sentimentalities and much wiping of the dim old eyes; but it had lasted long enough to give Robert the desired cue. She could not have picked on a better anecdote from his point of view, than the one which related itself to a reluctance to accept gold without working for it.

Pride stood nobly upright in him like a wheat-field in August, as he said:

"So *he* knew all about it. . . . I thought he must. All about wanting to work, and hoping and thinking you were strong enough, and then that damned cough again"— He recollected with dismay that he had forgotten to cough since he had entered the room; and though, goodness knows, he had been at it good and hard, and often racked his body to pieces during his attack of 'flu and ever since, yet just this once when it might have been useful, that damned ungrateful symptom had gone away and buried itself. But Robert was too clever to start coughing now merely because he had mentioned it. His effects were more subtle than they used to be while he was a beginner. Perhaps Marcus had taught him something, after all. So he went on, only with increasing shortness of breath:

"He hated having to write to *his* father. I think I could have brought myself to write to mine . . . if I'd had a chance. *He* would have understood right enough that it's only because I've been ill again. You can't help running up debts of honour when you're always ill; but to ask s-s-strangers for money, or accept it when they almost cram it into your p-p-pocket"—Robert made a gesture indicating the impossibility for one of his nature to accept even six-pence and even when "crammed into his p-p-pocket" . . .

And stood erect and silent, waiting for developments.

But he had not reckoned with Madame de Beaupré being

so very very old. He was forced to make it all considerably plainer than that, especially as to the "debts of honour". Though a deadly destroyer of good fiction while alive, Marcus was a live and useful asset to such fiction now he was dead. Robert confessed under pressure (having himself to supply the pressure that should have come from Madame de Beaupré) that his friend Marcus had *insisted* on giving him all sorts of presents not yet paid for, letting him run up heavy accounts ("Don't worry your head about them, Robert; this is my concern, not yours"). And now he was dead—(Robert bowed his head; then once more became a wheat-field, upright before the reaping)—he was not going to allow any lawyer to pay on his behalf what he had even been reluctant to accept from Marcus.

Yet what was he to do? Work, of course; work like hell; work till every sou was paid back, work till his lungs burst. . . . And here the good old cough came in of its own accord, in consequence of so much pent-up emotion.

Madame de Beaupré had at last got the idea; she could hardly have failed to do so; but Robert naturally presented a scene of stifled agony before he could bring himself to accept her really handsome offer, cash down and no tiresome visits to French banks. Even then, it was necessary for his benefactress to receive his solemn assurances that this was a loan which he would pay back when he was strong enough; and that only from an old poll-parrot who had personally known his father and was succouring him for his father's sake, only from her could he bear such generosity. Had he guessed beforehand, he said, that she would tell him the one story to break down his sturdy independence— ("Marcus always called it my damned obstinacy, but I believe, you know," with a rueful smile, "that he liked me better for it")—had he guessed, wild horses would not have brought him to Roquebrune. No, *Sir*.

While Robert was paying his call, several callers had been to the Château: Interviewers who had decently waited until the funeral was over before they came along to get their story on the Marcus Powell Library, tolerably well-known in the South of France. The sensational manner of his death had already been covered by local reporters; and the sober little band who now awaited the return of Milord Falcone had a literary and less flamboyant outlook. They were all French except two; one an English journalist on holiday; the other a cosmopolitan hybrid, more than half American, who had rented a villa at St. Raphael while he did a series of articles on behalf of a wealthy impresario hoping to work up a rival casino further along the coast. These, therefore, were doing the Powell stunt as a sideline, and hoped drama might emerge to justify their interest. The French journalists, however, really did know about rare editions, and principally desired information as to what was to become of these? were they, *par exemple*, bequeathed to the nation? And if so, which nation?

Forewarned by Amadeo, Robert found them prowling about the library. And without exactly saying that he hoped his butler had seen to it that they were given a courteous welcome and proper refreshment, he did somehow create an impression in his very first speech that here was the man who had been nearest to Marcus during his lifetime, and who certainly was now lord of the Château, if not of the Collection. Had the American only known it, Robert was certainly a satisfactory answer to his desire that something striking and dramatic might turn up from which a good story could be made.

He told them modestly that a rolling stone like himself— journalists like rolling stones, and the announcement made him instantly popular—a rolling stone like himself knew very little of the inside of precious volumes; and that the deep friendship between him and Mr. Powell had existed on a more human basis. Or words to that effect.

No, the Will had not yet been read; they were waiting for the Toulon lawyer to return from Brussels. No, he was afraid he could not produce the keys of the locked book-cases where the best stuff was kept, for he had begged Monsieur le Préfet to take them provisionally, to relieve him, Robert, of a grave responsibility.

Actually, he had asked Amadeo where Marcus kept the

keys "of everything"? and the Prefecture had been the major-domo's idea, to free himself of a worrying burden till *Il Colonello Inglese* should arrive. Robert did not much mind. He was perfectly comfortable without any keys, and at present asked for no more. When it came to cash, he preferred to get it in his own way; and that way was not to steal—except by the careless code of ratiocination.

The press departed, thanking Milord Falcone for his charming treatment, and depositing their addresses, if he would further put himself out and let them know when the formalities permitted them to come again and inspect the treasures now locked away? Robert promised. The English journalist was a little puzzled by the title, but the episode was not important enough for him to pay it any further attention while he was not professionally on the job.

Robert went to bed early, tired from unaccustomed driving, and from having mopped up a quantity of limelight, and the equivalent of £20.

On the following day Colonel Powell arrived to take charge of his nephew's affairs; and it was no use pretending that he found the presence of Robert necessary either to his comfort or entertainment; which was ungrateful of the Colonel, for Robert did his best to make him feel at home.

At once Amadeo was called aside to answer various testy questions: "Look here, who *is* this fellow? He walks about as if the whole damn place belonged to him. How long has he been here? Where did my nephew pick him up, d'you know? Who said he was a lord? Falconey? Fallconi? That's not an English title; how does he spell it?" Amadeo did not know how Robert did or did not spell it; and neither he nor the Colonel thought of looking it up in *King John*. However, Amadeo was able to state that it had been his employer, not Robert, who had told him the name; he was afraid, humbly, that "Falcone" was not quite right; it had been a foreign name and impossible to pronounce; that is, foreign to him, not to *il Colonello* to whom no spelling could be difficult.

"Well, but good lord," the Colonel barked, not at all placated by the compliment, "you must have seen it on his letters? No good my asking him straight out; I'll get a pack of lies. I know that sort of fellow; couldn't tell the truth if he tried." He really was too improbably representative of the orthodox retired officer of the old British regular army, with his neat figure, clipped white moustache, precise clothes, and a neck which turned pink at the nape when stirred to any emotion; not that he had a long list of emotions that could be stirred; chief of these were embarrassment and indignation; and indignation prevailed on hearing that this wayward and unidentified Milord had been over six months at the Château without receiving a single letter to settle even the elementary matter of how he spelt his name.

"If you ask me, he's nothing but a fraud, and I shouldn't be surprised, a thief into the bargain. Are those his own clothes he's wearing?"

Amadeo shook his head, doubtful what to reveal and what not to reveal. He evaded further barking by referring the Colonel to la Signora Dale-Carrington who at one time had been often in the company of Milord Falcone, and was also an old friend of *il povero signore*. So the Colonel marched off to Brenda's villa.

He returned rabid. And braced for immediate action.

"You'll be off at once, my man, and thank your lucky stars if you escape police prosecution."

"If that's what you think of me," said Robert, going terribly grand, "then I'm not stopping another minute. What's more, I'm not going in these clothes. They're not mine," taking the wind out of the Colonel's sails. "My own were taken away from me, and I'll have 'em back before I budge. I happen to know they're hidden somewhere in the shatto."

The Colonel gasped. He could not compete with such impudence.

"Let me tell you," Robert went on, "I'm not the sort of chap who enjoys wearing another chap's clothes, so you'd better get busy, because these are coming off here and now."

And he began to take them off there and then.

[278]

Aware that Robert had a right to claim his property, the Colonel decided it had better be found and restored as soon as possible, and so put an end to this disgraceful scene. Amadeo and Giuseppe were hastily summoned; and Robert, stripped and wholly unashamed in his nakedness, lounged against the *chauffage* on the landing, not joining in the quest himself, content to mock their failures and general inefficiencies.

Believing little else that emanated from this insolent swashbuckler, the Colonel *did* believe his statement that the clothes were hidden somewhere in the place and that they were not hunting for a chimera. And at last they were discovered, as Marcus had bundled them up in the pillow-case from the pavilion and thrown the bundle to the bottom of a cupboard not often used, in a recess of the hall. Gingerly wrapping his handkerchief twice round his hand to escape contamination, the Colonel fished out the ragged, greasy trousers, the shirt dingy and patched, the filthy old overcoat, and dropped them quickly on the mosaic floor: next came a hat, a wonderful hat, and a pair of boots still caked with ancient mud, flapping despondently where the live toes would presently protrude. Handling these recovered treasures as though they were new from Savile Row, Robert pulled on the boots, the shirt, and the trousers; and with a gesture of derision towards the Colonel, picked up his over- coat and knapsack which Amadeo had brought along from the pavilion, and began tô swagger off.

"Oh, no, you don't!" shouted Colonel Powell, suddenly noticing the bulging knapsack. "Just you wait a moment, my fine fellow. If those are your own clothes you've got on, and just what I expected they would be, what have you got hidden away in there? Stolen stuff—eh?" And with Giuseppe to help him, disregarding Robert's loud assertions that his knapsack contained only what he had brought with him and what he bloody well intended to carry away, they went through the contents of his pack.

A shabby velvet coat—("I'll put that on"); corduroy trousers . . . the Colonel growled a little, but passed both these articles, for though not bad, they had hardly the appearance of having ever belonged to Marcus. He was more than sure of a vile pair of boots which followed, and as his growing preoccupation was to get rid of Robert, he raised no question about the coat and trousers. But then came several books, and the Colonel really was startled; he had hardly expected books, and immediately supposed Robert had somehow managed to get at the Collection and that these must be stolen volumes. Silently suffering from this slur cast on his spotless character, Robert opened the volume of *The Ebb-Tide* and pointed to the inscription: "To my dear friend Faulconbridge . . ."

"Faulconbridge?" the Colonel repeated, puzzled and somewhat quenched by the evidence indisputably in Marcus's handwriting.

"My property," said Robert. "So what about an apology?"

"I'll see you in hell first." The Colonel picked up a copy in faded peacock-blue and gold, of *A Child's Garden of Verses*.

"That's my own as well." And indeed, Robert believed by now that it was.

"So you say. Don't know much about these things, but— Hey! this is a what-d'you-call-it? a signed edition. I shouldn't be surprised if it was worth a lot of money. Don't tell me *this* doesn't come out of my nephew's Collection."

But Robert did tell him. And for a short while they shouted threats at each other without getting much further . . . till Amadeo diffidently suggested that the matter be referred to the catalogue in which he knew *il signore* very carefully entered all the valuable books in his possession. He brought along the catalogue, and there was one staggering moment in which *A Child's Garden of Verses* by Robert Louis Stevenson did appear listed as a first edition. The Colonel lifted his head and took off his glasses to glare triumphantly at Robert.

"Go on, read what more he says about it," for Robert could see over the Colonel's shoulder that details were appended for the benefit of experts, and was wickedly confident that these details of Marcus's copy would not be likely to contain a description of the details of Miss Gibson's copy; the autograph, for instance.

A moment later he had the satisfaction of seeing the poor Colonel's face fall heavily.

How just like his cynical nephew, who could never be relied on to help when most needed, now and once more to fail his family by seeming even after his death to be backing up the word of a ruffian, first by the testimonial to Faulcon-bridge, mentioning him specifically as a "dear friend" and then by making it quite clear in the catalogue that this same dear friend had *not* pinched one of his treasures.

"And if you care to trot along and look in the library," laughed the ruffian, now definitely no longer Milord Falcone, or Lord anything-else, "I can show you through the glass the back of that copy which looks just like mine." He slightly emphasized the possessive pronoun. "Marcus wouldn't have *two* copies, would he, and not put the auto-graphed one in his catalogue?"

"Get out," bellowed Colonel Powell.

Robert put on his horrible hat for the express purpose of sweeping it off with a low bow towards the Colonel, and a piece of advice to keep his wool on. He remembered the effect that same remark had had on Marcus, and hoped it was in the family to be exasperated by the suggestion. Then he grinned at Amadeo; and jaunty and uncrushed, departed from a residence where, he declared, he had been well looked after and free from care, so that he would kindly overlook the high-handed treatment of the last half-hour.

It was perhaps Robert's luck again that the discovery of *The Ebb-Tide* and *A Child's Garden of Verses* had kept Colonel Powell so busily employed that he had not reached quite to the bottom of the knapsack, where a battered tin tobacco-box contained evidence that Madame de Beaupré was a rich and sentimental old poll-parrot; together with a more perplexing testimonial (or the reverse) to Robert's identity: a crumpled illustration from a book, showing a man with long hair, gaunt face, and brilliant dark eyes that with a sidelong smile mocked at the whole world.

[281]

The Colonel's unjust slanders, his reiteration of the word "valuable" in connection with that first edition of *A Child's Garden of Verses*, gave Robert the idea of using his own copy to further advantage. He had quite forgotten this asset; so a blessing on the Colonel, dear old fellow.

For Robert was firm in his intention not to let himself sink back into that easy slouch through life in a state of perpetual insolvency, which had contented him for so many years; working where there was no help for it; dropping work at the first chance; scraping along somehow; tramping; cadging bread and meat, or doing without; letting himself be adopted and educated till restlessness cut short those domestic interludes. Looking back on all these years, it seemed to him now that he had cheated himself. He would do so no longer. As for that preposterous impulse towards righteousness last spring in Provence, when he had voluntarily renounced a really paying proposition, to lie instead under the olives and read and dream and see his small store of capital dwindle to nothing while he tried out what it felt to be an honest man—Robert failed to recognize himself in such an utter fool.

But now, while superficially a picturesque gipsy laughing at the turn of fortune's wheel and all the rest of it, his spirit would not answer to that old stale song of the vagabond; it had hardened into granite determination not to be any longer swindled out of his birthright, true or false; it was for him to dictate what spoil he would extort from the world, and by what methods; for him and no one else. He knew what apostasy was in his heart . . . directly he slipped off Marcus's clothes and stood naked on the marble staircase, disdaining to retain what belonged to the Château; proudly insisting that Marcus's uncle should hunt for the wretched pauper odds and ends of raiment that let the rain soak in and the icy gales bite his wincing flesh. For in a wicked joyful flash it had come to him: *he would be needing those clothes again.* Half-way to Gehenna might as well be the whole way, and he had no more to lose. In his headlong dive from grace, he bitterly hated Marcus as its origin. Hating Marcus hurt no one; but it would have been an

unendurable hurt to himself if he had owned that by compromise, twice staying on in luxury at the villa when twice
he should have left immediately, he had everlastingly forfeited . . . something of real value. But Marcus had driven
him right back over the rim of time, till he returned to being
dead and useless. And Robert was left to his desperate
loneliness; loneliness which Lucifer had known; belonging
to no one, answerable to no one; his own master again at
last.

Yet once and for a little while, he had acknowledged
authority.

Never mind that now. Forget it. And as the Colonel
fished up a bundle from the bottom of the cupboard, Robert
was able to draw on his raiment with jaunty indifference
to any man's opinion of a beggar.

("The rant and cant of the staled beggar stirs in us a
shudder of disgust. . . His ragged boots were, in the stage
phrase, 'properties.'")

To hell with regrets. Leave them to rot. Robert cocked
a snook at the Château as he paused just beyond the wrought-
iron gates, and had a look through the pack of cards which
the journalists had left on him while they still mistook him
for the missing heir. Yes, this was the winner, the ace of
trumps: Alfred H. Ingleby; Mon Repos; St. Raphael.
He scattered the rest on the dusty road.

Ingleby was only mildly astonished at Robert's present
piteous appearance when compared with the figure in
decorous well-cut mourning who had so amiably received
him and his fellow-journalists in the Château library only
the day before. His own life of ups and downs had accustomed him not to pay much heed to what a man wore, but
rather to how he bore himself; he had more respect for
self-confidence than for a well-pressed suit, and there was
nothing humble in Robert's demeanour as he produced
a small faded peacock-blue volume lettered in gold across
the back:

"Thought as you were so interested in the Marcus Powell
Collection, you might care to see this. No, make no mistake,
it's mine, not his. First edition, and, as you can see, auto-

graphed"—Robert paused for a fraction of time—"by the author."

From then onwards, it was easy as cutting soft cheese. Ingleby's nose for a story, in the newspaper sense of the word, was far more developed than his interest in bibliography, and Robert provided a swell story pent-up and only waiting for release. Yet oddly, here was one of the few encounters where he actually had to declare in plain words his romantic identity. Ingleby was tickled to death by the inscription on the title-page: "For ▮▮▮" (a name heavily blacked out). "Affectionately from Robert Louis Stevenson." But he did not then, as Robert had fully expected, stare and stare at the other's face, till at last daring to ask breathlessly: "Are you Stevenson's son?"

In fact, Ingleby had apparently been remiss in studying photographs of R.L.S.

Robert was nonplussed; it was never effective to have to supply both sides of the dialogue, as: "Do you know whom I look like? *Don't* you? Well, I do!" Nevertheless, having all his wits about him, he scrabbled again in his knapsack, and triumphantly produced and smoothed out the crumpled frontispiece of the Nerli drawing; handed it over without a word of explanation, and savoured Ingleby's loud astonishment at the likeness. . . .

"That book," Robert spoke with apparent unconcern, "that book belonged to my mother. It was all she had to leave me. Naturally I crossed out the name—well, you can see for yourself—so that nobody should be able to read it." He appeared to hesitate on the verge of confidences, having quickly made up his mind to use a still virginal variation of his usual story, one which had come to him when Miss Gibson had first shown him her copy—his copy— of the verses. For the enlightened, the dates had been all against poor sweet Kirstie's little boy of five remembering how the parcel had reached her shortly before she died, and her tremulous hands as she opened it, and her pretty flush at the sight of her name written on the fly-leaf in that handwriting. . . . But he did not think that Alf Ingleby was particularly hot on dates. All the same, you could hardly

[284]

make yourself too cheap; to tell a story as tender and as intimate, you would require pressing. So: "Reckon I'd better be going. I haven't spoken about this for years; not since . . . my mate was drowned. I told him most things. Just now I felt somehow it would be a relief, but after all, you're a stranger and— Goodbye, sir." He took back the book; and with lingering touch, as though the very handling of it meant more to him than he could ever express in words, thrust it back into his knapsack.

He had already limped to the door . . . before Ingleby stopped him.

*　　*　　*

Ingleby wanted Robert to stay with him at Mon Repos until they sailed for San Francisco, a month ahead; he had already booked their two passages on a small but comfortable cargo-boat going the whole way by sea via the Panama Canal (which Robert had helped to build). But his protégé refused; he had had enough of staying with people who, in his cynical summing-up, each only wanted him for a reason of their own: Miss Gibson for romance; Marcus for entertainment; Ingleby for profit. Here, not a doubt of it, was the Big Scoop at last. Meanwhile, and pending their departure, for Ingleby was pledged to clear up various negotiations connected with his publicity campaign in St. Raphael before he felt free to leave, Robert installed himself independently in quite an elegant little hotel on the sea-road, and averred that he would pay for himself until his cash ran out. Not that he was doing his proud-and-tall-as-a-wheatfield stuff with the publicity man; on the contrary, when they went out together he did not in the least mind being an expense to his future impresario and lecture agent. After all, he, Robert, was the benefactor in consenting to let himself be exploited at all, when the moment came.

Professional impostors usually try to leaven a fairy-tale with truth, to help it rise. But in this instance, his narrative of how he came to leave the Château so suddenly could be all sob-stuff and nearly all factual as well.

Marcus had taken him in when he was on his beam ends, said grateful Robert, but of course had not provided for him in his Will—"I hadn't expected it," said diffident Robert, his gaze limpid with sincerity. Yet the Colonel had supposed that he was a crook and a go-getter, and gave him marching orders: "So of course I could hardly walk out wearing any of the kit poor old Marcus had had to provide me with," said sensitive Robert.

He put up no objection to letting Ingleby buy him a trousseau, neat but not gaudy; though once they were in California, he was prepared to revert quite happily to whatever rags or velvet coat his spicy rôle might demand. For Ingleby, chuckling in anticipation, made no secret that these were worth a million dollars and more, in the colossal bluffing act ahead of them.

Ingleby had sent no cables to announce their impending arrival in California; for he planned to wait till he could personally display his valuable acquisition. Then and at once, having the necessary contacts, his fingers on all the ropes, there need be no delay in carrying out their plans for the Big Scoop. He boasted, not aggressively but simply as second nature, that he had the press in his pocket; lecture agents too, and publicity agents everywhere in the Western States. Of these he talked freely and intimately, sketching out the sensational production of the lean figure of a tramp in a velvet coat, with his romantic history attached for all who cared to pay and hear it; maybe in a series of intimate "talks"?—Ingleby perked an enquiring eye towards Robert to see how that went? He looked rather like a jolly plump little sand-hopper, as they walked along the beach at Saint Maxim. "A nice select audience limited to two hundred and fifty, let's say, till you get into the way of it?"

Robert was not in the least intimidated at the idea of audiences; "Reckon I just got to be myself," he remarked; and Ingleby approved of him with the heartiest "Attaboy!" of his vocabulary. Robert, he said, would have to be interviewed first, to prepare the public for the début of a rough, picturesque hobo from Scotland. . . . "And believe me, they'll fall for you like a ton of bricks." His notions of their prospects were flamboyant and optimistic; not bogus, for he believed Robert's story, backed by the evidence of the book and the photograph. But his was a single-track mind; and having stumbled on such a spectacular history, what else should be done with it except use it? Did that make sense, or did it make sense? Especially as Robert himself put up no bashful objection to being publicized; some of these human gold-mines were awful shy. Ingleby liked this bold buccaneering creature; liked him very much indeed; a real privilege to make a fortune for him and come in on a percentage. Much better than moaning round with a lot of sentimental hero-worship for a dead man's son, and no profit at all at the end of it.

Sweetest of all, in Robert's ear, were Ingleby's prophecies of what would certainly happen when they confronted William D. Gosham and his daughter. He talked for hours about William D. Gosham, a veteran Californian millionaire, patron of literature and the arts; an ardent Stevensonian; he had been pointed out to Ingleby as one of the most melancholy pundits at the unveiling of the San Francisco memorial.

"Yep, I remember," from Robert. "Sailing-ship on top of a column." He made a mental note that when they got among the more accurately informed Stevensonians such as old man Gosham and his daughter, the book with its date of publication which would not tally with his own probable age, must be suppressed by some such expedient as pretending to Alf that it was too precious to let any newspaper men get their paws on it, literally or figuratively: "You do understand, Alf? It was my mother's, and so . . . Well, just never mention that book to anyone. Go on, tell me more about the old billy-goat."

Ingleby chuckled again; "old billy-goat", as a label chosen at random for a benevolent and slightly absurd Mr. Gosham, was not inapt. He continued the biography: There was one daughter, a middle-aged spinster lady who had written and published some quite good poetry about Stevenson. Ingleby had already visualized this pair as Robert's godparents, patrons and sponsors. They would relish the showman importance, the reflected limelight; enjoy being in on things that money could not buy, quite as much, though less consciously, as being in on a spectacular renaissance. Not only, Ingleby promised enthusiastically, not only would they be likely to adopt him—Robert grinned; how many more? the Merrills, Miss Gibson, Marcus— Ah, but the rich Goshams would take him cruising to the South Seas in their famous yacht—"Unless you can afford a yacht of your own by then, my lad." Robert mused about this yacht of his own till he could almost believe he was already aboard, sailing with a favourable wind through the Golden Gates, south-westward to the vivid islands of the Pacific . . . "Honolulu, Tahiti, the Galapagos, Guayaquil"—

For since that attack of 'flu, his tubercular symptoms had come back; and joined to his naturally sanguine temperament, may have accounted for his jubilant high spirits during these last weeks on the Mediterranean coast, before they embarked for the New World. Every day on waking, he congratulated himself anew as though it were the date of his birthday: Many happy returns, Robert, many happy returns. Nor was he in the least appalled by the bigness of the Big Scoop; by the possibilities of discovery, of having his bluff called. On the contrary, he had an inflated sense of power and eloquence to a degree that had never possessed him before. He could carry it off, and if he made a mistake— that too could be bluffed. Talk about fun, this was fun with a vengeance! It did not occur to him to repeat the phrase slowly, as though each word counted: Fun . . . with a *vengeance*.

Nothing, he reflected, could now go wrong with the scheme that was presently to be the grand fulfilment of all he had most ardently longed for. *Nothing*. But then he remembered Marcus's fatal accident. That time it had played into his hands, marked him anew for luck and his name on a white stone. . . . Was he confusing luck with something religious he vaguely recollected from Mr. Merrill's numerous discourses?

" *To him that overcometh will I give to eat of the hidden manna, and will give him a white stone, and in the stone a*

[288]

*new name written which no man knoweth saving he that
receiveth it. . . ."* The text and promise lingered in his
mind where so much had sunk in the quicksands. Always
Robert visualized a heap of dullish stones, grey and brown,
among them one gleaming white, and that was luck and
that was for him, some day. As for the new name—
Arrogant now, he told himself to read it boldly and to see
that others read it too.

Yet Ingleby too might die before he had achieved what
was obviously his mission of launching Robert into fortune.
All the same, given the right data, he was quite capable
of launching himself. Take precautions, that's all. So
in view of what had happened to Marcus, Robert carefully
extracted from Ingleby all the Californian names and
addresses that he might possibly need on arrival, and noted
them down afterwards. Naturally he did not say to old
Alf: "In case you fall overboard or get bitten by a snake
or swallow a rotten oyster." . . . Instead, he put on an act
of childlike eagerness, bursting with questions, enthusiastically demanding every detail of the wonderful treat ahead
of them.

Only another five days. As the sailing date drew near,
Robert began to think about his début. Hitherto he had
relied sometimes successfully and sometimes unsuccessfully
on pure improvisation to capture at last that elusive silver
ship dancing in readiness on the harbour waves. The vision
lured him on: for the sake of a yacht to carry him to the
humming-bird archipelago of the Pacific where he could
rest in the sun and be well, he dared not risk any little
slip-up; you could not rely on *all* the Stevenson enthusiasts
in California to be as conveniently ignorant as Alf. Ingleby
had repeated many times: "It's the personal touch that gets
'em," and that being undoubtedly true, Robert thought he
had better start mugging up his part. A pity he had not
Miss Gibson's library out here for purposes of research.
Which led him to recall that he had, after all, a small
portion of the old camel's library in his knapsack. Surely in
A Child's Garden of Verses he might discover a plausible

[289]

incident which he could introduce as though he had only just remembered one of the make-believe games a young father used to play with his happy little boy? And if any busybody in the audience identified the source of this touching memory—what the hell! A man could play it first, and write it as a poem long afterwards, couldn't he? And he'd invent games to amuse little Robin that he had loved to play himself when he was a kid, wouldn't he?

Robert sat down by his window and began to hunt through the pages.

Not bad, some of the pieces that his eye picked:

> I should like to rise and go
> Where the golden apples grow ;—
> Where below another sky
> Parrot islands anchored lie. . . .

But no use for his purpose; it had to be action, not the mere dreamy longings of a loony kid (for he still kept to his original judgment).

> We built a ship upon the stairs
> All made of the back-bedroom chairs. . . .

That would do fine. And yet—it was little more than a year since the new 1911 edition of the Letters was published and widely read, freshening the public interest in Stevenson; might some hag in the fifth row get up and call out: "You got that out of a book." Yes, but he had his answer: "*I* came first and the book afterwards." It was a perfectly good answer, and he added in gay parenthesis: "—And just you sit down and don't ask questions or I'll have you put out of the hall."

Powerful Robert!

Pleased as a child who thinks up some preposterous gesture of defiance, he went on turning the pages, and grinned again as he lit on the verses which had started up that jovial argument in Edinburgh; jovial for him, not for Miss Gibson; she had got the worst of it, and had to pass on to something else rather quickly.

When the grass was closely mown
Walking on the lawn alone,
In the turf a hole I found
And hid a soldier underground.

Spring and daisies came apace ;
Grasses hide my hiding place ;
Grasses run like a green sea
O'er the lawn up to my knee.

When the grass is ripe like grain,
When the scythe is stoned again,
When the lawn is shaven clear,
Then my hole shall reappear.

I shall find him, never fear,
I shall find my grenadier. . . .

"This is meant for me," said Robert.

And all that had gone before, slowly crumbled and collapsed as at a charge of dynamite a house can give way, storey by storey, windows and walls seeming to melt and fall outwards; the explosion so loud that the street was strange and soundless afterwards.

"*This is meant for me.*"

His name had come up on a white stone, and not in the way of dazzling luck, as he had foreseen it.

He had absolutely no doubt. It was an intensely personal communication by a poem which when he first read it, had signified nothing to him beyond the odd, fussy, solemn little acts that children do, ever incomprehensible to grown-ups. Yet now the meaning was bare and crystalline; near as the hills when they give an aching certainty of rain to come. A writer has his own means of carrying on a tireless pursuit through life and after death; and a man may find his son at last down dingy improbable ways: through dishonour scoffing at his very memory and using it as a racket to cash in; through the conflict in one body of God and the devil, allowing no respite for evil to enjoy his hard and careless gains; through living pages of print where even a few lines insisted on getting read or recollected or quoted at the most disconcerting moment and from the most irrelevant sources; through the unwearying siege laid to Robert's peace and pleasure, his merry successful fraudulent career. . . .

"You might have known you wouldn't get away with it!"

Burying a soldier and leaving it underground. Punk! But punk had taken its revenge. If Robert failed to follow the lead now, it would haunt him until at last he yielded. That's the way it happens when you choose to pay no heed to a delivery meant unmistakably for you and you alone. He knew with that queer inner authority which he was beginning to recognize, that the little boy, the loony kid, had himself once buried a soldier in darkness and obscurity, as men bury their seed not seeking where the impulse has its secret spring, nor how it may mature years and years afterwards at some mysterious sudden moment, under no visible control, by no audible command, yet for a clear purpose.

> When the grass is ripe like grain,
> When the scythe is stoned again. . . .

Well, here he was, found and rescued at the eleventh hour from his dark underworld. But though dumb as the Dumb Soldier for want of proof as to whose hand had put him there, he *must* testify to that unconscious faith.

> When the lawn is shaven clear . . .

He was not a fanciful sort of bloke. You invent fanciful reasons only when they tend towards your own benefit, not in self-robbery of all you stood to gain. For he still wanted desperately to be taken to California, to make him rich and well again.

Those jingles were sent to plague and torment him. If he had not fooled the old camel, if he had not stolen her treasure— Look how they turn on you, these inanimate things, when you propose to use them as no more nor less than stage properties. Or if he had trusted to his own wits when he got to San Francisco, instead of sitting down—was it only a few minutes ago?—sitting at the open window with a book in his hands and a lesson to learn.

"Thanks, I've learnt it."

. . . Broken fragments of Greek and Roman myth jumbled in his mind with the parables taught to an unheeding boy who had preferred the "heathen deities", as Mr. Merrill called them, mildly reproving his turbulent charge for being attracted by those ancient stories. Demeter, goddess of corn and fruit, who lost her daughter in the sombre regions of hell and went on looking for her; went on and never gave up till she brought her back in triumph with the bright green grass. Sowing the seed, reaping and garnering of the sheaves, and at the end of it all, a pagan festival to celebrate the ripe harvest. A sower went out . . . and some fell upon a rock and some fell upon thorns. . . . And at the end of it all, a child's voice to celebrate the resurrection in confident triumph:

> I shall find him, never fear,
> I shall find my grenadier.

A likeness can prove nothing; they had existed all down the ages. Why, you had only to raise the question in a pub, for instance, and anecdotes sprang up all round you: "Like as two peas in a pod. . . ." "Might have been twins. . . ." "And no relation, mind. . . ." "Couldn't tell 'em apart. . . ." Faces were not the same as finger-prints, proudly unduplicated. Jam for the swindler, these accidental likenesses. In books, too; what was the tale Mr. Merrill had given him as a prize? *The Prince and the Pauper*, by Mark Twain; nobody knew which was Edward VI of England and which the ragged boy outside the gates; swopped throne and gutter, they had, and still folks didn't guess. And that other book he had read at the Home: *A Tale of Two Cities*; a chap escaped from a French prison and wearing another chap's clothes, walked straight out past the jailor, simply because they looked alike.

Looking alike did not count unless you could feel as Robert felt now, from a deeper conviction than any physical resemblance had given him, that truth had run him to earth and raised him from the earth.

He thought a little sadly, how strange that the young male compulsion to sow his seed and achieve immortality, should have come up as rotten as himself. A pretty poor immortality for a great author. Nevertheless, Robert was met now with an authority which he dared not leave unanswered. Religion? He had no need of religion; could never have been capable of sacrificing all he had for an unknown cause, a far-off Damien; yet for this direct affiliation, impact of a father's creed on a son prodigal and discredited—"*I will arise and go to my father*" . . .

Robert damned and swore at the insolent intrusion of these half-forgotten tags of the gospels; swore especially at the prodigal son for having been not as bad as himself, with no record that he had begged and cheated and swindled, or spread a greasy layer of lies all over his father's name; why, he had actually worked, tending swine. He, Robert, was a dirtier swine than any prodigal son. And though his own father was apparently alive enough to stop him by stern intercession from crashing on in his own way, now the job was done there could be no joyful running to meet him and falling on his neck, no best robe and ring and shoes and fatted calf, no tender compassion. The fun was over, that was all. He had been claimed.

This time dangerous delays and half measures would not do. This time he dared not fool round with temptation. Temptation in his case had proved itself not merely a meaningless word in a block of words used over and over again by the New England minister in the pulpit.

So better not see Ingleby again.

Then better not remain in France.

Where should he go? Scotland flashed before him as a solution; Scotland, representing not so much the land of his fathers, as the one place where he had incredibly been told he might return and find a job waiting for him. Scotland and the farm at Gleann Bàn.

On the verge of the Big Scoop; about to be adopted by a

doting millionaire, presently to sail Southward in a luxury yacht to a new home on a tropical island; Robert Black, Merrill, Gibson, Faulconbridge, Robert-soon-to-be-Gosham dared not miss this one threadbare hope of honest work, digging ditches at twenty shillings a week.

Cash for the journey? He had just about enough left of what Madame de Beaupré had given him, to take him to Argyll by rail and sea and rail. He was sharply aware that he should return her the sum; but unless he were to get right up North at once, the job might be filled, for this was within a few days of the time of year when they had told him he might come back. Robert decided (without ratio-cination) that it was justifiable and more important to escape in the swiftest possible span of time, than to give back a few pounds to an old lady whom it would merely bewilder, and who would not be lacking any comfort for want of those few pounds. If he covered the ground only by slow and tramping stages, Ingleby might track him and follow him, Ingleby persuasive and genuinely affectionate: "You're not deserting me, Robert, old son? Think of the Big Scoop."

Of course he could take nothing along that belonged to Ingleby. What was his own? Still functioning in that odd methodical way, he made a rapid inventory: The four volumes of Letters, they were undoubtedly his, earned and paid for . . . Robert went rather white as he remembered the savage toll on his strength, during those drab weeks at Gleann Bàn last year; but he had been buoyed up then and even amused at the thought that this was work to put an end to all future need of working. He hesitated as he picked up the Pentland Edition of *The Ebb-Tide* by Robert Louis Stevenson and Lloyd Osbourne. That surely was his own? his "patron" had given it to him, and though he certainly had not read it, he might without undue casuistry put it among his baggage. But *A Child's Garden of Verses*? You can't pretend, son, that that's yours. Yet there might be a chance of leaving it on its rightful owner if he could manage it without seeing her, so he packed it with the few clothes that he had bought at the Port of Geith— Then grimly pulled them out again, corduroy trousers, decent shirt and velvet coat, and put them on in place of those Ingleby had bought him. His cast-off rags he left behind on the floor; long past even a tramp's use except for the one unspeakable and now forbidden purposes.

Impossible to leave any more explicit account of what had become of him, for poor puzzled old Alf. Alf had been very decent to him. Easier if his actual body could have been left lying behind on the floor, to explain what had happened: "He must have been struck by lightning."

❧ 17 ❦

He let his draining-spade fall by its own great weight into
the squelchy ground, and leant for a moment on the crossbar,
panting, exhausted, the sweat pouring down his face; too
spent even to look round him with loathing for the expanse
of grey beaten water and dark hills washed and all but
blotted out by rain and darker cloud; a scene spongy and
colourless which was all Robert had had to look at for nearly
three weeks. Here he had toiled from the instant of his
arrival into the urgent flurry of a crisis, when the two
women at Gleann Bàn had seized upon this man sent them
by Providence, clutched at his strength, a male dropped on
them from the outside world and asking for work; yes,
asking for it and curiously willing to cope with it, just after
the frost had cracked the hillside above the farm, and the
heavy downpour started a landslide perilous to the water
supply, which came bursting down from the heights. This
time by a miracle the pipes were spared; and by an even
greater miracle the neglected draining of the steep slopes
could at last be dug by the tramp who had turned up at the
same time as last year, looking for casual labour. Last year
he had only stayed a short while, though he had done his
job well enough. This year Nellie, the younger sister,
prayed fervently both to the Almighty and to Isa (who was
inclined to be mean in payment) that he might be persuaded
never to go away at all. For last year their brother had still
been with them, and the spate of winter's catastrophes could
be met. This year Gleann Bàn would have been overwhelmed before even the snows began. So quick, give him
the draining-spade.

You dig a leader drain about eighteen inches deep in an

[297]

irregular zigzag down the hill face behind the farm buildings, and then a herringbone pattern of side drains running into it. If you tried to save yourself trouble by digging the leader perpendicular, it would confine too violent a collision of water with earth and then the poor silly sheep would fall into the scooped-out pot-holes. Robert knew; he remembered what his boss had taught him twelve months ago, when he had barely listened to the reasons involving all that extra sweat; for twelve months ago it had been sweet to think that he would never need to work again.

But one is never safe from change. Leave things for a day or leave them for a year, and come back to them, and have they sat still? No; all twiddled round again on purpose to cheat a man so desperately weary of changes in his own life that at least here, at Gleann Bàn, he might well have expected to find them still the same if only because they were too darned dull to be otherwise. Bad enough to have worked under Fenwick who spared not others nor himself; but at least Robert could do as he was told, sleep heavy afterwards, and reflect that nothing but his own will obliged him to stay digging for one moment longer. Somebody should have warned him that Fenwick had gone off months ago; married to a giddy wench who had him under her thumb and made him move to her father's farm near Dublin where city pleasures were accessible.

Gleann Bàn had belonged equally to Fenwick and Isa and Nellie. He had left them his share in it; and as happens when a man falls for a girl many years his junior, he was too infatuated to care further what might happen to those two bleak middle-aged women, his sisters; lame Isa was not without knowledge and character; she could supervise hired labour; he forgot, or did not care any more, that Isa was also too obstinate to understand that the only attraction they could offer a hired labourer to remain and work for them, would be decent pay and shorter hours. Nellie knew, but Nellie was frightened; frightened all the time: this farm had to be made to pay or they would go under, she and Isa; it represented both capital and income.

Gleann Bàn was isolated on the shore of a small sea loch,

cut off by folds of the hills. They had found themselves, when the dark weather began, with no help but the rheumatic shepherd Macnair, close on sixty-five, who had been there most of his life; and a strong lout, too dumb stupid for responsibility. So—

—"It's your *duty* to stay," cried Nellie Fenwick, desperately hurling her fears and all her hopes upon Robert.

"Shucks!"

This was still his automatic reaction to reminders of duty. Yet he stayed. What else could he do? The draining-spade had become a symbol. Even now, during these brief moments of rest, he had leant upon it too long. With an effort he lifted it, dropped it again into the moist earth, and with both hands on the wide crossbar, rocked it, and lifted it, and dropped the blade again; rocked it, and lifted it, and dropped it . . .

He remembered Marcus had said that work itself was a very different thing from thinking about work: "The life contemplative, one might say. Actually to do it and go on doing it, my dear Robert, will prove a rather more difficult matter. And you're not as tough as you were, are you?" He could hear that mocking tone now. Damn Marcus for being right. Marcus would be glad to see him soaked through on this steep slope of a hill in the western Highlands, plodding at his unsensational job; plodding away at it for no reason at all save a dogged acceptance of what was keeping him here on a sheep-farm in the dank air and cold sleet, instead of letting him clear off to the brilliant golden warmth of California and the South Seas.

The very thought of Marcus brought him from sodden despair into a more savage mood. For it was true that work, though disagreeable in prospect, came nowhere near the bitter confirmation. As for this filthy climate and those two unspeakably dreary women—we'd all be better dead, muttered Robert . . . (" *The best way to make a mucker is with your back to the wall and a few lead pellets whiffed into you—*")

Nevertheless, he went on with his digging.

The farm consisted of about five hundred acres of rock, five hundred acres of bracken, and the same of grazing, with only about twenty acres under plough. The bracken had not been broken down in the summer as it should have been under proper direction. Tough work, beating down bracken. Old Macnair told him they did it in this part of the world with a sort of Egyptian flail; a short stick on a long stick, hitched together. This winter the farm would have to pay for the neglect, and if the land were allowed to get water-logged, that would be the end of it. Sheep had to have somewhere safe to graze, and the snow, though mercifully late, could not hold off much longer; grand sport that would be, climbing in the tense darkness to find where the frightened animals had huddled together in a hollow and got covered with the drifting snow so that nothing of them might be seen, according to Macnair, but the blow-holes in the snow where they breathed.

Robert, you darned fool, finish your draining and ditching if you must, and then get out before the snow comes; it's not too late; you have all those addresses—Pop Gosham and the rest. Robert mused on the lucky chance which had forbidden him to take along money or gifts from St. Raphael; now he might turn his abrupt departure into a fresh asset: go to Ingleby and pitch him a plausible yarn. . . . From sheer habit, Robert began to compose what would be his sensitive excuse for quitting: "Alf, old man, I had to! It was too like begging, d'you see, and—I can't stomach begging. If I'd stopped to say goodbye and all that, you might have talked me over; and gosh, you *can* talk! So—I just vamoosed."

Yes, but along the same lines, how could he explain a re-entry? It could be manœuvred, of course, by a bit more twisting. Mechanically, his brain occupied by this con-genial tax on its inventive powers, he counted the waterfalls plunging down the hills; streaks of pewter brightening to silver when a shaft of sun pierced the drifting mists for an instant and then vanished again. Two, three, four water-falls; the nearest and loudest, the cataract which crashed all through the night in his ears directly behind the farm buildings, was audible from where he stood, leaning once more the draining-spade.

Vailima. It meant five streams: "Five streams, whence the name. . . . The island has beautiful rivers . . . with pleasant pools and waterfalls and often a great volume of sound. . . ."

Robert could imagine only too vividly the cool solace of those torrents heard at Vailima flinging their spray at tropical noon, out there where he might be journeying now but for that mad compulsion to put himself under orders from a father dead too long ago to care. As a swift getaway from the temptation to complete a racket so prosperously begun, Scotland did well enough for a start. But having once broken that glittering string to California, and on discovery that the job of work he loosely chose had meanwhile resolved itself into a harsh unpleasant entanglement—What in hell was still keeping him in hell? He could get out to California easily enough on his own; Glasgow and the Clyde were no formidable distance from where he stood. He had all the essential addresses from Ingleby. And working his passage out on any sort of steamer or cargo-boat would seem light as building card-houses, after this.

I didn't say I was going to tell lies again, did I? I only said: Get out of this, into the sun; you'll die here, pretty soon.

Yet *had* he finished with lying, who only a few short moments ago had been plotting to twist himself right with Ingleby? retrieve the idiot honesty of his departure? Had every son of God the devil in him as well, and just as strong, maybe stronger? Robert was again haunted by the feeling that he had heard of such a case, apart from his own. Surely his father must have gone through it himself, to disconcert Robert by showing where it led if he chose to ignore that strange feeling renewed and renewed again, of a covenant between father and son, invisible to all others. So was Apollo exiled by Zeus from golden Olympus, and sent as a penance into slavery, tending flocks on the dull earth. But Robert was not acquainted with mythology, and his slavery on the sheep-farm was nothing so submissive nor so patient

[301]

as a penance; simply he *had* to stop because Fenwick had gone; because this was a piece of Scottish soil in danger; because though he hated Scotland, he was responsible at this moment and in this way for this small sad portion of Scotland neglected. To those two tiresome women, he appeared indeed to represent a god; a god underpaid and overworked, but indispensable. He must not give in so soon. Yet as the very phrase shaped itself: "so soon", Robert saw in it further damning evidence how he was not to be trusted: "So soon"—but by that token it appeared horribly likely that he intended to give in at some future period, further away. When he had refused Marcus's money but gone to stay at the Château, and when again he had quitted the Mediterranean and all the glory that Ingleby had promised him, Robert had put faith in his own impulsive break from evil. Now he had no such faith; humbly and for the first time, he foresaw and admitted the possibility that he might still at any moment take a monstrous plunge back into a paradise forbidden.

So that night he begged ink and paper from Nellie, and an extra candle; and in the draughty loft where he slept above the byres, he wrote painfully a full confession to Ingleby (surely the oddest priest ever chosen by a sinner): A confession of his fraud and his lies, putting him wise to the fact that he, Robert, a foundling, a charity brat, had really not the remotest notion whose son he was.

The Big Scoop, the millionaire and his daughter, the whole San Francisco racket, the white yacht to the South Seas, had been still accessible, yesterday and today. By this letter he put them finally out of his reach.

And now that the way to the South Seas had been blocked by a barrier thick and strong as only the intangible can be, nostalgia for the home which had never been his home became so cruel that he could neither read the Letters nor leave them alone. The Brownies had got hold of those volumes again, and were up to their old unbearable tricks, charming and amusing, no doubt, but driving Robert nearly distracted. For as once in Provence they had aggravated his special fever by throwing up in scarlet, as it were, only the letters which concerned the writer's love for children and his games with children, sinking all the rest; or earlier, while staying with Miss Gibson, Robert had sought in vain for traces of the gay rebel whom he supposed was his mate and affinity, and the pages had revealed instead only a man who thought seriously, acted seriously and made unthinking sacrifice of self . . . so now at Gleann Bàn in grey winter, his Brownies delighted in nudging him to open any of the four books at passages (and these were many) about islands in the South Seas:

. . . and our fine days are certainly fine like heaven ; such a blue of the sea, such green of the trees, and such crimson of the hibiscus flowers, you never saw ; and the air as mild and gentle as a baby's breath, and yet not hot ! . . .

. . . The whole bottom of the valley is full of various streams posting between strips of forest with a brave sound of waters. In one place we had a glimpse of a fall some way higher up, and then sparkling in sunlight in the midst of the green valley. Then up by a winding path scarce accessible to a horse for steepness, to the other side, and the open cocoanut glades of the plantation. . . .

. . . In front of our house is a broad stretch of grass, dotted with cocoanuts, breadfruits, mangoes, and the strange pandanus tree. I wish you could have seen them, their lower branches glowing with the rich colours of the fruits. . . .

. . . There was nothing visible but the southern stars, and the steersman out there by the binnacle lamp ; . . . the night was as warm as milk. . . .

. . . We see the sea six hundred feet below filling the end of two vales of forest. On one hand the mountain runs above us some thousand feet higher ; great trees stand round us in our clearing ; there is an endless voice of birds ; I have never lived in such heaven. . . .

. . . The house is three miles from town, in the midst of great silent forests. There is a burn close by, and when we are not talking you can hear the burn, and the birds, and the sea breaking on the coast three miles away and six hundred feet below us, and about three times a month a bell—I don't know where the bell is, nor who rings it ; it may be the bell in Hans Andersen's story for all I know. It is never hot here—86 in the shade is about our hottest—and it is never cold except just in the early mornings. . . . I won't tell you if it is beautiful, for I want you to come here and see for yourself. . . .

Close the book and pick up another. But even in Volume One were happy gleams from Mentone; and in Volume Two, from Hyères. True, these were less perilous to his peace of mind than the four tanned and barefoot years at Vailima; but the Brownies saw to it that even when Robert believed he was picking up Volume One or Two, he usually found himself with Volume Three or Four in his hands.

Futile to escape from the waterfalls of Gleann Bàn by reading of the five waterfalls at Vailima. Yet as he had to stay, so he had to read. The beastly habit had hold of him again by the throat.

Then, in Volume Four, he became aware of a recurring note which chimed in more sympathetically with his sombre mood. They referred to a book called *The Ebb-Tide*.

. . . I have a tale, a shortish tale in length, but it has proved long to do, The Ebb Tide, some part of which goes home this mail. It is by me and Mr. Osbourne, and is really a singular work. There are only four characters, and three of them are bandits—well, two of them are, and the third is their comrade and accomplice. It sounds cheering, doesn't it ? Barratry, and drunkenness, and vitriol, and I cannot tell you all what, are the beams of the roof. . . .

. . . Well, it's done. Those tragic 16 pp. are at last finished, and I have put away thirty-two pages of chips, and have spent thirteen days about as nearly in hell as a man could expect to live through. It's done, and of course it ain't worth while, and who cares ? There it is, and about as grim a tale as was ever written, and as grimy, and as hateful. . . .

. . . Since you rather revise your views of The Ebb Tide, I think Lloyd's name might stick, but I'll leave it to you. I'll tell you how it stands. Up to the discovery of the champagne, the tale was all planned between us and drafted by Lloyd : from that moment he has had nothing to do with it except talking it over. . . .

And this was really funny: that of all the works of Robert Louis Stevenson, a good plenty, Robert should have had

[304]

The Ebb-Tide there in the knapsack, his own undisputed property. Remember, Marcus had chosen it to plague him, bound up with some other tale, just because "Lloyd's name" was on it too. The Brownies could laugh that off as they liked, and so could Marcus. But it was meant that he should have it to read, now, during what might easily be the last few weeks of his life.

For he had made up his mind that he would carry on grimly in this place which had become a horror of waking in the dark whistling hours before dawn with a grim day before him. Carry on and get these women through the winter; drain the sodden slopes, and stagger through the streaming dusks of January to withdraw the tups which had been put to the hill early in December. Sheep-lore . . . Macnair, steeped in it, told Robert (as though the story were rich and spicy as a seaman's yarn of the South Pacific) that sheep brought down in October for dipping and keeling, always tried to return to the hills from whence they had been taken, and for that reason it facilitated the business to push them backwards into the dipping-trough on the hill-ward side of the fank, and heave them over and make them swim out to the keeling-pen where they dried and were keeled. . . . Endless sheep-talk—how long would a man have to endure it? February an eternity of twenty-eight days—no, curse it, twenty-nine this year; March and April, they prophesied, were often the worst months of all. But then, if he were not dead by May, he would deliberately go to his drowning. "When the scythe is stoned again"— Fair enough, wasn't it? If he promised to wait till then, could any father expect more?

No dry and sticky end on earth, for him. Robert had learnt to love the clear flow of water on his naked flesh, water never stagnant. Even up here by the ice-grey tumble of burn and fall and Northern loch, its mysterious property of healing and oblivion still held a promise of comfort to a tramp's tired body. Surely then, water would be glad to do one last little job for him?

With this curious consolation lapping him round in an almost voluptuous certainty of rest, not many months longer to be withheld from his aching bones and cracking skin, Robert read *The Ebb-Tide*, in a lull between rain and snow:

... all was well; no eye must see him in that last act. He slid silently into the boat, thence, silently, into the starry water. Instinctively he swam a little; it would be time enough to stop by and by.

The shock of the immersion brightened his mind immediately. The events of the ignoble day passed before him in a frieze of pictures, and he thanked ' whatever Gods there be ' for that open door of suicide. In such a little while he would be done with it, the random business at an end, the prodigal son come home. A very bright planet shone before him and drew a trenchant wake along the water. He took that for his line and followed it.

That was the last earthly thing that he should look upon; that radiant speck, which he had soon magnified into a City of Laputa, along whose terraces there walked men and women of awful and benignant features, who viewed him with distant commiseration. These imaginary spectators consoled him; he told himself their talk, one to another; it was of himself and his sad destiny.

From such flights of fancy he was aroused by the growing coldness of the water. Why should he delay? Here, where he was now, let him drop the curtain, let him seek the ineffable refuge, let him lie down with all races and generations of men in the house of sleep. It was easy to say, easy to do. To stop swimming: there was no mystery in that, if he could do it. Could he? And he could not. He knew it instantly. He was aware instantly of an opposition in his members, unanimous and invincible, clinging to life with a single and fixed resolve, finger by finger, sinew by sinew; something that was at once he and not he—at once within and without him; the shutting of some miniature valve in his brain, which a single manly thought should suffice to open—and the grasp of an external fate ineluctable as gravity. To any man there may come at times a consciousness that there blows, through all the articulations of his body, the wind of a spirit not wholly his; that his mind rebels; that another girds him and carries him whither he would not. It came now to Herrick, with the authority of a revelation. There was no escape possible. The open door was closed in his recreant face. He must go back into the world and amongst men without illusion. He must stagger on to the end with the pack of his responsibility and his disgrace, until a cold, a blow, a merciful chance ball, or the more merciful hangman, should dismiss him from his infamy. There were men who could commit suicide; there were men who could not; and he was one who could not.

For perhaps a minute there raged in his mind the coil of this discovery; then cheerless certitude followed; and, with an incredible simplicity of submission to ascertained fact, he turned round and struck out for shore. There was a courage in this which he could not appreciate; the ignobility of his cowardice wholly occupying him. A strong current set against him like a wind in his face; he contended with it heavily, wearily, without enthusiasm, but with substantial advantage; marking his progress the while, without pleasure, by the outline of the trees. Once he had a moment of hope. He heard to the southward of him, towards the centre of the lagoon, the wallowing of some great fish, doubtless a shark, and paused for a little, treading water. Might not this be the hangman? he thought. But the wallowing died away; mere silence succeeded; and Herrick pushed on again for the shore, raging as he went at his own nature. Ay, he would wait for the shark; but if he had heard him coming! . . . His smile was tragic. He could have spat upon himself.

About three in the morning, chance, the set of the current, and the bias of his own right-handed body so decided it between them that he came to shore upon the beach in front of Attwater's. There he sat down, and looked forth into a world without any of the lights of hope. The poor diving-dress of self-conceit was sadly tattered! With the fairy tale of suicide, of a refuge always open to him, he had hitherto beguiled and supported himself in the trials of life; and behold! that also was only a fairy-tale, that also was folk-lore. With the consequence of his acts he saw himself implacably confronted for the duration of life: stretched upon a cross, and nailed there with the iron bolts of his own cowardice. He had no tears; he told himself no stories. His disgust with himself was so complete, that even the process of apologetic mythology had ceased. He was like a man cast down from a pillar, and every bone broken. He lay there and admitted the facts, and did not attempt to rise.

So his father had known about this too, and seen to it that the final way out was barricaded. He had even saved Robert from a futile swim: "There were men who could commit suicide; there were men who could not; and he was one who could not."

For of course Stevenson, in a dark hour, had tried it himself— ("Up to the discovery of the champagne, the tale was all planned between us and drafted by Lloyd; from that moment he has had nothing to do with it except talking it over. . . .") That the experience on record was personal, Robert knew with that queer inner authority which he had by now learnt to recognize: once a small boy had made a hole in the ground and buried his grenadier so that he might find it, never fear, when long afterwards he went to look; and equally, once a man in a black hour when the burden was too heavy, must have swum out into deep water to fling away his life, and could not do it, and had written down his failure for a son to find.

Not that way out. The covenant still held. Obedience again was claimed. And of course it had been Marcus who in giving him that book, no other, was the instrument to carry out these merciless instructions. And of course, as his own property, Robert had brought it away with him.

It was all perfectly simple, terribly lucid.

*   *   *

The lull was over; heavy rain had left a collection of slush round all the farm buildings, mucking up the gutters, clinging to the cart and barrows and implements, clogging the boots of the men and the skirts of the women; filth and manure on the midden, in the byres; the pipes were choked with dirt, and the white collie's coat brown and matted. Somehow and by pulling in help from Nellie and the boy Jim, Robert succeeded in getting most of the stuff shovelled away before the snow came twirling down, light and dry at first, hardly more than a powdering, its whiteness a relief after so long spent in raising his eyes to the hills and seeing only grey and drab and indigo. But Robert had barely time to be glad of the snow's momentary gaiety, before that too turned into an enemy, implacable, gaining weight and potency with every hour of daylight or dark. You could never hope to conquer the weather, here in the western Highlands; only just save the farm and its animals from being utterly overwhelmed. After almost half a century of monotonous experience, Macnair had to consent this winter that his active work must be done vicariously by the stranger who had wandered in only just in time. For the Fenwick women could not afford to lose valuable sheep.

Drifts and blizzards and more blizzards and deeper drifts, and hard chips of ice that were blown against the skin of your face and stung it as though they hated you, as though the elements were finding words for their hatred of man:

man who rescued sheep when the silly creatures were all balled up with snow and could make no move towards the track that led them home.

Work. Old Merrill called it the curse of Adam on man. What *I* want to know is, why did Adam put up with it?

Had to. What else could he have done?

Killed himself.

Then he'd have been separated from the love of his Father for ever; and he knew it.

See here, never you mind about Adam, nor about fathers. Adam's a long way off. Adam was O.K. He had a pack of troubles and found his own way out of it. He's not your business. Those bleating baa-ing blithering sheep—they're your business.

A few religious tomes in battered covers were the only books on the farm, and they stayed unread on shelves which were mostly used for litter; thereby declaring that though here were women, neither had a care nor a cure for ugliness and disorder. In a mood of desperate loneliness one night when there happened to be no need to go up the glen, Robert was impelled to test them with an anecdote of R.L.S. Longing for a human reaction, as a lover will, he mentioned the name casually, given an inadequate cue from a complaint by Isa that the cart could no longer be used as formerly, for the wheels were not mended, the traces broken, the flap hung creaking from its hinges, and they had no horse to put between the shafts—

"When Stevenson went to America," said Robert, and his heart thumped, "he made a damn fool mistake and took tickets for himself and his family on a cargo boat, thinking it was a pleasure steamer." He glanced sidelong at Nellie and Isa. . . . Had either sat up, their eyes sparkling, ready to be animated, to chatter tales of a favourite author?

"—They'd already sailed when they found out the boat carried a cargo of apes and stallions," Robert finished hurriedly; and added a shout of hearty unconvincing laughter.

Isa took no notice. Nellie blinked and murmured: "Eh dear, I never could have had a fancy to travel with monkeys, though I've not seen them but in pictures."

And that was all.

Despair was like a tight swelling in his chest. Somehow loneliness had to be assuaged, and the Brownies had got control of the Letters, and the women at the farm cared neither for books nor men who wrote books. Robert was driven to reading *Weir of Hermiston*, bound up in Marcus's edition with *The Ebb-Tide*. He knew little of *Weir of Hermiston* beyond a dim memory that someone, Miss Gibson or Mr. Renfrew maybe, had called it Stevenson's masterpiece; so it was the foulest luck that the writer did not live to finish it when after years of slogging along, barren of inspiration, work had begun to flow easily and joyfully once more. Though he knew nothing of writers nor writing, Robert had learnt from his odd affinity with the Letters, how much this must have meant to Stevenson; and perhaps how he must have hated being one of the holiday dead, his task left unfinished. This somewhat quaint theology was genuine enough from an idler who against the grain was idle no longer.

There was a touch of humour which for once Robert could not share with himself, in the industry and perseverance with which he tackled this fragment of a masterpiece; it is always a sorry spectacle, yet not unfunny, when a tale remains obstinate, *cannot* get read. Robert began with enthusiasm, which was soon quenched by boredom. He plodded on crossly; all this Scottish stuff, scenery and dialect . . . Not exhilarating like *Treasure Island*; nor like the Letters with their perpetual challenge of variety and laughter; nor could it ever stir his blood like the flight of Alan Breck and David Balfour across the heather; nor rouse him to shouts of acquiescence, as with Villon's *Lodging for the Night*; nor, finally, cause him to tingle with strange pride, as when against his will and for all the wrong reasons he had read *Father Damien*. Though he kicked himself along through the first chapter of *Weir of Hermiston*, he would have stopped short there, had he not seen the title

[310]

of Chapter Two: "Father and Son"; a phrase to quicken him if he lay dead in a snowdrift.

"My father, ever my dearest", Stevenson had quite simply confessed in a letter. But Chapter Two of Weir was still and in this too, a disappointment: Archie had a live father sitting there in flesh and blood; a grand coarse old fellow; any son worth his salt would have been pals with such a father. But that prig had gone miauling round, catching on to his mother's skirts— Robert had no concern with mothers; and Mistress Weir was a poor, puking body, not unlike Nellie downstairs. Archie neither realized his luck nor deserved it.

Yet, jealous and sore, he persisted from some buried motive of courtesy to the author, until he reached the line: "On he went up the great bare staircase of his duty—"

—And there he shut the book. He had no concern with duty, either. Duty bothered him like sermons and mothers. He sighed and stretched himself. Mothers . . . A name now was aggravating his memory like a bit of loose flesh on a cut finger. That woman in the book, Kirstie; he had never read *Weir of Hermiston* before, so what had caused him, Robert, to pick "Kirstie" as a random name for the wronged girl whom he had cast for his mother, in his old careless pre-reformation days?

Then the cogs bit on the wheel. . . .

The Free Library at Dumburnock; his fellow-readers round the table, their respectability shocked at this sudden appearance among them of a bona fide tramp. Much he cared! And then the very last letter of all, but the first to be read— How he had laughed to discover that R.L.S. had died believing himself childless. The joke was not quite so fresh and juicy now. To dodge his thoughts, Robert took up Volume Four of the Letters, and turned to the end to find what had been said about Kirstie, having so recently informed himself as to Kirstie's origin.

Nothing interesting; a bit of Latin that he couldn't pronounce:

. . . The case is that of a woman, and I think that I am doing her justice. You will be interested, I believe, to see the difference

in our treatments. Secreta Vitae comes nearer to the case of
my poor Kirstie. Come to think of it, Gosse, I believe the main
distinction is that you have a family growing up around you, and I
am a childless, rather bitter, very clear-eyed, blighted youth. I
have, in fact, lost the path that makes it easy and natural for you
to descend the hill. I am going at it straight. And where I have
to go down it is a precipice . . .

He pushed the book away and buried his face on his
arms. *Childless!* Could he ever really have laughed
uproariously at that?

"I will arise and go to my father."

There would be, of course, none of those rejoicing bursts
of trumpets and hallelujahs for *him*. Yet simply to hear his
father say: "Well, I'm not pleased with him, God, no!
he's nothing to be proud of: a sinner all right, not in any
big remarkable way, you know, just a mean, idle, scrounging,
dirty little ruffian and windbag and cheat and liar and
scallywag; but by Jupiter Ammon, he *is* my son, my only
son, and one would rather have even this sort of a son than
be childless."

. . . "The infernal nuisance is, Gosse, that if he keeps on
with this racket, he can't be a son of mine. Oh, I'm not
casting him off in righteousness, nothing like that, but face
facts, man, he *can't* be. See here, my father was one of the
best of men, and I was perhaps one of the worst, anyhow
in my younger days; idle and impudent. But *that*, making
up lies about him and my mother for money, it simply
couldn't have been in my flesh and blood and bones."

. . . It sounded so real in Robert's mind, that he could
hardly believe that it did not exist as a letter, say in Volume
Four; that he had not actually seen it listed in the Index,
printed on the page.

If he could do something *physical* to this rod of time which
prevented him with its rigid indifference from tackling the
more indulgent barricades of space; prevented him from
bursting into the study at Vailima with: "You're not
childless. Here I am, your son, the son you wanted so
badly." . . . The rod of time—he was bloody well not going
to kiss *that* rod, not he; it would never break for him nor

[312]

anyone, yet if only he might bend it and twist it, venting his impotent fury that the man of all men who cared for truth should have been so cheated and mocked as to die untruthfully writing himself down as childless.

Robert was terribly alone. He cried.

. . . Comfort crept in, like slow warmth on a body cruelly chilled. At first he could not imagine whence it came. Then he remembered: Lloyd had been there. The women, mother, wife, Robert carelessly discounted. But Lloyd at least had loved Louis and was with him till the hour of his death. With absolute sincerity, his jealousy all drained away, Robert thanked God for Lloyd, grateful to him for easing his own torment into quieter sorrow. He could now bear to be alone, if he had not to bear thinking that his father had been alone.

*   *   *

But for the stress of labour involved by the approach of the lambing, Robert could never have guessed that winter was nearly over at Gleann Bàn. The days were longer, but you hardly noticed the widening edges of light between dawn and dusk, when you had to learn how to be a shepherd and be one, both at the same time in severe weather. The constant pressure of your stiffened limbs against wind and snow; using all your remaining strength to tackle each accident as it came along, as though it were the first, with none behind and no more to come; never really dry, never really rested; carrying burdens, alive or dead, when you felt you could not stumble a yard further; groping, shuffling, painfully climbing, steeply descending, Robert thrust his body inch by inch through the cheerless months.

(. . . Ill as Louis was . . . he has gained health and strength every day. He takes sea baths and swims, and lives almost entirely in the open air as nearly without clothes as possible, a simple pyjama suit of striped light flannel his only dress. As to shoes and stockings, we all have scorned them for months. . . .)

He could not think why he stayed. It didn't make sense. Even though these women had nothing but the farm and only one able-bodied man to depend on, why should it be himself? Hell! *was* he able-bodied, coughing his chest raw every night? Yet never quite ill enough to lie there stretched out and fallen and finished; ill, dying, dead. Dead as a soldier from his wounds, that's what he'd have liked best.

Suddenly he remembered how Mr. Renfrew, ages ago, had chattered of the British nation on the brink of war: the Kaiser at loggerheads with the French over Morocco, sending a German squadron to—what was the place?—Agadir, to impress the world with his strength. Mere empty talk to Robert then, intent on a new and delicious method of getting his living without working.

To be in a war again, and this time to be killed— If war ever came, and if he were still alive, and if they would take him in spite of his rotten health,—oh, if he could get into it somehow!

A surge of "ifs" . . . Turning the ewes on to their backs to cut away the matted wool, a muddy tangle that would have to be sold separate from the rest and cheaper than the standard 1s. 2d. a pound, he muttered that given a war he *would* get in somehow. . . . And added an affectionate, half mocking "Never fear!" to a father whom he seemed to hear replying ruefully: "I'd like to see a son of mine a soldier, if I can't be one myself."

"The-minstrel-boy-to-the-war-has-gone-in-the-ranks-of-death-you'll-find-him-his-father's-sword—" When he had gabbled verse fast enough, at the Home where he was educated, he gained kudos and occasionally even a prize for memory. What came next, after "his father's sword—"?

The gallant picture flickered . . . and changed to a grotesque little minstrel brandishing a weapon many sizes too big for him. . . . Smoutie, aged six, with a sword huge and unwieldy and a shawl wrapped tightly over it, with tears of wrath struggling to explain to his mother and Cummy that soldiers fighting in the Crimea *never* wore shawls. . . . He had been only half asleep while Mr. Renfrew was telling this story about Smoutie.

"His father's sword he has girded on—" The line would

[314]

not be so easily rubbed out of mind. It pursued Robert
till at last it reached the stage where it lost all significance;
and he was able to throw it away and be rid of it, sword
and all.

A whirlwind twisted down the glen to the loch, carrying
panic and destruction at a pace of a hundred miles an hour.
It laid flat the only wooded strip of land on the farm, and
as though this trivial feat had hardly used up any of its
pent-up strength, raced on across the shining water.

It happened that Robert was not there at this crisis, but
behind a fold of hill on the further side of the loch helping
another farmer, behindhand through rheumatic fever,
collect his herd from the snowy hills and drive them down
to prepare for lambing. Macnair had passed on that Old
Dougal was in trouble, for even at such distances apart, a
curious communal sense carried the tidings from each
solitary farm to another. By putting on extra pressure the
day before, Robert decided he could spare the time, and
went off with Lassie before the household was awake and
stirring.

When he reappeared, he was confronted by a scene
tousled and scattered by the gale; Nellie sobbing, and the
elder sister in hysterics, for she had lost all dignity in her
own sight by her automatic obedience to a shout from
Macnair: "Down on y'r face—quick!" When she could
rise again, plastered with mud, she saw a shed torn up and
blown out into the middle of the loch, where it drifted limp
and ridiculous; saw the trees of the little copse wrenched
up by their roots and flung broken and splintered on to the
earth. Isa had been superstitiously fond of her copse;
though unprofitable, it was wooded land. So now she
screamed at Robert, blaming him for his absence when the
whirlwind came:

"Taking our good money, and away on pleasure without
asking leave, as though ye were not a hired man but your
own master which the dear Lord knows ye'll never be with
your idle habits!"

"Oh hush ye, Isa, hush—" But white-faced Nellie had

[315]

no power to keep her sister from railing, and could only cling to her, repeating "Hush." She was more sensitive than the older woman, and guessed that even after five months, their saviour at Gleann Bàn could not be taken wholly for granted, nor assessed in terms of weekly wages. Both times, Nellie felt, there was something odd and opportune about the way he had arrived. So should he not be treated with more gentleness? He had worked hard and done no wrong; the whirlwind that had laid the trees flat was an act of God. But terrified as usual, she remained mute in his defence, watching the strength on which they leaned ebb and recede as a rapid tide that leaves the strip of pebble and rock and seaweed more than ever desolate.

"I couldn't have held it back if I *had* been here, could I?" His reply, though reasonable enough, did nothing to soothe Isa. Robert was the man on the farm; it was his duty to support them in a catastrophe, to be on the spot, to lift things, to display his rough male substance. She had forgotten that scared helpless interval between the going of her brother and the arrival of the tramp. A man on the farm had become again the normal thing, and this man was in her pay; let him earn it and not be saucy:

"And if ye can't earn it by honest work, better be off to the scruff of the city where ye came from, with your dirty old velvet coat."

In silence Robert turned his back, walked off and left her. He had had enough of Gleann Bàn and this sort of woman. Another sort in the big cities; he laughed to think of them. He'd got a bit of cash too, earned by such sweat as now seemed incredible; it would get him by train from Arrochar to Glasgow, and then on to Edinburgh, and keep him there for a bit without begging. For he wasn't going to be a beggar again, but he meant to enjoy himself and be happy in his own way. And presently perhaps . . . presently . . .

(. . . you should see the turquoise mountain tops of Upolu coming hand over fist above the horizon).

He went round and up to his bedroom in the loft above the byres to fetch his money. Mocking at the queer bad habits which had grown on him since he had first landed on Clydeside sixteen months ago, he determined this time to get out free from conscience or baggage. Except for Miss Gibson's copy of *A Child's Garden of Verses*. As he was going to Edinburgh anyhow, he might as well return it to the old camel. And at the very instant of thinking he would do so, ratiocination leapt up like mad and consumed all honesty of purpose: of course, *that* was why he was going! That was why he was leaving the farm. Time she had it back; it was her treasure, and a valuable treasure too. Why be decent and go on saving sheep and land for a woman who could not be decent to him the first time a blasted wind came along to upset her? The poor old camel had been decent to him for months, and look how he had treated her: lugged her book all the way to Scotland from the South of France to return it to her, and there it lay, still at the bottom of a knapsack chucked in the straw of a loft. And he could not send it back to her either; no post-office for miles and miles; none on the shores of this desolate loch. And moreover, Robert went on arguing hotly, if he were to tramp for hours to the nearest post-office of the nearest village, was it likely he would trust it with a parcel containing an autograph of Robert Louis Stevenson? Not he.

The way to Edinburgh was plain now; and the reason for going, sound and good and watertight. Not trusting his torn pockets, Robert shook all the rest of his possessions out of the knapsack, put the *Child's Garden* tenderly back in it with his billy-can and a few other necessaries; and slinging it across his shoulder, the rest of his library tipped out and strewn over the boards, took his stick and set out on the journey, whistling.

Books! By God, he needed no more books ever again for the rest of his life; a life bound to be short and damn well going to be merry.

Yet on the threshold, a foot already on the rung of the ladder down to the yard, he turned back, picked up at random one volume of the Letters, and thrust it down into the knapsack as well. A trifle ashamed of the slight blemish on his swaggering exit into liberty, he strode out from Gleann

Bàn, and protected from sight by the farm buildings, reached the road.

The wind had subsided, and a pale gold sunset squeezed its way through straight bars of cloud. Robert drew a long breath. It was grand to be off.

❧ 18 ❦

"Frae a' the Airts" was only one of many waterside taverns down on Geith Harbour, refuge for the jetsam common to any seaport not frequently visited by the police; but it happened to be the one which had profited for several weeks by the hilarious generosity of a tramp who had strolled in on a March night and stood treat all round. He made it his headquarters, and wherever else he squandered his money in the "lands" and alleys of Auld Reekie's thicker regions, or in other of the small marine inns along the shores that faced across the narrow Firth to the coast of Fife, he continued to pour it out as though from an inexhaustible fund. For indeed, it gave Robert a saturnine pleasure to use up in this bounteous fashion the wages that Isa had grudgingly doled out, week after week. In her own harsh Puritan idiom, he was wallowing in the sty. The ripe and easy women who slid into his arms and out again, with no reproach for the mutability of his passion, were hags well past their prime, or they would not have sunk to this low-class line of trade where seamen from all ports of the world stayed for too short a time to be fastidious. So they chuckled, gratified, at what he put into their hands for pay, getting through his store quickly; what did it matter? it was earned money, and he was in no mood to respect and hoard it for such a stupid reason.

Over a glass of rum or raw brandy, Robert often affected a pious upper lip as though he were in the pulpit, while with pointed finger he burlesqued for the company the inverted moral of Roslyn Chapel's Industrious Apprentice who had been slain for performing his duty too well; telling those who were sober enough to care, that the money paying for their jollification had been earned by honest and un-

remitting toil; for since last November he had been draining and herding and cleaning out the byres on a desolate
farm in the West; but now he had sworn repentance and
would never commit such a mistake again. They bawled
with laughter, not believing a word of it; nor had Robert
intended they should, for it amused him to speak the truth
to this rowdy gang of thieves and smugglers and receivers,
pedlars and stowaways.

Rejoicing in his freedom regained, sleeping sound and
long, popular with the jolly old couple who ran "Frae a'
the Airts", the farm had faded like a nightmare from his
mind: "Must have been mad!"—and so forgot it in the
congenial atmosphere of blended sweat and drink and oil
and tarry corduroy; while the slatterns shuffled to and fro
carrying bowls of swilled barley and scraps to the sprawling
sailors who had gulped down so much drink they could
hold no more without disaster unless they were promptly
given food. Memory skipped the recent fantastic interlude
of his life, from the day he had landed at Greenock eighteen
months ago until the present moment; but recalled scenes
in the saloons along the waterfront of San Diego or San
Francisco, with the same sounds and the same smells and
the same women. . . . Women, for instance, like this Morag
whom he had known intimately for forty hours, till now
after a glorious day when spring had trickled down all the
steep cobbled alleys and blown in at every crack of door or
window, she was overwhelmed by a mood of maudlin
sentimentality which bored Robert. His haggard good looks
may have had something to do with it, and the tumblers
of Red Biddy she had chucked down her throat at his
expense: knock-out stuff, methylated spirit and dregs;
Robert had never cared for it himself, preferring rum. He
wished Morag would keep her paws off him, and tipple herself
into the next stage where she would be too sodden to keep
on entertaining him—the poorest entertainment—by an
endless tale of how she had fallen to her present squalor;
a tale with the flavour of a stale ballad whined in the street
to make tipsy men weep more copiously. The oil lamps
swung in gimbals, and the glass of their chimneys gradu-

ally grew smokier and sootier, dimming the room; whenever a boat moved slowly past the window, the riding light sliced the fug with travelling red or green; and a stream of icy air cut through comfort each time the door opened and a figure stumbled in from the outside world. At these interruptions and when the tide was up, Robert could hear the masts sway and creak like trees of the forest, the harbour bilge slapping against the wharf, the clank of the anchor-chains that held the schooners, and the restless gulls screaming derision at his snug sanctuary. He paid little attention to Morag drivelling along about having been a good girl once when she lived on the banks of Allan Water . . . and every Sunday after kirk they would go for a walk, she and her old dad, along the river bank, under the pine trees and the ash trees. . . . When you stopped and looked far down at the water it danced clear over the rocks and pebbles as though it were spilt brandy—"That colour, look in your glass; better than gold. It's the Waters of Allan I'm telling ye of, Robin me lad, not, ye understand, the drink itself. 'Tis cool and sweet there in the shadows under the branches, but always a glint on the river, and lovely now in April. I'd like fine to go with ye walking on the Sabbath at the Bridge of Allan, and I'll show ye where I was born, too. It'll cost but little; please, Robin, take me," she wheedled. He laughed and promised and humoured her. Morag was tiresome in this mood, but presently she would sleep, and if ever he saw her again there would be no more chatter of the Waters of Allan.

Yet the name and what she had said of it stirred in his mind as though it were familiar, as though he might once have walked there himself. Probably, he thought with a sardonic grin, his father's legacy again; that lad was for ever taking long walks, not because he had to, but because he liked it, and then writing enthusiastically about them to some long-suffering friend. Call himself a tramp! As though a real tramp ever footed it where there was a chance of a lift. Idly, from old habit, Robert thought he would look and see if he could find the letter. No, damn, his library was miles and miles away and inaccessible.

But then, with a quickening of his pulse, he recalled that of the four volumes of Letters, one (only one) was not abandoned to the rats in the loft of Gleann Bàn, but here and upstairs, in his knapsack. Which one? He had not the remotest idea; funny if it happened to be the very volume with that letter in it. Lifting Morag with as little ceremony as though she had been a parcel, from where she lolled against his arm and shoulder, and dumping her head on the table instead, he got up and ran upstairs, eager as a schoolboy; though why he should be disappointed if the letter proved to be in one of the other volumes, as was much more likely in the three-to-one chance, he simply could not imagine.

Ten minutes later, he brought his clenched fist down on the rickety table, with a triumphant exclamation. For here was the letter itself on page two-hundred-and-fifty-one of Volume One, the very volume he had brought along:

. . . On Friday I went to Bridge of Allan. A beautiful clear sunny winter's day, all the highland hills standing about the horizon in their white robes. It was not cold. I went up my favourite walk by the riverside among the pines and ash-trees. There is a little cavern here, by the side of a wide meadow, which has been a part of me any time these last twelve years—or more. On Friday it was wonderful. A large broken branch hung down over the mouth of it, and it was all cased in perfect ice. Every dock-leaf and long grass, too, was bearded with a shining icicle. And all the icicles kept dropping, and dropping and dropping, and had made another little forest of clear ice among the grasses and fallen branches and dockens below them. I picked up one of these branches and threw it on the ground ; and all the crystal broke with a little tinkle, and behold ! a damp stick.

. . . I am all right again, I think, though still taking eleven to twelve hours sleep per night. And I am quite strong and virtuous again, and determined to take no more money from my parents. It's all nonsense, it should be enough and shall.

Like a small shudder rippling the leaves on a windless day, Robert was moved by a premonition, familiar now, that after all he was not to be let alone; not free, but belonging; not cheerfully, recklessly lost, but far more disconcertingly found and claimed again. Found by the mere opening of a book to satisfy himself on a name raised by a wanton; as in the South of France last autumn, he had been stopped in full pace when doing nothing more deliberate than search for a fraudulent anecdote of a child and his father to please future audiences in California. These books— He should have brought none along, not one. No link at all. Would he never learn to play for safety?

Of course, it was just a rubbishy coincidence; a three-to-one chance often turned up; the odds were not heavy.

Yes, but what had made him turn back for a book? What or—who? No one.

Yet at least, he reassured himself—(choosing to ignore that uncomfortable decision of R.L.S. about taking no more money from his parents)—at least there was nothing in the letter itself to trouble him; only the tricky fact that it was there at all.

He read it again, and wondered whether he should conquer indolence the next day, and go himself for that walk by the river, starting from Bridge of Allan; though not, certainly, with Morag.

. . . And all the icicles kept dropping, and dropping and dropping, and had made another little forest of clear ice among the grasses and fallen branches and dockens below them. I picked up one of these branches and threw it on the ground; and all the crystal broke with a little tinkle, and behold! a damp stick. . . .

Robert dropped plummet deep into a reverie of a youth breaking the crystal icicles among the grasses, and with a rueful grimace, picking up a damp stick. A tinkle in his ears . . . and he became conscious of being well on the way to make the same sort of fool of himself as when he had obeyed directions of shutting his eyes and waited to open them on a figure laughing at him across the bank "where the road crosses the river below the old cruciform church at Glencorse".

He—and the old camel. To shake off memory of that discomfiture, he read on to the next letter:

. . . O, I have such a longing for children of my own; and yet I do not think I could bear it if I had one. . . . I sometimes hate the children I see in the street—you know what I mean by hate—wish

they were somewhere else, and not there to mock me ; and sometimes, again, I don't know how to go by them for the love of them . . . .

And now there was no longer any doubt : His father had
meant him to pick out this one special volume of the Letters
and bring it away with him; read it here and now, that
it might stop him from being happy and light-hearted and
following his luck.

After the sudden recognition of pursuit, doubt, as always,
came like a raging toothache. And in a queer way, he was
glad he might still be allowed this doubt of the unsubstantial
evidence; bitterly glad that no logical proof existed that a
man of his indelicate code and brazen behaviour, backslider
from truth so glibly and so often, beggar, idler, swindler,
fraud, impostor, cheat and libertine, could be for one moment
considered as sun-shadow of a man for whom honour sprang
from a live root.

Swing right over, and put an end to all this. Go out on
the racket again. Isn't a chance likeness of face and feature
still your luck and your fortune? Cash in on it, anywhere:
Scotland, America, the South Seas . . . "Are you Stevenson's
son?" And replying *"yes"*, he would prove the opposite,
and that would be the end of torment; the question finally
answered. For nobody's son could go on acting as though
nobody cared.

And disinherit yourself? Slam the door on any secret
moment of proud certainty?

You can't eat and drink and feel the sun and grow sound
in your lungs, on that "proud certainty", can you? It won't,
for instance, charter a yacht to carry you to the South Seas?

But here's a suave and pleasing argument, giving it to
you both ways: Louis himself was for years at odds with
his own father, sinning against Thomas Stevenson's high
sincerities of God and duty and right. "You can be no son
of mine"—the dramatic phrase must have been flung out
in anguish a hundred times in that household. Nevertheless, and in despite of such violent excommunication, who
would ever question Louis was a true son of Thomas? So
the test Robert had set himself was no test at all. If he
chose, he could be a bad son, but still a son.

[324]

And to begin with, chuck this rotten book out of the window. The tide was lapping just outside; the sea would take it and hide it, never fear.

He got up so impetuously that he knocked over the rickety table. The volume of Letters was in his hand. He had to stoop to fling it out, for the window was squeezed in as low as his knees, under the slanted roof.

He did not fling it out, but put it down quietly on the broad sill. Then with heavy tread he went downstairs and across the road to the barber's, nearly always crowded with sailors. Robert knocked on the door and went on knocking steadily till Mackenzie, surprised but not unfriendly, opened it and let him in.

Robert said: "Take off this moustache, old son. I'm in a hurry. Yes, I know it's struck midnight, but I'll pay you a bob extra and call it quits."

*   *   *

He had been tired out from morning till night during his months of labour on the farm, but never with that deadly weariness which was on him as he waited next morning for Miss Gibson to leave her rooms and go out to her shop, so that he could enter and give back her book without being seen; for he could not bear to be questioned by her, whether she reviled him as a thief, or rejoiced over him as a penitent; he rather thought it would be the latter, knowing women and the fuss they made; knowing old camels and last straws. Funny that he should have come to Edinburgh intending to restore the *Child's Garden of Verses* to its rightful owner, and then almost left Edinburgh forgetting to do so; he had had to come back when he was already at the station.

Train to Glasgow, and tramp from Arrochar to Gleann Bàn. Isa would have got over her temper by now; they would be glad to have him there when the sheep and the young lambs had to be dipped; far too much for old Macnair, and you could be dead sure they hadn't got anyone else. And next the grass would be ready for cutting. That rusty

[325]

scythe—he had meant to stone it, only he came away in a bit of a hurry.

Thank God, here she was at last, stump, stump down the stairs. He drew back further into the corner of the neighbouring doorway, taking no chances, though probably she would not have recognized him with his lips shaven clean. . . . Not likely he would ever be recognized again. When she was safely down the street and out of sight, and he had given her long enough to get on the tram and be jolted away, he went upstairs, saw the room, the horsehair sofa, the bookcase with its glass doors. Emotion had died in him, and things were quieter without it. He laid the *Child's Garden* on the table, and on top of it the latch-key which she had had made for him when he lived there. Lucky he had never thrown it away. When she returned that evening and found the book and the key, she would say: "He's been here . . . in the room . . . and I've missed him." Yet Robert supposed it would not matter to her much, having her treasure again with its faded autograph on the fly-leaf. But for that, he would never have pinched the book; never read of the child who had buried his soldier and left him in the dark, hoping to find him one day . . .

That was done, and he could go.

He was thirsty, and the branch-line train did not leave for Arrochar for nearly half an hour, so he went into the dingy station buffet at Glasgow, asked for some beer and a sandwich, and sank down at a table in the corner.

The small room was thick with smoke, and rain pattered on the smeared glass of the skylight. . . . It hardly seemed possible on such a dingy, sorrowful morning, that after death he might hear himself acknowledged by the father from whose integrity he had so often flung himself, a rebel: "This is my son"—protective, compassionate. Since it could not be otherwise, Robert acquiesced in an invisible father, but he could not help still wanting his salvation to quicken into a human kinship, and though defiantly homeless all his life, to know he was home.

Perhaps there was no "after death". Perhaps his bare shred of hope for an encounter that could no more happen to him down here, was utterly futile; worse, laughable. Nevertheless, he could not risk forfeiting even that last ragged shred. It stood for all he would ever care for in Heaven. Yet beyond even this tenuous argument, Robert saw in a sword-flash that if the Archangel Michael were to come to him and swear there was no chance in all eternity for that longed-for meeting, still he would have to go back to the farm, carry on with his desolate job, steadily testify to the influence of a father who could have done so little with him by admonition or conscious precept; but was now bravely, warmly alive to conquer that insidious demon tempting his son again and again into saucy indolence of earning bread and beer and skittles by exploit of a lie.

He became aware, as one is always aware of an intense scrutiny, that somebody was staring at him. And he raised his head quickly as though at a command. Yes, a traveller somewhat better dressed than the rest of the assembly at the buffet. When Robert looked up, the man gave a slight start, as though the face were not quite what he had expected to see. Then moved easily across to the table and sat down:

"The likeness," he remarked amiably, without any preamble, "is quite extraordinary."

Robert had never dreamt he would again hear this pleasant news. A wicked joy blazed up: So, though he had been such a darned fool, he had not irrevocably chucked away his living by a sixpenn'orth of the barber's razor? He grinned delightedly as he pulled from his pocket a crumpled illustration and flung it on the table in front of his companion. "Reckon this is what you mean," he drawled.

The other looked at the Nerli drawing, and shook his head.

"No, not that one; though," with another keen survey of Robert's face, "I can see a likeness there, too. But the portrait I meant—and it nearly took my breath away when

[327]

you looked up— Probably you don't know it? It was enlarged from a snapshot, and you find it as a frontispiece to the 1899 two-volume edition of the Letters."

Silently Robert stood up. He could not bear any more; the shock was too direct. Above the clanking and growling of engine and truck, they were bawling out his train to Arrochar. He had to go.

The man still remained seated at the table, one hand clinking the coins in his pocket: "You *are* Stevenson's son, aren't you?"

"I don't know."

But standing in the crowded carriage, jerking to and fro with the sway of the train, doubt spent itself for ever in a deep exultant shout of silent affirmation. For by the answer which had leapt out, not with the old calculated "yes" for profit, it had ceased to matter that no final proof could ever identify him to the outside world. He had identified himself. It makes sense, thought Robert, a little puzzled that it should.

THE END